Flawless

SA WOLFE

Published: S.A. Wolfe 2019
sawolfe24@gmail.com

Cover Design: Damonza
Editing: Emma Corcoran
Editing: Clio Editing
Editing: C&D Editing
Proofreading & Formatting by Elaine York, Allusion Graphics, LLC, www.allusiongraphics.com
Proofreader: Jovana Shirley, Unforeseen Editing, www. unforeseenediting.com

Flawless

For Emma Corcoran

Take one pretty chef with confidence issues...
Add one sexy restaurateur with blind ambition...
Untested recipes are always a risk ... is this one worth taking?

She's going to ask the arrogant hottie for a special favor...

Talia Madej, a personal chef, has kept a recent harrowing crisis secret from her friends and the local gossips in her small town. She has enough baggage to sink a ship which has crushed her confidence and makes her wary of men and relationships. The only way out of this is to start living again, and the first hurdle is to ask the new guy in town to help her get back in the game. Even if he is not her type, a cocky workaholic who always seems to be surrounded by beautiful women, he's the perfect candidate because he's temporary. He'll be a short-term player in her long-term scheme.

He's not about to refuse her and the intriguing offer she presents...

Peyton MacKenzie's star is rising. A hotshot restaurateur in New York City who is used to putting himself first, he just has to get his newest restaurant up and running, and then he's blowing this tiny bohemian tourist town and pursuing a huge career opportunity. But when the charming blond chef needs use of his commercial kitchen for her catering business, he surprises himself and doesn't hesitate to say yes. And when she asks for something bigger with no strings attached, he's definitely more than willing to oblige. Soon he realizes that simply being a pawn in her plan is not enough for him. He has to figure out how to hold on to her...forever.

Prologue

Talia

HE SAYS HE WILL stop my heart. That there is always a risk of death. And I imagine my unconscious body surrounded by strangers who must bring me close to death in order to give me life.

"Don't you have a heart whisperer around here, or anyone who won't kill me first?" I ask, wishing I could walk right out of his office and forget about my condition.

He smiles as if I'm joking. I can tell smiling doesn't come naturally to him. He's a serious man with strong physical features that match his profession. The slender build of a long-distance runner, the intense eyes bracketed with creases as if he's perpetually scrutinizing a challenge, and the perfectly shaved bald head all live up to my expectations of this famous, innovative expert.

Meeting with him should ease my fears. Baldy is the smartest, most skilled, and the best in the world, according to all the research. However, I'm still scared.

Baldy gestures to the video on the wall monitor where the blackish, gelatinous beating heart is stopped. His words become background noise as my brain tries to process all the medical jargon paired with the explicit images. It has real shock value, much like what TV shows do to get their ratings up.

He will stop your heart!

He continues with more unabashed satisfaction that resembles amusement, about sawing through chest bones and placing ice on the heart. *My heart.*

Who agrees to such things?

I mimic his calmness to mask my terror.

Sitting next to me, my fiancé, Marko, is unemotional, staring at the older man in the white lab coat with the fancy office overlooking Central Park. Marko's stoicism falters, though, when he lets go of my hand.

I'm not sure which man is upsetting me more. The cool, monotonous demeanor of Baldy who makes me want to throw the stapler at his smooth, shiny head. Or Marko, who should know better. He's supposed to be my partner in this, my reassuring support system, the man who loves me. Since the minute Baldy started speaking, though, Marko has kept his eyes averted from mine, and there is a shift in the room when his body, his whole being, seems to separate from me. That's when I know.

I'm in this alone. I am alone and scared.

• • •

Peyton

She wakes, stretching languorously, exuding a sensuality that would leave most men in a stupor, but my mind is elsewhere as I look out the window, watching Park Avenue come to life before the sun has risen.

I finish buttoning my shirt, then rake my freshly showered hair back with my fingers while I watch the people below. I like to see the traffic build and the throngs of fast-walking men and women race to work.

"Come back to bed. It's uncivil to get up this early." She props herself up on an elbow to study me.

Men never turn Flora down. She steals their attention with her exotic beauty and curvaceous body, and she keeps their attention with her brilliant legal mind, clever conversation, and uninhibited sexual appetite. I'm no different than other men, except I have already spent several active hours in her bed, and I feel like the early risers down below, the same sense of determination and eagerness to get to work.

I'm leaving today, spending the next few months in a small town in the Catskills, where I'm opening a new restaurant.

"Peyton," she says.

I grab my car keys from the dresser, hoping I can dodge out of her apartment without one of her lectures.

"I need more. This timeline isn't working for me. I like things to run efficiently, with more structure and agreements in place. We've been together for nine months already."

"We've been sleeping together for nine months. It's sex, Flora, nothing more. No timeline. We have an expiration date."

"Sometimes you can be the biggest dick," she says, throwing back the covers as she gets out of bed.

"The biggest? That's why you like sleeping with me." That was low, even for me.

I see the flash of red in time to bolt out of the apartment and close the door just as her shoe hits the other side. Flora has good aim.

1

Three months later...
Talia

Today is my big comeback, at least to me. To everyone else, I'm just returning from a long vacation. And it will be an exceptional day, I have decided. You cannot die on exceptional days, not when they signify your return to the living.

I have to keep giving myself these silly little greeting card pep talks. If I could summon a marching band with fanfare for my big return, I would.

On the way to town, I pedal my recently bought, used bike harder and faster, leaving the memories of dying behind. And as I enter the outskirts of Hera, the quaint little main street greets me like an old friend and lifts my spirits.

I have been absent for two months and had no idea how much I missed the sight of this tiny town with its quiet beauty and familiar businesses that bring a sense of safety to the fragile disposition I have adopted. *Note to self: stop being fragile.*

It's a pretty March day for this part of New York, where it's not uncommon to get a late snow or heavy rainstorm. I tell myself it's a sign that this is my lucky day.

The warmth of the sun on my face triggers an involuntary smile, something I haven't felt in months.

The new brewery and restaurant loom ahead in the distance. For the past few decades, it was a vacant warehouse, a historic building sitting behind our main street that fell into disrepair after it closed down as an ironworks factory in the 1980s. Now the building is spectacular, giving off its own energy.

The concrete building has been given a face-lift; the peeling paint removed, leaving the original brickwork exposed, and a steel-forged sign above the front door with an engraving of the goddess Hera opening her arms to the name below: SWILL, HERA TAPS. I laugh, remembering months ago when *Swill* was being bandied about with hilarity. I'm pleased to see my friends went through with it.

A hint of nervousness blooms as I get closer. The excitement of a new business venture to help rehabilitate Hera's commerce. When some of my friends started work on the project six months ago, I was distracted with my own problems and didn't give their restaurant much thought, but now that I desperately need the use of a commercial kitchen, I'm going to ask them for help, something I'm not good at.

Cooper MacKenzie's pickup truck is parked in front, where a tall, brawny man is unloading a large stack of barware racks from the back end. It's a heavy load. I've never even seen a bartender lift that many glass racks at once.

From the back, I know it's not Cooper, because the shoulder-length hair is almost black instead of blond.

I go in for a closer look, but since riding a bike is new for me, I cruise by him a little too close and let out a short squeal as my front wheel barely misses the back of Brawny's legs. Simultaneously, I look back at him, and he grunts with the weight of the glasses before he looks over at me. Our eyes lock for a moment.

Peyton. Cooper's younger brother.

He is glaring at me with his beautiful gray eyes, and suddenly I feel myself losing control of the bike. I whip my head back to face front and get the wobbly old bicycle under control. At the same time, I hear a loud crash of glass and an angry, hoarse curse.

Braking is something I haven't mastered. My sister makes fun of me with the fact that five-year-olds ride their bikes with more control than I do. Well, some people are afraid of spiders or stepping on sidewalk cracks; I have always been afraid to ride a bike. I was the neighborhood kid who ran on foot when everyone else was biking to the corner store for their candy stash. Buying this bike was my first step in putting several major fears behind me. The downside was I had to teach myself how to ride the thing, which I have seen very little improvement since I started secretly practicing a few days ago.

I instinctively let the bike slow down on its own before I hop off and let go of the handlebars altogether so I don't crash with it. The slow-moving hunk of metal hits one of the large tires on a parked SUV before it topples over to the ground with a creaky thud.

I leave it there and jog back to Peyton, who is looking down at the mountain of broken glassware in front of him. I haven't moved this fast in months, and my panting, mixed with the elation of today and the commotion I have already caused, produces a dull ache against my sternum.

Peyton takes this moment to give me a good hard look, as though I'm the culprit of this mess. I decide he probably can't be bothered for a glass of water, even though I'm sure I look exhausted, dehydrated, and a little breathless, but that could be from his disarming good looks and his striking long, dark hair that sets off his eyes and strong jaw. He's a fine specimen of masculinity, and after all the handsome men who never made me look twice, I'm self-conscious about my visceral reaction to him.

"I know you." His expression is rather cold. "You're that little Russian spy."

He's made of MacKenzie stock—tall and strong like his older brother, Cooper—but Peyton's dark features give him a more dangerous, maybe even sinister look, and much to my dismay, I find it appealing.

"We saw each other at Cooper and Imogene's wedding last year. You were showing off. Walking on your hands across the bar. And I'm not Russian. I'm Polish and a personal chef, not a spy."

His intimidating scowl softens. "I remember. You're *Tal-ia*," he enunciates slowly in his deep timbre.

I feel myself blush at the way he says my name and the very fact that he even remembers me. But then, I remember him, too.

"And you're Peyton, Cooper's brother. Big on handstands, big at parties, and big with the ladies, as I recall."

His eyes roam over me from head to toe.

Greedy men and their one-track minds.

I slowly look him up and down, intentionally being just as obvious as him, but I doubt I pull it off with the same unapologetic arrogance.

He pauses and a smile quirks ever so slightly. "So, what's the verdict?"

Have I been out of the dating game so long I can't tell if he's being obnoxiously forward?

"I think we both look good. I know I do," I say.

He opens his mouth, and I expect him to laugh at me. He doesn't.

"What the hell happened?" my friend Dylan shouts as he comes running out of the building. "I heard a crash—shit!" Dylan looks at the pile of plastic racks and glass shards.

"Yeah, I had a little distraction," Peyton admits. "This one nearly sideswiped me on her bike."

"I did not. I didn't even graze you," I say. "It's his fault for carrying more than he can handle," I tell Dylan.

Dylan shakes his head and smiles. "Talia, it's good to see you back." He steps forward and gives me a quick embrace and a kiss on the cheek. "Just so you know, this guy has a radar for every cute chick in the vicinity." Dylan gives Peyton a disapproving glance.

"Cute chick," I say in disgust.

"My keen observations aside, shouldn't we be more concerned that the little woman here can't handle herself on that sorry excuse for a bike?" Peyton puts his hands on his hips and stares at me. I stare back. After all, he's got my attention with the way his muscled arms fill out his snug, short-sleeved, gray T-shirt and how his long, athletic legs carry off his weathered jeans. I shouldn't engage in this childish behavior, but I actually like this little game with him.

"What's with the Huffy?" Dylan asks me. "It looks pretty crappy. Where's your catering van?"

"My sister has it. Aleska and the cleaning crew are using it during the day. She'll drop it off when I do deliveries in the afternoon," I explain. "I'm trying something new. Biking as much as I can to get some exercise."

"Hey! What's the holdup?" Carson barks as he and Cooper walk out to join us.

"Talia!" Cooper exclaims and gives me a strong hug.

"How was Florida with your dad?" Carson asks, putting an arm around my shoulders and pulling me in for a kiss on the cheek.

Although he's one of my clients, Carson is more like a protective older brother, and his wife, Jess, has become one of my closest friends.

I shrug to cover my squirming at the uncomfortable topic of my father and the information I've kept from my friends for the past three months. "It was fine. I'm ready to get back to work, though, and I have a huge favor to ask you."

"Shoot," Carson says as he kicks a rack aside, assessing the damage to the barware.

"The kitchen I rent in Woodstock—"

"Hey, I heard about the building fire last night," Dylan says. "I worried your kitchen would get trashed. The fire trucks were still there this morning when I went by on my run."

"The landlord called me this morning. He said the firemen saved most of the building, but my kitchen had a lot of smoke damage and the roof was destroyed. All the other chefs are running around the county, looking for temporary space to lease, so I wanted to get to Swill before someone else does. Everyone knows this place is huge and about to open. I'm hoping I have some leverage with you."

"Of course you do," Carson says. "Without you, Jess and I would be living off canned food and cereal."

"We'll take our little Russian spy over those generic wholesome chefs any day," Cooper says with a straight face.

"Oh, stop. I'm serious. I will pay you the going rate. My landlord doesn't have any idea how long it'll take to repair our part of the building and renovate the kitchens. And then they have to pass inspections, which could take months. I need a kitchen starting tomorrow. I can't have my mother filling in for me and cooking out of our home anymore. Two months of that while I was on vacation was long enough."

"Her food was awesome, by the way," Carson adds.

"I know. I learned from the best. But I need to get back to work, and I'm hoping your kitchen is up and running. I promise I'll only need it during the day. I'll be gone before you serve dinner, and I'll leave everything spotless." I give Carson and Cooper my best pleading, pouty face.

Carson and Dylan Blackard own Blackard Designs, a high-end furniture factory that employs many in town. Carson is also known for his generosity—hiring people who are down on their luck and providing financial backing to those who are starting their own businesses. Cooper MacKenzie is one of the company's principals. He convinced his brother, Peyton, to leave New York City to open a new restaurant with them in Hera. They're all backing the new venture financially, but I suspect that luring Peyton to join them is what will make their new business a success.

"Shit, a chef without a kitchen is like a sex-starved guy who's been told he has to be celibate." Dylan shakes his head. My comradein-arms, who is a gourmet cook in his own right, isn't always the best with words.

Everyone looks at Dylan and laughs. Everyone except Peyton.

"I don't see a problem with that," Carson says.

"Nope," Cooper adds nonchalantly. "We should be able to work something out. Can't have the best chef in town going out of business."

"Since I'm the biggest stakeholder and I'm managing this place for the next few months, you should be talking to me," Peyton clarifies. "Come inside and meet our chef, Sebastian, and let's see if we can come to an arrangement."

I look to my other three friends, hoping one of them will accompany me, but they're suddenly consumed with cleaning up the destroyed glassware, so I step forward as Peyton's eyes beckon me.

2

Peyton

TAKE IN HER blonde hair, tousled on top of her head and held in place with a blue ribbon. The blue of the ribbon matches her eyes ...

And I can't believe I'm going there. Comparing her eyes to a ribbon? She's just another woman, another *chick*, as Dylan would say, and I already got away from a demanding one in Manhattan.

Flora and I had a good run, but I don't need to be thinking about another woman. Sure, Talia's more than attractive, but beautiful women are everywhere, especially in my business. She's just another pretty woman who happens to have horrendous biking skills. Not to mention her timing sucks.

I'm trying to keep things on target for our opening day, and this little woman shows up for a big ask, batting her eyes at the other guys, who are pushovers for anyone they call a friend. I'm going along with it. Guess I'm a sucker, too.

I let her follow me through the cavernous hallway at the entrance, and then I lead her into the main dining area that is designed like a German beer hall. This morning we'll be bringing in the rest of the long tables made for family-style seating. Two walls are almost entirely windows; the original industrial checkerboard-style glass panes that offer plenty of natural light. Another wall has a long, rustic bar, an open fire oven, and rotisseries.

She stops and takes in all the work we have done to renovate the once-dilapidated warehouse into a trendy restaurant and microbrewery. It's much cooler than the bar I own in Brooklyn with my family, and it's very unique compared to the high-end restaurant we own in Manhattan, where expensively dressed, elegant people hang out and easily drop hundreds of dollars for dinner and drinks for two.

This is a good project, and people in the industry are watching. It's going to be a game-changer for me, opening the door for something bigger and more challenging. Everything I crave in this business—success, money, fame—will happen after I complete my stint in this miniscule tourist town.

"This is incredible." Talia walks ahead of me, her shoes making a soft clicking sound on the concrete floor. She runs a finger across the grain of the only table we've brought in so far. "I like that everything is unpolished. It's so ... raw." She turns around to face me.

The way she says *raw* makes me think of other things, things I need to stop thinking about. All I have to do to distract my brain for a second is to look at the funny bag she wears strapped across her body. It's shaped like a life-size rotary phone, except it has a big, hot pink receiver as the handle, and the fake rotary dial on the front is set against a tropical design. Flora would never wear something so zany. That alone makes me like it. And I like that Talia has the boldness to add such odd whimsy to her polished look.

"Unpolished and raw is the feel we're going for. It's casual. Easy for anyone to eat here. Families, couples, old, young. It's my first gut renovation, and it only happened because Carson has pull with the architects. I'm happy with the results."

"You should be. You have a talent for creating restaurants."

I brush past her and continue on to the kitchen, Bash's territory.

"Sebastian!" I shout as we enter the kitchen where every stainless steel area is gleaming with newness.

Bash, dressed in a white chef's coat, jeans, and work boots, is putting pots on a tall shelf. He turns around and studies Talia.

"This is Talia. Talia, this is Bash."

"Our first visitor," Bash says. He can be guarded when it comes to people outside of me and his cooking staff. Much of it stems from bad work experiences in our early days when he went on job interviews and people assumed he was an immigrant who didn't speak English. In reality, Bash is Native American and trained at The Culinary Institute. Our time together, working in various establishments, gave me daily reminders of how we were received differently, how he always had to work harder to prove himself. I knew he was the man to run my kitchens. "You look familiar."

"We were both at Cooper and Imogene's wedding. At Peyton's bar in Brooklyn." She smiles.

"That's it." Bash gives a hint of a smile, his dark complexion taking on a reddish hue.

For fuck's sake, don't tell me he's already crushing on her.

"I think we can all agree that we were slightly hammered at that wedding, so let's move on to business," I say brusquely.

Talia gives me a little frown, then steps forward to shake Bash's hand. "I was just telling Peyton that I could use a big favor from you guys."

"Oh?" Bash looks from her to me with a raised eyebrow.

"Don't get too excited there, buddy. She has a catering business, and her kitchen is incapacitated at the moment. She wants to know if she can use our kitchen in the hours before we start serving the dinner crowd. Not sure how we'd work out the weekend time, since we'll be serving brunch at some point down the line, but I told her to talk to you."

"Sure," Bash says rather too quickly. "I don't see a problem. Look at the size of our kitchen. We have room to spare."

"Don't worry," Talia adds. "I'll bring my own knives. I'll only need to borrow a few pots and pans. Some utensils. I'll clean everything, and I won't bother your dishwasher or your cooks."

"Hey, I don't mind having a sous chef around." Bash crosses his arms and leans against the steel worktable with a goofy grin. Bash, who has developed the best poker-face since our wild days as teenagers, has turned into a pile of mush.

I don't have time for his goddamn flirting. And if it were any other guy, I would feel like smacking that smile right off his face.

"Funny," Talia says. "But I don't work under anyone. I'm my own boss."

"Hmm," Bash responds.

"Are we done with introductions here?" I snap. "Bash, show her around, and you two work this out."

Bash is still gazing at her with a glassy-eyed expression.

"Bash?" I prompt, a bit annoyed.

"Yeah." He drags his eyes away from Talia and focuses on me. "Sure thing, boss man."

"Stop calling me that." I turn to Talia. "We good here? After Bash gives you the tour, I'm going to need you to sign some insurance waivers. Liability and all that crap."

"I understand." The words roll off her tongue in a well-practiced, clipped tone.

English may be her second language, but her Polish accent is barely noticeable, except when her voice drops a couple octaves to enunciate certain consonants in a sexy, Natasha the Spy sort of way.

I head back outside to help carry the rest of custom dining tables from the delivery trucks, which only had to drive from the Blackard's furniture workshop across the street.

The extra-long tables have benches that seat sixteen people, so they are hefty and it takes all of Carson and Cooper's staff to hoist and carry the furniture.

It takes four people to carry one table, but Dylan convinces me that we're strong enough to haul one between the two of us. I'm still thinking about Talia when I lose my grip on the iron table frame and jostle it enough so the other end drops and hits Dylan's shoulder.

"Mother of—" Dylan shouts as he drops his end and hunches over, holding his shoulder in pain. "What the hell are you doing?"

"Sorry, it slipped." I put my table end down, the heavy iron legs crunching against the gravel.

Dylan takes off his T-shirt and studies the bloody gash across his shoulder. "Thanks a lot," he growls. "We can't afford your sloppiness."

"I said I was sorry. It was an accident. No need to be a prick about it. Why don't you sit down and take care of the blood? I'll get Bash to help me carry this in."

"I've had enough of you calling the shots!" Dylan yells. "You've been acting like the fucking boss since you came to town."

"Oh, fuck off. I'm the only who has experience starting and running a restaurant. That's why Carson and Cooper put me in charge of this. And if that hurts so much, why don't you run to the ER and get some stitches?" I should have tried to deliver it with a little more diplomacy, but I'm just as tense and exhausted as Dylan.

I see the others trudging around two other delivery trucks with the rest of the tables. Carson and Cooper are carrying a table together, and they both shoot me looks.

"Knock it off, you two!" Carson yells.

"We're all tired and stressed out over finishing this. We don't need you two going at each other's throats every second you get," Cooper lectures.

Emma, Dylan's wife, suddenly appears from behind a truck. "Yes, I'm sick of all this, too." She's angry. "Dylan, I mean it. We're all getting a little punchy and on edge for the opening day. You're not helping by flipping out."

"I apologize. It was my fault," Dylan mumbles.

"Not good enough," Emma says. "We need a break, hon."

"I'm sorry ... too," I say to him.

He waves me off and lets his wife lead him away to his Jeep.

Dylan has struggled in the past with bipolar depression, but he's managed to do well with treatment. I feel some responsibility for pushing his buttons. I've been aggressive and confrontational with everyone since they made me the lead project manager.

"It was an accident," Carson tells me in a low voice. "Sometimes he slips up, and he has to deal with it."

I nod warily. This is supposed to be an exciting time—getting close to the grand opening—but we keep running into glitches, like the faulty tap lines our brewmaster, Zander, needed days to repair, and getting the permit on the new gas lines. It keeps us all in a perpetual state of high anxiety and short fuses.

"Asshole," Cooper says as he cuffs my ear. "We'll take care of the tables. You go inside and cool off."

Behind him, Cooper's wife, Imogene, puts her hands on her hips and smiles at me knowingly. Marriage has given her the siblings she never had, so she treats me and my unmarried brothers and sister as her pet projects; people she must fix before finding us suitable matches.

I turn back to go inside the restaurant, seeing both Talia and Bash standing at the entrance, watching me. From Bash's smile, I assume they saw my juvenile argument with Dylan. Talia looks disappointed.

"Come back to the office and sign some papers for me before you leave," I say curtly.

"Of course," she says, following me back inside.

The office is a small, windowless room between the restaurant and the actual brewery. I yank open a file cabinet drawer and pull out an insurance folder. "Here, this waiver should be enough." I toss the paper on the desk and hand her a pen.

"And what about the rental fee? Do you have a figure in mind?"

"How about zero? Will that work for you?"

She looks at me, perplexed.

"I'm not going to charge you to use our kitchen for a few hours a day."

"Why not? I pay a competitive rate in Woodstock for something much smaller."

"You're good friends with Carson and the other guys. I've learned they don't charge friends." I sigh. "They give the house away. Besides, you saw how big our kitchen is. You won't even take up five percent of the space. So, if you want it, it's free. Sign the paper and you're set."

"That's very generous of you." She leans down to sign her name with a big flourish.

"Wait. You didn't even read it."

She looks up at me with those big, baby blues of hers. "I trust you." She hands the form back.

"It's interesting how people here are so trusting." My tone suggests a bit of cynicism.

"Small-town life. You're not used to this kind of close-knit community."

"You're right. I prefer the city. It's less predictable, more exciting. And there's definitely more privacy."

"You mean there are less nosy neighbors and people up in your business?"

I shrug.

"I love Hera. The camaraderie here is borne out of something different and special. We're not connected by blood bonds, but our relationships are just as strong, if not stronger. You see, Dylan is more than a friend to me. He's easily provoked ... We all try to help him."

"What are you saying? You have something going on with him? He's married."

"Ew." She grimaces. "I meant he's like a brother to me. I don't like seeing you two fight. You taunted him, and it made me—"

"Ah, you're pissed at me."

"A little ... for hurting my friend."

"If it's any consolation, I like Dylan. Otherwise, I wouldn't be going into business with him and his brother. I also don't think he's hurt at all. Well, other than his tough ego. The guy is built like a boulder. We both lost our temper. We'll all get past this and move on to better times. Besides, it's only temporary."

"What's temporary?" She brushes back a loose tendril of hair.

I'm momentarily tantalized by the movement as she curls the tendril around her finger. I have to shake the visual from my mind or I could be here all day, wasting time with chitchat.

"Me. I'm temporary. I'm a joint partner, but I'm only staying in Hera for a few months until everything is running smoothly. Then I'm going back to the city. I have two restaurants there to deal with. And I have a big business opportunity that's in the works. I'm counting on a deal to come through in Los Angeles."

"Oh." She sighs.

Is that a hint of relief in her voice?

Her rigid shoulders relax a bit, but she still holds herself with a graceful posture. "I'm going to go pack my things up at my kitchen … whatever was saved after the fire. I'll be back early tomorrow with them. Bash said everyone will be here in the morning, working on the kitchen setup, and he'll give me a set of keys then."

I stare at her for a moment, thinking about how she said *Bash*, as if they were already good friends. She's relaxed with other people, but not with me.

"Do you want me to come along and help you pack? I have a truck," I blurt out. It's not like I have any time to spare, but at this very moment, I want her to see me as a decent guy, not the jerk who just got into a playground shouting match with one of her good friends.

"No," she says. "Thank you for the offer, but your presence isn't necessary." She delivers this statement politely, without realizing how demoralizing it strikes my ego. I chalk it up to her formal English language skills that lack subtlety.

The restaurant has plenty of room to accommodate her, but I can tell she's going to be highly inconvenient for me personally. Extremely distracting.

I'm in trouble here.

3

Talia

"HE MUST BE VERY nice to let you use his kitchen," my mother muses as she watches me collect extra aprons and supplies that I've been storing in our cramped utility closet.

"Yes, Bash is nice. He'll be pleasant to work with. Well, I mean be around, since we're not really working together."

"I was referring to Peyton. You said he's the primary owner, and he's managing the restaurant. I think it's very generous of him to let you use his kitchen. I know I don't like anyone futzing around in my kitchen."

"No, you don't. You yell at everyone when they put things back in the wrong place. Maybe a few breadcrumbs on the counter wouldn't make you so crazy if you had something else to do. Like getting out of the house once in a while." I'm entering dangerous territory, but I keep thinking it's my duty to push her instead of pretending that she leads a normal life.

"I don't have the energy to have this argument again. I'm going for a run." My mother crosses the kitchen to the family room, where the treadmill takes up entirely too much space.

"You can't say you're going for a run unless you actually go *outside* to run. You're just going to the treadmill. There's a difference."

My mother ignores me, putting on her headphones and starting up the noisy treadmill. She has become surprisingly fast, and she's definitely more fit than me. What's the point, though?

My mother's world is very small. You could say she lives within the four walls of our little home, sequestering herself.

It wasn't always this bad. Years ago, there was a time when she was a very industrious woman, someone who had a full-time career working as an office manager for a growing tech firm while raising two young daughters. She was still able to cook big dinners for our family, and she and my father had a social life. She was admired by friends and family for her education, her career, her remarkable culinary skills, and the generosity with which she dispensed home-cooked dishes to anyone in need. That was a different time, a different city, a different country, where Mila and Damian Madej were popular among their friends and neighbors.

Now my mother spends every day living through the same routine. She showers and dresses as if she's going to work, wearing nice dresses or pants with a silk blouse, elegant pieces of jewelry, and fixes her mid-length hair in a stylish wave of loose curls. She's meticulous about her appearance, yet she can't step foot outside our home.

We left Lublin, Poland, when I was twelve. Our optimism fortified us, believing our strong work ethic would propel us into a better life, an American dream. Our friends warned us that it would take time and there would be bouts of fear and uncertainty.

Those first few exciting, but scary, months turned into several miserable years. My father couldn't get work as a civil engineer or anything close to what he did back in Poland, but a friend from our Lublin days got him a low-level management position with a grocery distributor out of Queens, a job he disliked and complained about every day.

I thought my parents were both strong and confident when it came to doing what was best for the family. They had the idealistic conviction that they would both be able to go back to school during the evenings and work on advanced degrees so they could get better jobs. Their simple plan never came to fruition, though. They didn't really have the opportunity to enroll in night classes. They were beaten down, stuck in a routine of low-paying work and putting in overtime to cover our monthly expenses. It strained the marriage and their motivation.

It was the lowest I had seen my parents, but I assumed that, once we gained our citizenship, they would recover emotionally and get back to being the optimistic people who had bounded out of our former homeland as if they were off to conquer the world. They were going to be the risk takers.

I imagined a scenario where they could buy the deli and sandwich shop that was for sale in our Queens neighborhood. My mother could put her own twist on the food, and they would build a name for themselves and expand on their reputation with one or two more locations. As a teenager hungry for my family to be whole again, I imagined all this good fortune on the horizon. But it wasn't happening. The challenges in the years leading up to our citizenship had already taken its toll on their marriage. There was less affection, more fighting, and a general sense of giving up on their big dreams. They were merely trying to get by.

Initially, my sister, Aleska, was excited to finish her middle and high school years in America. She had already seen herself as an American kid as we waved goodbye to friends and boarded the plane. She held on to that hopefulness longer than I did. Coming to America was a big blow to our disintegrating idealism. We all became fragile in our own ways. I acted out in school, becoming angry with my parents and scared that I didn't know what to do. My teenage rebellion started early—poor work habits in school, dating troubled boys when I was barely fourteen, and a penchant for smoking with the older high school kids just to shock my peers. It all felt out of character even to me, but I did it anyway.

The whole time we lived in Queens, I was the outsider, the foreigner, the one who didn't speak like everyone else, no matter how hard I worked at it. I have an ear for music, and learning the piano was easy, but my special ability to hear notes and chords never translated to hearing and comprehending English as well as my family. I think my fear of making mistakes and being judged made it worse.

One boy used to mock everything I said with a Dracula accent, and the other kids would laugh along. I was so embarrassed by my accent, and for a long time, it clouded my ability to move past my shame and anger. I'm amazed I managed to graduate high school. The administration must have been as eager to get rid of me as I was to leave.

It didn't help that Aleska had to start working part time at sixteen while she was just a high school sophomore to supplement our parents' incomes. By then, I was a sullen eighteen-year-old with no college prospects, so it was easier for me to join the full-time workforce. My expectations were so low at that point.

We tried to scrounge up enough money and financial aid so we could both attend state college, although there was little chance for me, but there wasn't enough money. And cutting down our work hours at the Greek restaurant where Aleska and I bussed tables meant reducing our family's ability to pay bills. *We're all in this together*—that was the mantra my father kept repeating to us.

Frustrated and tired of the endless cycle of work and growing unhappiness, my father negotiated with a produce distributor he knew to get a job out of the city. It meant a slightly lower salary, but we'd be able to cut down on our living expenses and save money if we were careful.

After Aleska graduated high school, we moved to the little town of Hera, New York—less than a thousand residents, tranquil in the winter but bustling with tourists in the summer. We arrived without knowing a soul, rented a small home, and once again let our hope fuel the motivation we needed to get through each day in our new, lousy jobs.

My mother, Aleska, and I cleaned houses for a disreputable firm based out of Yonkers that pilfered our wages. Five days a week, we cleaned other people's toilets and tried to perform miracles of getting cat and dog odors removed from their carpets and upholstery. On our two days off, we started our own part-time housecleaning business, and the first client I secured was Carson Blackard. When I saw how he didn't keep his kitchen stocked and rarely ate at home, I started offering to cook for him and the other busy professionals he hooked me up with. It was slow going, but it was the new beginning I needed.

Four years ago, and one year after coming to Hera, on a morning like any other, my mother took off her housecleaner's uniform and refused to leave the house. My father assumed she was having a midlife crisis, a mild breakdown, and it would pass. It didn't.

Her undiagnosed situation became worse as she rose each morning and got ready for the day, inventing dozens of excuses why she couldn't leave our home. After a year of rapidly dwindling income, my father could no longer contain his exasperation, which had transformed into indifference toward his wife and daughters. Instead of physically hauling her off to a doctor as Aleska and I begged him to do, he chose to move out and leave his family altogether.

I think my mother's behavior was the opportunity he had been waiting for all along. My father could go much further in his

American life without the burden of an unstable wife and children who were dependent on him. He was willing to give up our love in return for bearing no responsibility for anyone. The bastard also left with most of the money in the family's savings account. So much for the college fund.

Since I already missed those golden years of college and was well-ensconced in an unfulfilling job that would offer no future or security of any kind, Aleska and I devised a new survival strategy so we could take control of our lives and take care of our mother. When you're not given a choice in the matter, you take the one path in front of you and figure out how to make it work.

While our father was basking in the Florida sunshine—his idea of getting as far away from us as possible—Aleska and I took the risk of quitting the insufferable cleaning job and taking our business full time. By then, I had become more ruthless and had no moral dilemma about stealing away clients from our former employer. I also expanded basic meals into more refined gourmet dinners with place settings and linens if the client needed them. And after Carson had me cater a few company dinners, things really took off. That's how I became the local, personal chef in Hera. It's not a career I planned on. I fell into it out of necessity.

I can cook like no one else. While I was a terrible student in school, I was also my mother's helper in the kitchen. I paid attention and learned how to cook like Julia Child. Much of it was watching and practicing, and the rest was instinct.

After three years without our father, and our mother's inability to work, Aleska and I had done fairly well. We could support our mother, pay for Aleska's night classes, and even give me a couple days off a week to spend time with my fiancé, Marko. It wasn't magical or perfect, but my life seemed pretty damn good after all those years of uncertainty with our father.

It was good, not great, until three months ago, when Baldy delivered the scariest news I have ever received.

4

Talia

I AWAKE WITH THE familiar sharp pain that shoots up my breastbone like a hot rod permanently welded to my chest. I turn on my side, silencing my desire to cry out as the pain radiates around my rib cage until I can come to a full sitting position. I breathe slowly and raise my arms to stretch as far as I can.

The doctors gave me Percocet and other drugs, trying to find one that will subdue the extreme discomfort until I heal, but we discovered I can't handle anything stronger than Tylenol without severe, adverse effects—vomiting and dizziness to the point that I feel like my body has aged a hundred years and death is imminent.

I shower, then eat breakfast with Aleska and my mother, who still likes to cook for us. She searches my expression for any sign of pain before putting more scrambled eggs and avocado toast on my plate. It embarrasses my mother to have her daughters supplying the only income, but she puts on a stoic face every morning as though this will be the day that she leaves the house.

Plans to bring in a doctor for a house call were met with angry resistance. Aleska gave in immediately, not willing to battle it out with our mother every day, and without Aleska, I don't have the strength to do it on my own.

As of today, I haven't worked in two whole months. My sister and mother performed my catering job, with my mother doing all the cooking from our small kitchen because I couldn't even lift a frying pan, and Aleska delivering the meals. They also covered up my secret—the real reason for my absence—so well that no one thought to ask questions about me. Everyone thinks I was in Florida, visiting my estranged father. As if I would ever spend money on a plane ticket to visit that bastard.

I've been going crazy holed up with my mother in our house, working ferociously on my excruciating rehabilitation. I made a name for myself, and having my mother doing my work illegally from our residential kitchen made me uncomfortable and eager to get through my physical rehabilitation.

We each have our specialties. Aleska is majoring in accounting and loves numbers, so she manages not only the cleaning crew, but also the overall business finances. I don't get that at all, so I stick with the food, designing the menus and cooking at the fancy, high-end, commercial kitchen I've been renting in a nearby town. Except that fancy kitchen, the one I love so much and depend on, caught on fire the other night.

Of course it did. I can't go back to work without more bad news to screw me over.

When the landlord of the kitchen called me yesterday about the electrical fire, I wasn't even surprised. It's like I just expect bad things to happen to me. I know this is a shitty way to think about yourself.

Now Aleska drives me to Woodstock so we can see how much damage was done. The landlord, Mr. Ricci, gives us hard hats and escorts us inside. The fire was put out in time to save my cookware; however, the walls and floors are scorched beyond repair. It all needs to be replaced and rebuilt. The chemical stench is pungent.

We gather my good knives, the stainless steel and copper pots, and load our company van. Then I look back at the old building, a place for small, start-up businesses, a place that made me happy while I was cooking and filling my brain with ideas for my future. I feel sentimental about losing it.

"At least you weren't in there when the fire started. Things could have been worse," Aleska remarks. "And you've already been through enough."

"True. Besides, Carson's new kitchen is better."

"You mean Peyton's." Aleska smiles. "He's running Swill, Talia, and he's the one who allowed you to use the kitchen."

I look out the window as Aleska steers the van onto the road, my thoughts turning back to Peyton. He's gorgeous. He's also not the type a woman looks for if she wants to settle down and have a family. That doesn't mean I can't fantasize about him.

"And you have to admit he's hot," she continues.

I feign shock, and then we both laugh together. It's been a long time since we've done that.

"Seriously, I've seen him around town for months now, and he is scrumptious!" That's Aleska's favorite word for handsome men. "When we started cleaning his house—"

"Wait. He's one of our clients?"

"Yes. He called me two months ago. He wanted the dinner service, too, but I told him we could only offer cleaning at the time."

"Because I was sick."

"I didn't tell him that. But we definitely couldn't add more clients for Mom to cook for. Not in our little kitchen. But now you can add him to your roster."

"No, absolutely not. Besides, he lives in a restaurant. He can get his meals at Swill. He doesn't need me delivering meals to his home when he has Bash cooking for him."

"Well, all right then. So much for cooking for the hottie."

We make several stops at a few grocery stores in three different towns so I can get all the produce and special cuts of meat I need for the next few days. Aleska tries to carry most of my bags, but I remind her that I'm permitted to handle grocery bags now. I won't collapse, or faint, or go into cardiac arrest. This doesn't stop her from hovering, though.

When a butcher hands me several pounds of lamb chops, Aleska sweeps her arms in front of me, grabs the brown paper packages, and puts them in the cart. I don't tell her that her overprotectiveness makes me feel like I'm her frail grandmother instead of her big sister.

When we arrive at Swill, Bash is outside inspecting crates of produce brought in by a vendor I recognize, a local organic farmer. Considering it's not summer, these must be some of his greenhouse produce.

Bash looks over at me, then says something to the farmer, who then picks up his crates and begins carrying them inside. Bash heads my way with a shy smile.

"Let me help you," he says, pulling the back doors of our van open.

Just as Bash is about to lift up one of my boxes, Peyton comes out of the restaurant, strolling with purpose. I hesitate for a moment to watch him and judge his expression.

"I'll take care of that, Bash," Peyton says. "Go in and handle the produce guys."

Bash looks surprised. "It's no bother. I'll help Talia, and then I'll deal with the deliveries. The guys know where to put everything. We've already gone over—"

"No, you're needed in there. I'll take care of this." Peyton doesn't acknowledge Aleska or me as he hoists two boxes up, one on each shoulder.

Bash's mouth quirks as if he's going to laugh or challenge him, but then he seems to decide against it. "Sure thing, boss man."

"Knock it off." Peyton gives him a hard look.

"Oh, man, I've been usurped by a MacKenzie." Bash shakes his head.

Peyton wins the stare down as Bash chuckles and leaves.

"Tell me where you want this stuff," Peyton directs at me.

"And good morning to you, too," Aleska says brightly.

Peyton's expression softens into a blip of smile. "Good morning. So where am I taking this?"

"To the kitchen, of course," I respond.

"Duh," Aleska adds.

"Of course." Peyton locks eyes with me for a moment, and I study his light-gray eyes, surrounded by his long, dark hair. He's striking, really, if you like good-looking men who have a wolf-like appeal.

Inside, the restaurant is buzzing with activity. The new servers and kitchen help are trying on aprons over their Swill T-shirts and setting out the final touches in the dining area. The bartender, a young lumberjack of a man, is lining a row of scotch behind the bar.

"You're almost ready to open," I say to Peyton's back.

With the boxes on his shoulders, he swings around and walks backward. "Almost." He gives me a devilish smile, knowing that people are jumping out of his way so he doesn't crash into them.

"Be careful. You could hurt yourself."

Peyton is amused by my concern and fakes a stumble. My jaw drops and panic grips me.

"Gotcha," he says.

Behind me, I hear Aleska giggle. However, I don't find it funny at all.

Being around Peyton makes me nervous in unexpected ways.

The box I'm carrying grows heavier and pulls at my sternum. I'm not exceeding the weight limits my doctor gave me, but I hoist my box uncomfortably anyway. Peyton notices and frowns.

When we enter the kitchen, I put the box on the long, stainless steel worktable before he can take it from me.

"Talia, I need to run," Aleska says. "Marguerite is picking me up here. We're going to use her car today so you can have the van and figure out your new runs."

"Thanks."

Aleska gives me a hug, with an extra squeeze on my arms so she doesn't touch my tender chest.

Daily hugs aren't our thing, but since it's my first day back at work, I think my sister is worried about my endurance.

"Let me know if you hit a snag. One of the girls can give me a ride, and I'll come help you."

"Got it." No need to discuss this in front of a kitchen full of people.

After Aleska leaves, Peyton rests a hand on one of my unopened boxes and looks at me as though he deserves some answers.

"What does she mean by *new runs*? And what's this about you hitting a snag?"

"I have two new clients: a family and the man who bought the huge house down the way from Carson's place. I have to figure out a new delivery schedule based on who needs what and when. Some people like a simple drop-off service, while others like for me to heat the food and place it out at a certain time, so I have to factor these things into my deliveries. I have fourteen clients receiving dinner tonight. Those are the runs."

"Busy woman. Sounds very profitable, too," Bash says as he fires up the grills.

"Huh," Peyton says with narrowed eyes. "Why would you hit a snag?"

"She just meant if I got too busy and needed help." I shrug.

"Right," he says. "So then, you are taking on new clients? I tried to sign up."

"I was on vacation then. Aleska couldn't add any new clients with me gone. And now you have this kitchen and Bash cooking for you."

"Maybe I want to eat dinner at home."

"You can bring meals home from your own restaurant. You don't need my services."

"Maybe I want a woman in an apron serving me dinner."

"Then that would be a hard *no*. I'm a chef. I do not provide entertainment."

"Watch yourself, MacKenzie," Bash says, eyeing Peyton with disapproval.

"I'm joking," Peyton says. "But I really did want your chef service. Everyone in town swears by it. But I guess I'll have to just settle for having a clean house."

"You'll survive. Bash will make sure you don't wither away."

Peyton raises an eyebrow at me. Did I win this round?

Then the persistent hottie opens one of my boxes and begins to take my utensils out, but I quickly place a hand in front of him to stop. "Please. I'll do it. But thank you, anyway."

Peyton is a little put off by my abruptness, but he isn't discouraged. He doesn't leave the kitchen, even though he's got bigger problems to deal with in running a new restaurant.

"Chefs don't like their personal tools touched. You know that," Bash tells Peyton as he shuffles a few hot sauté pans around on the range.

"Fine," Peyton says.

"We're very territorial about our knives." I smile, picking up my two new knives, a Yoshihiro Gyuto and a Misono Gyuto, and holding them in a cross in front of my face. "It's all about the knives."

Peyton stares at me for a moment. "Twisted girl. I like that."

"Oh." I put the knives down with a shaky carelessness. "Don't get the wrong idea about me."

Peyton looks at me with that particular smug satisfaction a man gets when he flusters a woman. "Bash, let's get all the dishes out within the next half hour. I want every server and bartender to know what they taste like. And I want you to make sure they know the ingredients and how they should describe the dish to the customer in the most concise manner possible without sounding like they memorized the menu."

"We're on it. Almost ready." Bash casually checks over his other cooks' shoulders to see how their dishes are coming along.

"I'd like your opinion, too," Peyton tells me, "since you're here. How about it?"

I look at Bash. Honestly, reviewing another chef's food makes me uncomfortable.

"I'm fine with it," Bash says, sensing my apprehension. "I'd like to know what you think of our menu."

"Ah, well, I can tell you right now that I love the menu, and everything you're cooking smells divine. I really don't think you need me to do a taste test."

"Chicken?" Peyton asks.

"What?" I reply, confused. "Chicken? Are you referring to a chicken dish on the menu?"

"He wants to know if you're too scared to tell me the truth about my food," Bash clarifies.

"Oh." I think about that for a second. Why don't I know this chicken expression?

"What's wrong?" Peyton laughs. "You're making a face."

"Ease up on her, buddy." Bash winks at me. "You threw her off with *chicken*."

"Remember, English isn't my first language." I give him a good poke in the shoulder and almost break my finger on his hard muscles. I pull back my hand, a little embarrassed that I touched him like that and also concerned that I sprained my finger.

"Hmm," Peyton studies me. "And yet you speak English so beautifully. Almost perfect, most would say." I don't know if he's mocking me, but the way he says this makes me feel rather lovely inside. It's definitely better than his sexist apron remark.

"I've had a lot of private English lessons," I say. "And I watched a lot of *Gilmore Girls*. Those marathoning shows."

"Marathon reruns," Bash corrects.

"Yes, that. They talk really fast, so it was good practice. But I didn't understand a lot of the humor."

Peyton moves closer to me. "So then, you're not too chicken to try Bash's food and give us your real opinion on our menu?"

"No. I'm not too—why do you keep referring to poultry when talking about fear?"

Bash and Peyton both laugh while I stand there dumbstruck. Then Bash is quickly distracted by the various burners and prep stations he's got manned with very quiet, industrious young men and women who cook alongside him, but Peyton continues to watch me.

"You're interesting." His voice is lower, as if he doesn't want the others to listen. They should be too busy cooking and can't possibly hear us over the sizzle of the grill and the repetitive sounds of metal blades hitting plastic and wood cutting boards, but they seem to watch Peyton, their boss, with side-eye, anxious glances. "This is an unusual day. Normally during this time, only Bash and I will be here, so you'll be able to cook without this crowd in your way."

"I only hope *I'm* not in *their* way. I can step out for an hour so they can finish their forty or so menu items."

"Don't leave. You need to get to work." He picks up one of my large knives and twirls it on its side against his palm. It's a frenzy of light reflecting off the shiny blade like a magician's trick, and then he catches the handle and places it back down as though it was nothing.

"How did you do that?" I ask, stunned that he didn't lose a finger, or worse, lose the knife and accidentally stab me.

"I worked in quite a few restaurants before we bought our first one. I had to start as a dishwasher and work my way up to the salad station. I did all the prep work for the chefs."

"Nice. You're very handy, but don't ever do that again around me. That's reckless, and if I was your kitchen manager, I'd fire you."

Bash laughs from across the worktable. So much for our conversation being drowned out by the buzzing kitchen activity.

Peyton leans over, his long hair brushing my cheek as he whispers in my ear, "Good thing you're not my boss. I'd miss seeing you every day." Now I understand the expression *smooth talker*. Peyton's words and voice are so smooth I practically sway.

"Peyton! Phone!" a pretty waitress shouts as she pokes her head in from the dining room. "It's your sister. Greer says she's back in the brewery, and Zander is still having major electrical issues." The waitress leaves as quickly as she entered.

"Why can't we get decent cell service in here!" he shouts to the room. "This business of running to a landline is archaic."

So much for his playful flirting.

He stalks across the kitchen, grabs the phone off the wall, and pushes the blinking red button. "What?" he asks tersely.

Tying my long apron around my waist, I jump when he hisses, "What's the problem this time?" Pause. "Damn!"

I look at Bash, but he doesn't seem concerned in the least about Peyton's issue. I should know better, really. Restaurants are full of one mini drama after another, and those in charge tend to be emotional, hyper, control freaks who keep the stress and tension level high. Peyton fits the young, cocky, overachiever role perfectly.

Bash, on the other hand, is Peyton's opposite. Unlike most restaurant chefs who tend to be short-tempered, Bash calmly moves from station to station, assisting his cooks.

Peyton slams the phone back on the wall, causing the kitchen staff to glance his way.

"Excuse me," he says directly to me as though we were in the middle of something important.

I almost want to laugh at his gruffness, but I don't. I'm glad I'm not in his position of putting out a million fires before opening day.

"You're excused," I reply, perhaps a little too coyly.

Peyton looks at me and hesitates a moment. "Oh, we're not finished, Natalia Madej," he says coolly and then leaves the kitchen.

• • •

"He's not always so serious," Bash says as he arranges dozens of entrees on the counter. He wipes the plate rims with a clean towel and adorns the food with various herbs. His crew is done with the grills, so I move in to take one over with my pans of lamb chops.

"I really only know Peyton from witnessing his outrageous behavior at his brother's wedding. Peyton was the jokester entertaining the crowd, but we've never actually spoken, and until now, I've never seen him in his work element." I jostle a few sauté pans and turn back to the worktable to set out the delivery containers I need to fill.

Bash sneaks glances my way and watches with interest.

"At work, he's usually all business," he says. "The family bar he owns with his dad and uncle wouldn't be successful without him. Neither would the Midtown Manhattan restaurant he and I run together. He's the driving force behind them."

"I remember the bar. When I was at the wedding, I took a good look around and thought Peyton did a very good job restoring the place. Cooper said it had been rundown and hadn't changed since it opened in the 1960s."

"Peyton has a head for business, and when there are rough patches, he's good at adjusting quickly to market trends. I've known him long enough to know that, when it comes to restaurants and bars, he's the guy I'll follow anywhere. Starting a brewery on top of all this is a new thing, but I have faith that Peyton is going to crush it. He's that good."

"He's fortunate to have such loyal friends and employees. But I guess he really sees you as a partner, not his employee." Bash is so large and imposing that it's hard to imagine anyone delegating orders to him.

His sweet smile breaks through his rough exterior. "Peyton gives me free rein to do whatever I want in the kitchen and with the menu. He doesn't mess with my area, and I don't advise him on his, unless he asks."

"Does he ever ask for advice?" I'm genuinely curious.

Bash smiles. "Only once. He asked me how he should politely break up with a woman who thought she was his girlfriend."

"Seriously? How does that work?"

Bash shrugs. "Women like him. He went out with this one woman a couple of times, and she assumed she was his one and only."

"She was really one of many, right?"

"Maybe not *many*, but a few. He did have a girlfriend—a woman he dated for almost a year. But enough about him. Try this." Bash takes a forkful of food from a plate and cups it with his palm, walking over to me. He feeds me directly, and I oblige. When the flavors merge in my mouth, I am delighted.

"Chicken pâté," I say with my mouth full.

"Yes, with truffle oil and lingonberries. What do you think?"

"It's delicious. Pâtés are not my specialty. This is excellent, Bash."

"It's one of our appetizers. I think it'll do well. I'm glad you like it."

Bash and his cooks finish putting out all the menu dishes, and then servers come in to sample the food and listen to Bash explain the ingredients. I try all of his dishes as well and give approving nods to the rich entrees, such as the Wiener schnitzel and the Hungarian beef goulash. There's nothing ordinary about these classics, a testament to Bash's talent.

As the servers eat their way through all the heavy food, then clear away the empty plates for the dishwasher, Bash begins cleaning his kitchen, and I help with the pans and utensils.

I finish packing all my individual dinners of lamb chops and rosemary potatoes and the various side dishes while Bash watches me arrange and cover each container, treating them with care and a ridiculous amount of attention, as though they are precious.

They are my babies. Each dish I make and deliver is something I'm keenly proud of. At the same time, I'm always conscious that something can go wrong and a customer may be unhappy.

"Now your turn," I say to Bash. Using tongs, I hold out a fried pepper to him.

It's cool enough that he takes it between his fingers and pops it in his mouth. He looks cute as he tries to decipher the ingredients.

"This is good," he says while chewing. "Red cherry pepper stuffed with prosciutto and ..."

"Fontina cheese," I add. "I serve it with a balsamic reduction and cucumber yogurt. It's not a fancy dish, but it's always a big pleasure for crowds."

"A crowd-pleaser," Bash politely corrects me. "I love this. If Peyton gets his hands on one of these, he's going to demand you put it on the restaurant menu."

"I'll give you the recipe. And you'll have to give up one of yours, too."

"Whatever you want. I'll swap recipes with you any day."

"Who's swapping what?" Peyton demands as he enters the kitchen. He looks around, surprised that the kitchen is spotless and all my food is already packed in insulated tote bags.

"You missed the taste-testing," Bash remarks, hanging up a knife against the magnetic strip on the wall. "It went well. I think everyone is prepared ... to sell food, at least. How are the tap lines?"

"Wouldn't you know, the pilsner line is the only one that isn't working. A German pub without a pilsner. There's a sad joke for you," he says. "At least the electricity is back on in the brewery." He shakes his head. "All these fucking problems."

"Try this," Bash demands as he pings one of my stuffed peppers at Peyton. I think it will hit Peyton's chest and drop to the floor, but his reflexes are quick and he catches the golf-ball-sized pepper. I'm surprised he pops it in his mouth without questioning Bash.

"This is damn good." He finishes eating it. "Did you add this to our menu?"

"Nope. It's Talia's."

Peyton casts an undecipherable expression toward me. "You see, Ms. Madej? This is why you and I have a few matters to discuss."

"Peppers?" I ask with a light laugh. I pick up one of my delivery bags, realizing I can only carry one at a time to the van.

"Peppers are just the beginning." He picks up my other bags, stacking them, and then proceeds to follow me out to my van. "You're full of surprises."

"I don't know what you're talking about. They're stuffed peppers. Nothing more."

Peyton balances the bags in one hand and opens the back of the van for me. I start to place the bags inside, but he takes over, arranging them in a way so they won't move during transport. This is something I always do, but he beat me to it, as if he could read my mind and understands my system. Then he closes the back doors and leans against them with his arms crossed.

"It's more than that."

He's waiting for me to say something.

"Now you've lost me. You sound like Cooper when he goes off on one of his abstract, philosophical rants."

"You're mysterious. I like that. And it's also why everyone refers to you as the little Russian spy. I'll figure you out, though."

"Once again, I'm not Russian," I say in annoyance. "And I have nothing exciting to hide. Besides, people in Hera can vouch for me. They know there's nothing mysterious about me. Nothing."

His gorgeous smile is sinister. "This is going to be fun."

5

Talia

T HE DELIVERY ROUNDS ARE more wearing than I anticipated. Something I've been doing with easy vigor for the past few years exhausts me in my current condition. I'm in good shape, but my energy level is not where it should be for simply driving around, delivering meals. Maybe the few hours I spent in the steamy kitchen over the hot grill was all I could handle for today. Still, I only have one delivery left for this evening. I timed it so a certain new customer will be the last one of the day.

Adam Knight's home is spectacular. It was one of the first contemporary "green" homes built by one of Carson's other businesses, a home development group that specializes in LEED construction, using sustainable materials and creating these modern, box-style homes with soaring windows to capture natural light and garden rooftops to recycle rain water. Carson and Jess's home is similar, and after working there for a few years, I've grown accustomed to the serene simplicity of the minimalist style. The poured concrete floors mixed in with bamboo woodwork and forged metal fixtures blend in nicely with the surrounding green shades of nature.

The original owner of this home was an executive at a Manhattan firm and only spent weekends here before being transferred to San Francisco. The home never made it to market. From what Carson told me, Adam Knight bought it from photos off the Internet and moved in two weeks ago.

I park my van in the unpaved driveway and take in the tall home of glass. I can see all the way through the two-story front windows to the back of the house and its impressive views of the hilly valley below.

All I know about Adam Knight is he's a rich CEO of a successful hedge fund, which he runs out of a converted warehouse in Tribeca. I don't recall the name of the company, but in his email to Aleska, he mentioned living in a loft above his firm and plans to spend at least three days a week working from his new home in Hera. He said we came highly recommended from Carson. Of course we did. He had house keys delivered to us and had the home security system disarmed since he didn't think it was necessary. A lot of people in Hera sleep with their doors unlocked. It's one of *those* towns.

I carry the insulated bag to the front door and have no problem unlocking it. Everything seems brand-new, as if never used, but then the previous owner was rarely ever here.

As I push open the door, fortunately, no alarms go off.

Once, when I was younger, I was picked up by a deceptively friendly cop—it was such a minor incident! But sometimes I still think I'm going to be stopped by police and questioned by the authorities, and they'll tell me my citizenship was a mistake and I have to go back to Poland.

Even though I've been in America for over ten years and am a citizen, I still have some doubts about where I belong. I want to belong to Hera, and the people here make me feel like I do, but there's another part of me that still feels like a misplaced foreigner, the person who doesn't always understand their inside jokes or how they maintain strong family relationships. Somehow, they do.

Carson has held on to his younger brother through Dylan's years of struggling with bipolar depression. Jess, who is truly a genius, gifted in math and computer software, has managed to strengthen her relationship with her standoffish, academic parents despite leaving her big New York City life behind for Carson and a career in art. And Lauren and Imogene always knew they would come back to Hera after college, get married, and start their families and business here.

They reeled in men from outside of Hera. Leo and Cooper both came to town to work for Carson at Blackard Designs, but they stayed for the women they had fallen in love with. Sweet courtships I watched from a distance.

I'd like to think I'm like my friends, that I'm building a life here. But, if I'm being completely honest, when it comes to fitting in, I have a problem. While the rest of my family can easily pass as native New Yorkers, I'm the only one who still sounds like I just arrived in this country. And I still make the most ridiculous mistakes. I don't think I will ever live down the number of times I referred to the old reruns of the TV show *Family Ties* as *Family Thighs*. For years, I mispronounced *T*s for *th*'s, much to Imogene's delight. She loved doing impressions of my faux pas, entertaining the lunch crowd at her family's diner. However, I believe I have remedied this situation by taking online speech and dictation lessons for the last year, working diligently to get rid of my accent.

"*Family Ties,*" I say clearly to myself as I step inside Adam Knight's home.

I can smell the natural eucalyptus cleaning products that Aleska uses. Windows have been washed, rugs have vacuum cleaner tracks, all surfaces are gleaming, and no dust is free-floating in the last rays of sun spiraling through the immense windows. As I expected, the home is minimally furnished. Not stark, but just enough furniture and artwork to make it comfortable.

What catches my attention is the grand piano at the far end of the living room. It's showcased in a semicircular glass alcove that overlooks the woods off to the side of the house. I wonder if the master of the home can play or if it's for show.

My temptation to inspect the piano up close is brushed away with the need to do my assigned job. I find my way to the kitchen, where high-end appliances have that fresh-from-the-store appearance of never being used. I check the metal filters under the range hood and, sure enough, they are spotless. This has to be one of the easiest cleaning assignments for Aleska's crew.

The enormous refrigerator holds a few bottles of mineral water and beer. Unless he plans on eating most of his meals out, he's going to need some groceries. My two or three dinners a week can be eaten as leftovers, but even I would get bored eating the same thing for three meals in a row.

He's wealthy and he's single—obviously, look at this place. If there were a woman involved, there would be photographs of her with him on exotic vacations. There would be throw pillows and a few vases. There would be something personal to show that she's here and this is her man. Unless he's gay.

I contemplate this for a moment, because the truth is, I'm hoping he's not. It didn't occur to me to do some internet research on this man. Aleska replied to his emails because I was too busy doing physical therapy and sleeping for the past two months. I assumed, and hoped, Adam Knight would be a nice, easy, no-fuss client like Carson was when I first started.

I spot a magazine on the far end of the kitchen counter. It's out of place in this overly sanitized home. Aleska must have placed it just so with its bottom edge sticking out over the lip of the counter so I'd notice it.

I've never heard of this magazine because it's about finance. *Bloomberg Markets, ANNUAL HEDGE FUND ISSUE, THE TOP 100* is splashed across the cover with a model-handsome man underneath. He's in a black suit, arms crossed, with a Rolex gleaming from underneath his shirt cuff. The man gives a smug smile, projecting enormous confidence and ego, everything this magazine is about. My sister is clever, and I'm on to her.

The subheading on the cover confirms my suspicions. *WHAT DO YOU THINK OF ADAM KNIGHT NOW? He makes enemies, instigates controversy, and runs KNIGHT, the world's best-performing hedge fund.*

My gaze is glued to his sharp, hazel eyes and handsome face. His light brown hair is cut short and parted to the side, but not too short, so the ends curl slightly above his forehead, giving him a deceptively boyish appeal.

"There's nothing boyish about you, is there?" I ask the face staring back at me. "You are definitely smart and handsome, and probably a bit ruthless to be where you are." I search the glossy cover for any sign that he may also be *kind*. I don't open the magazine because I already know the article will tell me how wildly successful Mr. Knight is, with no mention of his kindness, if it does exist. This is a magazine about titans and winners on Wall Street. It does not measure people on a kindness scale. That, I will have to do myself.

I put his food in the oven, then set the table for one. Then I tidy up so the kitchen is as clean as Aleska left it and walk back into the living room to admire the piano. It's a Steinway, a rather old but well-maintained one from the looks of it. The keys haven't yellowed with age; they look like perfect white teeth against the gleaming black wood. Me alone with a glorious grand piano is too tempting.

I run a finger along the keys, firm enough to check tone. Someone has been keeping this beauty tuned. I slide in between the piano and the bench and sit down, but I pause with my hands poised above the keys, almost talking myself out of doing this. Too late. I've broken my silent pledge never to touch a client's personal belongings, but I justify it by believing that tuned pianos must be played and enjoyed.

It's easy. My fingers remember everything as they slip into Chopin's Piano Concerto No. 2. Years of lessons with my father on our flea market baby grand piano back in Lublin, which was then replaced with an upright piano when we moved to Queens, are burned into my brain and fingertips.

When we moved to Hera, our piano, along with a few of our other valuables, had to be sold off at our one-day garage sale so we could pay off the rent that was overdue. My father had ignored the daily calls and letters sent from the collection agency, but when an intimidating man showed up at our door, and argued with my father about "a debt," I wondered what kind of trouble my father was in. The kind of trouble that requires you to sell your family's prized possessions.

I miss having a piano. It's not that I only miss playing it; I miss hearing my father play and my mother sing. Those were the good times.

Leaving Queens felt like we were giving up as a family. Whatever was once good—my parents' marriage, our music, our American dreams—seemed to have vanished instantly the minute we moved.

I continue to play Mr. Knight's piano. It's as though my fingers have a mind of their own as they switch to Brahms. The melody is lovely and makes me smile from the inside, even as I think of my father's betrayal that changed my family's path.

I'm sorry we weren't enough for him, but I really try not to dwell on him too much. I imagine he doesn't think about us that much either as he moves from one Florida beach town to another, engaging in his never-ending, money-making schemes with women who help him forget us.

"That's superb." A deep voice startles me from behind.

My hands slam down, causing the keys to shriek. Then I turn around and face the man who runs the world's best-performing hedge fund. Whatever that is.

"*O Boze!*" *Oh God, oh God.* I stand abruptly. "I apologize. I shouldn't be playing your piano. Excuse me." I rush toward the kitchen.

"Wait. Somebody should be playing that thing. I certainly can't."

I pause and turn around. Normally, I'm very composed, but I'm shaking slightly in his presence. *Maybe because the good little girl got caught again.*

He tosses his keys on an end table and slings his suit coat on the couch.

"I'll set up your dinner and get out of your way," I say hurriedly, silently cursing my unprofessional behavior.

"Wait." He laughs as he removes his tie and tosses it as well. "There's no rush. I don't mind you playing the piano. It was nice to walk in and hear music instead of the usual dead silence. I'm Adam, by the way, since we haven't formally met."

"I'm Talia. You've corresponded with my sister, Aleska."

He walks toward me and extends his hand, which I take. His handshake is warm and firm, and his eyes lock with mine. A business handshake, I remind myself.

"Your food is ready. Let me get it." I waver a bit since he's sending my hormones into a fit.

Shaking those untrustworthy emotions aside, I remove his food from the oven and plate all the courses, arranging them on his kitchen table.

Adam washes his hands at the kitchen sink, watching me with a casual curiosity.

"I didn't think to ask if you'd rather eat in your dining room. I assumed you'd prefer this smaller table."

"This is perfect. I've never had a real meal in this house. Thanks." He sits down at the small table made for four and studies the cloth napkin. Most of our clients are quite affluent and have fully stocked cupboards of monogramed linens, including napkins. If they don't, Aleska stocks their kitchen with ivory linen napkins, which we supply at no charge to the clients. Aleska washes them with the rest of their laundry, and it allows me to dress up their table setting beyond using paper napkins.

Adam nods approvingly and snaps open the napkin and places it on one leg. "Aren't you going to join me? There's enough food here for more than one." He gestures to an empty chair.

My hand covers my slight laugh. "No. I don't dine with clients. You have extra food to eat on the evenings I'm not here. The heating instructions are on the counter, along with the rest of the food and containers. Whatever you don't finish, just put it in the fridge. I try to make this as simple as possible for everyone."

"So I have to eat alone." He leans his tall frame against the back of the chair and rests an arm casually across the empty chair next to him. I can see how he'd be a good negotiator in business with his cool confidence and persistent tone.

"Please, eat," I say.

He cuts into a lamb chop and takes a bite. "Excellent." He drops his cutlery and picks up the chop with one hand, tearing into it like an animal. I can't help laughing, and it makes him grin. "You don't know what you're missing."

"I think I do."

"Not the food, which by the way is truly superb. I was referring to dinner with me."

"Oh." I laugh. "You definitely aren't shy."

"Never. When I'm in the city, I always have a dinner date. No one wants to eat alone. Ms. Madej, you've crushed my ego."

"Doubt it. Your ego has a really good appetite." I resume gathering my catering bags so I can leave.

"Look, I was kidding. Being too forward. The truth is, when I don't have a client dinner, I usually hit the gym before grabbing a bite to eat sometime around midnight. Sometimes I get bored of my own company, so a dinner companion who isn't a client would be nice right about now."

I smile and shrug.

"But of course, I'm your client, so this would be like a client dinner for you." He grins. "I guess I can't win this, but at least it's a night away from the city and a great meal that doesn't involve my work."

"Is that why you bought this place? To get away from the other sharks?"

"The other sharks? I like that. And that's precisely the reason. I haven't taken a vacation or time off ... well, I don't know when, but now I'm in a position to work two to three days a week away from the office."

He hasn't stopped eating since he took the first bite, and I notice his plate is almost empty. "Why did you choose Hera? Why not Woodstock? Or the Hamptons, a beach home?"

"I didn't want a town populated with celebrities and socialites. I met Carson Blackard when I was passing through once. I liked him right away. I bought some of his furniture for my place in the city, and then I found out about this house and decided to look into buying it. Hera is a fairly short commute to the office if I leave early. I like to drive into the city around four a.m., when everyone else is still sleeping. And this house, the photos online, sold me. And it has that view." He juts his chin toward the floor-to-ceiling window that overlooks the pastoral landscape.

"You're a workaholic." I sigh, wondering if a man like him will always love the challenge of his career more than his marriage. That's if he ever gets married.

"I'm learning how to relax. That's what this home is for."

"Working from home doesn't sound relaxing to me."

"Having a nice home-cooked meal in my new, peaceful house is very relaxing. Hopefully, next time I'll have a dinner date."

I look at him for an extra beat. Is he going to start bringing women here for me to feed? To serve?

Recognizing my confusion, he smiles. "Once again, I'm referring to you. It would be nice if you'd join me sometime for dinner. Since you're here and all."

"I don't eat with the clients," I reiterate.

"Client? I'm a shark. We're predators, Talia, and we're really good at getting what we want."

6

Peyton

FOR THE PAST TWO weeks since she started using our kitchen, Talia has been cordial with me, but pretty much keeping a safe distance from having to converse with me beyond a morning greeting.

When we're near each other, there's an electrical charge between us, surrounding us, that seems to make her nervous. When I catch her looking at me, she quickly averts her eyes. I'm not blind, there's a mutual attraction, but she seems to be trying very hard to avoid it. Why does it make me more interested in her? She's not the type to have a casual fling to amuse me for the next few months while I'm living in this dull town. That doesn't deter me, though.

I've tried to insert myself into her daily life, which is highly uncharacteristic of me, but here I am, every morning, checking the time on my phone because I know when she bikes to Swill ... and I just happen to be passing through the kitchen when she arrives.

I get the polite hello before she gives her attention to Bash, continuing a conversation from the day before. And I look like a putz if I hover around them in an attempt to be included when I have a shitload of tasks to be completed on a tight deadline. Yeah, but that doesn't stop me from trying, again with the fucking clock watching.

I'm always in the kitchen when Talia is packing her delivery bags, and I always carry them outside to load them in the van. She's appreciative, but still distant, and I don't push it because I honestly don't know why the hell I'm doing this or what I expect to happen with her.

So here we are, one day before our grand opening night, and everyone insists we have to spend tonight at Carson and Jess's home for *movie night*. I've been so busy overseeing the remodeling of the restaurant and hiring staff the last few months that I haven't spent much social time with my new business partners or even my brother and sister.

The timing for this party couldn't be worse. I'm surprised they aren't more hyped up about the opening like me. Anything can go wrong and often does with restaurants.

The food industry is a tough business, and I feel too pumped up to settle down with a bowl of popcorn and watch a movie, but Imogene is the pushiest sister-in-law I have ever had. She's also my favorite. I can't say no to her. My brother is a lucky guy for landing her. I'm betting they'll have the only marriage in my family that doesn't end up in divorce court. Unlike me, Cooper wants to settle down, and he found the perfect partner.

I'd consider making an actual effort to talk to Talia, who's hanging out in the kitchen with the other women, but I remind myself that I'm not like my brother. I'm not like any of the married guys here. Talia doesn't need me wasting her time.

"You should socialize," Greer says when she catches me eyeing Talia a little too long. My sister has her twin three-year-olds, Nikki and Owen, in hand. "We can't stay for the movie. I have to get the monsters to bed."

"We're not really monsters," Nikki clarifies primly.

"No, you're not monsters." I bend down and kiss them both.

"Why don't you go talk to the pretty chef you're looking at?" Greer says.

"I was thinking I should go to the restaurant."

"Because the employees haven't had enough of you running them ragged? You should take a break tonight and get your rest, because there will be plenty of time tomorrow for you to act like the boss from hell. Stop worrying. I'll see you in the morning, and everything will go perfectly tomorrow. You'll see. You were made for this business, Peyton." Greer kisses my cheek, then leaves with her kids.

I don't really want to talk to anyone tonight unless they want to commiserate with my opening-day concerns. They don't. They all look happy to put aside work and talk about other things.

I'm operating on less than four hours of sleep a night, and when the day-to-day problems of uncooperative appliances or contractors get to me, I take off on runs with Dylan. He needs the daily runs and rigorous workout schedule before, during, and after work hours at the Blackard Designs factory—where he's also head of their sales division—to help manage his depression and mood swings.

I appreciate his silence when we're both in a foul mood and all we want to do is run it off. Dylan doesn't pry, and when he does ask me questions, it's more out of thoughtful curiosity than judgment. However, we're similar enough that, when we disagree, our explosive arguments can be heard across town. At least we never hold a grudge.

Barefoot, Carson plops down on the massive couch and fiddles with a remote that rolls down a full-size theater screen from the ceiling. Cooper and Leo take over another side of the sectional while Dylan heads into the kitchen to get the food he's prepared. The guy can cook just as well as any of the trained chefs I've worked with, and he shares the same territorial behavior as Talia and Bash about his knives and food.

"Don't fuck with my stuff," he snapped at me once when I made the mistake of picking up one of his paring knives. *Chefs and their fucking knives.* That immediately makes me think of Talia.

After some major explosion happens on the movie screen, I make my way to the kitchen, where all the women are gabbing over platters of sandwiches and appetizers that Dylan is arranging.

"Hey, help me carry this stuff out there. Those bastards started the movie without me, and I can't listen to these hens clucking and gossiping anymore."

That gets him a nice, hard jab in the ribs from his wife, Emma.

"Sorry." He smiles at her.

We take the food out to the living room, and the platters are swarmed by the hungry dudes before they're even set down on the oversize coffee table.

Still anxious, I can't sit down to watch the movie or eat. I don't know if I want a beer or if I should head home to try to sleep.

I walk back into the kitchen for a bottle of mineral water. I pull it out of the fridge and guzzle all twenty-five ounces without stopping.

"A little tense?" Imogene asks as I toss the empty bottle into the recycling bin underneath the sink. "Worried about tomorrow?"

"Maybe." I shrug and run my hand through my hair. Christ, did I forget to take a shower after my run today? I can't remember half of what I'm doing unless it's directly related to the restaurant. I spent the last few days fixing every crisis that popped up, and they seemed to happen every hour.

The work distractions have been good. They keep me on a nonstop schedule, preventing me from saying something stupid to Talia when I run into her.

The urge to spend more time with her and the discipline I use to stay away from her are making me fucking irritable. There were a few times when I thought I could smell her perfume, or maybe it was her natural scent, as if she had just left the space. It drives me insane. This instinct to search for her and sniff the air makes me feel like a fucking wolf.

Maybe I just need to get laid. In that case, I should call Flora and have her stay with me for a few days for *friend* sex. That would go over really well. The image of her causing me bodily harm—castration comes to mind—leaves me tense all over again.

Talia is bouncing Jess's baby, Scotty, on her hip while she gently holds the back of his head and talks to him in a soft voice. The baby smiles, then begins wailing, surprising Talia, who thought she had the infant under her soothing spell.

"I think he needs to be burped," Jess says. "He just ate like one of those guys who wins hot dog eating contests."

"Yuck, and ouch," Imogene says.

"You're telling me." Jess looks frazzled, the right side of her shirt covered in spit-up. Not to mention, two enormous wet spots are blooming across her chest where she's leaking.

I remember when Greer was going through the nursing stage with the twins. The sleep-deprived mother with that glassy-eyed stare of both amazement and frustration that her body had a new purpose, one controlled by two fifteen-pound babies.

I love all my nieces and nephews, and playing with them can be a hoot, but I have no interest in tying myself down to a family and staying in one place, living each day by the same routine.

"Burp him," Lauren directs at Talia. Lauren's own toddler is asleep on her shoulder, making parenting look easy.

Talia pats Scotty's back firmly, but the chubby little man won't give it up. He's wailing now, and Talia looks a little petrified.

I cross the room to her and reach for Scotty. "Give him to me."

She lets me take him and looks up at me, curious if I know what I'm doing.

"The MacKenzies are pros," Imogene adds, patting Talia's shoulder, then taking a swig from her wineglass.

Jess looks on wearily as I lay her son facedown against my forearm and rub his back. "It's the football hold," I explain. "It pushes the gas out quicker."

Scotty calms down immediately and, within seconds, small burps are followed by a loud belch. The baby smiles and closes his eyes, enjoying the back rub.

Jess tilts her head in wonder. "Football hold? Why didn't Carson tell me about this? He loves football."

Talia lets out a husky laugh. "How many babies has Carson held?"

"Other than Maisie and Scotty, none," Jess says. "Look at him. My baby is happier in Peyton's arms than mine."

"No, you just don't know anything about football and burps," Talia tells Jess. "He loves his mama more than anyone."

"You're his food supply," Imogene snorts.

"Here." I hand Jess's sleeping baby back, and she takes him in her arms with a weepy desperation.

I need to get away from these women and their baby conversation. It's making me edgy, as if Flora will show up any moment and scream, *Ah-ha! You can do this, so why were you making my ovaries wait!* Thinking of that last blowout with Flora makes me shudder.

"Stay away from our women," Cooper says half-jokingly as he enters the kitchen, clamping his hand on my shoulder and giving me his big brother *don't fuck up my life* look.

"I was only burping a kid."

Cooper grunts and moves on to get more drinks for the guys.

I pull my phone out to check if there are any emergency messages from Zander or Bash, who are both at the restaurant doing final checks. Nothing terrible yet, just a lot of group texts from them talking about things to buy or do before tomorrow night's opening.

I back myself against the far end of the kitchen to get some space from the women and give myself a chance to think.

The chatter and energy of the women surges when Aleska arrives.

"*So?* How was Adam Knight?" Imogene asks Talia enthusiastically while winking at Aleska. "Did you see that magazine cover he's on? I saw a copy at Jess's house and, oh my God, the man is awesome!"

I've heard about Adam Knight, the CEO who bought one of Carson's expensive homes. He's a few years older than me, but he's got the Wall Street job and Ivy League education that husband-hunting women want. Fine by me. I don't want to be a husband, not when I've got my time committed to my businesses.

Fuck all, then why do you keep trying to get Talia's attention?

"He's arrogant in a funny way, but nice, too," Talia says to the women. "I only got to see him on my first delivery to his place. Over the past couple of weeks, I've had to set up his dinners before he gets home, so I haven't seen him.

"The Garcia family put in a special request for my last time slot. Every night for the past ten days, I showed up and put the kids' favorite foods out, and their dad chased after the toddlers and got them to the table so his wife could sit and nurse the baby at the table. The kids were having a really difficult time adjusting to the new baby in the house, and dinnertime had become a screaming match, but after four days of me asking the kids to help set the table—I call it *decorating* so they're more interested—the kids stopped screaming. And now they're happy to help with plates and napkins, and they sit right down and eat. I think I'm pretty good at it, and the two families I've done this for seem grateful."

"You can charge more for that!" Imogene says. "Do you have any idea how many families around here with little kids have the same problem with dinners from hell?"

"No, I don't," Talia says, sounding concerned.

"Neither do I," Imogene adds. "But there has to be buckets of money to be made from some of these rich families."

"I like working with the parents and kids, but I'll be happy to put Adam back in my last time slot." Then she breaks into a smile and says in a low voice, "He *is* very attractive."

The way she says this makes me feel a sliver of contempt toward Adam Knight. I don't know the guy or have anything against him, and I certainly don't have any claim on Talia, or plan to be caught up in this small-town soap opera, but something about this rubs me the wrong way.

Talia isn't a naïve, innocent girl. She's a very capable woman, at least from what I've seen and from what I remember at my brother's wedding. I have no doubt she can handle herself, but I'm also pretty sure that a man like Adam Knight has the practiced skills of getting what he wants. He's got to be tempted by a beautiful woman like Talia coming into his home, cooking for him, doting on him like a pretend wife. Knight's a Manhattan guy, and he probably would love to get a little, pretty country ass on the side, especially since she's conveniently showing up on a regular basis.

"And Adam has slightly wavy, brown hair. But it's short, the way Talia likes. A clean-cut man," Aleska explains to the others.

I don't know how I went from not giving a shit to reading too much into this, but suddenly my fist is squeezing my cell phone.

7

Talia

PERK UP WHEN Aleska starts talking about Adam. But as the women circle in closer to hear more about Hera's new resident, I notice Peyton leaning against the far wall, his expression intense as he reads his phone, and have a momentary lapse, forgetting about Adam. Instead, I observe Peyton, his tall, brooding form gripping his phone as though it is life and death, his dark hair falling forward, covering part of his face. I can see how his staff finds him intimidating. The truth is, under that dangerous-looking facade is a fair-minded man who spends an inordinate amount of time helping others. I've watched him—okay, spied on him—when his sister's young children visit Swill and Peyton fills in for their absentee father. He isn't only protective of family members; he treats his employees with remarkable concern.

In the restaurant business, there's a high turnover of staff. Everyone seems to be expendable because it's not a business where people aspire to be food servers or dishwashers for a lifetime. Peyton seems to think he can beat those odds by making his restaurant a desirable place to work. I've seen countless restaurant owners attempt the same thing, but they don't have Peyton's appeal. It's Peyton's job to make the environment exciting and a place you want to come work at, and he makes it his business to know all of his employees, their work needs, and schedule issues. I admire him for that.

I even catch myself admiring *him*, his rugged handsomeness. No wonder the younger waitresses flitter around him, hanging on his every word. A few years ago, I would have, too, but I know his type. All work and too much careless play. Career ambition is the name of the game, and Peyton seems to be set in that area, with a girlfriend who is a successful attorney in the city, someone who also works long hours and is just as driven as him.

I'm not putting Adam Knight in the same category. He's already shown the first step of being different than guys like Peyton by buying a big house in the country. You don't do that unless you're looking for something beyond your work life, like putting down roots and having a family.

It doesn't necessarily stop me from thinking about Peyton. Despite his ambitious goals to rise to celebrity ranks in some type of restaurant conglomerate, the man possesses a special, deep bond with his family and the people who work for him. It's appealing, and I wonder if it will be hard for him when he eventually leaves Hera and all his new friends behind.

As if he senses I'm thinking about him, he looks up from his phone and shoves it in his jeans pocket. He smiles at me, all cocky and gorgeous as he makes his way over.

His self-assurance makes me roll my eyes. I've met so many men like Peyton.

His eyes lock on mine, and he's about to say something when Scotty suddenly wails in Jess's arms.

"Oh no," Jess moans. "Why doesn't my son sleep?"

"I thought newborns slept all the time, well, that and poop and eat." Imogene's comment makes Jess grimace. I can tell she's insecure about her parenting, especially when Lauren and her baby make it look effortless.

"You have a special baby, my friend," I say. "Someday his energy and stamina will evolve into something unique. It's going to pay off in a big way because he has your brains and Carson's brawn." I hope I've delivered a compliment, but it's hard to tell with Peyton's chuckling.

"You have a bionic baby, pure and simple," he says. "They eat and rule. Wait until he's a teenager."

"Great. Now I'm terrified," Jess says.

Scotty grabs Jess's damp T-shirt and stretches it with his meaty fist as he lets out a growl.

"He is the cutest brute I've ever seen," I say, and Jess looks at me with pleading eyes. "Oh, give him back to me. You go change your shirt, take a shower—anything. I can handle this tough guy for a while."

"I really thought this not-sleeping business would settle down after two months. At this rate, Carson and I are going to go stark raving mad from lack of sleep. I don't know how to do this," Jess's voice falters to a whisper.

"Just go upstairs for a while," I urge.

Jess doesn't argue. By this point, her shirt is soaked, and she's so haggard that the last thing she needs is to entertain guests.

She shuffles out of the kitchen just as Carson enters. He looks at her, but before he can say anything, she brushes his shoulder lightly with her hand as she passes and leaves the room.

"What's going on?" he asks.

"Talia thinks she can head off your wife's breakdown," Peyton says offhandedly, and I shoot him a look.

"You're not helping," I say.

"You want my help?" he asks coolly.

I scoff and turn my attention back to Carson as I juggle his hefty baby on my hip. "Your wife needs a break, and you do, too. You both need sleep."

"Tell me something I don't know," Carson grumbles.

"You do look pretty bad, dude," Peyton adds.

"Thanks." Carson leans against the counter in silent defeat and watches his robust baby play with my hair.

"I think I have an idea that will help you—at least for tonight. I'd like to pitch in and help get the baby on a more reasonable schedule."

Scotty twists my earlobe in his little fist, and I wince.

Carson watches and shakes his head. "He's not like other babies. He doesn't sleep twelve to fourteen hours in a twenty-four-hour period. He doesn't take long naps during the day either. He sleeps in sprints, either when he's feeding or when we're in the car, so it's not like we can sleep when he's sleeping. He eats constantly, and then he wants to play, even at three in the morning. Look at him. He's huge. He's measured out of his age group in weight and height. He's off the charts."

"And look at that big head," Peyton says. "He could be a bouncer at a bar."

"You're not helping," I snap at him.

"Seriously," Carson continues, "I estimate that Scotty's cumulative hours of sleep in a twenty-four-hour period are seven or less. Maybe five hours at night, three of which occur while he's nursing, and then maybe two hours in the car if Jess drives to the store. He falls asleep in grocery carts, too. The car is his favorite place to sleep, though."

"Maybe we should rig up his crib, motorize it and put it on wheels and a track so it rolls in a circle around his room all night." Peyton is only half-joking, I think.

"I've actually considered that." Carson smiles. "Baby on wheels didn't fly with Jess."

"Well, the car is the only thing that sedates him," I say, getting us back to my idea. "It's simple. I'll drive Scotty around for a few hours tonight so you two can sleep. People drive their babies around all the time to get them to sleep. Or so I've heard."

Carson frowns, and Aleska shakes her head in disbelief at me.

"I'm not talking about a road trip. I'll just circle your property. It's a few miles, nice and empty, and I'll put on his favorite music and we'll loop around your land. When he falls asleep, I'll keep driving until morning."

"Talia, as much as I want to turn my baby over to you for a night so I can sleep, my wife wouldn't be able to bear it. Jess has serious separation problems with this boy. We haven't been able to hire a babysitter to go out for a two-hour dinner because Jess starts crying five minutes after we leave the house.

"Her mom stayed with us two weeks ago, and she was terrific with Scotty. And she and Jess got along great for the first time in years. The baby mended a lot of tension between those two, so I thought for sure that Jess and I'd get a night out for a quiet dinner. We got in the car, and Jess immediately called her mom to see if Scott reacted badly to Jess's leaving. I mean, we were sitting in the driveway! Then I drove past the property line and Jess burst into tears. That was that. We went back home."

"I should have been here to help her for the past two months."

"Hey, she's not blaming you. You were here for the birth, and she needed that the most. This isn't your problem. Jess and I had a baby, not you. This is our job, and it may take a while to get this down to a viable schedule, but billions of people have done this and we can, too … I think."

Peyton puts his hand on my shoulder. I don't mind it one bit.

I glance up at his sly smile, dreamy eyes with long eyelashes— good God—and the dark scruff that accentuates his strong jaw and cheekbones. So sexy. I'm not immune to his gorgeousness, and even though I normally prefer short hair on men, Peyton's shoulder-length locks give me stupid, little happy shivers.

He's been so helpful the past few weeks, carrying my delivery bags and loading them in the van. Every single day I'm cooking at Swill. And every day, I thank him, careful to sound professional and polite. I don't want him to know how he makes me dizzy when he's hovering around me, taking heavy objects from my hands and unintentionally smothering me in a wave of arousing warmth. Calming breaths are a necessity whenever Peyton makes an appearance.

I attribute this attraction to being holed up for too long. So many weeks sequestered at home, recovering, feeling that emptiness and loneliness of being hidden. I don't know how my mother manages to live like that without losing her mind.

For a moment, I am silly enough to believe Peyton's sexy smile is just for me, and then I remind myself that this is how so many of the younger women at the restaurant think of him. I can't afford to be a young, wide-eyed ninny again.

Yes, I happen to know that odd word *ninny*.

Aleska didn't approve of my previous relationship, said I was being a ninny so many times that I couldn't possibly forget that word. Sure, I had to look up the definition and still didn't fully understand the context until the infamous ordeal that ensued preceding our breakup. I never want to be a ninny again. *Says the pathetic woman who swoons at Peyton's touch.*

"Babies are boss," he says in that low, seductive voice of his.

As soon as I begin to fantasize about kissing him and what it would feel like to have his rough, unshaven face against my skin, I wrench my gaze away from him.

"I want to help, Carson," I repeat. "And I think Jess is exhausted enough to say yes."

"Say yes to what?" Jess returns in a clean T-shirt, and her hair has been brushed and styled into a tidy bun.

"You're supposed to be napping," I tell her. "No wonder you're exhausted."

"I can't sleep when there's a party downstairs and people are talking about me."

"Talia wants to kidnap your baby and take him for a drive so he'll sleep," Peyton explains.

Everyone watches as he takes Scotty from my arms and gently cradles his head before giving the baby a belly rub with his own head. Scotty's gurgles turn into giggling delight.

"Her plan isn't perfect," Peyton continues, "but she might be on to something."

"What's the plan?" Jess asks.

"The word *kidnap* didn't bother you?" Imogene asks. "You must be desperate."

"I am, because this little guy is going to want to eat in another hour or two, and I'll burst like Old Faithful on cue. And then Carson and I will do the zombie walk around the house, trying to entertain our wide-awake baby. It's the same script every night. Look at me. I'm a wreck. I don't sleep. I feel like the crabbiest mother on the planet. I don't have any energy, and I still have this muffin top!" Jess grips the extra flesh above her jeans and shakes it for proof.

Imogene laughs. "Are you still wearing maternity jeans?"

"Yes. That's my point. I don't sleep, so I can't do anything else, including exercise. I planned on not working for a while, but I need sleep, and I need exercise. And Scotty's ravenous appetite makes me hungry, too. That whole thing about 'nursing burns so many calories and gives you your body back' is not working for me. And no one told me that the pregnancy would make my curls go flat. I'm tired, flat, fat, and leaking all the time. So, yes, I'm game for a new strategy."

Carson hugs Jess from behind and cocoons her in his big arms as he plants a kiss on the top of her head.

"I'm sorry for sounding like an ungrateful whiner." Jess reaches out to stroke her baby's cheek. "I love him more than anything, but the sleep deprivation is causing me to deteriorate more and more each day."

"Then it's a plan," Peyton says. "Talia and I will drive Scotty around so the baby and you two will sleep."

"What?" I jerk my head toward Peyton.

"We'll do four hours and return him when he's settled and calm. Hopefully snoozing," Peyton explains.

"Okay, before anyone changes their mind, here are my keys." Carson pulls them out of his pocket and tosses them. Peyton, still holding the baby, manages to catch them before I can. Carson looks pointedly at his confused wife. "They are going to drive Scott around our property. You and I are going to bed now. Got it?"

Jess nods. "Wake me for the handoff. I'll be in better shape by then. I hope."

"There's a fridge full of liquid gold. Bags and bags of milk," Carson explains. "He only lets me give him a bottle every few days. He's a boob guy and usually puts up a fuss if I try to feed him from a bottle, so you may have a real problem there."

"I'm not worried. I've done this with plenty of fussy nieces and nephews. I'm good at getting them to take the bottle," Peyton says smugly as he locates the bottle cooler bag on the counter, and then he holds the baby out for me to take. It's like being handed a huge boulder, but clever on Peyton's part. This is how he disables his opponent and takes charge.

"I can't believe two big dudes are discussing this. It's hilarious," Imogene says.

"Honey, stay out of this one," Cooper says, making his way across the kitchen to his wife. "For once, the men saved the day."

"And me." I glare at Cooper.

Scotty takes that moment to smack my cheek with a chubby hand.

"Oops," Cooper says. "That looked painful."

"You don't need to go with me," I tell Peyton while trying to wrestle Scotty's hand away from hitting me again. "How hard is it to drive in circles? And I can always pull over to feed him a bottle."

"I have at least a hundred thousand hours of baby-feeding time over you."

"You are in charge of opening a very big restaurant tomorrow night. You cannot stay up all night babysitting. I, on the other hand, have tomorrow off because all my customers are going to be at your restaurant. I can handle this." I glance at Carson to take my side, but the big oaf just shrugs.

In a frenzy, as if they think we're going to back out, Carson and Jess jump to grab the cooler from Peyton, and they fling open the fridge and quickly load it with baggies of milk and cold packs.

Even with Scotty in my arms, I'm able to grab the diaper bag off the back of a chair and beat Peyton to the cooler, taking the handle as Jess zips it closed.

Peyton watches me with amusement and waits until I'm struggling with the weight of the baby and the two bags before he approaches. "Give me the bags or the baby," he says with a palm out. I hand him the baby who happens to weigh a lot more than the bags.

"Well, that's that," Carson says. "Let's leave it to them." He grabs Jess's hand and pulls her along.

Before she's yanked out of the kitchen, she turns to me and Peyton and whispers, "Thank you, thank you, thank you."

"That's a first," Imogene remarks. "That's a really big deal—Jess handing her baby over to you."

"Love of my life," Cooper says with exasperation, "let's finish the movie, then get everyone out of here so Jess and Carson can have a quiet night. And you two on baby detail, good luck and don't call us for help."

"Screw you." Peyton smiles. "This is going to be a piece of cake."

"Good. Hand over the keys," I demand.

"Hell no, woman. I'm driving." And with that, he snatches both the diaper bag and bottle bag from my shoulder, hitches Scotty up in his other arm, and heads out of the house, with me trailing behind in quick steps.

8

Peyton

I SETTLE THE BABY in his car seat as Talia gets in on the passenger side. Scotty is facing backward, so I adjust the special baby mirror on the back seat so he will be able to see my face when I look in the rearview mirror. Talia observes with a perplexed expression.

I've got this covered. I did the same setup for my sister with her car, and I handled my brothers' kids when they were newborns, too, so all this baby gear and the parenting tricks are very familiar. Doesn't mean I want it for myself, though.

I buckle myself in and look over at Talia. She's the opposite of every woman I have ever pursued. I have always been attracted to tall, voluptuous brunettes, but I constantly find myself staring at Talia, a petite blonde with slender arms that are deceptively strong when she's hauling stock pots of boiling water or chopping vegetables like she's handling a machete.

Talia scrolls through her music library as Scotty squeals and kicks behind us.

"We can use my playlist." I hold out my phone.

"Scotty likes Earth, Wind and Fire, according to Carson. And Jess said 'Baby Beluga' drove her over the edge, so I think—"

"'Boogie Wonderland' it is." I start the song on my phone before Talia finds it on hers. Then I start the engine and set the volume to low.

As the upbeat music fills the eight-speaker stereo system, Scotty lets out a happy sigh and burps. Talia smiles at me, pleased that we seem to be handling our babysitting duties quite well so far.

The private road that circles Jess and Carson's property is rough, unpaved terrain, surrounded by pitch-black darkness with no moon to light our way, only trees and brush that ominously reach into our path.

I turn the music down to the lowest possible notch and turn off the front speakers so it only plays softly next to Scotty, who is finally quiet, his chubby legs no longer kicking in the air.

"I think it's working," Talia whispers.

"So it seems. But don't be fooled. Babies always trick you into thinking they are content, and then ... *bam*. It starts again."

"I suppose." She turns to study our subdued passenger then she settles back into her seat. "But this is kind of fun. Weird, but fun."

"It is." *What the hell is wrong with me? I'm bragging that I'm great with babies and I'm driving around with this woman to prove my point? Jesus.*

"Thanks for volunteering. This is easier and more interesting with you helping."

"My pleasure," I say. *Because I'm an idiot.*

I glance back at Scotty, whose eyes are fluttering with sleepiness. When I turn back to Talia, she's staring at me, her eyes unblinking and her pink lips frozen and slightly parted. It takes me a second to register her expression, the way she's looking at me. It's attraction and curiosity rolled together, and it triggers the same response in me. It's lust. Experience has taught me that, when it comes to women, I really do have a one-track mind.

A sudden rocky patch in the road causes the truck to jump and land with a hard thud. Scotty giggles, but Talia yelps and grabs the dashboard with both hands.

"It's fine," I assure her. "This vehicle was made for this, and the baby likes it."

"I'm not sure I do." Talia puts her hand protectively against her chest, and I wonder if she's about to cross herself and say a prayer.

"Sorry if that scared you."

"I'm fine. A little startled, that's all. It's so dark out here and the road is ... rough."

"We're safe," I say, and she nods, albeit apprehensively.

9

Talia

"So, you like guys with short hair. That's the extent of your criteria?" Peyton cocks a brow at me and then returns his attention to the road.

I don't know where he's going with this, but I'm quite sure it's one of his games. He's a *smooth operator*.

I love that expression and only know it because my mother used to play the Sade song "Smooth Operator" over and over when I was little. I'd dance around the apartment with her, singing the lyrics, which didn't hold any meaning for me. How ironic and prophetic since my father was the ultimate smooth operator. Needless to say, my mother stopped playing that CD when he left, when her favorite song became just a little too real.

When it comes to women, I think Peyton is the same. Not that he's a louse—another word I love, right up there with *rat*—but Peyton is too irresistible to women. Even I'm finding him a little too irresistible.

I don't think he's a bad guy, but I know quite well that he's not the type of man I need in my little world of dysfunction and neediness. I have to fix my situation, my life, with a different approach and a different kind of man. Of course, I'm thinking along the lines of Adam Knight, a man who exudes stability, whereas Peyton is the type who would gallivant all over the world, from restaurant to restaurant, woman to woman, following his dreams. I don't need a self-involved dreamer, but for kicks I can play along with Peyton's game. It's harmless flirtation.

Says the former ninny.

"Sure, I like a nice, clean-cut guy in a good suit. Worn with confidence and a good sense of humor, most intelligent men can pull it off, and what woman doesn't find that attractive? Not every man has to wear jeans and boots to look cool."

Peyton looks down at his own jeans and work boots. "Ah."

"And my criteria is a lot stiffer than that."

"Is it now?" Peyton begins to laugh before I realize why.

"I didn't even try to make that sound sexual," I say. "I must be picking up those dirty innuendos from Imogene."

"I love my sister-in-law—she could make a mobster blush—but I like your subtlety, too."

The smile fades from my face. I'm not sure if he's paying me a compliment. And I'm really not sure what he means by my *subtlety*.

"You've got men eating out of your hand, willing to do anything for you."

"I do?" I stare at him, waiting for him to explain.

"Oh, come on. You've noticed that Bash lets you do whatever you want in his kitchen. No one has that power over him. And Zander always finds a reason to visit the kitchen. Whenever I'm looking for him in the brewery, I find him there, either eating your food or pretending to search for a tool that doesn't exist—at least, not in the kitchen. And Oliver, the bartender? The guy keeps walking through the kitchen with single glasses for the dishwasher. He doesn't even bother to carry a rack to make his trip look legit. He's always talking to you in his broken English, Pepé Le Pew act."

"That's no act. He's still working on his English. He says this job will force him to improve. I speak French fairly well, so I understand him, and he isn't flirting. He's passionate about soccer. I don't know how to tell him I'm not a big sports enthusiast, so I go along with whatever he wants to talk about. He's a little homesick. All of his family is in Grenoble—he's just trying to connect to people here." I pause and take a breath, realizing I'm rambling.

Peyton doesn't say anything, just listening and waiting for me to continue.

"Zander gets lonely back there with the beer tanks, so he pops into the kitchen to hang out with humans for a change of pace. And Bash ... well, we are becoming friends. There's no attraction for either of us. We just like talking."

"Well," he finally says and gives a small smile. "You sure know a lot about my male employees, but you're not as astute about the male species as you think you are."

His warm, inviting eyes shimmer with a bit of mirth behind them. He makes me feel exhilaratingly nervous, and I let out the breath I was holding. So much for resisting his magnetism.

"Oh, really?" I say. "I disagree. I can also tell you a few things about your female employees."

Peyton raises an eyebrow, again in a perfect challenge.

"Melody just had her twenty-second birthday, and she confided to me and the other women that she'd love to bag her boss. Only her words were, 'Do you think Peyton would notice me if I got a boob job? Having a mild crush on my boss makes it easy to come to work.'"

"Jesus," Peyton mutters. "Really?"

"Really. And Grace has to take care of her grandchildren because her daughter is an addict. She has been late for a few shifts and is terrified that you'll fire her because she's not young and perky like most of the servers, and she's not skilled for any other line of work."

"I would never fire her for being late, especially since she takes care of her grandchildren." He looks wounded.

"I know," I say matter-of-factly. "You're a decent guy."

"You think so?"

"You gave me a kitchen when I needed it, and you have a whole host of nutter heads working for you, and they really do like you. Not many bosses can say that. But then, like I said, your staff is full of nuts. Nice nuts, but still."

Peyton lets out a deep laugh, and I have to shush him so he doesn't wake Scotty who drifted off during the thirteenth replay of "Boogie Wonderland."

"So, tell me what happened to the knucklehead, the one you dumped?" he asks.

"What?" I'm shocked.

"I remember that guy you brought to my brother's wedding. Big dude, buzz cut. He was all over you. I was thinking of asking you to dance, but Imogene said that the walking refrigerator was your boyfriend and you two were serious."

"Marko." Saying his name out loud makes me nostalgic and sad. Marko is a reminder of who I was before I got sick. We were happy, and I was sure we were in it for the long haul, as they say. "I didn't dump him. Life took us in different directions. You should know what that's like."

"What's that supposed to mean?"

"You're here and your girlfriend is in New York City."

"She's not—"

"I'm guessing when you're not at work, you spend all your waking time thinking about work. Even now, you're driving around with me, but you're obsessing about tomorrow night, wondering if you'll fill the house—and you will, by the way. You're a workaholic, and your girlfriend is a workaholic, and you rarely see each other. But what do I know? I'm only guessing because I know how hard the restaurant business is and ..."

"And what?" he asks with a tinge of irritation.

"And I've never seen your girlfriend here."

"She's not ... She'll be here tomorrow night," he mutters.

"Good, you'll have to introduce us."

"You're saying you and this Marko guy decided your careers were more important? What does he do?"

"He works for a heating and plumbing company, and ..." My words drift off when I run out of ways to defend my ex.

"Wait a minute. He does installation and repair jobs and probably works eight to five, right? And no offense, but you've established quite a nice career for yourself. You've got your cooking and deliveries down to about eight hours a day on average, add on an extra ten hours a week for parties. But seriously, I don't believe for a minute that your careers were a factor. What do you have to say about that, Ms. Madej?"

"Will you stop saying my name like that? You're giving me flashbacks of a terrible man I once worked for. He'd line up the employees for weekly inquisitions. He constantly accused us of being thieves when customers called him about items missing from their homes. Whenever a client misplaced their jewelry or tchotchkes, they'd chew our boss out because it had to be his cleaning crews stealing their paper clips. You know, us immigrants are all shifty con artists. We'll take anything that isn't tied down or locked up. We're especially fond of pencils with zoo animal erasers."

Peyton's deep, rumbling laugh stops me from blabbering.

"It's true," I say. "A client actually accused me of taking her daughter's new box of pencils and erasers, so my boss gave me the fifth degree."

"Third degree," Peyton corrects.

"Right, third degree." I get a little angry thinking back to that incident.

"Did you take the animal erasers?" he asks in amusement.

"Of course not. The mother found them still in the shopping bag on the back seat of her car. She never apologized."

"Sounds like it was a shitty job."

I sigh. "It was."

"Yeah, but that doesn't explain why you and the refrigerator broke up."

"His name is Marko, and it's the same reason other people break up. The relationship ran its race."

"Course."

"Fine. It ran its course and that was that. It happens, and I'm okay with it. I don't hold a fire for Marko."

"A torch."

"What. Ever." This makes Peyton grin, and for those few seconds, I memorize his magnificent features, and especially the way he makes me feel right now—relevant. I inhale all of it.

This man whom I so easily judged is really pleasant to be with, and it suddenly dawns on me that maybe I don't want to see him leave Hera.

This little revelation reminds me of the loneliness I've endured over the last few months. Restricting my confidences only to my mother and sister created a terrible isolation.

"What's your favorite movie?" I'm determined to get to know him better, starting with the safe questions.

"Easy. *Jaws*."

"I thought you'd pick one of the Bond movies. Men always want to be James Bond."

"Nah. *Jaws* is the best. It's the ultimate battle, man against beast. What's yours?"

"*Eat Drink Man Woman*."

"Never heard of it."

"It's about family bringing people together with food. Food is the glue and a symbol of love, like in many cultures."

He acknowledges it with a "Hmm," but his mind seems elsewhere. I let it go. Maybe he's not interested in the topic, or he's really too preoccupied about the restaurant.

• • •

The baby sleeps soundly as we listen to "Sweet Dreams" at the lowest volume. Annie Lennox's voice lulls both of us into a trance as Peyton navigates the dark terrain. At some point, Scotty wakes with a deafening scream, and Peyton calmly pulls the SUV over and climbs in back to feed him a bottle while I drive. After an hour of the baby slurping his way back to sleep and another belch, Peyton takes over the driving again while I stretch out lazily in the passenger seat.

"Get some sleep," Peyton says.

"That wouldn't be fair. I should drive since you have to work tomorrow. Today, actually."

"I'm too wired to sleep. I've got lists running through my head of everything I need to do once we open the doors."

"Are you nervous?" I ask through a yawn.

"No. I'm excited. Bringing in the people is the fun part. Now get some rest. You can barely keep your eyes open."

I'm twisted on my side with my cheek buried in the soft leather seat. "If I do fall asleep, promise you'll wake me in a couple of hours so I can drive."

"I promise," he murmurs while the rhythmic crunch of the gravel road and the sway of the vehicle coax me further toward sleep.

10

Peyton

IN A DEEP SLUMBER, Talia is curled up like a cat, her toes pointed as she hugs her knees. She pushed her shoes off an hour ago when she changed position, never opening her eyes, never waking. Each breath she takes causes a wisp of hair to float up and down against her cheek.

I've been driving like this, studying her face and listening to her talk in her dreamworld. Neither the bright morning sun nor the squealing baby rouses her.

"Hey, Sleeping Beauty," I say as I brush the hair off her face. Her skin is as soft as it looks. "It's time to wake up."

Her eyes part, then close quickly at the harsh sunlight. She yawns and stretches her limbs. "Oh my God," she groans. Her hand goes to her chest as she struggles to sit up. "God, that hurts. What an awful position. How long was I out? You promised to wake me up. We were supposed to return to the house after four hours."

"I did. I drove back to the house and texted Carson, but he didn't respond. Everyone was asleep, so I kept driving. You and Scotty looked pretty comfortable, too. And I just woke you now, so technically, I did wake you."

"Well, now everything aches." She keeps one hand firmly planted against her chest as if she needs to hold it, protect it.

"Are you okay?" She looks like she's in serious pain, and I wonder how I missed this while she was sleeping. But she slept like the dead, at least the contented dead. "Did you hurt yourself? Your hand? Your chest?"

She puts her hand down as she rights herself in the seat and begins to smooth down her hair and make a new ponytail. "My hands and chest are fine. I feel a bit mangled," she says, wincing and cracking her neck.

"You were out for hours. You even slept through a diaper change and another feeding. Scotty woke up two hours ago, and he's been jabbering away the whole time. You didn't budge. And, by the way, you talk in your sleep. You were having whole conversations in Polish, I'm guessing."

"My mother says I've been doing that since I was two." She rubs her cheeks and eyes to wake up.

The color comes back to her fair complexion, and the sight of her in the naked morning light is nothing short of breathtaking. A slight smudge of mascara, a tangled mane of hair, her eyes slightly crusted with sleep—she's beautiful.

I feel a familiar, swirling ball of yearning, the same feeling I had with my first crush in sixth grade. I'm too old for crushes, but all I want to do is enjoy this moment with the woman sitting next to me.

As we cruise slowly up the long driveway to Carson and Jess's house, I try to redirect my thoughts about the big day ahead of me.

"I guess my great idea proved that I'm not much of a babysitter. I fall asleep on the job. But you were terrific," she says, lightly touching my arm for a second before she unbuckles her seat belt.

"I wouldn't have done this if you hadn't initiated it. We make a good team." I sound like a sappy fool. The truth is, I'm completely wired now, and I wouldn't mind if we kept driving. She's easy company, and my brain seems to downshift on its own from high speed to a low-gear comfort zone when she starts talking. I like it. I like her.

"Still, you should have woken me up. Jess and Carson will think I'm too incompetent to babysit." Her mouth quirks into a small smile.

"You were so tired that I even took two phone calls from Zander and Greer, and you slept through it all. They were talking pretty loudly, but I could barely hear them over the argument you were having with someone in your dream."

"Oh." She thinks about that for a moment. "I was probably arguing with my father. He and my mother are divorced, and he lives in Florida, but we still push each other's levers."

"Buttons."

"Fine, we push each other's buttons. You sure don't give me any breaks."

"Can't help it. You make it so easy." I can't tell her I actually look forward to her vocabulary screw-ups.

When we park in front of the home, Jess runs out in slippers to meet us before we even step out of the vehicle. A mother's intuition; she knew her baby was near and coming home.

She runs toward us, her arms open with a big smile, while Carson leans against the front doorframe, sipping a mug of what I presume is fresh coffee. He looks content and rested, smiling as he watches his wife.

Scotty squeals in delight as he's removed from his seat harness and returned to his delirious mother. Jess raves on and on about how well they slept before she practically squeezes the life out of her baby with a joy that borders on hysterics.

"So, you're available to come every night and drive Scotty around so he snoozes?" Jess jokes.

"Right." I smile. "I think we've discovered that he needs motion, or at least the feel of it, and some white noise to keep him asleep."

"What about putting a vibrator next to him in his crib?" Talia adds.

Jess's brows come together and she purses her lips. I don't blame her. What mother wants to share with her Mommy & Me class that her baby sleeps soundly every night with the aid of a big dildo?

"A big fat dildo," Talia clarifies in a serious tone as if she read my mind.

"Oh boy," Carson mutters, going back into the house.

"It sounds pree-verted, but ..." Talia's explanation dies off as she studies Jess's skeptical expression.

"*Perverted*," I correct. "Really, it's not such a bad idea. There's probably some other kind of device out there that creates the right vibration and noise and is safe to put in Scotty's crib."

"True." Talia nods. "Some guys can be very jealous of dildos—cocks bigger than their own. Right, Peyton?" Talia looks at me with a pert smile, her eyes lingering longer than normal, and so do mine.

"I'm not jealous of a dildo. I've got the real deal." Wow, I sound like a first-class moron. Then again, I do feel exposed, the workaholic guy who doesn't have time for women is staring just a little too long at the pretty woman next to him. I have to shake this off. "We have to go. I assume you need me to drive you home."

I hear Talia's soft chuckle behind me as I head to my truck. She follows and jumps in the passenger side, then waves at Jess as we pull away.

• • •

"That was fun," she says. "The drive, not the movie. I didn't even see the movie."

"You thought the drive was fun? You slept through most of it. Didn't I do all the work?" I look sideways at her. She's grinning. The sleep creases have faded from her face, and she's glowing.

"You did," she replies. "And teasing you back there was fun, too. I've never seen you embarrassed before."

"Not embarrassed. A little amused that you would suggest a baby sleep with a dildo. At first, I thought you were joking, but you said it with a straight face."

"I was serious. A big, fat, fake cock—"

"You sure like saying cock a lot." I speed up on the bumpy dirt road, trying to remember the turn to Talia's house. I've never been there, but I have her address mapped out in my mind. I'm curious to see where she lives. "Jesus, why can't this town or county pave these roads?"

"You sound a little angry. Is it because I said cock and it riddled you? Too much cock talk?" She laughs.

"*Rattled*," I say forcefully.

Talia rolls her eyes.

"I have no problem with you talking about cocks. I have my own and am damn happy with it." Great, I'm a raging idiot and a moron.

Talia covers her mouth and laughs.

I laugh, too. "Yeah, that sounded stupid."

"No, it's nice that you're proud of your cock."

Every time she says it, my dick gets harder.

"Turn left up there." She points. "Hey, how do you know where I live?"

"From the insurance paperwork."

"You memorized my address?"

"Hell, there are only, like, five roads in this town. I think my GPS and I can find your house."

"Don't you like Hera? Or are you getting crabby because you didn't get any sleep? This is such a beautiful place." She has that wistful look again.

"I love it," I deadpan.

We come to a row of small homes in a cul-de-sac. It looks like a planned community that was started then left unfinished, as if the developer ran out of funds and walked away. There are four, ranch-style homes each on a small plot of land, equally spaced, all similar to one another with their 1980s facades. If it weren't for the landscaping connecting them together, they would look really sad and depressing, as if they were the town cast-offs, left to fend for themselves.

Someone next door to Talia's house has been tending to their home with care. It stands out as the only non-depressing house. The shrubbery and trees are healthy, and the house looks freshly painted in white with gray shutters and flower boxes under the windows. The other homes, including Talia's, look a little neglected in comparison.

I recognize Talia and Aleska's company van, so I pull in behind it.

"You don't need to park. I can get out here," Talia says with an air of urgency.

The front door to her home opens, and a woman steps into view just behind the threshold. She looks like an older version of Talia. Blonde, willowy, dressed in jeans and a white blouse. She smiles when she sees Talia jump from the truck.

"Your mother, right?" I ask.

Talia shoots me a look. "She's not the most social person ..." She stops herself from saying more. "Thanks for the ride, and for the interesting night."

I kill the engine and step out quickly, rounding the truck so I'm by Talia's side in a flash.

"What are you doing?"

"Going to meet your mom."

Talia looks stricken, nothing short of sheer panic.

"What's wrong?" I stop, and Talia bumps into me.

"My mother is not well. She doesn't go out."

"She's an introvert, or are you saying she's agoraphobic?"

"Agoraphobic." She looks uncomfortable with the admission.

"It's all right. I want to meet her. I promise to be nice. I know what it's like to have a mom who isn't well."

She still looks uncertain, but she accepts that I intend to meet her mother.

I stride toward the house with my hand on Talia's back. She glances at me warily, no doubt wondering what I'm trying to prove. I'm wondering the same thing.

As I approach Talia's mother, I put my hand out, and she immediately takes it.

"Good morning, Ms. Madej. I'm Peyton MacKenzie."

She beams, not at all like someone who's afraid to meet people. I don't know anything about her disorder or what has her trapped here, but she comes across as friendly and open.

"Wonderful. Call me Mila. It's a pleasure to finally meet you. Can I get you to come in and have some breakfast with us? Aleska told me that you two were taking care of Scotty last night. You must be hungry."

"He can't stay," Talia stresses with a hint of urgency. "Tonight is his big opening. He has to get to the restaurant."

I can't believe she's trying to get rid of me so fast.

"I have twenty people over there setting everything up. It's not like I'm pulling off the halftime show at the Super Bowl. This is Hera, I can fit everyone and their cows in the restaurant. It should be easy."

Talia scoffs.

"I can spare a little time to eat. I'm starved, Ms. Madej—Mila. Thank you."

Mila steps aside so we can enter.

I hear a low groan of disapproval from Talia, but I ignore her and follow her mother through the formal living room in front and down the hallway to the back of the house that opens into a bright, cozy kitchen. I'm ushered into a chair at the table, and then Mila begins to serve me coffee from a French press.

Talia excuses herself to go change while I start up a conversation with her mother about life in Hera. Talia returns in loose-fitting sweatpants and a short T-shirt that keeps rising, showing her belly button. She catches me looking her over before sitting down next to me.

"You're so obvious. How do you manage to work around all those pretty women at the restaurant without coming on to them?"

Mila is busy at the stove, flipping pancakes and frying bacon, but she hears every word. "Sounds intriguing," she adds, returning with a plate of eggs, bacon, and pancakes for me.

"Not really. Strictly business. We always end up with more female staff than male. I don't get involved with employees." I keep my eyes down on my plate so I don't have to see the mother-daughter team scrutinize me.

I don't know their position on men at the moment. Talia alluded to arguments with her father, and Mila divorced the man, so I'm potentially another untrustworthy guy to them. However, Mila is feeding me and doting on me like the guest of honor, so there's that.

The attention reminds me of how my mother treated me. As the youngest, I got away with too much. I could piss my mother off, but most of the time, she would laugh and pull me in for a good, hard embrace.

It's been more than a year since she died. The grief is fresh if I summon it, but I push it back. I try to remember my mom the way she was before she was too sick to leave her bed, when the cancer made its final stand.

"This is great, Mila. I've been living on restaurant food and haven't had a home-cooked meal in a long time."

She joins us at the table with her own plate and a fresh pot of coffee that she passes around. "Talia hasn't prepared any of her dishes for you? She's the best cook in this house."

"No. My mom is the best cook," Talia says with a mouthful of pancakes. "Where do you think I learned how to cook? The Cordon Bleu?"

"I tried to sign up for her dinner service, but she couldn't take on new clients at the time. Aleska keeps my house nice and clean, though."

"You do need Talia's meal plan," Mila interjects. She likes me; I can tell.

"No, he doesn't." Talia gives me an exasperated look. "You own a restaurant. You are fed well every day. Besides, I'm booked solid. I can't take on any more clients right now."

"You managed to squeeze in Adam Knight, though, right?" I lean back in the chair and stretch out my legs under the small table, careful not to kick the women.

"He got the last seat on the train, mister. You missed takeoff."

I have to hold back a laugh. "You mean he got the last seat on the plane. Planes take off. Trains just kind of rumble slowly out of the station."

Mila laughs, and I see how much she and Talia resemble each other, with the same mannerisms and graceful tilt of the head.

I realize I want her mother to approve of me. I shouldn't care. I shouldn't be interested in what Talia or her mother thinks. I never put this much thought into Flora's family. *Yes, that's right, asshole, you had your chance with a girlfriend.*

I liked Flora's family, but I weaseled my way out of most of their invitations because if Flora and I had become regulars at her family's gatherings, people would assume I was going to pop the question soon.

As platonic as this situation is supposed to be, the air is charged when I'm near Talia. At Swill, at the party, in my truck, hell, right here in her home, the energy between us is palpable.

"Fine," Talia clips. "Trains, planes, whatever."

Mila is still smiling. I'm sensing she's aware of the energy, too. Mothers know these things.

"Oh, honey, did you tell him about *Family Thighs*?"

The exchange between the two has me completely fascinated.

"God, no." Talia glances at me.

"What did I miss?" I nudge Talia under the table with my boot.

"Nothing. It's one of those stupid, humiliating things that any nice mother would not bring up," Talia says to Mila.

"Oh, it's funny." Mila gets up and clears my empty plate before I can protest.

"Tell me." I'm already overstaying my welcome and taking advantage of Mila's hospitality, but I don't want to leave yet.

"Well," Mila begins, and Talia sits back in her chair with a disapproving sigh. "Years ago, back in Lublin, we used to watch the show *Family Ties*. It was dubbed in Polish. And we all spoke English quite well, but Talia had convinced all of us the show was pronounced *Family Thighs* in America."

"I like this story already."

Talia flings her hand at my shoulder, and I have the urge to catch it in mine. I am behaving like a young teenager developing his first hopeless crush on a girl.

"It was apparent we had a few incorrect pronunciations when we moved to the States. Talia and Aleska were trying to impress some older neighborhood girls and rattled off the American shows they knew. The neighbors couldn't stop laughing when Talia mentioned Michael J. Fox and *Family Thighs*."

I imagine this serious, pretty little girl in a huff, indignant.

"It wasn't that funny." Talia raises her chin and purses her plump lips.

"Goodness, it went on for years. Talia couldn't break the habit. It was just as adorable when she tried to order chicken *ties* from the butcher. She must have been eighteen then. He thought she was so delightful and kept asking her out after that. Sometimes *Family Thighs* still slips out and we all have a laugh."

"Not all of us," Talia reminds her mother.

"Did you go out with the butcher?" I ask, curious.

"No." Talia winces. "He was almost twenty years older than me. I had to start shopping at another grocery store." Talia looks down and fidgets with her hands.

"Thank you for the excellent breakfast, Mila. And thank you for a sleepless night, Talia." I can only stall so long—I have to get to work.

A deep blush blooms across her cheeks, and I feel a little smug about making that happen.

"I need to get going." I stand, and Talia follows my lead, probably relieved to get me out of her home.

"It was so nice having you visit. You have to come back." Mila surprises me with a kiss on the cheek. "I make the girls stay in on Sunday nights for a family dinner. You have to join us sometime."

"Oh, Mom, Peyton has to be at the restaurant every night. Dinner is their thing."

"I'm definitely coming back for dinner—family thighs, chicken ties, I'll take anything. If Talia is going to blackball me from her food service, I'll come directly to the chefs."

Mila picks up my hand in both of hers and gives it an encouraging, motherly squeeze. "I hope tonight is spectacular for you. I'm sorry I can't be there."

"You really know how to pile the shit on with mothers, don't you?" Talia says when we're outside by my truck.

"It's called piling on the charm, and my mother happened to love that shit."

"Oh God." Talia puts her hand to her mouth. "I shouldn't have said that. I wasn't talking about your mother." Talia crosses herself, and a little ache makes me appreciate her gesture.

"I know you weren't talking about my mother. She had a great sense of humor, and she would have liked you."

"I told you, my mother doesn't get out. Ever. This meant a lot to her—to be able to cook for you."

I remove her fingers that are poised near her mouth, hesitating there as if she's worried that she'll say something else. "I like your mom. I like you, too." I step closer to her and move her hand down to her side, entangling her fingers in mine.

There's an overwhelming pull, an electrical charge that lassos us in. I'm walking into trouble with this. I'm setting myself up for major drama ahead, but I can't resist.

Talia senses it, too, and tilts her chin up. Her eyes meet mine, and before she can stop me, my lips capture hers. She's soft, as I expected. I barely graze her at first, then my ego takes over and I want more.

I crush my mouth against hers. She's receptive and allows me to put my other hand on the small of her back and pull her closer. Suddenly, her tongue becomes my focal point as it explores mine.

I slide my hand up her back and it gets tangled in her hair. She lets go of my other hand and reaches up, both her hands on my shoulders. My head is spinning with sultry images of Talia entwined with me in so many possible, desirable ways, and my body reacts in kind. I'm so hard that I'm practically throbbing against her waist.

Any obligations I have today are pushed from my mind. All I see and feel is Talia.

"Stop!" Talia gasps as she pushes away from me. "You have a girlfriend, and I'm not the kind of woman who screws around with another woman's man." She puts a couple of feet between us and looks down, clenching her jaw.

I'm all worked up and still feeling the desire to throw her in my truck and take her home with me, but the last thing I want to see is her disgust. I haven't been serious about any woman, but I believe in trust and honesty. And even in my flimsy book, this was a bad move on my part. I haven't been upfront.

"I don't have a girlfriend. That ended when I moved here."

"But I've heard people mention your girlfriend. Everyone thinks you have a girlfriend."

"Because I don't bother correcting them. It's none of their business."

"If you're kissing me, then it is my business."

"Hello!" an old woman yells as she pushes open the door from the nicest looking home next door. She waves her cane at us.

"Hi, Norma!" Talia waves back. "I'm just saying goodbye to Peyton! He has to go to work!" Talia points at me awkwardly like I'm a prop.

"I'd love to meet him! Maybe next time when you both have time to stop in for a visit," Norma shouts, her voice cracking. She makes her way back inside and closes the door.

Talia looks relieved. One less person she has to introduce me to, I suppose.

"Sorry. This was my fault," I say. "I'm not looking for a relationship again. My life is chaotic with work."

"Exactly. And I don't want to get involved with a guy who's just passing through town, so no more. Okay?"

"I agree, but that kiss was like rocket fuel, sunflower. Do it again and we may have to sleep together just to get it out of our system."

Talia narrows her eyes. "I bet you say that to every woman." She lets out a huff as she storms back into the house.

I used to, but not anymore.

11

Talia

I STAND AGAINST THE back of the door long after Peyton drives away. The house is claustrophobic again, so I step back outside onto the front stoop to reclaim the memory in case the incident was a trick of the mind. The sensation of his kiss lingers, and I foolishly enjoy the moment, thinking of his two-day-old scruff against my cheek and the way his eyes looked hungry for me. I forgot what it's like to have a man show interest.

So, no girlfriend, but there is Peyton's desire to climb the restaurant ladder of fame, and he's only going to be here for a short while.

Try not to get all swoony when you're around him, you and your stupid, misguided hormones.

As I lean against the doorframe, fantasizing about the solidity of Peyton's broad shoulders and arms embracing me, a sleek, car comes slowly down the road toward my cul-de-sac. The car doesn't belong to one of my friends or neighbors, and tourists don't come down this road, not even by mistake.

I'm pretty sure it's a woman behind the wheel. I try to get a good look at her, but she's wearing large sunglasses. She must notice I'm watching her, but she doesn't change her speed as she rolls around the cul-de-sac. She turns her head as though she's studying me for a moment, then turns the car back the way it came, picking up speed and leaving a dusty cloud in its path as Peyton's truck did less than a few minutes before. How odd.

My first thought is she might be looking for real estate, but Archie Bixby, the town lawyer and our friend who owns these four rental houses, has no intention of selling. He rents these homes to us and our ancient neighbor, Norma, at stupid low prices, and he has never raised the rents. The two other homes have been vacant since the renters moved more than a year ago, but no one who drives a new Mercedes is looking to rent one of these.

"Honey, close the door! You're letting bugs in," my mother shouts from the kitchen. I go back inside and close the door. Once again, it feels like closing the door on our own cage.

From where I stand, I can see down the hallway and into the kitchen, where my mother frantically moves about, wiping down counters. How can she stay holed up in this house without breaking down? She carries on as though it's perfectly normal that she hasn't left our home in four years.

She pays no attention to me examining her routine cleaning process, the speed and vigor she exerts, which offers little reward. Aleska and I appreciate everything she does for us, but neither of us thinks thrice-daily cleanings between manic assaults on the treadmill is healthy.

My mother picks up her cleaning caddy and takes her mission into the bedrooms, which are already spotless.

The rotary phone mounted on the kitchen wall rings. It's cracked, the plastic casing is the color of faded bananas and has one of those long, coiled cords—that's always tangled in knots!—that can be stretched to any room in the house. It produces the loudest, shrillest ring, like any 1982 mechanical device should when it's outlived its era and has mutated into something out of science fiction. That's precisely why we never got rid of it—we can always hear the ring. Plus, Aleska and I discussed years ago that the phone may be our mother's only source for help in an emergency if we're not at home and she's trapped in the house.

Who am I kidding? I'll be trapped with her if a storm brings a tree down on the house or a blizzard buries the small home in an avalanche. I'll be home with Mom, and Aleska will be trapped at a bar with the fun people. Aleska and I joke about that, but there's some truth to it.

"Get the phone!" my mother shouts from Aleska's bedroom as the irritating ring continues.

I pick up the receiver, which I kind of love since it's like the old-fashioned handle on my funky telephone purse, my most precious gift from our only neighbor Norma.

She's a century old, shrunken as you'd expect at that age, but she isn't as frail as she looks. For the past few years, Norma has been helping hold our little family together by being a grandmother figure. We watch out for one another, and she pays special attention to our housebound mother.

"Hello?"

"Is this Talia? Or Aleska?" my father asks with a gentle laugh, as if he can break the instant tension that comes with hearing his voice.

"If you lived here, you'd know."

"Talia!" he guesses happily. "Tell me how things are going with—"

"Mom!" I shout toward the bedrooms. "It's for you!"

"Who is it?" she sings in response. This game of pretending she has a full social calendar and couldn't possibly know who is calling is getting on my last nerve.

I storm down the hall with the phone gripped at my side. "Who do you think?" I snap when I find her re-tucking a perfectly made bed.

Her bewilderment gives me a pang of remorse for being so short with her.

I toss the phone on the bed, but it slithers quickly back toward the door. "It's the Dark Side. They want to know if you're available for cocktails next week."

"Oh, Nat." My mother's tone is tender and apologetic. She picks the phone off the floor. "This feud with your father is pointless. It doesn't help anyone, least of all you."

I stalk off to my bedroom and close the door so I don't have to hear her talk to my father in that kind, forgiving voice. It makes me want to scream at her. It makes me want to punch him, if only he were here so I could do that. And sometimes, it makes me want to leave Hera.

How could two people who treated each other like the world for most of their marriage decide abandonment and living two-thousand miles apart are acceptable solutions when life gets hard? Of course, now that my father has established himself as an unreliable salesman for various questionable businesses, and his personal life revolves around an ever-changing stream of young girlfriends, why would my mother want him back?

I don't want him here, yet I'm still furious at him for leaving. I'm angry he ruined any sense of family and security Aleska and

I had. We went through some difficult times as a family—the financial instability, sharing the burden of the economic strain with our friends and family in Poland, holding each other up. That's what we did as a family. We weathered the bad times with constant hope and laughter because we believed in our family and what we could accomplish together. Or, at least, that's how my teenage self remembers it.

Thinking about him spikes my blood pressure, and I growl at myself for letting him get to me. I slam my drawers as I hunt for clothing and rifle through my closet, looking for the right outfit to wear to Swill tonight. I settle on a gold silk blouse and skinny jeans with a little cardigan draped over my arm for the late evening chill. The gold brings out the white-blonde in my hair, and the jeans make my legs look long and athletic, which is ironic because I'm often wheezing after I climb stairs or walk too fast these days. I'm healthy and getting my strength back, but I still sometimes feel like a granny.

I dig a pair of gray booties out of the closet and inspect them. They have a three-inch heel, which will help give me a boost. That conjures up an image of being closer to Peyton's face, his lips ... *that kiss*. I should be putting those thoughts into getting closer to Adam Knight.

If I ever want to feel normal again and find a man who's relationship material, it's him I should give my full attention. I haven't found anything on the Internet about him being a playboy, nothing scandalous, and it's quite possible he could be someone who likes me as I am. Doesn't that happen in the movies all the time? Aren't we supposed to believe that we don't have to change for someone else and that we deserve to be loved for who we are?

There is a list of things I wish I had accomplished, namely college, but otherwise, I'm a fairly decent catch if you don't expect to marry a rich, Ivy League woman, and I don't think Adam is looking for someone like himself. I think he's like most people underneath his expensive Italian suits and posh homes. He's searching for someone to share his life with, someone to sit at the kitchen table with him and share a dinner and a conversation about everyday things. I could be that woman. *Yes, I could.* The way he spoke to me, the way he looked at me, wasn't he flirting? Adam Knight could be the one.

You and your inane analysis. You met the guy once!

I turn the shower on to scalding, the way I prefer it, and step in.

Adam creeps into my thoughts again. More than his good looks, that confident way he laughed and tried to get me to join him for dinner. And just as I imagine sitting down to dinner with him, another image pops into my head.

Peyton.

He leans all his weight down on the table and says, "You sure about that guy? Because I'm pretty sure you had an orgasm when I kissed you. If I can make that happen with one kiss, imagine what else I can do."

Boy, I do imagine. And that's exactly how I'd expect Peyton to act. And unfortunately, I like it. I like him in a way I didn't think was possible. He's hard to ignore, especially after the kiss, but I have to keep reminding myself that I'm not one of his young, college waitresses who can afford to have a fling. My life has real responsibilities. Then there's my health, my fears—more reasons I can't have a typical relationship.

You're not a hopeless mess. Repeat that mantra a few times because you're slow. And not all men are like Dad. They don't all leave when they discover their woman is imperfect.

Imperfect, I think as I rinse the shampoo from my hair. My mother and I are both imperfect. Who isn't?

Damian is my father, whether I like it or not, and he did leave my mother when she became ill, for lack of a better word. And when he was informed of my hospitalization and surgery, he didn't care enough to come see me. He didn't care enough about anyone but himself.

When I get out of the shower, I discover two texts on my phone.

"You're shittin' me," I say to the phone, uttering the only appropriate Aleska phrase that comes to mind.

The first text is from Adam Knight.

The second text is from Peyton MacKenzie.

12

Talia

AT SWILL, THE PARKING lot is packed, with cars overflowing into the grassy field beyond the graveled lot. Aleska and I hop out of our ugly, clunky van.

It's times like these I wish we had my mother's old Camry, but we had to sell it, along with the piano and other personal items that could fetch a good price for a family like ours that was descending into divorce and poverty.

I glance down at my phone and read the two texts that make my heart race a little too fast for my liking.

Adam: *Hope to see you tonight at Swill.*

Peyton: *See you tonight.*

One is hoping, and one seems sure. The sure one is hardly the epitome of a settle-down kind of guy.

"Wow, this is the place to be." Aleska strides toward the restaurant, swinging her hips, knowing she looks beautiful tonight.

I admire that about my sister—her ability to love herself. Earlier today, she had grabbed the extra flesh around her waist and said, "I'm still hot, even if I have some new waffle and bagel fat."

It's true, she is very pretty, and wearing a dingy bandana around her head while she scrubs a client's toilet until it shines doesn't diminish her sparkling beauty. It's partly her pretty face, but it's also her self-assured smile. She knows who she is and knows her self-worth. She's doing so much better than her big sister.

The restaurant is so crowded no one could possibly notice my entrance. I was shamelessly hoping to see Adam Knight when I walked inside and get a reaction to all the effort that I put into curling my hair and walking in heels, which I haven't done in a long time.

The hostess is seating people in front of us, so Aleska and I start wandering around the tables full of boisterous people. I recognize a lot of Hera residents and plenty of the part-timers—the city couples and families. I'm pleased to see Peyton has the staff all dressed in identical black oxfords and black jeans. Thank God there are no tight tops with cleavage shots for the women. I have to give Peyton credit for that. He also has female staff over the age of fifty, a rarity in newer restaurants.

"It smells good," Aleska says, swiveling her head around, looking for eligible men no doubt.

"Hey, you two lovelies!" Eleanor shouts from a nearby table. She stands and waves to get our attention. "Don't you want to sit at the fabulous table with the fabulous people?"

Eleanor is sitting with every Hera person I know who's over the age of sixty. Archie; his wife, Emily; dear, raunchy Lois; and a few other seniors. Behind them are Jess and Carson and our usual gang. They've all managed to squeeze into two large, picnic-style tables. But, if I sit with them, there's little chance I'll find Adam or any other single man.

Aleska sighs. "We'll have to do a few walk-arounds to check out the men."

"This isn't a nightclub. We'll look stupid roaming around the tables while everyone's eating."

"No, we'll look like we're very popular women, and we're visiting people so they can bask in our popularity," she says.

As we walk over to our friends' table, I take one last look around for Adam in the huge, German beer hall before I squeeze myself between Jess and Imogene.

"Where's Scotty?" I ask Jess, who looks extremely rested and happy.

"My parents showed up after you left. They're spending the night and watching Scotty."

"You must be pleased about that."

"I am, and I told them what you and Peyton did last night. I don't want them to try to replicate your magic, but they are going to try to help with the sleep situation in the house. I figure four adult brains should be able to master one baby. We'll see. Oh, and your knight is over there." Jess smiles and points to a table of men closest to the open, wood-burning ovens.

My gaze lands on Adam's profile. He's lifting a pilsner glass to his lips but then pauses and laughs. He must have invited friends from the city. It registers with me—all men, no women. *Thank you.*

"He's the man you're looking for, right?" Jess asks.

"Whom are we speaking about in secret?" Imogene nudges her head into our huddle.

"Adam Knight." Jess tilts her head in his direction, and Imogene looks him over.

"Right. The handsome, rich, hedge fund guy. Are you really interested in him, or are you bored?"

"What?" I glare at Imogene.

"Imogene, really uncalled for," Jess hisses.

"I don't mean to be rude. Really. Last night, I was excited to hear what you had to say about him, but I've been thinking about this. I think you should be cautious with him. He's a powerful guy, and—"

"And what? I'm a lowly serf?"

"In a manner of speaking, yes. You know what I mean. It's often not simple when there's an economic imbalance."

"Because he's rich, and I'm not?"

"Yes. You've only met him once. Texts and emails don't count. I would hate for you to get hurt by him. Trust me; there are a lot of men who would love to have you serve them dinner, they own their own houses and businesses, and they aren't boyfriend material and definitely not marriage material. So I want to know if this is just a physical thing because you want to get your rusty parts back in action."

"Thanks, that wasn't rude at all," I say.

Cooper and Carson are moving steins and pilsner glasses around the long tables so everyone has a fresh beer. I take a sip of the amber liquid in front of me and consider what Imogene said.

"Who says she's rusty?" Jess asks, starting an unflattering topic I'd rather not hear.

"She broke up with Marko months ago, and then she was vacationing in a retirement community with her father in Florida for two months. Unless she's a gold digger looking for a future husband with a short expiration date, she hasn't met anyone." Imogene guzzles half her beer then slams her stein down with a soft belch. "Whoops."

"My father is forty-nine. He doesn't live in a retirement home. Since Marko and I broke up, I've been too busy with work to think about dating."

"You weren't working in Florida. What the hell did you do there for two months? You didn't meet one single guy on the beach or at a club or go on a date?" Imogene pushes.

"Nope. Not one."

"But after three weeks back in Hera, you latch on to the idea of this one guy you've met once. You need sex, that's what I think."

"Imogene," Jess says sharply. "Who made you the dating police?"

"We don't know Adam. I'm sure he's a terrific client, but you're entering dangerous territory. Do you really want to have a hookup with him? Won't that make things weird?"

"I don't want a hookup with him. I actually think Adam is nice, and maybe this could have potential without the weird stuff. He texted me a while ago, saying he'd like to see me here, so I thought it sounded promising."

"He did?" Jess lights up.

"I could be wrong. Maybe he doesn't look at me other than in a neighborly kind of way."

"Yeah, no. He's not being neighborly, unless neighbors stare at you like they want to lick you. Hundred-year-old Norma is a sweet neighbor. This guy is sex and money." Imogene nods with her chin, and Jess and I turn our heads to look at Adam's table. He's smiling at me and raises his beer in acknowledgement. Then he extricates himself from his table of rowdy friends.

"Yay! He's coming over here," Jess whispers loudly.

"I can see that," I counter with relative calmness. I'm not as nervous as I thought I'd be.

"Nice build, nice face," Imogene assesses a little too loudly, but the rest of our table is completely involved in their own conversations. "Nice package."

"Imogene," I snap.

"Oh, look, he's going to be proper and say hello to everyone at the table before he calls on his *purdy* lady."

"Knock it off." I elbow Imogene in the ribs, but she just laughs.

"He does have a nice ass," she adds, and of course Jess and I check out his backside as he turns to talk to Carson and Dylan. "Man, he fills out those jeans perfectly. And he's the only guy in

Hera who doesn't have sawdust or drywall caked on his legs. Those must be the three hundred dollar kind of jeans that repel dirt."

Imogene is right. Adam fills out his jeans well. I check him out as I pretend to scan the restaurant and bar for people I know. He's wearing a fitted, gray shirt that gives a hint of a body that probably spends a lot of time at the gym, and those jeans—well, designer or not, they wrap around his muscled thighs perfectly.

"He's handsome," Jess confirms.

"Yes, he is, and he's *nice*," I remind Imogene.

"You'll find out if he's nice in bed very soon, methinks." Imogene snorts. "He's coming your way."

Adam works his way down the crowded aisle between other tables to reach my end of the table. I would be more comfortable if I wasn't sitting with my nosy friends. He flashes a beautiful smile of perfect teeth, and his hair is ruffled perfectly as though he's been staged, primped, and groomed for a modeling session to look like he's the average, everyday man.

"Talia." His smile is for me, and my heart accelerates, but I'm not overwhelmed. Deep down, I must think he talks to everyone this way and knows how to make a person feel special. This is partly what makes him successful. He's perfect on paper and in person, but my heart isn't soaring the way it should be if I were a normal woman. Any other woman would throw herself at this man, so either I'm scared to get back in the game, or I'm defective.

"Hello, Adam. This is my friend Jess, Carson's wife. And this loudmouth on my left is Imogene, one of the town gossips. Don't cross her or you'll find yourself on the receiving end of creative storytelling."

Imogene smiles and shakes Adam's hand. "It was only one guy, and he deserved it."

"She spread the rumor that he left his wife to live with a goat," Jess says softly, and I cringe. This is not how I want Hera to be presented to this man.

Adam grins. "Will you come join my table for a bit?" he asks me. "I'd like to introduce you to my friends. They came in from the city."

"Yes, I'd like to meet your friends ... and talk to you," I stumble.

"How about now?" He takes my hand and steps back so I'll follow him.

"Sure." I stand up, wobbling a bit on my heels. Jess and Imogene slide to the side as much as possible so I can climb up off the bench in an ungraceful manner. Adam quickly puts a hand on my lower back to steady me and holds his other hand out to lead me.

"Have fun!" Imogene waves as we walk away.

I quickly look down to make sure my blouse is buttoned up to my collarbone, then touch the top button. It's becoming a habit.

"You look great," Adam says, pulling me against his side as we walk the narrow path toward his table.

The restaurant is loud, bustling with servers carrying beer steins and trays of food, and customers moving between tables as though it's one big, community party. No one notices me with Adam, other than Jess and Imogene. I prefer it that way.

I haven't thought this completely through. Imogene is right. Am I really trying to pursue a relationship with a guy I just met because he seems like someone good for the long-term, or am I looking for an affair, someone to get me back into the swing of things?

I've never slept around. I've always had long-term boyfriends. But after the last few months, my confidence has been at an all-time low, and some people swear by the emotional benefits of hot, sweaty sex. Who am I to question science?

Adam introduces me to the men at his table—all who are in their thirties like him, quite a bit older than me. Some are wearing wedding bands and have graying temples, but they are all fit like Adam and exude confidence and wealth—the hallmarks of hedge fund managers, I suppose.

We don't sit down and join his friends. Instead, Adam pulls my hand and whispers in my ear, "Let's head over that way for some privacy." He nods toward the hallway that leads to the back offices.

"Uh-huh," I respond as his smooth-shaven cheek brushes mine and I inhale the exotic scent coming from his soap or shaving balm. He smells good, he feels good next to me, and he looks beyond good. *Jump for joy, Talia!*

I don't jump. In fact, I feel a little strange.

As we walk past the rustic ovens, I see Bash manning the rotisserie with his team. He sees me and waves. Then he does a double-take, checking out Adam. Bash doesn't meet my eyes again, but I see something uneasy in his expression. This certainly is not helping my confidence. First, Imogene thinks Adam couldn't possibly be interested in me other than for sex, and now Bash, too?

Adam leads me into an alcove off the hallway. It was part of the original building, and the brick walls and carved, wooden beams above us make it feel rather medieval. Everything about Adam fills the alcove, but in a good way, as if I'm safer.

Servers are rushing past with heavy trays through the swinging kitchen doors. I remember Peyton discussing the alcove with the staff and telling them to direct customers to the small, isolated place if they're having loud, cell phone conversations.

"Finally. Our paths didn't cross for two weeks. I was really looking forward to seeing you tonight. I've been thinking about us," he says.

"Us? There's an us?" I laugh a little, and he chuckles.

"The whole thing about you not dating clients. I get it. Excellent policy, by the way. But a funny thing happened. After I had your great meal and we talked for a bit ... after you left, I couldn't stop thinking about you. I drove back to the city and put in two, sixteen-hour days, and I was still thinking about you. Why do you think that is?"

"Because you're trying to figure out how I put all that magic into my cooking?"

"Right, it's sorcery." He places his hand on my shoulder. "Listen, I know this is a little short notice, but I wanted to ask if you're available next Saturday."

This is it. He's going to ask me out. A little rush of pleasure boosts my ego.

"I have some friends coming to stay with me next Saturday, and I would like to hire you to cater the dinner. A dinner party, actually. About fifteen or more people. I would get the exact head count to you as soon as possible."

Idiota! Idiota! I am an idiot. He doesn't want to go out with me; he wants to hire me to cater his party. I suppose I should be grateful for the business.

"Yes. I can do it. One dozen or two dozen, it's no problem. I do dinner parties all the time." I try to sound professional and not at all bothered by the fact I thought this man was planning on asking me out. Aleska and Imogene will get a really good laugh out of this.

"Thank you." He puts his hands on my shoulders, making the situation more awkward for me. Does he touch everyone like this? He certainly has a talent for seducing his audience with the way he uses his body to give you his full attention. Hands, elbows, shoulders. I keep thinking he's going to kiss me.

"You're very welcome," I reply.

Just then, the kitchen door swings open, and Peyton strides out, looking very much like he owns the place. Adam's back is to Peyton, so he doesn't notice, but my eyes lock on to Peyton instantly.

He cut his hair! All that long, dark, sexy, gorgeous hair is gone. There's less than two inches left, brushed off his face in short waves, making his features more prominent. On top of that, he's dressed like a man with power. He looks like money. Expensive, black dress pants, polished black leather shoes, and a fitted cashmere sweater that flatters his athletic build. But it's that damn hair. I can't look away. I loved his long hair. I fantasized about running my fingers through that hair. I fantasized about what that hair would look like if Peyton was naked ... on a bed ... with me.

And now I love Peyton's short hair.

I'm practically holding hands with Adam, hoping he'll ask me on a date, while staring at Peyton.

That's when Peyton looks up from his phone and notices Adam and me huddled privately in the dimly lit alcove. In that split-second, Peyton frowns with disappointment that surpasses Bash's reaction.

I'm too startled to say hello, and soon he's lost somewhere in the crowd.

Hopefully, I was only ignoring Adam for a few seconds and not minutes as it felt like in real time. I turn my attention back to him, and he lets go of my hand and shoulder.

"I'm not planning a wild party, just close friends who are curious about my new house and my new favorite chef."

"Me?"

"I told them Hera is unique and so are you."

I'm totally confused by this man and his flattery. Either I'm an employee he's winning over with praise, or he's building up slowly to something else. Maybe I should remind him that English isn't my first language and telling me that I'm his favorite chef and that I am unique is like sending me a giant bouquet of red roses on Valentine's Day.

"Don't worry about a thing. I love cooking for dinner parties. I'll be there with horns on," I say with a smile.

Adam laughs. "You mean bells on. You're cute."

Puppies are cute. When a man tells me I'm cute, it usually means they see me in a way I dislike.

"Yes, bells, not horns. That doesn't present a pretty picture, does it? Some of these things I'll never get right."

He smiles and touches my arm, leaving his hand there. Again with the touching and holding. Someone should tell him that he shouldn't touch a woman this way unless he intends to kiss her, because there's only so much ambiguity a woman can take.

You're a paid servant, Talia. He's a client. Get over it.

"You should get back to your friends, and I need to get back to my table," I say like it's no big deal and like I rub elbows—or is it rub shoulders?—with rich CEOs all the time.

"I thought you could join me and my friends for a bit."

"I don't think so. Not tonight. A bunch of men drinking, and … I work for you. I don't think I should since I'm someone on your … personal staff." I didn't intend for it to sound mean, but Adam blinks once and says nothing for a few seconds.

"I understand," he says. "Go back to your friends. I'll see you in a few days when I'm back in town. We can discuss what you need for the dinner then, or you can certainly email or call me at work."

"I doubt your secretary is going to let me call you at your firm. I've had a few of them turn me away when I tried to contact my clients at work."

"My assistant has you on my approved call list. You can call me anytime."

He makes these kinds of arrangements all the time. It's business.

"Good. I'll talk to you soon." I bow my head slightly, then turn and walk away as gracefully as possible, wading through the standing crowd and the servers.

I never look back at Adam. I'm trying to mix business with pleasure. It seems to be much like the *Titanic*—people are dancing in the ballroom as the band continues to perform while the boat is most definitely sinking. And that's what I can't decide. Should I keep dancing, thinking something is happening with Adam? If Aleska was in this situation, she'd ask Adam directly and not waste time with trying to interpret every little thing the man says or does.

I have become such a coward.

As I squeeze back into my seat between Imogene and Jess, Cooper places a pint of beer in front of me. "It's a Hofbrau Dunkel," he says as if it means anything to me.

"Well, what did the stud want?" Imogene inquires.

Thankfully, Carson interrupts by handing her two platters of food to pass around. They've ordered everything on the menu and are passing it around the table family-style.

Imogene pushes a dish in front of me. It's loaded with kielbasa and sauerbraten. She scoops my favorite currywurst onto my plate, but I don't have much appetite. I watch Bash's staff prepare these foods every day and enjoy sampling everything until my stomach protests, but tonight, my stomach is jittery and I don't think I could keep down even the lighter appetizers. When a plate of Bavarian pretzels is passed down, I grab one, hoping the bread will help settle my nervous belly.

Bash makes a walk through the dining hall to see how the food is going over with the crowd. As he passes near our table, he raises a hand and smiles as if he's relieved to see me sitting with my friends. I take a small bite of the chicken pâté and give him a thumbs-up. He looks pleased. The restaurant is packed and the food is being enjoyed. He heads toward the kitchen, and I return to sipping my beer and playing with my food.

"Is he the chef?" our friend, Kimberly, asks as she approaches our table, a little out of breath as if she couldn't make it to us fast enough. She points at Bash's back as he disappears into the kitchen.

"Yes, that's Bash," I reply.

"I thought so!" Kim fans herself with her hand.

"Simmer down," Imogene says. "What are you so excited about?"

"I saw him at the gas station once and wondered who he was, and then I saw him with Peyton outside Swill a couple weeks ago. Wow, he's cute. How did I not meet him before tonight?"

Imogene and I share a smile.

"I think you need to go into that kitchen right now and introduce yourself, missy," Imogene says.

"Oh, I'm definitely going to. But first, I want to run an idea by you guys. Do you think Peyton would let me host an auction here to raise money for the library we want to build?"

"He better," I say. Kimberly is the most enthusiastic librarian in the county, and Hera could use its own little library. I also picture it being the perfect place for my mother to work if we can ever get her out of the house. She loves romance novels and thrillers, and working the circulation desk would be a great job for her, if she can be persuaded to join the human race again.

"I don't see why not. It's the closest property to Swill, so when that dumpy old house is renovated into a charming new library, it will also improve Swill's curb appeal," Jess says.

"Did someone mention something about a fundraiser for the new library?" Lois shouts from the other end of the table.

"Oh God, not Lois," Kim mutters. "That woman."

"Tell me about it," Jess and Imogene say in unison.

"You should get to Peyton before Lois does," I whisper.

"Yes, you're right." Kim looks around. "I'm going to ask Peyton about the auction, and then I'm going to go compliment the cute chef. Wish me luck."

"You go get 'em, girl." Imogene pumps her fist, and then we watch Kim dodge past Lois's waving arm.

"She certainly doesn't waste any time," Aleska says. "She sees what she wants and goes for it."

"I'm not brave like her," I say. The temptation to check out Adam's table is strong, but I don't look.

"Are you going to tell us what Adam wanted?" Aleska demands, and both Imogene and Jess look at me.

"It was indeed a neighborly offer. He gave me a catering jig," I reply.

"Gig. It's a gig, not a jig," Imogene says testily.

"Does it matter? I made a big ta-da about him texting me, thinking he might be asking me out. I was wrong."

"It's a fucking *to-do*." Imogene slams her hand on the table.

"Will you stop, or I'll *to-do* you," I tell her.

"Oh, now I'm scared," Imogene shoots back. "It sounds like you're threatening me with sexual favors."

Aleska and Jess laugh.

"It's nice that he offered you a job," Jess says in that tone friends use when they are trying to cheer you up.

"Oh, please," Imogene says. "She'd rather *to-do* him, or even *ta-da* him."

"It has been a while since I did any to-do-ing with anyone."

The women laugh, and I choke on my sip of beer with a giggle.

Groups of men and women keep entering the restaurant, and we get caught up in people-watching and gossiping. It's a welcome change from the isolation I've been experiencing the last few months. I forgot how much I missed my friends or being around lively people, in general.

The noise level is high. I can't hear what Dylan and Emma are saying at the far end of the table, so I pretend to listen intently to Jess and Imogene drone on about a killer yoga class I have to try. They explain it's a cross between yoga and acrobatics, and the yogi, Anima-Christi, teaches the most grueling sessions. Personally, I think it sounds awful. And physically, I'm in no position to be airlifted into handstands.

It's not until they both gasp and say, "Wow!" that I pay attention.

A gorgeous, exotic woman enters the restaurant. Tall and curvy, with an ample bosom and long, dark, flowing hair. She walks into the great dining hall as if she *owns* sex. Her smoky, dark eyes search the restaurant, dismissing everyone she sees until her gaze lands on Peyton, who's at the bar, talking to one of the bartenders. When he notices the beautiful bombshell, there's recognition in his expression, so I assume this incredible woman must be Flora.

"Look at her," Imogene says.

"I am," Jess replies.

She is dressed in black leggings with high-heeled, thigh-high boots, making her look like she has ten feet of leg. I would look like a little troll standing next to her. A *cute* troll.

Her top is maybe a size too small, but it's the kind of snug, formfitting blouse that looks good on sexy women with large breasts and tiny waists.

I'm hiding behind my big, fat, Bavarian pretzel. I keep it against my face like an eyeglass, peering through the pretzel twist like a child as I watch Flora make her way to Peyton. I grab my beer and take a quick swig, and then I take another. The bitter liquid does not go down smoothly for this non-beer drinker, but I'll do anything to keep busy so I can spy on Peyton without being obvious.

"What are you doing?" Imogene asks.

"Watching Peyton and his girlfriend. She's more glamorous than I expected," I say.

"She's a stunner," Imogene adds. "But I'm pretty sure she's his ex-girlfriend. It's a hunch, but my hunches are usually spot-on."

"Interesting. Well, you definitely notice her walking into a room," Jess says.

"It looks like they're arguing." Imogene smiles. "This is like a soap opera. I love it."

"We shouldn't watch," I say, but all three of us keep watching, and I'm absolutely enthralled with Peyton and how hot he looks tonight.

Together, he and Flora make quite a beautiful couple, another reason I think he's better suited to a flashy lifestyle. Hera isn't flashy, which is why wealthy city dwellers are buying up country homes here, but not Peyton. He wants to be a part of a restaurant empire and travel from one big city to another, and he's going to want a high-end girlfriend to go along with that lifestyle. Apparently, he doesn't need to love her; he's not looking for that. Sex and a superficial relationship will suit him just fine.

Listen to me, sounding bitter and disappointed. Itch that—no, scratch that! I sound bitter.

I'm only partially listening to the conversations around me. Lauren and her husband, Leo, have arrived, and they're going on and on about how the grandparents compete to babysit their little toddler, Maisie.

I wish I had such problems. Even if I'm fortunate enough to have a child someday, they would soon get bored of visiting Grandma Mila and her little prison of a home.

Oh, I am bitter!

I gulp down some more beer and raise my glass when Cooper makes a toast to the group about their great investment.

I haven't finished my beer, but someone takes my glass and replaces it with another. It's a different color with a long German name that sounds like a witch's incantation when I try to pronounce it. Imogene laughs because everything is a tongue twister for me.

And then another swig of beer tells me I'm tipsy. I haven't had anything to drink since my diagnosis over three months ago. I'm not on any medication, and I was given the go-ahead to eat and drink what I want, but it's odd not to have Marko babysitting me, getting me drinks and telling me when I've had enough. I always used to take his monitoring as concern for my welfare and not control over my choices and behavior.

The beer is giving me a new perspective, and I think I like this tipsy Talia who is a little less polished and likes eating slouched over a table with greasy fingers. Marko liked me made-up, and it used to make me laugh when he'd say, "That's not very ladylike of you." It never bothered me at the time. I thought he was bringing out the best in me, when he was really doing it for himself. It makes me furious to think I was stupid enough to agree with him and change my behavior, my clothing, my posture, and my language, for his approval. If he could see me now, he'd really disapprove, and that makes me a little happy. It's a little taste of freedom.

My second beer is mostly full when someone removes it and passes around little shot glasses of all the varieties of beers on tap.

"More samplers!" Eleanor shouts from the other end of the table, and I wonder how a woman in her sixties can outdrink me and still walk and talk.

"You've had less than one beer," Aleska says, watching me, trying to assess the quantity I've consumed.

"I guess I'm a light ... a light something. A lightsaber? A light ..."

"Lightweight," Aleska says.

There's so much going on in the restaurant, between the live music and the table-hopping customers, but Peyton and Flora stand in the middle of it all, having a heated argument. I'm probably the only one who is watching for any sign of affection between them, silently hoping they walk away from one another.

Flora doesn't seem to be short on words, and she's gesticulating and flailing her hands and arms everywhere. Peyton looks as though he's trying to calm her down by using firm, terse words. It's not working. Flora seems to be the type who will say whatever she wants and doesn't care who's watching. Me—I'm watching. But I'm a very small person in Flora's world. She takes up a lot of space and air and demands attention.

Peyton listens to Flora's rant with a resigned weariness, then crosses his arms as if to ward her off. Flora gets in the last word, then storms past all the dining tables, with every man and woman watching as she heads down the hallway toward the restrooms.

Feeling fairly brazen with the alcohol surging through my bloodstream, I extricate myself from the table, ignoring Jess's questions, and walk over to Peyton, who is already in a new conversation with Zander, the brewmaster.

"Looks like you've got big trouble in a little town, mister," I direct at Peyton.

Zander leaves, and I step closer to Peyton, teetering in my heels and trying to strike a natural pose, even though my feet are in agony from the pointy boots.

Peyton looks at me slowly, studying my face, then working his way down to my heels. "You should take those off. You'll be more comfortable."

"At the moment, I would love to go barefoot, but restaurants frown upon that."

"I'm the owner. I'll let you."

"I'm assuming the woman you were fighting with is Flora. What's the game with you two?"

"You mean the *deal* with us?"

"Sure, make fun of me."

"The deal is I disappoint Flora ... a lot."

"I bet. All you do is work. You never have fun."

"I have fun," he states.

"When do you do anything besides work?"

"First of all, I think my work is fun. Second, I had fun on the night drive with you."

"Then your life is almost as dull as mine. What kind of relationship is that ... with her?"

"It isn't a relationship. I told you last night. Flora and I broke up when I moved here."

"So you said. But then, why did you let everyone assume you were still together?"

"Because Imogene and Greer are always on my case about settling down. I decided not to tell anyone and let them assume what they want. This way, no one tries to fix me up, and I don't have to get involved in Hera's wild dating scene."

"Very funny. I wish there was a nightlife with a dating pool of men to choose from."

"And now I've created one," he says. "Lot of guys here, Talia."

"So, why is Flora here? If you broke up ages ago, why is she here and why is she angry with you?"

"We've stayed in touch. We're still friends, in a sense. We talk on the phone and catch up on business. She's here to support us, and she also wanted to give me a piece of her mind. That's what Flora does best."

"Really?" I ask, feeling hopeful at the news of his single status.

"Really. She's dating a lawyer we both know, and she decided to tell me what's wrong with me and all men."

"She looked *pissed. Off.* I was waiting for her to slap you."

"That's how she is. Flora doesn't have reasonable conversations, unless she has her lawyer hat on. The real Flora is emotional and high-strung. She's angry because the guy she's seeing was half an hour late to her apartment, so she left without him. That's why she's here alone."

"Oh," I say, realizing I misinterpreted the whole interaction between them.

"Are you having fun?" he asks, looking a little peeved himself.

"I am."

"Anything else you want to tell me? Like why you're interested in Adam Knight?"

"Why wouldn't I be? What woman wouldn't be interested in a man who's successful and just bought one of the most fantastic homes in Hera?"

"Maybe a woman who doesn't want to be one of his *many*."

"Look who's talking. You're the one with a *Playboy* centerfold following you around."

"Flora?" he scoffs. "She'd punch you if she heard you say that. And she's not following me around."

"Oh, right. I'll bet she broke up with you because ..."

"Because why?"

"Because you like having different women on your arm. Flora is gorgeous and smart, and you ..."

"I *what*?" Now he's irritated.

"Nothing. This isn't worth arguing about." I'm a little too tipsy to summon a good comeback.

"I don't have different women on my arm. I haven't gone out with anyone since Flora. You have this image of me that's both insulting and wrong."

"I remember you at Cooper and Imogene's wedding. You were—"

"I was dancing, like you were. I danced with different women, and you danced with different men. I drank and danced at a wedding, just like everyone else. Then, one day at a business meeting with our attorneys, I met Flora. We dated for nine months. And, by that, I mean we went out to dinner together and we slept together."

"If it was getting serious, what happened?"

"It was never serious. But Flora wants to find someone older who's ready to settle down at some point. I'm not that guy, and she's smart enough not to waste her time on me."

"I'll say." I poke his chest.

"And I hope you're smart enough not to waste your time on Knight."

"I thought he was flirting with me. I thought he was going to ask me out," I say, thinking about that moment that turned into a job offer and not a date.

"What?" Peyton stiffens.

"I hadn't planned on telling you that. I thought Adam asked to speak to me privately because he was going to ask me out. I look pretty stupid now, don't I?"

Peyton doesn't respond. His jaw tightens.

"Well, he wanted to hire me. Not a date. It's a work jig. Gig."

Relief seeps across Peyton's face. "Good. A catering job?"

"Yes. Next Saturday, he's hosting a dinner party, and he hired me. Lucky me."

"Sunflower, there are a lot of men who would like nothing better than to be your boyfriend. Men who are better than the walking refrigerator you were with before, better than a rich CEO who has people—women—falling at his feet. I don't know why you're trying so hard to get his attention." We both look over at Adam's table, where he's clearly involved with his friends and not noticing me.

"I'm not trying that hard. I thought he'd be somebody to consider," I say, finishing with a loud hiccup.

Peyton smiles, and I don't think he could be more gorgeous.

Adam is handsome, too, but Peyton has that extra punch of sexy muscleman and a mind-blowing smile. I'm standing next to the hottest man in the room, and the most dangerous.

Maybe it was easy for Flora to walk away from Peyton, but he turns me inside out, upside down, and every which way, scrambling my brain and my hormones. And that's when I decide I should return to my table.

"Hey," he says as I start to walk away. "Where are you going? I thought we were talking here." He grabs my hand and stops me.

"I thought I'd hang with Imogene and the rest of my friends."

"Get back here." He pulls me back to that space where I can breathe him in.

I don't like this attraction to Peyton. Well, I do and I don't. I'm worried. It feels too one-sided, and I'm the type to get hurt.

"You don't understand how unfair this is," I blurt out.

"Holding your hand? That's unfair?" He smiles and squeezes my hand. I yank it away from him.

"I understand how Flora feels. I think women have it harder, that's all."

"I think you're drunk."

"A little tipsy. That's why I can talk to you like this—about Flora, about Adam, about men and women. Otherwise, I'd be sitting with my friends, talking about babies, hemorrhoids, geriatric yoga, and listening to all these couples be lovey-dove and affectionate with each other."

"If Knight is so great, why aren't you sitting with him? Why didn't he invite you over to his table?"

"He did. He offered me the catering job and invited me over to sit with his friends. How confusing is that?" I laugh.

"Ah, hell," he says gruffly.

Veronica, one of the waitresses, approaches Peyton. "We have an issue," she says urgently.

"Is it a homicide?" he asks dryly. I'm surprised he's not more concerned on his opening night.

Veronica thinks about it for a second. "Yes, it's a homicide."

Peyton sighs. "What's the problem?"

"We ran out of mussels. They were a huge hit. Bash wants to know if we need to make a run, because the only place he can get them is from another restaurant in Woodstock."

"No, we're not running anywhere. If we run out of an item, just tell the customer we're out because it's so popular. Push the oysters and whatever Bash thinks is easiest to produce. If any customers complain, let me know. I'll comp them an app or a dessert."

"Thank you," she says with relief and leaves.

"You're a really nice boss. I've worked for some awful managers who'd scream at the waitstaff if customers complained about anything."

"That doesn't fly here. Nobody screws with my employees. I treat them well, and I expect customers to be respectful, too. It goes both ways. This is a nice crowd. I don't expect the food police or sleazy, rich guys pawing my waitresses. Well, except one guy."

"Adam?" I say with a laugh.

"He's not the Boy Scout you think he is."

"I have no idea what a Boy Scout is, or why I'd want one, but Adam is a gentleman."

Peyton shakes his head. "I watch out for my employees. And my sister. I've spent enough time in bars watching how these guys with money make their moves. I'm trying to give you some advice because I don't want Knight to string you along."

"Because you have so much experience as the guy who knows how to make moves on women? Like Marko?"

"I can see you've put me light-years away from the moral high ground. Fair enough. I'm not perfect or anywhere close. But did you ever consider you deserve better than Adam Knight?"

I open my mouth to say something, then shut it promptly when every possible response escapes me.

"I'd love to talk to you all night, sunflower. Really, I would. But I have to play manager and attend to some matters." He leaves, moving across the room in long, elegant strides.

Aleska finds me and protectively guides me back to our table, where I spend the next two hours sipping beer and acting like the old Talia.

"I think you're done." Aleska moves my beer stein away and pushes a glass of water toward me.

"I'm tired," I say, propping my head up with a hand. "Let me close my eyes for a few seconds."

"God, is she drunk?" Imogene asks.

"No, she's not drunk. She's tired," I reply.

"You're sleeping," Jess says.

"No, I'm resting with my eyes closed."

"Talia, I can't carry you to the car, so get up and let's go," Aleska says.

"If Mom sees me like this, she'll be angry at both of us," I reply sleepily with a yawn.

"She barely drank anything. Why would your mother care?" Imogene asks.

"Our mother hates when we come home late from bars," Aleska explains.

I can hear Aleska trying to cover for me with silly little lies, but I'm too tired to help. I really would love to lie down somewhere and sleep.

"You're adults. I think your mom will manage. Talia's real problem is being attracted to two different guys," Imogene says. "One is a little unmanageable, even though I'm rooting for him because he's my brother-in-law, and the other man doesn't seem like he could possibly be in the market for the sweet type."

"Talia likes Peyton?" Jess asks.

"I can hear all of you. I'm not unconscious yet."

"I think she likes him, too," Aleska says. "She's in a very vulnerable position right now. After Marko—"

"Stop it. I'm fine," I say, sitting up and firmly forcing my eyes open. "Imogene, can I stay in your guest room tonight so my mother doesn't give me the degree ... the third degree, for getting buzzed?"

"Off less than two beers," Aleska mutters.

"We're under construction," Imogene replies. "The guest room and the living room are ripped up."

"Our guest rooms have been overtaken by my parents and all the extra clothes and office equipment they brought with them," Jess says apologetically.

"I need some air." I stand, and then both Aleska and Imogene take one of my arms and help me walk out of the restaurant. It's almost closing time, and people are slowly making their way out into the night.

Aleska holds up my cardigan as I squeeze my arms into the snug fabric that seems much tighter than I remember. I button it all the way to the top.

"This is ridiculous," Aleska says. "Let's just go home. You can't be afraid of Mom."

"Are you kidding? When I'm exhausted, she takes it as a personal failure. She's smothering me. I don't want her to see me like this, not until I've had a good night's rest ... somewhere else."

"We should be able to find someone who can let you crash at their place," Aleska says, searching the crowd walking to their cars.

"Throw me on the back of Dylan's Harley. I'll stay with him and Emma. I'm really tired. It hit me like a ton of wet towels."

"A ton of wet towels?" Imogene laughs.

"Towels actually makes more sense than bricks, if you think about it," Jess says. "A person is more likely to get hit by wet towels than a ton of bricks."

"Who cares? Where are we sending this woman?" Imogene asks. "Dylan and Emma left a while ago. Lauren and Leo left before them. We could send her home with Lois."

I lean most of my weight on Aleska. "No way. I am not going home with Lois and her date."

"How about I drag you by your feet over to Adam's car and he can take you?" Imogene is enjoying herself.

"No." The thought of Adam witnessing this would be too much. I'd have to quit working for him.

"Don't worry." Imogene sighs. "He's gone."

"Hey, sunflower. Looks like you could use my help," Peyton says, appearing by my side.

"May I use your guest room tonight?"

"I'd never say no to you."

13

Peyton

THIS ISN'T WHAT I expected to do at one in the morning after a spectacular opening night. I should be with the staff, pouring a round of drinks for their hard work and success. However, if this pretty blonde needs me to hold her fine ass next to me, I'm not complaining. She looks worn out but grateful as I walk her to my truck.

"Thanks for understanding." She yawns for the umpteenth time. "My mother ... I just need to be away from that house for tonight."

"Understood."

Aleska runs over to us, looking relieved to see Talia about to get into my truck. "You forgot this." She hands that crazy telephone purse to Talia.

"Ah, yes. Your phone," I say.

Talia hugs the purse to her chest and waves her sister off.

"Your chariot awaits," I say.

She's in the passenger seat and has it reclined before I can do it for her. Her eyelids flutter close. It looks like sleep has overtaken, so I buckle her in.

As I walk around the truck to the driver's side, Aleska pulls her van up alongside me.

"Thank you. Really," she says. "Maybe this was meant to be."

"What do you mean?"

"I think you know what I'm talking about. You two have become very chummy."

"What has she said?" The adrenaline begins pumping through me.

"It's what she doesn't say. Every day when I come here to drop off the van for her, I always offer to help load her deliveries, but there you are. *Poof.* You and Talia are like a team, and the looks that pass between you two ... I can only imagine what goes on in that kitchen all day."

"Nothing goes on. She cooks and mostly talks to Bash. Besides, she told me she's interested in Adam Fucking Knight. Speaking of which, why is she cooking for him if she's interested in him? Isn't she breaking your company policy or something?"

Aleska looks amused. "I signed him on as a client. Talia never met him until his first delivery. He's not her type."

"Tell that to her. I distinctly remember you and her fawning all over the guy last night at Carson's."

"He's good-looking. That's all." She grins and peers over at her slumbering sister. "She's sound asleep. She trusts you."

"What are you getting at?" Is it a subtle warning not to touch her sister, or is she speculating on our relationship based on the fact that Talia can drop off to Snoozeville within ninety seconds of being in my presence?

"I'm just pointing out that she would not ask to crash in Adam's guest room, and she definitely would not let herself fall asleep in his car. She wouldn't."

"That just means she's comfortable with me. I could be Dylan or Cooper or any other guy who's like her brother." *Except for that kiss. Is that how friends kiss?*

She laughs. "Keep telling yourself that, big guy."

"I'll bring her by in the morning. You can come up with a story to tell your mother."

"I'm telling Mom that Talia spent the night at Jess's and you showed up at their house for breakfast and offered her a ride home."

"Outstanding." What parent would fall for that nonsense? I keep my opinions to myself, though. The Madej women are a mystery to me.

"Peyton," Aleska says firmly.

I'm on to her. She has a fiery streak like her big sister, and no one's going to hurry her along, not while she's lecturing me on women.

"You really could have Talia if you wanted."

I stare at her. Is she offering her sister up for sex, or is this country speak for something else? *Jesus.*

She registers my confusion and laughs. "I'm not talking about hooking up." She laughs some more. "You should see your face. For a big city New Yorker, you sure can blush. I'm saying I could totally see you and Talia together."

I sigh. "I just got out of a relationship."

"No, you didn't. That little show ended a long time ago, and it was never going to be the real deal. I have eyes. Flora never came to Hera until tonight. And I talk to your sister-in-law." She grins. "Obviously, you and Flora must have been pretty together, but that's all it was."

I falter and smile. Her unrelenting quest to be a matchmaker is charming.

"If you're so insightful, why would you want someone like me to be with your sister, assuming it's true my relationships are purely superficial?"

"Because you're both different people when you're together. It's up to you how you want to play this."

"Aleska, I'm here on business. To get this place up and running, and then I'm gone. I'm not staying in this town longer than I have to. It's actually written in my business contract."

She shakes her head. "I'm going to say goodnight now, and you're going to take good care of my sister." She drives off, leaving me to contemplate what she said.

Most of the parking lot has cleared except for the employees' cars. Talia is sleeping peacefully. I lean against my truck and call Greer and Bash, who are inside doing the closing. I should be helping. I like putting effort into working side by side with the servers doing the general cleaning, but it's not like I can leave Talia sleeping in the parking lot.

Greer's end of the connection is silent while she thinks about my predicament, and then she sighs heavily as if this is typical of me. Next, I call Bash, and he laughs and says I'm a lucky bastard.

That's that. I take off for home.

The rough dirt road leading to my house causes Talia to stir. She looks sleepily out her window. "I like night driving," she says, then closes her eyes again.

When I park in front of the house, she wakes again and opens her door. I hustle around the truck to help her. It would be easier for me to carry her in, except it looks like she wants to do this on her own. Besides, carrying a half-conscious woman in this situation could be misconstrued as sexually aggressive. I don't want to be that guy.

She slips her arm around my shoulders, and I hold her waist as we walk inside. Again, I have to deliberate over how to handle this. I decide not to put her in the guest bedroom. The couch in the living room seems like a safer bet.

"Have a seat here." I untangle her arm from my neck and ease her down onto the couch.

"Wait. I thought I'd get the guest bed," she says in a groggy voice.

"I think it would be wise for you to sleep here. You're not in any condition—"

"I'm fine!" Her sudden energy startles me. "Hey!" She grabs my hair, tugging it on both sides of my head. It's actually painful.

"Hey, sunflower, you're going to pull my hair out," I say, trying to figure out how to extricate myself from her grip.

"I feeeeel like kissing you." Her Polish accent is more pronounced. A hard *G* instead of a *K*. "Gissing you," she repeats again.

"Please don't. Let's save it for when you're completely sober."

"You are a *prigggg*," she mumbles.

"Prick. I'm a prick."

"That, too." It looks like she's going to drift off to sleep, but then her eyes pop open again.

"Jesus," I mutter. "Are your eyes on a timer? You need to go to sleep."

"Peyton," she says, "I do love your short hair. Love, love, love."

"Thank you." I chuckle as she pinches my earlobes.

"Your hair goes good with your ears. I love your ears, too." And down she goes. She releases me, and her arms flop to her sides.

I lift her legs up onto the couch and put one of the decorative pillows under her head. I unzip her ankle boots and tug her narrow feet free, stabbing myself with a sharp heel in the process. Her snug little sweater is buttoned up to her throat, the collar twisted around her neck. It looks like it's strangling her, so I unbutton it completely and straighten her blouse underneath so she'll be more comfortable. When I tug the hem of the blouse a second time, the top button comes undone and opens the blouse neckline into a deep

V-shape down to the front clasp of her bra. It reveals a surprise. I've stumbled upon a secret, of that I'm sure.

It takes me a few seconds to grasp what I'm seeing. I have been with all types of women, and I'm never surprised by flesh, soft or firm. I particularly like the expanse of flesh from the top of a woman's neck down to her breasts, that imaginary center line with delicate skin made for tender kisses that mark the trail for even the novice teenage boy. Those kisses to the prized breasts. But I am not prepared for what Talia exposes.

I lean over, my hands on either side of her still form, and I study her chest. There's nothing lascivious or perverted about it. The need to know what happened is killing me. I almost feel like shaking her awake so I can ask her to explain what I'm looking at.

Her long, graceful neck arches down to the smooth, unblemished skin on her chest, but between her breasts is a bright pink, jagged line of flesh at least four inches long, covering the length of her sternum.

I have no intention of changing her into a T-shirt or something more comfortable. She asked for a place to sleep, not a nurse, and now there's an uneasiness that I've invaded her privacy. I button up her blouse the way she originally intended to cover the scar.

She is sleeping so soundly. It gives me time to pause and consider why she has a fresh surgical scar—and why nobody knows about it, at least not her friends. It explains a lot, though. She was supposedly gone for two months, visiting her father in the Florida sunshine, but she returned looking pale. And then there was the issue of her friends, particularly Jess, complaining they couldn't reach Talia during her absence. It's apparent I've stumbled upon her secret. The question is: why has she kept it a secret?

As I gaze at Talia, not only does her beauty floor me, but her vulnerability makes me want to protect her. I'm never that guy—the knight in shining armor, the savior. Upon seeing her scar and thinking back to all of her kind and hopeful remarks about Adam, I understand why she's looking for that type of man, and it makes me both jealous and envious of him.

In another room, I have a few more hushed conversations with Greer and Bash about the closing process. Then I talk to Zander, who assures me that every tap line is functioning perfectly and he'd like to pursue the hot topic of bottling growlers—large jugs of fresh draft beer that customers can take home with them. It's another legal can of worms I have no interest in thinking about at this moment when I have this woman in the next room.

Without a doubt, I'll call it a first that I'm not racing back to the bar to sit with the others for a drink and go over the numbers and production for the evening in my usual, obsessive way. Unlike New York City, being in a laid-back, little town that prides itself on taking it slow even when you're opening a new business makes it that much easier for me to push my business duties to the next day. And I can't walk out the door when I have my own real-life Sleeping Beauty crashing on my couch.

I walk back to the living room and hesitate at the threshold. From here I can see Talia is sleeping peacefully. What am I doing?

Focus. Work.

I can't stare at her all night. This is not who I am.

For all those months I slept with Flora, not once did I watch her sleep. I was too tired from our waking hours together to waste my sleeping hours admiring her beauty. We were a volatile pair and spent more time in disagreement than in bed. The two states of our relationship were verbal sparring and sex.

Flora is conventional. She wants the high-powered career, and after making partnership, she'll buy her way into marriage and family. Not that she'll settle for any guy, but she won't dillydally with indecisive men or those like me—guys who aren't interested in settling down with mortgages and babies. For all her beauty and sex appeal, not once did Flora bring me to my knees. Not that I'm a great catch.

But this woman who regularly butchers the English language is opening a hole in my chest. Something that started as a pinhole is now a gaping wound the size of a basketball. I've opened myself up to her without trying, and somehow, I need to shove the genie back in the bottle.

Between tonight's event and bringing Talia home, I'm too wired to sleep, so I go down to my room and change into jeans and a T-shirt, then grab my laptop and head back to the living room. Talia hasn't moved.

I plant myself in the big, upholstered chair next to the couch and begin reviewing the financials that Greer is posting to the restaurant spreadsheets. The opening day numbers are excellent. Overall, the night would have been perfect if I hadn't had that public tiff with Flora. But she likes to make a grand entrance and an even grander exit. This way she got to make sure everyone noticed her, and they did.

I push Flora and work out of my mind when I look up from my laptop and see Talia sprawled in front of me.

When I run through the list of women I've been with, which isn't a huge number by any means, they all fit a certain mold physically—tall, with dark hair and dark eyes. I didn't see my own pattern until I found myself fantasizing about Talia's blonde hair wrapped in my fists, envisioning her creamy-toned flesh turning flush when she climaxes, and her petite stature that has enough curves to fill my palms as I grip her in various positions while I take her from behind. Sure, she's definitely my type when my thoughts about her go all X-rated and give me an unbearable hard-on.

And then there's the unexpected chemistry. I'm not talking about the desire to have a good fuck. That kind of chemistry can happen with hundreds of women, whether I'm under the influence or not. Basic animal urges don't count; as humans, we can replace one sexual partner for another if the primary goal is sex and fulfilling a physical need. It doesn't mean I've slept around with scores of women lined up at my door. No, I've been a serial monogamist, staying with one woman for a few months before the sex cravings run out on my part. And sometimes I would make life simple by avoiding sex with women altogether. Naturally, there are health risks involved with abstinence, such as severe carpal tunnel.

I've admitted noticing Talia, but I never expected to feel this way, to have this longing where I need to be around her and wonder where she is at every waking moment.

The discovery of her scar speaks volumes about a woman who everyone in this little town thought they knew. Maybe I should feel guilty for having some insights into something she's been trying to hide, but I don't. I feel oddly proud and entitled. Something deeper inside makes me believe I have a right to know what happened to her and a right, more like a duty, to help her deal with it.

There's really no comparison between the two women, and Flora would fucking kick me to the curb if she knew any of this, but I do have to ask myself why I couldn't feel the same way about Flora. They have universal goals, but Talia and Flora are so very different. They both want the same things in terms of career success and a solid relationship, and family is important to both of them. But Talia is a giver, while Flora succeeds at taking. Don't get me wrong, she's a good person, but there's no way in hell she'd live with an agoraphobic mother, and she'd never worry about an aging neighbor who lives alone, or a younger sister who depends on her.

Talia takes care of people; she thrives on it. It explains why she's so disciplined and can run her own business, even if it won't make her rich. It allows her to help others, and I admire her for a virtuous trait that I don't have. I'm more like Flora—taking what I can get from others.

As the youngest in my family, I got the easy way out too many times. When my mother was dying of cancer, I was there for emotional support, but Cooper and Greer shouldered the burden, handling her round-the-clock nursing care and settling her estate. I loved my mother more than anyone, including my father, but I was really only good for hand-holding. While Cooper and Greer and my brothers, Evan and Neil, were dealing with the tough shit, I used the time to run the family bars and meet with prospective investors for future projects.

I've always been a bit of a selfish bastard, and it's only recently, being around Talia, that I've been rather ashamed of my arrogance. Little did I know she would become part of my daily routine; that I'd look forward to seeing her walk through the doors at Swill in the morning, having our first conversation of each day, whether it's kind or sarcastic; watching her cook when she doesn't realize I'm there; or simply hearing and seeing her throughout the day. Every day. She has become an elixir, illuminating another side to me that was never apparent.

Whatever I'm feeling has to get shut down real fast. I have to keep my eyes on the prize—everything I've been working toward, the career I want more than anything, more than any woman. And Talia deserves better than someone as selfish as me.

• • •

The stiffness in my legs wakes me, and when I open my eyes, I'm still slouched in the chair with my outstretched legs resting on the couch where Talia is still sound asleep. I glance at my phone and realize I've been asleep for six hours with my legs crossed at the ankles and my hands clenching the sides of the armchair.

The glorious, vivid dream I was having is beginning to fade. I try to grasp the last remnants of it before it's gone for good.

Talia was kissing me and running her hands down my back. We were in my bed, so perfect. Then that awesome image was interrupted by Greer walking into the room, disgruntled about numbers she had to discuss with me. Suddenly, Zander appeared in his gray, industrial jumpsuit, stinking of beer and trying to talk to me about the fucking tap lines again. Yeah, the dream was really good and starting to get hot and heavy before all the work shit came crashing into it.

I pull my legs off the couch, stand, and stretch, arching as far as I can to work out the kinks.

A soft intake of breath takes me out of the moment, and I look down to see Talia watching me.

She looks down at her fully clothed body, then back at me.

"We didn't sleep together," she says matter-of-factly.

"No."

"I remember all the beers being passed around, but I was mostly sipping. I don't feel hungover."

"It went right to your head. I didn't mind. I got to carry you to bed."

"You mean the couch. You didn't carry me. I remember asking to stay in your guest room. Why did you put me here?"

I sit back down and lean forward to get closer to her. "That would be pushing a boundary I'm not comfortable with. You weren't drunk, but you didn't have full control ... I wanted you to be comfortable ..."

"Oh, you were afraid to put me in the bed. Afraid of how it would look to me."

"This is new territory for me—bringing a woman home. And it isn't about jumping into bed."

"I asked you to put me in a bed because I know you have an extra one. I wouldn't have asked you if I thought you'd take advantage of me while I was sleeping." She sighs. "Your concern is sweet. And being called sweet must make you uncomfortable."

"Not at all," I say unconvincingly, and she laughs.

"Can I ask you a question? Something that's been bothering me."

"I suppose it's going to make me look bad, but sure. Ask away."

"I'd like to know more about why you would let Flora get away. Why do men do that?"

"Christ, Flora again."

A slight tilt of the head and raised eyebrows. She expects me to explain something I really can't, not if I want to retain the perception of my humanity. It's also my only leverage for information. She wants to know *why*, and I want to know *what*.

"Okay, sure. I'll tell you my story if you tell me yours."

"I don't have a story. You know the dull details about my life. I live with my recluse mother. Nothing else to tell."

"I don't think so. That scar on your chest is pretty fresh."

She immediately puts her hands to the front of her blouse, checking to make sure her scar is covered. "How did you know?"

"Last night you were tangled in your sweater. I was adjusting your clothes so you wouldn't strangle yourself. I straightened your blouse, and I saw the scar. You had surgery recently, didn't you?"

She hesitates, then nods slowly. "I did. Only my mother and sister know—and Norma. My father knew about the surgery, but he chose not to be here, so I don't count him. I wanted to keep it a secret from everyone else, at least for a while. Now that I'm completely sober, tell me about Flora, and then I'll tell you about my scar."

"Why do you care so much about Flora?"

"I don't. I'm trying to work some things out. I'm trying to understand why men do what they do. I think you can give me some perspective on them. You broke up with a very successful woman, who's gorgeous, like out-of-this-world, stunningly gorgeous."

I shrug. "Sometimes that's not enough."

"I'd like to understand why, because if she's not enough for a man, then how does a woman like me stand a chance?"

"With me?" I ask, surprised.

"With any man," she replies, each word clipped as if she can't believe the audacity of my question. "There had to be something specific that would break you two up. The woman is an attorney, so I know she has a brain. And when she walks into a room, she owns it. My God, every man in the restaurant was looking at her last night. No, itch that. Every person in that restaurant was looking at her. Why does a man reject a woman like Flora?"

I start laughing, and her mouth tightens into a narrow line.

"Now what?" she snaps.

"Sorry. You said, 'Itch that.' It's *scratch* that."

"Yeah, yeah, yeah. So, what happened? Why can't you fall in love with a woman like Flora and be with her forever? Why did you have to end it? And why did she look so angry at you?"

I laugh. "She's been pissed at me since the day we met. It never stopped us from having fun."

"Stop laughing. Why are guys always so nonchalant about their exes? And they laugh them off as if they were the problem? That can't be the whole story."

"Look, it's pretty simple. We hired a law firm to handle compliance for us, and they sent Flora. We hooked up, and next thing I knew, I was her boyfriend. We were strictly professional when she came by one of the restaurants or if we had meetings at her firm. We were kind of an after-hours-only couple."

"And ...?"

"Jesus, you're pushy. What do you expect to learn from me?"

"Why men do what they do. Why they fall for you, then drop you."

"Hey, I didn't drop Flora. It was mutual. Flora has always known what she wanted. First her career, then a family, then she'll conquer something else. She's one of those people who likes having a lot of balls in the air."

"So you were one of the balls?"

"I've got two, thank you."

"But your balls weren't enough for her?"

"You're something." There's no way to make her or anyone sympathetic to my side of this story. "Flora has always been very clear about what she wants, and I told her I wasn't interested in settling down anytime soon. Hell, I wasn't really in the mood for a girlfriend. Not a high-maintenance woman like Flora anyway. But that didn't stop her. After we slept together, she carried on as if we were already a couple, and I didn't really try to stop her. I was busy running two restaurants and was in the middle of blueprints and raising capital for Swill. I figured, who am I to shit on her dreams? Let her fantasize about the multimillion dollar condo or brownstone she'll buy for her future family. She's the type who, if she could, would control the sex and hair color of her children. Honestly, I didn't give it a thought. I loved being at my restaurants, and when I was with Flora, the sex was great. That was enough for me."

"You're making yourself sound awful. I hope this story has a good ending."

"It does have a good ending. Flora doesn't have to keep trying to make me into something I'm not. She'll be happier with someone else."

"I still feel bad for her. She's trying to do what many women are trying to do. It's hard to find the right person you want to have children with, and then hope you can have a long, happy marriage. Then she figures out she was being used for sex."

"Hold on," I say harshly. "I didn't force her to stay, and I never once said or implied that we had a permanent thing going on."

"You slept with her for years!"

"Years? It was nine months, tops. And remember, we called this whole thing off before I moved here. Give me some credit."

"You should have stopped it from the beginning, but I think you were drunk on sex. You like having women like Flora available for when you need it."

"You don't know what you're talking about."

"I was raised by a man like you. They can only do the family thing for so long, and then they need to roam. They have wandering balls."

I burst out laughing. "You mean wandering eyes?"

"I think it's *balls*, because they end up in other women's beds."

"So I'm not allowed to have sex with a woman unless I'm willing to marry her?"

"Don't be silly. But you took it too far with Flora. You knew what she wanted."

"And she knew what I wanted. Don't make me out to be some evil guy. Flora liked having me at all of her corporate parties and benefit dinners. And she had her moments, plenty of days and nights when she wanted to be alone. I spent time with her because I liked her. She's intelligent, funny, and extremely emotional and loud, like the rest of her family. Sometimes it was a blast, and sometimes it wasn't."

"Did you love her?"

"No." I clasp my hands together and look down at the floor. "Maybe I thought if I stuck it out, I'd fall in love with her. Isn't that how it works?"

"But you never did." She huffs out a breath, sending a few wisps of hair floating up, then down.

"No. And Flora always knew it. It's not like her world would end without me. She was destined to find someone better suited to her. She was there last night as a friend to wish me well. I told you this."

"I know, but it didn't look like a friendly visit. Did she really wish you well?"

"Yeah, she did."

Talia studies me, and I use the opportunity to get up from the chair and stretch again. She keeps looking me over from head to toe, and a little grin blooms across her face.

"What are you looking at?" I smile because I'm good at this kind of flirty game.

I push her legs over and sit down on the couch next to her.

She shakes her head. "I know what your problem is."

"Christ, here we go again."

"Your problem is you're not serious about women. Flora was probably your first grown-up woman, and you couldn't handle what she wanted, what most people want."

"Ah, you've been coached by my sister."

"No, I came up with it on my own. You can sit here and think about that while I go freshen up. I assume I can use the guest bathroom," she says as she stands up. "I used to work here before Carson finished his new house."

"Of course. Towels are clean. No one has used that bathroom ever, and your sister keeps cleaning it."

"Thank you. You're an excellent host. And I see my sister is keeping this place in great shape."

"I only sleep here. She's basically cleaning the clean. No time for dust mites to move in on her watch."

Talia smiles and saunters off to the bathroom with an extra sway in her hips.

I head down to the master bedroom to take a shower. Even watching her sleep gave me a raging hard-on, so I spend the first five minutes under a cold waterfall of pain. When I step out of the shower, I wrap a towel around my waist and walk down the hall to listen in at the guest bathroom. I hear Talia shut off the shower. She's singing.

The bathroom door swings open, and she stands there frozen, in my bathrobe. Her hair is dry, piled on top of her head in a messy bun, but the rest of her is swimming in the giant robe. Even in the thick terry cloth, she looks sexy as hell. A man's robe or sexy lingerie, it doesn't matter, my brain is getting all fired up and signaling the rest of my body to follow suit.

She stares at me long enough that my cock comes to life again. I know when I'm getting the once-over from a woman, and this is more than a once-over.

"Why can't you put on a robe like a normal person?" she asks with a hitch in her breath.

"You're wearing my robe. Your sister accidentally hung it in here, I guess."

"Oh, I assumed it was for guests."

"Hmm" is all I can get out, imagining her naked body underneath my robe.

My towel slips lower on my hips, and Talia tries to avert her eyes from my obvious erection tenting the towel. I grip the towel before it slips off completely and release a tight, slow breath, weighted with arousal.

"You look really hot in my robe. You have no idea what you're doing to me, sunflower."

"I think we're both suffering from dehydration. We need water." She edges around me, and I follow her to the kitchen. She opens the fridge and grimaces. "Gatorade, Tabasco, and water. Why don't guys ever buy groceries?"

"I work in a restaurant. But I'd sure love to eat at home, if only there was a local chef who delivered home-cooked meals."

"Nice try." She hands me a bottle, and we both guzzle our waters in tandem. She wipes her mouth on the sleeve of the robe. "That tastes so good. But seriously, too bad you don't have eggs and bread here. I would have cooked you breakfast. I used to do it for Carson if he was still asleep when I showed up to clean."

"Lucky guy." I adjust my towel. "He must have loved that."

"Don't look at me like that. I never slept with Carson. And he didn't love it when I surprised him with a breakfast tray in bed. He practically jumped out of bed. I think he felt guilty about not being at work when I showed up, but I usually got to his place before seven in the morning because I knew he was an early riser. It made him feel weird to have me serve him, so after that I would leave the breakfast in the kitchen and go about my cleaning. He lightened up after he started seeing Jess."

"That's sweet. Really," I say, sarcastically. "You still owe me an explanation."

Talia narrows her eyes and walks past me. Again, I follow her around my own home.

She walks right down to the master bedroom and stands in the middle of it, surveying the walls. "There's nothing here."

"There's a bed and a dresser and a nightstand."

"That's all Carson's old stuff. The room is spotless, and the bed is made. I recognize Aleska's signature fold-over style. There's nothing personal of yours in here. It's like a hotel room, and I can tell by the bed that you didn't sleep here."

"I slept in the chair, in the living room."

"Peyton," she says softly. "What are we doing?"

"You're the one who asked me for a place to sleep, and I gave you one. I fell asleep in the chair. It's no big deal. But if you're interested in something more, I'm half-naked and horny as hell, and you're making it worse by parading around in my robe."

She waves me away and walks to the dresser, searching through my paltry wardrobe. "Here, put on these sweatpants. The label says Big Cocky Dude. They must be yours." She tosses them to me.

The towel around my waist drops to the floor as I shake out the sweatpants. Talia's eyes widen before she turns her head as I dress in front of her. Then I push my damp hair back and hop on the bed, settling myself against the pillows and the headboard.

"What are you doing?" she asks.

"I'm waiting for my story. I gave you shelter, water, and my best robe, so you owe me the story about that scar." I pat the bed next to me. "Sit down. I won't bite. Unless that's your thing."

She huffs and hoists the thick robe up so she can climb on the bed. "Don't you need to go to work?"

"Not for a few hours. And I know Sundays are your day off, so we have plenty of time to talk."

She settles herself onto the bed and, for a moment, we are both quiet. I've just invited a woman to my bed to talk, something I never do. All I can think about is kissing her again.

"And then you can have your way with me," I say, thinking my smart-ass remark will break the tension. It fails miserably.

Talia forces a weak smile and looks down at her hands. At least I know it's not my imagination; the arousal is mutual. And I know this is where everything can go wrong.

14

Four months earlier...
Talia

Marko lives by a strict routine, and I like the structure he creates for me, something I never had with my own family. I spend four nights a week at his apartment in New Rochelle, and three nights a week he has dinner at our house in Hera. He's polite, and my mother dotes on him with big dinners, feeding him like a son who has just come back from a long journey.

Marko has always worked for his father's plumbing and heating company, and he always will. He will eventually buy a home in New Rochelle, within walking distance to his parents, and he will continue to work out at the same gym with the same schedule, even when he gets married and has children. We don't discuss dreams. He has none.

This effortless life plan has been explained to me countless times. The self-serving rigidity with which he keeps everything simple and tailored to his needs might annoy other women, but Marko's bluntness is easy to live with. There's safety in knowing exactly what he wants and when he wants it. I lived with so much uncertainty when I depended on my parents; Marko has removed that fear. He is uncomplicated in every way, and he suits me.

A couple of weeks before Christmas, I have to cancel every evening with him because I have a cold that turns into an aggressive cough. Marko begins to find the whole thing inconvenient. A simple cold shouldn't prevent me from going to his friends' holiday parties.

I'm more upset that I can't see Jess, but I can't risk getting her sick. I don't care about the Christmas parties, but I worry I'll miss her delivery date if the baby comes early.

When Marko does finally see me, he keeps his distance. He wears his disdain like polished armor ... on an arrogant warrior who never sees battle. My mother and sister witness this, and after he leaves, I fall into the old ninny trap of apologizing for his selfish behavior. Finally, Aleska convinces me to see a doctor, and it all ends there. Or you could say that's the beginning. In either case, it's the defining moment that changes the course of my life.

"I'm hearing something unusual," the doctor says. He's one of the generic doctors supplied by the walk-in clinic where I go only out of necessity, one of the few places that takes my insurance.

"What are you hearing?" I ask as he probes under my blouse, placing the stethoscope on various parts of my chest. He tilts his head each time and listens with deep concentration.

"I think there's backwash. Regurgitation," he says, matter-of-factly.

"I don't understand what you're saying."

He removes his stethoscope, and I pull my blouse down. "It's possible your blood is being regurgitated. Your heart is pumping very hard, and it sounds like a murmur."

My eyes must be popping wider with alarm, because his generic, non-emotional, physician expression softens into something more human. "I'm not an expert on hearts. I can only tell you what I think is there. It sounds like a heart murmur, and in simple terms, the backwash sound I'm hearing could be caused by a valve that isn't functioning properly. Does anyone in your family have a history of heart problems? It wasn't listed on your chart."

"I don't think so. Did I do something to cause this? How do I fix it?"

"This could be something you were born with, and unfortunately, sometimes these things go undetected until there are symptoms like shortness of breath or even a heart attack."

"But other than a cold, I feel fine. I exercise, I run, and I'm never out of breath. I'm here because I can't get rid of this cough."

"I know. I think it's the cold and your persistent cough that may have shown us the underlying problem. But I need to send you to a cardiologist to check on your heart function. I think your cold symptoms have been getting worse because your heart is struggling. The murmur is very loud now. Otherwise, I may have missed it."

I no longer like this generic doctor. No diplomas are displayed on the wall, so I have no idea if this man actually went to medical school.

Panic is consuming my brain, and this pale, skinny man with his unremarkable face and blasé manner is making it worse. It amazes me how he can be so unconcerned after giving me news that feels like a death sentence.

After I hand the receptionist my copayment, I walk to my car, dreading telling my mother and Marko the news.

"Talia!"

I turn around to see Dr. Pasty Face walking briskly toward me. He holds out his hand with a business card. Seriously? He thinks I need his business card? Am I supposed to recommend him to my friends?

"This is who you need to see." He hands me the card, and I study the name of the doctor and the prestigious New York City hospital. "I just spoke to him. He's expecting a call from you. He's the best."

As Dr. Pasty Face pushes a swath of hair off his worried face, I suddenly want to apologize for thinking nasty thoughts about him, and I want to tell him I'll be fine.

"He's the best doctor?"

"He's the best cardiothoracic surgeon when it comes to mitral valve repair. I'm pretty sure that's what you need, but he has to see you and run his own tests."

"Oh." I don't know what else to say. There's a bit of shock that accompanies the word *surgeon*.

"Call today," Dr. Kind Pasty Face pleads. "His assistant will get you in since I referred you."

"Thank you."

He smiles at me for the first time.

• • •

The famous Dr. Allen will see me.

Marko thinks this will be no big deal. Nothing ever really bad happens in Marko's world. He comes from a big, healthy family. No one gets divorced; no one moves away. They live a very simplistic life. When they aren't working hard at their day jobs, they spend all their time with the family. Or, I should say, families. Everyone from his parents to his siblings, grandparents, uncles, aunts, and cousins all live within two miles of each other. They have their own Polish community, and when I'm among them, it feels like Lublin, where the Polish language flows freely.

I'm convinced Marko knows best. Big and strong men provide us with a sense of protection, but it's Marko's idealism about us and his army—that big, nosy family—that instill a sense of comfort. I am one of them; therefore, I will be fine.

This is real. I'm seeing a heart surgeon, one of the top five in his specialty in the world, and I hope he tells me it was all a mistake, that Dr. Kind Pasty Face did not hear a murmur.

Dr. Allen's office arranges for a meeting with me, but first, they send me to a cardiologist on their team, Dr. Cho. I thought I was going for a simple checkup, another groping session with the stethoscope, but no. Dr. Cho, who looks like a teenager, arranges for me to have an echocardiogram, which is easy; and a catheterization, which is not. It puts Marko and me through our first uncomfortable medical procedure together.

I lie on a cold, metal table, and a young male nurse gives me a Brazilian. He shaves my pubic area completely, and then a team of doctors and nurses insert a long, thin tube through my groin and guide it up to my heart.

Dr. Cho's head pops in front of my face with his big, friendly grin and says everything looks great. My arteries are spectacular. Dr. Allen will receive the results of my spectacular arteries and an enthusiastic thumbs-up from Dr. Cho. He tells me I'm a perfect candidate for Dr. Allen's surgery. Instead of being happy or even relieved, I'm simply terrified.

Hours later, after I spend time in the patient recovery area with Marko at my side, I am released.

On the drive home, Marko says, "That was easy. There's nothing to worry about."

It was easy for him. For me, it was like an alien abduction, getting probed by a bunch of strangers who are fascinated with the inner workings of my body. I give Marko a pass, though. This is new to us, just the beginning. He's treating this upcoming surgery like a trip to the dentist. No one likes it—the flossing is painful, as if the dental hygienist is using razor wire on your gums, and the toothpaste is gritty and gross—but you do it. For Marko, my surgery is nothing more than bad toothpaste. For me, this surgery puts my whole life in a different perspective.

The meeting with Dr. Allen is more emotionally harrowing than I expected. He's in his fifties, very fit, with a shaved head, and is meticulous in his speech and mannerisms. His personal office overlooks Central Park, and it's bigger than my home. With this kind of real estate, Dr. Allen is obviously a king in his field. There's a combination of old-world wealth and advanced technology in the expensive credenza and the elegant bookcases that have been paired with high-tech equipment. Large flat-screens line his walls, with statistical spreadsheets and images of a beating heart, presumably mine. It's nothing like I expected.

I feel so small and helpless, and the sanctity of the doctor's office reminds me how fragile the human body is.

Dr. Allen proudly explains the images of my heart that are on the various large monitors. The term *mitral valve prolapse* is explained to me again, and he assures me it's genetic, and it indeed often goes undetected. Because of that, people refer to it as "the silent killer."

Silent killer.

Defective heart.

Silent killer.

My body is rigid, gripped by fear. Put heart and killer in the same sentence and I assume my life is over.

Marko seems mystified that he cannot prevent this. His questions focus on the genetic aspect, asking why my parents and my sister don't have it. Dr. Allen says everyone needs to be tested.

Tested. Like I'm Patient Zero. Everyone related to me will need to be tested to see if they have a heart valve silently leaking blood.

Marko has been holding my hand the whole time, but now he doesn't look at me. It's as if he's questioning the doctor relentlessly when the answer is obvious. I need surgery. *Now.*

Dr. Allen comes across as delighted and confident—traits you want in a surgeon—and he has no doubt that, because of my young age and good health, the surgery will be uneventful. We caught it in time, unlike those poor young athletes who drop dead on the football field to the shock of everyone. I'm lucky, and my arteries are beautiful, according to Dr. Cho, so Dr. Allen is pretty certain when he opens me up, he'll find a good valve that can be repaired rather than replaced. Apparently, that's a big deal.

Most heart patients with valve issues end up with pig valves, which have a limited life span, or the patient receives a mechanical valve, which requires the patient to be on blood thinners for life. So I'm supposed to be happy about saving my own valve.

Marko once again moves the conversation toward my future. I won't need to be on any medications long-term. Marko nods at this but doesn't seem to care. He pushes to know more about the genetics. Not my current family's health, but my *future* family's health.

And then the realization hits me. Marko is worried I will give him defective babies. He doesn't say that out loud, but it's clear that's what he's concerned about. His family is full of healthy people. Even his grandparents are robust, energetic, and mobile. How can he tell his parents, his whole family, that I could give them children with a life-threatening defect?

Marko's line of questioning is making me just as paranoid as he is about our future children.

But this is also the moment, the pivotal point in our relationship, when I feel sad that I'm with him. Marriage is about supporting each other in sickness and in health, and it's already apparent I'm getting the Marko who thinks marriage is about bouncy houses and backyard cookouts.

As Dr. Allen talks about the actual surgery, cutting me open, putting ice on my heart to stop it, I think of how easy it would be to throw the stapler at his head and run out of there. But the urge to throw a hard object at Marko's head is stronger.

I get Dr. Allen. He's a surgeon, and like he said jokingly, he likes to get in there and cut (doctor humor). I respect his passion, just as much as I'm beginning to hate Marko's doubts about me. Because that's what is coming across loud and clear in the room.

When we leave the hospital, he decides it would be best if he drops me off at home rather than bringing me to his apartment. This is supposed to be one of my "Marko nights" and why I keep clothing and toiletries at his place.

A forced cheeriness creeps into his voice as he says without looking at me, "I want to get in a good workout and go to bed early."

This from the man who has put pressure on me over the last year to move in with him, or at least spend every night with him. This from the man who has had me on a short leash because of his jealous streak. This from the man who wants sex every night, every day!

As we drive out of the city, I'm quiet as he rambles on. At first, he sounds encouraging and says I'm lucky the doctors found my heart condition early, and I'm fortunate to have doctors of this caliber, and that my insurance covers these huge medical expenses. Soon, everything goes from "we" to "you."

"*You'll* be fine."

"*You* have the best doctors."

"*You* have to let your mother help *you* in the recovery stage."

"*You* have a sister and mother who will do anything for *you*."

That's where Marko makes his mistake.

So, this is it, I think, when we are far enough away from the city to see the welcoming, snow-covered hills and open space of the approaching Catskills. It's like a trigger for Marko. He sees the exit signs for the surrounding small towns and launches into a speech about how he needs to do more research to see what the failure rate is on this procedure because, after all, some of the people in Dr. Allen's waiting room had the surgery in other hospitals and it failed.

Marko keeps his eyes on the road, anger beginning to curl around his words as he presents his concerns about doctors being wrong, and maybe my heart will have limitations, maybe it will drastically change my life. What he means is it will drastically change *his* life.

Before we reach Hera, he is so worked up that he says what he's truly thinking. "This fucking sucks. At least one of your parents caused this. They passed down this fucking gene. And you could pass this down to any children I have!"

"*You* have?" I ask. "I'm pretty sure I'm the only one between us who can give birth."

He doesn't apologize for his remark as he parks in front of my home.

I look at him hard, seeing the anger underneath his stony expression. All I feel is contempt for him.

"Can you imagine putting a little kid through major surgery like this?" he asks in an accusing way.

"No, I can't. I can barely imagine myself going through this." I grip the door handle, ready to leave. It's obvious he's not going to walk inside, sit down with my mother and sister, and explain what the doctor said. It's obvious I'm on my own.

"I need to do more research," he repeats, his jaw clenched, shaking his head.

"That's good. You do that." I swing the car door open and step out. "I'm scheduled for surgery in a few weeks, so I'm going to get my business in order and mentally prepare myself for when they saw my chest open and fix my defective heart that's screwing up your life. So you go work on that research." I slam his car door and walk into my house without looking back.

My mother and sister take the news surprisingly well. For someone who is terrified of the outside world, my mother shows great strength and comfort inside her domain. At last, she has something meaningful to do—she must help save her daughter.

Up until the surgery, it's business as usual. I let my customers know I'll be visiting my father in Florida for a long break, but that Aleska will be running the food deliveries and my mother, who really is a better cook than me, will make sure their meals are spectacular.

Jess goes into labor before my surgery date, and I peek at the baby among the other infants from the glass window that protects the newborns from the visitors. If my friends think it's odd that I'm going to spend so much time with my deadbeat dad, they don't say anything. Jess is too busy with Scotty; Imogene and Lauren are buried in their jewelry business; Emma, Dylan, Carson, Leo, and Cooper are busy jumping into the restaurant business; and the town snoops, Lois and Eleanor, are busy gossiping about Peyton, the man who's in charge of Hera's biggest coming attraction. All this activity is the perfect cover for me.

Marko sends periodic texts with an alarming number of sympathetic clichés. Either he's improvising with his own versions or he really isn't as bright as I thought.

Take one step at a time.

A journey begins with the first step.

Take it one day at a time because each day has a thousand steps.

What the hell?

I ignore his texts. And he doesn't call.

I can't wait around for him to feel better about this. It's not my job to cheer him up, not when he's being an awful person.

My mother makes it her mission, her job, to lead my recovery phase. We order an expensive treadmill from a shop that will deliver and install it in our family room the next day. My mother loves it so much that she starts using it every day. She's never been a runner, but now she hops on the treadmill a few times a day. I get used to the sound of the hum of the motor and the pounding on the rubber belt.

As the surgery date approaches, my anxiety escalates, but my mother is becoming very fit. She also takes over the wall calendar with our business schedule. She plans out the food she will cook and schedules my morning and evening walking sessions on the treadmill, which will be supervised by her in case I suddenly feel weak and fall. She has my post-surgery all planned out. She's here for me. She's nervous but confident.

Unfortunately, the revelations about this type of genetic heart disorder are not enough to compel my mother to have her own heart examined. She will not leave the house.

Aleska is scared for me but tries not to show it. She does see a cardiologist and returns home, relieved when all the tests conclude that her heart is fine.

It's Aleska who drives me to the hospital at four in the morning. It's Aleska who waits in the family room from when they wheeled me away at seven thirty in the morning to when surgery was completed at two thirty in the afternoon. She spends the hours sitting in a crowded room with other worried strangers, watching the patient names on the electronic board that indicates the status of our surgery in real time. And it's Aleska who stands by my bed in the ICU after the seven-hour repair job, as we refer to it.

As a nurse and one of my surgeons try to wake me, it's Aleska's voice I respond to. I'm told for several hours my eyes would flutter open at the sound of her voice, but I kept slipping back into unconsciousness. When I do awake fully in the early evening, Aleska is there, saying, "Wake up, lovey. Talia. Talia. It's me, Allie."

I see my sister and, for a moment, I'm searching behind her to see if Marko is there, too. He was supposed to be there, but then I remember I was with the wrong person.

15

Talia

WHEN I FINISH TELLING the story, without omitting a single, gory detail of what I experienced in the hospital, there's a moment of silence where I'm wondering if I said too much and Peyton is merely trying to think of something nice to say.

He leans toward me. "You don't need anyone to save you. You saved yourself, Talia."

"And some hotshot surgeons helped."

"You went through some kind of hell. That's for sure."

Whatever strength I have been using to hold myself together these past few months is crumbling like a slow-moving avalanche of pebbles, rocks, and boulders. Instead of crying, my defenses go down. A soothing blanket envelops me so I don't have to keep up my tough facade.

Telling Peyton my personal story and reliving the unpleasant details was easier than I thought it would be. I could never speak this way with Marko about "bodily things." Marko would be disgusted.

Peyton is not repulsed by what I have told him, and his compassion makes him that much more desirable.

He has a capable body; strong arms I'd like to wrap myself in, to cocoon myself against the Pandora's box I've opened.

Revealing my secret to him is only the beginning. Soon, the "middle" of this secret will be the admission to my friends, and the "end" will be accepting what has happened and what the consequences may be in the future.

"That ex of yours ... what a shithead." Peyton's eyes flare with anger. "He should lose his manhood for what he did to you."

"His manhood?" I laugh.

"At least you got to see him for what he really is before you married the guy."

"I know I'm supposed to see that it was a real test of our relationship ... Aleska made a point of telling everyone in town that our engagement was off. She told them while I was on my fake Florida vacation. The idea was that, when I came back to work two months later after my recovery, my breakup with Marko would be old news and my friends wouldn't ask a lot of questions. I think all the activity around your restaurant helped distract everyone from the Marko issue, to be honest."

"I still can't believe you hid your surgery from your friends." He shakes his head in disbelief. "Seriously, you know too many people here, and everyone is in everyone else's business. I don't see how it was possible for you to keep it from them, and I don't understand why you felt the need to hide it."

I look down at my scar, then pull the robe closed more tightly to cover it.

Peyton moves closer and puts his finger under my chin, gently raising my head so I'll look at him. "You can tell me why—you've already told me everything else. And sooner or later, others will find out, too. You can only cover up the scar so long."

I don't want to be a victim, or someone sickly, in Peyton's eyes. The longing and desire for him is pure lust. It's juvenile and inappropriate since, realistically, he's not the man to pursue. Except, I don't want the teasing sexual tension to end because it's the push and pull between us that reminds me of my old self, the strong person I was. He makes me feel alive again.

"I didn't want my friends involved in my surgery and recovery because I would have become another town *project*. Considering my mother's agoraphobia, having people stream in and out of our house to help would only add to her anxiety. I didn't want to worry more about her than I already do. I didn't have it in me to take care of both of us. And besides, me being a patient gave my mother something to do. She got to do all the cooking for my clients, and she got to nurse me. She felt useful, and it's been a long time since she's felt that."

"You can't use your mother as an excuse." He rests his hand on my shoulder. "I think it was your pride. You don't want to need help.

"Still, how was it possible to stay hidden? Your house is less than two miles from my restaurant. I was there every day, and your name would pop up in conversation a lot when Jess was there. Everyone talked about you, thinking you were in Florida with your father. Jess couldn't wait for you to get home." He pauses and looks amused. "Wow, your covert techniques are spot-on. You really could be a Russian spy if you wanted to."

"Except I'm Polish."

"Yeah, I know. I like how it annoys you when I give you a hard time about it. I'm impressed with your ability to carry out your devious agenda."

"I wasn't being devious; I was being practical. Our neighbor, Norma, was in on it, too. She's always walking into our house unannounced, and my mother couldn't bear to start locking the door to prevent the surprise visits. She's like family, so we had to tell her.

"Norma kept me company while Mom was cooking and Aleska was doing double duty, cleaning houses and delivering the dinners. My agenda consisted of walking on the treadmill and sleeping. Every day, I'd do the same thing—walking, exercises with small hand weights, TV, and sleep. Two months imprisoned in my own home with the same boring routine, day in and day out, I was becoming claustrophobic."

"It must give you a better understanding of your mom's condition."

"A little. The urge to run out of the house and escape the boredom was so strong, but the fear of being on the outside was stronger. How does my mother not go insane?"

"Before you can help her, you need to get over your own fears."

"If I hadn't told you about my heart condition, would you think I was scared? Do I project fear?"

"Not at all." He lies back on the bed next to me with his arms behind his head, looking up at the ceiling as though he's studying the rustic wood beams. It gives me a chance to admire his long, hard, lean body.

He has taut muscles, ripped abs, and those fantastic lips I want to kiss again. It's funny and rather demented how I think more about Peyton than Adam Knight, or any other man, for that matter. *Lust* has no common sense; it has zeroed in on Peyton MacKenzie.

"I am afraid." I scrunch down on the bed and turn on my side, facing him. He rolls to face me and puts his hand firmly on my waist. It feels good, natural, like the satisfaction you get from sliding a puzzle piece into its proper place.

"Tell me what you're afraid of."

"I used to be a typical, twenty-five-year-old with no sense of mortality. Frailty belonged to other people, not me. Since the surgery, I feel scared and nervous almost every day. I know I'm lucky to be alive, but since I came closer to death than I've ever experienced, it's all I think about."

"Death?"

"I'm afraid of feeling weak, physically and emotionally, because my responsibilities to my mother and my sister are enormous. They can't afford to have me fall apart. I can't afford to be weak. I have to take care of my mother. And I have to help Aleska, to make sure she finishes college, because it's important to her and our business. And I also feel a great responsibility to Norma. She doesn't have any family, except for a distant niece in Arizona or someplace hot like that. She's this amazing hundred-year-old woman who has it all together and is able to walk around and speak her mind, but everyone needs someone to check on them and make sure they're okay, even Norma!" I'm so worked up I'm about to cry.

"Easy," Peyton says, putting his hand on my shoulder. "I was only asking a question. You don't have to justify how you feel."

I take a long, deep breath and exhale slowly.

"You're not weak, and you haven't failed anyone."

"But if I die, I'm worried about what will happen to these people. They're my family and none of us are very good on our own. We only function if we live and move like a herd. We're like a pack of helpless cows."

Peyton cracks a smile. "I had no idea you were this stressed out. You have everyone fooled. You come across as a strong person. There's no reason you can't feel that way again. The doctor said your heart is perfect. And you got rid of the crappy boyfriend who didn't deserve you in the first place. I can't believe you were with an asshole like that to begin with, and I should know—relationships have always been disposable to me. But that lowlife leading you on with marriage and the picket fence, and then dumping you because he decided your genes aren't good enough—well, he's wrong and you can't fall for any kind of that bullshit."

I like having Peyton defend my honor and get all worked up over Marko's bad behavior, but he's right. Peyton only has casual flings, so I need to be very clear with myself and know exactly what I'm getting into if I'm choosing the door labeled *I Want to Bang Peyton*. That's exactly what I'd get. An awesome banging before the door closes and hits me on the ass. It sounds pretty great, actually.

"I'm glad Marko is out of the movie—picture. I'm glad he's out of the picture. But he has made me see myself in a different way. I didn't think the scar would be such a big deal, but he would cringe every time he mentioned it. He couldn't hide his revulsion."

"He was wrong. Stop worrying about what he said or did. He no longer matters. Maybe one of your kids will be born with the same defect, but now they can detect it and fix it. It's not a death sentence, especially since you're aware of it. So it's not an issue."

"But it is. Don't you see? Any man I consider marriage material will have to be told about this, and he may have the same reaction as Marko. Maybe every future boyfriend and fiancé will see me as defective."

"*Every*? How many boyfriends and fiancés do you plan on having?" His joking is weighted with a tone that suggests he's also annoyed.

"I'm serious. I never worried this much about my appearance or thought that I could be undesirable, except for that awkward teenage phase. But what fifteen-year-old girl doesn't freak out over a patch of zits that appears overnight or her flat chest that requires an obnoxious padded bra?"

Peyton bites his lower lip, stifling a laugh.

"Don't laugh. Because of this damn scar, I hate looking in the mirror now. Every time I do, I see the tip of the scar dead center above every blouse. It pulls all the skin around it. My chest looks like it belongs to someone fifty years older than me."

"You're blowing this all out of proportion."

"I'm not. Maybe it seems superficial to you, but I'm worried what people will think of me when they find out. Am I going to be *Poor Talia, she's fragile, go easy on her*? Are most men going to be like Marko and be turned off by me physically? It's a horrible thought. That's why I hate looking in the mirror. I wear the stress and fear on my face. And who wants to look at that? Who wants to look at me?"

"I do. I'd love looking at you naked, too. Just try me."

Don't tempt me, mister.

There's nothing I want more than to have hard, sweaty, hot sex with Peyton. Nothing would make me feel more alive than heart-pounding—ironically—rough sex. The thought of our two bodies entwined makes me feel like my old self, the one before the disastrous Marko era.

I pause and study his eyes and lips. Slowly, I inch forward.

A slight smile tugs at the corner of Peyton's mouth. "What did I tell you about rocket fuel, sunflower?"

"You like kissing me ... I think you want to kiss me again."

"I do. But you need to think about what you're doing. Who you're doing this with."

"I'm tired of thinking," I say, moving closer until my lips brush his.

Peyton groans as I lightly trace his lips with my own. His grip on my waist becomes tighter as if he's working hard to maintain control and pace himself—at least, I hope it's how he feels, because that's exactly what's happening to me.

I want to push him back on the bed and climb on top of him, grab him, fondle him, strip him, and have my dirty old way with him. But this soft kiss is too intense, too perfect to break.

I always thought you get one first, electrifying kiss with someone, one chance when you touch and get lost in the mind-bending thrill of being with that person you've had a secret crush on. Except, these past few weeks, I had convinced myself that I didn't have a crush on Peyton because he's just supposed to be eye candy. I'm astonished how deliriously excited I feel kissing him.

"You're flawless," he whispers against my lips.

"You're such a good liar," I reply between kisses. "An amazing seducer, though. No one is flawless."

He pulls back and looks at me. "I'm not lying." Then, with all gentleness aside, he kisses me again with savage hunger until I'm wet between my thighs, and my lips and body beg for more.

He ends the kiss, and we're both breathing heavily. Why would he stop? Why can't we let it go all the way?

"Some of us are better than others," he explains, regaining his composure. "You're right, though. We all have marks on our character. It all depends how deep they go."

He stopped that incredible kiss for that?

"You think I have a flawless character?" I laugh. I thought we were talking about bodies. He's actually referring to my integrity?

"I do. I have a lot of black marks. Next to me, you're flawless, sunflower." He traces his finger from the tip of my scar between my breasts down the length of it. The rough pad of his finger is enough to raise goosebumps on my flesh and make me shiver. "Your scar is a badge of honor, the will to survive. It makes you that much sexier." He continues the invisible tracing, and then around my scar, lightly brushing against my breasts. Then he stops and looks at me as if he's trying to gauge my arousal. I want to tell him how much I need this—his words, his touch, his body. He's making all my senses go haywire.

"If we're being direct here, I don't want to talk about this anymore. What I really want ... what I really miss ..."

"What?"

"Sex. I miss sex," I say. "Nothing makes you question your health and strength more than the absence of sex."

Peyton stops touching me and pulls his hand back.

"I think I said that wrong. You don't have to have constant sex to be a strong person, but I was going through a period where everything was gray and scary, and it was dragging on for so long. I used to be full of energy. I could dance all night at a party. And sex was, well, I took it for granite."

Peyton bites his lower lip, his tell when I unknowingly say something funny.

"Oh God, did I just say granite? I meant granted. You know that, though."

"I do."

"It's true. I took sex for granted. Not that I was a nympho or anything, but who doesn't like great sex that makes you feel incredible? Those feelings vanished after my diagnosis. I felt the opposite of sexy. I should be grateful my body has survived, but mostly I think my body signifies doom, to me, at least. So my character isn't as good as you think. The truth is, I'm fairly egotistical."

"Missing sex doesn't make you egotistical. It makes you human."

"You're not disturbed by what I said?"

"Not at all. I always want sex. I'm surprised you'd tell me, but then, I'm glad you did."

"I like to think we're friends now, right? You have your big, ambitious career plans, and you won't be in Hera for long, so I suppose I can tell you things I wouldn't tell someone else who lives here year-round."

He's quiet, but he stares at me, waiting for more.

"My goals are smaller. I'm building my life here. I hope to find someone better than Marko. I won't make that mistake again. I'm telling you these things not because I think that person could be you, so you don't have to worry about that. I know it's not you. But that doesn't mean I don't want to sleep with you."

He moves his hand to rest firmly on my hip. "So, let's be clear here. You want to sleep with me. You want me for sex, but you don't want anything else?"

"Yes. Sex. I have to get back in the game." I force a casual laugh.

"The game? Meaning sex?"

"Life. Nothing makes you feel like a part of life more than sex. That is, if you've been deprived of it and it's all you can think of. And I think we have good ... whatever that's called. And I think we'd have great sex."

"I know the sex would be great." He looks at me, so serious. His reaction is not at all what I expected. "There's just the issue of what happens after. It's hard to compartmentalize these things. I tried it with other women, and they changed. They wanted more."

"Well, I don't want more from you." The words fly out as if it means nothing to me. However, the truth is that it's harder making that statement than I thought. I like Peyton. He does all sorts of *things*, wonderful things, to my insides. But I am realistic. With Peyton, I know what I'm getting into. Sex. *Sex!* And Peyton is the perfect candidate for mindless bedroom fun. "Sex is what I need. Harmless fun for both of us, and then you can go to Las Vegas or Louisiana or wherever."

"Los Angeles."

I smile and push him back onto the bed. "It doesn't matter. We're adults. We can have some fun for a while, then go our own ways."

"You're sure?" He looks concerned, but his sweatpants can't hide the fact that he's hard.

"I'm sure. It's just sex. Nothing else."

A flicker in his eyes triggers the beast within. It's the green light. We're on.

I throw myself on top of him and kiss him. He pulls me in and pins me to his chest, taking on all my bravado, kissing me back more fiercely than before. I can't get enough of his lips, his firm hold, as I grind myself into him without restraint, without shame. I want Peyton to do everything to me, to blind my senses with an immeasurable intensity to the point that everything else fades away.

"Talia." He's breathing hard as he pulls away from the kiss. "Slow down." And with that, he easily flips me over onto my back as if I'm a weightless rag doll, and then he props himself over me. "We're not going to rush this. I don't want a two-minute fuck with you."

With my newly repaired heart pumping rapidly, I whisper, "Yes."

Peyton yanks down his sweatpants and tosses them to the floor. I smile, almost perversely. He's too sexy, too perfect for me not to be ecstatic over this mountain of a man.

His thick, corded muscles bulging across his broad shoulders and legs work to steady him above me. His eyes are locked on mine, not blinking, watching my gaze take in all of him, from his long, powerful legs to his full, thick cock, up to his washboard abs, to his gorgeous face. Those gray eyes, glinting with hints of silver as though he is going through a metamorphosis from the busy restaurant manager that I see every day to this wild beast who has one person in his sights. *Me.*

I'm not timid about staring, about practically panting. I don't have to care with Peyton. This is all about our basic animal instincts, our bodies, and nothing of the world and people beyond this room.

As I loosen the belt of the robe, Peyton grabs the collar and pulls the whole robe out from under my weight, then tosses it onto the floor.

He studies my body in that primal way men do when they see a naked woman and it short-circuits their brain. A visual comedy, except for the fact it also provides them with a generous erection.

I smile to myself, thinking about the male brain depleting its resources and sending all of its energy and blood supply to his vital appendage.

The desire gleaming in his eyes is what makes me feel beautiful. We're not supposed to feel anything beyond that.

Maybe I like him more than I'm willing to admit, and it's fine as long as it doesn't turn into *caring.* Caring is a dangerous place to go, a place where emotions get muddled and stretched to sometimes unbearable limits. This is a lesson that *every girl* dismisses, but it's a lesson that *every woman* is conscious of. I'm also aware each caress from Peyton is only adding to this concern of involvement, and yet, I'm still not going to stop us.

Peyton tortures me by making another slow, sensual inspection of my body from head to toe. He takes his sweet time, intensifying the craving I have for him. I want him to move faster, to run his strong hands across my skin and ravish me without restraint. I want him to be rough and hard.

"You're beautiful," he says slowly.

Under the weight of his intense stare, I flush.

He smiles, then unexpectedly runs the tip of his tongue lightly around my scar. My arousal heightens, and I lose my ability to utter any words. His tongue circles around my nipples and gently sucks on each one before releasing it. My perfectly repaired heart is beating wildly in appreciation, and my ears feel as though they have been flooded with the overpowering thumping rhythm of the blood rushing to awaken every part of me.

I reach for his cock and wrap my hand around his hard length, stroking the velvety soft skin, causing moans to escape him.

"I want to devour you," he whispers in my ear. "I want to be inside of you and fuck you until you don't even know your own name."

"I don't think you own that phrase," I taunt as I rub the tip of his cock against the wetness between my legs.

His deep chuckle reverberates against my ear before he sucks ferociously on my neck and squeezes my breast, making me ache more for him.

"But make me forget everything. *Please*," I urge, not caring how desperate I sound. I have no doubt he can deliver the pleasure that has been absent from my life for far too long.

As I continue to stroke him, I grab a fistful of his hair with my other hand and pull his mouth back to mine. He tries to keep it gentle, but I'm testing his willpower, teasing his cock, stroking and pulling it until it barely enters me.

"Wait, wait," he says, pulling away from me. He grabs both of my wrists and slams them down above my head, restraining them in his tight grip.

"What?" I smile. "Is this too much for you? Can't hold out for longer than a few minutes? I thought you excelled in this area."

He smiles but can't hide the fact that he's trying to catch his breath and control himself. "Believe it or not, it's been a few months. I haven't gotten any action since I've been here."

"Was that intentional?" I arch into him, hoping his mouth will descend on a breast—anything to get him to touch me.

"Yes, this town is too small. I can't afford to screw where I work. At least in the city, there are plenty of women outside of work, and it doesn't interfere with my job. That's not going to work here without compromising the business. Everyone here knows what's going on with me. I'm pretty sure they know everything I have in my refrigerator, too."

"I don't care about anyone else."

"For the moment. You may change your tune later. So I'm going to ask you, are you sure you want this? With me? Because eventually, everyone will find out."

"Yes, I want this. I don't care what other people think of ... this. Are you worried they'll think less of me? You're concerned about my reputation?" I laugh lightly and struggle against his restraints on my wrists. "This town isn't as provincial as you think."

"No, I'm concerned you'll regret this. We're connected by this town and by a very small circle of friends, so I don't want it to become uncomfortable for you. I want nothing more than to fuck you right now, but I don't want us to do this at the expense of any of our friendships, especially mine and yours."

"Okay, sure, you're a good guy. I won't think less of you and me. You're a nice, concerned guy. Thank you," I say hurriedly. "But, yes, we can screw. And yes, we can still be friends. I won't have regrets or hate you later. I want to boldly go where other women have gone before."

"Did you just try to quote *Star Trek*?"

"God, would you shut up and do this already?" I shout.

"Gladly."

He releases my arms and settles himself between my legs, propping his arms under my thighs so I'm fully exposed to him. I'm thinking I really want the *wham, bam, thank you, ma'am* kind of sex. Nothing romantic, no special requests, just the quick and dirty, basic sex to get me through this miserable dry spell.

Peyton has other ideas. He slips his fingers between my legs and begins stroking me. I catch my breath, and his eyes meet mine. It's like a challenge. I told him to give it to me, plain and simple, and he's showing me that nothing is *plain* or *simple* with him, especially when sex is involved.

I'm about to tell him that I don't want to drag this out. I don't want to make it personal with extra care and attention—we've had our foreplay; we're ready for the actual screwing part. But I lose that train of thought when my arousal heightens and Peyton continues to touch me in all the right places.

When he finds my sweet spot, a small yelp escapes me, and he smiles.

Looking at him makes my breasts swell and my nipples harden into pink buds again. All this buildup is going to kill me.

He watches what he's doing to me, so I look away and focus on a wood beam in the ceiling.

"Look at me." His voice is husky, seductive. "You want to feel alive, and I'm going to make you feel that again, but I want you to watch me."

"I'm ready. Really. Get the condom and we're good to go."

"No, that's lazy sex. You deserve better than that. Look at me."

I pull my eyes away from the ceiling and look at him. He has a devilish gleam in his eyes before he dips his head down and replaces his fingers with his tongue.

I knew he was experienced, but I didn't equate quantity with talent. And he is talented. He titillates and taunts my clit with his tongue like he's got a black belt-level certification in this particular activity. My heart is pounding, my limbs feel boneless, and my mind is dizzy with images of Peyton's tongue—the way he's licking, probing, sucking. And then, when I start to imagine what he looks like thrusting his cock in and out of me, I climax hard ... and long. I know I moan and maybe openly praise Peyton along the orgasmic journey, and when I recover, Peyton looks pleased with himself.

He swiftly puts on a condom, hooks his arms under my knees, and hikes my legs up on either side of him. He enters me in one hard, swift thrust, watching me as he pumps into me with smooth, quick, elegant hip swivels. It's just like I imagined moments ago.

It goes on and on. He's controlled, thrusting and striking my clit perfectly. His face tightens and he grunts the closer he gets to his own release. I feel my own body pulsate, bringing me to the edge of another climax. Except, this time, Peyton's inside of me.

I never climax this way. I've also never told my partners. It's as if Peyton knows this about me and wants to right the wrongs.

His expression becomes more intense as he works to bring us both to climax, and his thrusting loses some of its finesse when it turns into pounding. It makes me smile. I'm not the only one who's losing control here.

He lowers my legs a bit, with a hand under each knee so he can move faster, pumping into me less like a guy who has a black belt in the female orgasm and more like a guy working on a red belt. Props to him for trying. I'm just not one of those women who can reach orgasm this way. I always hope it will happen. I'd like to think a guy's cock could be enough ... *and so would they*. But it never is.

Until now.

Peyton throws his head back and groans. "Fuck, this feels good."

My own temperature seems to be rising, and instead of hovering at the edge of a climax like I always do in this situation, a new sensation takes over. The tingling wave of ecstasy is taking me on that wild ride to euphoria again, and I can't believe it's happening.

I reach out to touch Peyton, grasping his shoulders. His muscles give me something to hold on to as an orgasm thunders through me. I make some incoherent sound, and Peyton watches me crumple into a blissful state before he has his own explosive release.

He takes care not to collapse on top of me. *Perks of having a giant scar down my chest!* He sidles up to me, nibbles my ear, and kisses my neck. He drapes his arm across my waist, and we both wait for our breathing to return to normal.

This is the part that surprises me the most.

Peyton is a snuggler.

16

Peyton

"**D**ON'T YOU NEED TO get to work?" She swirls her finger around my chest. We're both in a sated fog, and I really don't want to interrupt this bliss unless we're going for another round.

"I'm the boss. I can go in whenever I want. Besides, Greer is pretty high-strung, so I know she's already there. I should be, too, but I needed this."

"I can't argue with that." She angles her head to look up at me from the crook of my arm.

A million things are running through my head, like how I didn't expect to get involved with anyone, how I thought I would blow through town, how I haven't been able to stop looking at Talia since she almost ran me over, and how this feels so right. I've never connected this well with another woman. It's never been this easy. I'm pretty sure that's my cock talking, because he's just happy to get some long-needed action.

I should feel some guilt, or maybe even remorse, for jumping into bed with her, but she's the one who initiated it. She asked for it and was adamant about it being casual. This is music to my ears—having a woman tell me she expects nothing but sex. I'm also surprised that my ego is a bit deflated at the thought of her plans to give more to some other guy—Mr. Perfect, the one she's searching for.

This is good, though, I tell myself. I'm not worthy of her, and as long as she knows that upfront, she won't be disappointed when this ends.

Since I was teenager and started working in one of Danny Bourdain's restaurants, I knew what I wanted. I saw how Danny and the chefs put their careers above their families and the toll it took on their marriages. I'm not going to make that mistake.

I want the career with the money and the status among my peers in the industry. That requires a lot of time and devotion, and means putting friends, family, and women on the back burner. I'm selfish. I can do this because it's easier to succeed in business than deal with complicated relationships, especially marriage. It's been an easy mantra to live with.

Talia sits up and looks back at me with her long, wavy, blonde locks all tousled, framing her flushed, heart-shaped face. With her fingers, she makes her way down to different parts of my body.

I'm pretty much useless at this point. Between her sultry expression and her light touches, I feel like I have invisible shackles. I can't move.

Her gaze doesn't break from mine and, at that moment, I feel my gut clenching, almost a tightening pain from my chest to my stomach.

It's her. I want her, and not only in the carnal sense. *She should be mine.*

I give myself an invisible smack of reality. I've been out of action for too long. My body is simply reacting to this sexy woman in my bed.

I pull her back down to me and roll on top of her, conscious of her scar and keeping my weight off her. As she wraps her arms around my neck, I'm lost in her beautiful blue eyes. *Yes, I have to have more of her. Her body, only her body.*

I'm as hard as I can possibly be and could come in a matter of seconds, but I do everything to control myself so I can take this long and slow. I don't know how much time I'll have with her, how many weeks, or even days, our little game of casual sex will last, so I'm going to make sure I don't waste our limited time together with quick, sloppy fucks in a janitor's closet or a car. For now, I want to claim every part of her and record this, brand it in my memory. It seems vitally important to know what it is to be with her, to remember everything about her. To *remember* Talia. Because, at some point in the near future, I will be nothing more than a passing memory, a guy she spent some time with before the "right guy" came along.

Fuck that. Where's that easy mantra of mine when I need it?

Feeling irate and horny at the same time, I reach over to the nightstand and pull out the whole box of condoms. The thin cardboard crumples in my angry fist, and condom packages fly everywhere. Talia laughs.

I grab the closest condom, rip it open, and put it on as fast as I can. Then, before this woman beneath me can finish her laugh, I slide back into her. She moans and glides her hands down my shoulders, gripping my forearms tightly as I thrust completely into her. I hold still, my arms and jaw tight with control as I study her relaxed, euphoric expression.

"Don't stop," she whispers.

"I didn't plan on it. But I like looking at you. Give me this moment."

"Aw," she teases. "How sweet."

As I move slowly inside of her, she moans again and closes her eyes. I lean down and lightly kiss her eyelids, then her soft lips, and then her neck. She moves slowly with me, arching her back, moving her hips against mine.

Lowering myself down on one arm, I fondle her breast and begin caressing every part of her that I can reach with one hand. She escalates her hip action, trying to get me to move faster, but I control the pace with long, slow thrusts. Her frustration shows, and I enjoy this temporary power I have, my own way to consume every part of her.

The animal in me wants nothing more than to flip her over and take her from behind, but I can wait until she's satisfied. I'm feeling grateful and sentimental; uncharacteristic for a guy who likes to serve himself and get back to business, the kind that doesn't involve romantic entanglements.

When she shudders to a climax and clenches around me, I lose myself in my own release. It's a grunt and a yell as I finish with the urge to collapse.

I quickly assess the slight woman beneath me as I throw myself to the side before landing on the bed. Then I pull her in for a tight hug because I want to keep touching her. She looks up at me and gives me a contented smile, and it feels good.

I'm generally not a hugger or cuddly person, especially after sex. I like to have the rough-and-tumble sex, shower, and be on my way. Sex is a way to recharge my batteries, but there are a whole host of emotions coming into play with Talia, and the desire to hold her is one of them.

She moves up and kisses me, her lips persistent, and I give in completely, kissing her back, enjoying it all too much.

Jesus. I stop the kissing altogether. Sex is one thing, but a kiss is the worst thing that could happen, worse than having sex with a *friend.* A kiss is too intimate. It says so much more about how a person feels. The last thing Talia and I need is to confuse our casual sex with something more.

Talia disengages herself from me and gets out of the bed. She saunters into the bathroom, allowing me to admire her ass as she walks with a sexy sashay. I take note that I'm usually the first one to leave the bed. Clearly, Talia is the one in charge and my confused ego didn't get the memo.

While she showers, I collect some fresh towels and an extra toothbrush for her. When I walk into the steamy bathroom, the only thing that separates us is a flimsy, vinyl shower curtain around the big clawfoot tub. I'm tempted to step in there and soap her up.

Talia is humming to herself while I stand there thinking of what I'd like to do to her body. A few exciting thoughts take over my brain. It would require a bit of gymnastics, but I'm ready for more sex. Instead, I drop off the bath items for her, sneak back out, and head toward the other bathroom to take a very cold shower.

Twenty minutes later when we walk out of the house, the bright sun and the dewiness of a spring morning makes us smile at one another. It's a corny moment, and it's also the best fucking feeling to be with someone who makes you feel incredibly high on life.

Shit. I'm living in a Hallmark card. Well, except for the sex.

"Can I drive?" she asks, beaming and doing a little skip and jump toward my truck.

"Why? I thought I'd drop you off at your house, then head to Swill."

"I never get to drive anything fun. I'm always in that big, boxy, nerdy van. I'd love to drive your truck and take you out for breakfast."

"Really? You want to head over to Bonnie's and get some eggs? I like hanging with the senior crowd at the diner."

"I love Bonnie's, but no. I'm craving fast food," she says as I toss her the keys. She gets in the driver's side, and I slide into the passenger side, waiting for her punch line.

She looks at me and laughs.

"I'm sorry. I can't believe you want fast food. You're a chef; isn't it illegal for you to eat Hot Pockets?"

"I can eat whatever I damn well please and, right now, I want some greasy cheeseburgers from BooHoo Burger. They serve twenty-four-seven to people like me."

"Whatever my lady wants, my lady gets." Too late for me to take those words back. I should have said *the* instead of *my*.

Talia pretends she didn't hear the possessiveness and drives us out onto the interstate. I use the time to check my phone and catch up on messages from Greer and Bash, who are indeed both at the restaurant.

"Time to put your phone away. I'm treating you to breakfast burgers!"

"Sounds awful."

She pulls the truck into a drive-through, a relic from the 1970s with a giant, creepy clown statue right out of a B-movie.

There's a dilapidated playground that's closed off with caution tape around it. I guess, back in the day, families hung out here on summer evenings. The clown must have been the main attraction. He's holding an old speaker box with one hand. The other hand is broken off, along with his red ball nose and part of his painted white face. It makes him look menacing, the kind of clown that lures kids in and eats them. The burgers must be out of this world for this dump to still be in business.

Talia pulls the truck right up to the clown, and I notice the speakerphone he's holding has dangling cords and there's a large, unappealing dumpster right behind him.

"Are you sure this is where you place the order?" I ask. The proximity of the dumpster to her window is alarming.

"Sure. I mean, I've never used the drive-through before. We always eat inside." She sticks her head out the window and speaks right into the rusty black speaker, the clown grinning down on her as if this is a trap. She orders six cheeseburgers and fries, and I laugh, wondering where the hell she's going to put all that food.

There's a crackling sound a distance away, and then we hear a young guy's voice. "Ma'am? Ma'am? Can you hear me?"

Talia pops her head up and looks up at the clown as if he's the one speaking to her. I suppress a laugh.

"Ma'am," the teenage voice says again. "Could you pull up to the window? You're talking to the garbage can."

Talia notices the dumpster behind BooHoo the clown, and I roar with laughter.

Talia glares at me with pursed lips. "Well, how was I supposed to know it's broken? There's a big clown with a microphone!"

"I could have told you it's out of order. The cables are cut. Go ahead and drive to the window; give the kid your order," I say, grinning.

In a huff, Talia guns it and squeals the wheels for the next fifty feet before slamming on the brakes at the window.

The kid appears as I imagined—a young teenager with acne and a dorky paper hat.

She places her order and asks him to add two strawberry milkshakes. I keep my opinions to myself about the bright pink drinks and the greasy bags she hands over to me. I grab a few salty fries and hold the bag open so she can help herself while she drives.

"You are planning to share this with your mother and sister, right?"

"No." She waves a french fry in the air. "This is for us, and I want to take you someplace special where we can eat it. Something I want to show you." She looks over at me and widens her eyes in delight.

"I'm intrigued." Truthfully, I don't know what to say to a woman whom I just had amazing sex with, the woman who instigated the unusual just-sex agreement.

"Don't get too excited. It's nothing kinky. You got your sex quota for today," she deadpans, and I smile at the easiness with which she jokes about us.

"I tossed my quota. The goal is never-ending." My attempt at humor falls short. I haven't figured out what I'm doing yet, or how I'm going to manage the restaurant and see Talia every day, acting nonchalant about sex meet-ups. That is, if it actually happens again. Maybe she intended this to be a one-time thing.

I'm about to turn on the radio to break the weird silence when Talia begins humming again. A few words in Polish escape as she studies the road, appearing oblivious to her own singing. I sit back and listen, watching the expansive landscape of the countryside unfold before us.

I still don't know the area that well. I spend all my time at Swill and have yet to venture out of town for anything other than vendor meetings. When I was a kid, a trip to the country was taking the D train down to Coney Island for the day. We weren't much on hills and pastures and fresh air. This is all new to me, but I can't help being moved by its beauty.

And her beauty.

I steal a few glances at Talia, who is completely enamored with driving my truck. She powers her window open and flicks on the radio. When she finds a country song to sing along with, her accent is more pronounced. The whole scene is pretty comical. I'm more of a hard rock guy, so this image of her singing about drinking whiskey and eating biscuits and gravy is adorable, especially with her hair whipping wildly around her face as she tries to keep up with the tune. There's a smile on her face as if she's dreaming about something better. I doubt it has to do with me.

We take a long, rambling dirt road up a slight incline until a stately Victorian comes into view. The home has seen better days. The white exterior has aged to a dirty gray, and the black-trimmed shutters are missing on half the windows. It's four stories high with turrets, a crow's nest, and widow's walk on the top floor. The home looks as unsafe as the BooHoo Burger playground and clown. It's abandoned.

"It's the old Pickwick estate. It used to be grand. What do you think?" she asks happily as she parks the truck near the grand front steps that are severely warped.

"I think it needs caution tape around the whole property." I get out of the truck with the food bags.

"Aw, don't be so negative. I love this house. Don't you think it has potential?"

"Potential as what? The backdrop for a horror movie?"

"Imagine it completely renovated with all its natural woodwork restored. That huge porch brought back to life with wooden rocking chairs and hanging flower baskets."

"And then what? Do you have the kind of money to live in a house like this?"

"No, I think it would make a great bed-and-breakfast, an inn that also has fine dining, and an organic farm."

"Are you serious?" I ask too sharply.

When she flinches, I hear my mistake, my judgmental tone.

"Yes." She hoists herself up on the hood of the truck and begins divvying out the burgers and fries between us.

"Why the need for all this farm-to-table nonsense? Pretty soon, restaurants will start putting live chickens on the tables and asking customers to kill and pluck them. You could call it The Feeding Trough. Or Pigs to Pots."

She laughs. "Or The Purposeful Pea." She bites into her burger with gusto.

"You're kidding, right?" I take a bite of one of the burgers dripping with grease. "How about Organic Shits? Man, this burger is good." The post-sex hunger sets in, and I'm suddenly ravenous. I polish off the burger and start on another.

"The Spotted Sparrow," she states.

"Why not make the name appealing? The Organic O. People would come just to find out about the O."

"Talia's Edible Inn."

"I don't think you get it, sunflower. Talia's Outhouse."

"Talia's Greenhouse."

"Boring. Where the Swine Meet the Fiddleheads."

Her laugh is infectious. "You're making fun of my dream. I need real names."

"You mean you want something safe, like The Fermented Fig? You'll draw more attention with Orgasmic Organics."

"Stop!" She laughs as I finish my third burger.

"You know your fast food. That was great. I'm stuffed."

She has a spot of ketchup on her cheek, and I wipe it off with my thumb. This should be awkward—sharing a laugh and a meal after really hot, sober sex with someone from my workplace—but it's not. Not awkward at all. I'm enjoying her company so much that I wish I could ask her to spend the day with me while I work.

"Don't forget to dip your fries in the shake." She demonstrates.

"Looks revolting. And you call yourself a chef."

"It's excellent. The sweet and salty effect. I wouldn't lie to you."

Those last three words grab me in a place that's usually off-limits. It's the place in my soul only a few people can touch—my family, and that's about it. The intimacy outside of the bedroom is what I'm afraid of.

Something has changed between us. If she'd let me, I'd take her right here. We'd be naked in a heartbeat, and I'd have her bent over the hood, giving our nature friends a nice show.

Chemistry seems to be key here. Atoms and cells screwing with my head. Those tricky, little bastards aren't acting casual and cool about hooking up. They're making it more complex. I keep reminding myself this is about two people who like each other enough to have sex but not enough to get involved. Good policy if it works.

Something is wrong with me. I am definitely on the precipice of being more involved than I should be.

"It's a dream, not something I'm planning on," she continues. Her cheeks are pink; she's glowing. I'd like to say it's because of the sex, but I think she's over the moon talking about her dream career. She's a good sport for putting up with my harsh jokes.

"Sorry if I came across like a jackass. I'm not putting down your idea. You're very creative, and an excellent chef like you should have ambitious plans. I guess it's the practical side of me that looks at every business opportunity with a lot of skepticism."

"Why? If anyone should know about living your dream, it's you."

"Right, but it's also not that easy. My dad and uncle are retired cops now, and the restaurants they run are doing well. But we learned the hard way.

"The first place we bought was a bust. They sank most of their savings into it. I was finishing college, and I'd come back on weekends to bartend and help with inventory. We didn't know enough about our market or branding, so they had to bail before they lost all of their money.

"I was scared that my dad and uncle were leveraging their pensions, gambling away their future security. Fortunately, my mom's corporate job paid the bills for my divorced parents to hold on to our two brownstones. Two mortgages, second mortgages, and college loans. So much debt, and so many kids to support.

"My brothers and sister had all moved out, but I was still living with my mom, and Dad was across the street with his new wife and new kids. It was insane. The downsizing didn't happen until after my mother died. My dad finally got his shit together."

"Your parents had a unique relationship. My father doesn't help us financially."

"My parents stayed friends. But, man, my mom was furious with my dad for being unprepared and throwing money at a bar he didn't know how to run. And he has too many kids to be that careless. He and my uncle really fucked up, and I was too green to know better. I had more to learn from the pros running the best restaurants.

"After college, I got a good management position at a high-end place. That's where I did my best networking. I made friends in real estate and met people who believed in me and who had the cash to invest. When we bought our next place in Brooklyn, I became the primary owner, and then we moved into the big leagues with our restaurant in Manhattan. My brothers are investors, and my dad and uncle technically work for me now. I love this business, but I worked my tail off to get here."

I also vowed to never fail at business again.

To never let my family lose their money again.

Talia slurps down the remains of her milkshake and waits for me to say more. I'm not going to share with her how scared I was about my family coming close to being wiped out financially and that it motivates me to be highly focused, driven, and selfish. She already knows what it's like to be scared of the future.

"Enough about that," I say. "The point is, I had a lot more to learn, and I needed a strong network of people to back me."

"So, what if I got that, too? I have a lot of restaurant experience, and the organic farm-to-table dining is profitable. And I know some people with money. Kind of."

"You're talking about running three businesses in one location. Three of the hardest businesses to operate. An inn, a restaurant, and a farm, of all things. A farm." I laugh.

"Stop laughing." She takes my remaining fries and eats them, chomping like she's still hungry.

"I don't want to stomp on your dream. It's a big one."

"But you do think it's interesting, right? You can see how it would be appealing to city people who want to get away and want something smaller than the Mohonk resort. And local people would like to have another dining experience option. Something very different than Bonnie's diner or Swill. Right?"

"I see the appeal. It's a great idea. In fact, Dan Barber has something similar at Stone Hill Farm. Did you think of that? And he's something of a celebrity in this business, so you have to consider that. Not to mention all the other farm-to-table restaurants in the other towns."

"This would be different than Stone Hill, and we're far enough away that we can serve people the other places can't accommodate. Everyone tells me how dense the Hudson Valley is, and it's ripe for business. I think there's room for all of us who want to have a restaurant."

I like her spunk and how she doesn't give up or let a jerk like me dissuade her.

"Fair enough. How did you come up with this idea?"

"Pickwick has been abandoned and on the market for years. Most people don't want to buy a rundown estate with forty acres of farmland. Before we moved to Hera, my dad drove us here to see the countryside. It was a day visit, and we happened to stumble upon this place. So we stopped and had a picnic, like today. We thought of all the ways we could fix this house up. My father had outrageous, fun ideas, and my mother and sister laughed along, but it really made me hopeful that someday we would be able to have a family business.

"When we did move to Hera, though, things were already pretty bad between my parents. I was the only one who thought about Pickwick. I was the only one fantasizing about a beautiful inn where we could live, and where my mother and I could cook for guests. I didn't realize when my dad brought us here all those years ago that he was just getting my hopes up and blowing smoke up ..."

"Your ass. He was blowing smoke up your ass. Sorry."

"Yeah, the whole smoke-up-the-ass part really hurts when it's your own parent letting you down."

"No kid deserves that."

"I come here a lot. It cheers me up. It's gorgeous," she says, beaming at the wreck in front of us.

"Sure is." I'm looking at Talia, not the house. "But this needs a few million in renovations to start. To build a small hotel, a restaurant, and a frigging farm? An organic farm. You are so far out of my expertise on this one.

"You haven't told me much about your dad. Was there a time when he took on big projects like this?"

She's quiet for a moment as she reflects. "There was a time when I did believe in him. He was funny and enthusiastic, and as far as I knew back then, he put all the stars in the sky. I adored him. Once. We depended on his spirit and determination to leave Poland and start over here."

I reach out to touch her hair, twisting it gently in my fist. I feel I've at least earned this right since we slept together. "We all think our parents are heroes when we're too young to know better. You have to be realistic, though. Most restaurants fail. Farming is hard, and many farms fail, too. Don't get me started on the hospitality industry and hotels. It's twenty-four-seven. Put all three of these businesses together in one place and you've got yourself one of the most challenging, stressful operations possible."

"I understand." She looks down at her lap. I keep bursting her fucking bubble.

"Don't forget, you're already a success. You have a great business with your sister. An in-demand personal chef with a wait list is a big deal. You've cornered the market in this area."

"I want to do more than work in other people's kitchens and cook for them, and Aleska doesn't want to clean houses forever. I want a restaurant of my own. You don't think I'm a complete fool, do you?"

"Never. I think you're ..." I want to say *fantastic, amazing, sexy, beautiful, and you're starring in my fantasies.*

She tilts her head with a slight smile.

"You're perfect the way you are."

I slide off the truck and step in front of her, positioning myself between her dangling legs. She gazes at me, her lips parting slightly. I don't want to miss this chance, so I grip both her knees and move in slowly to kiss her, first on the cheek. Then I kiss her tenderly on the neck, where I see her pulse. I glide my lips over to her mouth, our lips mingling, gently tugging. She tastes salty and sweet as she returns my kisses with a slow, restrained pressure.

My hands are eager to journey up her body once again as the kiss deepens and she cups her hands firmly around my neck. The kiss builds, my heart races, and I place my hands on the back of her head, crushing her lips to mine so I can explore every part of her mouth. I grab her ass and slide her across the truck hood until our bodies are pressed together and my cock is hard, straining against my jeans.

"We have to stop," she says, pushing back. "We can't do this in public."

"You want this as much as I do. No one is around for miles." I keep my hold on her, kissing her neck, right below her delicate earlobe, and feel the heat of her flesh.

"No," she says, pushing me away harder this time. "I don't want this kind of relationship with you in front of everybody else. The sex stays in the bedroom. There will be no public flirting. No public kissing. No public touching of any kind. And most definitely no sex where we can be seen. This is the only arrangement that will work if we still want to maintain a professional working relationship. You know it as well as I do. You're the one who said you don't sleep with people you work with. We may not be working *together*, but we are working side by side almost every day."

I sigh and straighten myself up. I make sure she notices that I have to stick my hand down my pants to adjust myself because it's so goddamn uncomfortable. She gives me an understanding smile.

We've barely started something, yet we've already come across a problem with our friend-sex setup. And the truth is, I know she's right. The boundaries need to be clear. It's sex and nothing more. I remind myself there are different agendas at play. She wants a guy who can commit to the same future she wants, and my commitment is to my career. What I want won't fit in Hera. I'm glad she's the one setting the parameters so I don't have to play the asshole role.

"Sorry. Let me just pour the rest of my milkshake down my pants to put out the fire below."

"Very funny." She blushes, reaching for my arms until she slides her hands right into mine.

"Hey, no public touching," I say, shaking her hands off as if her touch doesn't affect me.

When her cell phone interrupts us, for once, I'm grateful.

She takes the phone out of her bag, and her eyes light up when she looks at the screen. I'm pretty sure I hate whoever is on the other side of that connection. When she answers with a grin and a sultry *hello*, I feel a prickle of jealousy.

"Yes, of course I can do it," she says. "I take care of all the shopping, and I can pick up any alcohol you want to stock in your bar."

Shopping and stocking a personal bar?

Adam Fucking Knight.

The guy isn't wasting any time when it comes to Talia. And how convenient to hide his ulterior motives under the pretense of having her cater his party.

I begin cramming our garbage into the paper bags while she finishes the call. When I toss everything on the back seat floor, Talia hops off the truck with a faraway smile.

"Good news?" I ask dryly.

"As a matter of fact, Mr. Knight and I were finalizing some details. So, yes, very good news."

"Good for you. I mean that. Let's go. I'll take you home." All the excitement has completely fizzled.

Adam Knight sure knows how to ruin the mood, and the guy isn't even here. I try not to show my disappointment. After all, Talia is giving me exactly what I want. I guess I'm not used to someone else calling the shots.

As I drive us away from the battered old estate, my thoughts keep returning to Knight and if he has planned anything for her. Is he really only hiring her to cook, or does he plan on making a move? More importantly: why do I care?

"Why isn't Swill exciting enough for you?" she asks after she shuts off the stereo. "What's so special about Los Angeles?"

"Danny Bourdain is based there now. Hopefully, I'll be opening two new restaurants with him and his conglomerate, Bourdain-Torrance Enterprises."

"I ate at one of his Manhattan restaurants a couple of years ago. Lois and Eleanor treated a few of us at the yoga studio to a night out. The food was very good, very expensive, and Lois had to reserve three months in advance."

"When I worked in Danny's first restaurant, as a teenager, he was still the head chef. He's been my idol all these years. I watched him become one of the most famous chefs in New York City and then the country as he opened more restaurants in major cities."

"But he stopped cooking. Like you. He's not a chef anymore."

"True. He's a restaurant guru. He runs his own investment group, too. Everything he touches turns to gold. He visited my Midtown restaurant last year, heaped on the praise and encouragement, and dangled that proverbial carrot in front of me and Bash, letting us know he's been following our careers and would like to work with us in the future. He called soon after we bought the building for Swill and several times since. Initially, we discussed very detailed plans about two properties he wants to develop, and he liked my ideas and input and said he wanted to hire me and Bash. I explained that we have a commitment to Swill for a certain period of time, and then Bash and I can go out to Los Angeles. We haven't hammered out the contracts, but they will be executive positions. So it's different than Swill. I won't be managing an individual restaurant. I'll have a team."

"So the goal is to keep building restaurants for Danny Bourdain? You won't be the manager and get to know the staff of any of these restaurants? You'll finish one restaurant and move on to the next?"

"Yeah. Basically."

"But you're such a good manager. You're so good with the people who work for you. Won't you miss that personal interaction?"

"It becomes predictable and too routine. The development team under me will involve personal interaction, too."

"That's not the same as a big, busy restaurant."

"I'll be plenty busy. Scouting locations, working with architects, designers, and Danny, and dealing with city officials and the press. It will be long hours and a lot of excitement."

"I guess I don't understand how you can move across the country when you have everything here. Cooper and Greer live in Hera. Your sister moved here because of you. And your father and uncle, and your other brothers and all those nieces, nephews, and step-siblings are close by in the city. You have three successful restaurants here. You already have so much."

"You have to act on ambition when you're young. This is the time for me to go for something much bigger. And I can always see my family. That's what planes are for."

"Huh," she says warily. "You act like such a tough guy, but I think it's an act."

"Really? Well, speaking of acts, what was that little performance of yours on the phone a few minutes ago?"

"I wasn't performing. I was talking to a client."

"Is he just a client, or do you have an agenda for this guy?"

"Keeping my options open. Like you and your business prospects."

"What about not getting involved with clients? You said something to the effect of not mixing business with pleasure."

"Thankfully, I'm the boss, so if the guy fits, I'll ..."

"Wear him?"

She laughs.

"So, you'll sleep with me, ruthlessly use me for sex, while you pursue a more promising prospect?"

"Don't pretend to be indignant. You're a physical person, not an emotional one. You're getting exactly what you want."

"As I said, *ruthless*. But fair, considering my record."

"It's fair because we agreed upon the terms."

"For such a savvy businesswoman, tell me why you don't have a company name."

"Oh." The word deflates as she says it, along with her confident, verbal sparring. "That was my mistake. We did have a name."

"Go on," I prod, eager to hear what's made her clam up. She looks cute when she's trying to hide something embarrassing, so I know this has to be something good.

"When we started the business, Aleska and I discussed using our first names. I got carried away and went out and made business cards." She looks at me for a moment before wrinkling her nose.

"I want to hear this," I say.

"Instead of our names, I used our first initials, like contractors do. I had *T & A Services* with *We'll Meet All Your Needs* printed on a thousand cards, and I left stacks of them at shops all over Dutchess and Ulster counties and, well, let's just say it's good I ran out of cards."

My laugh is pretty ear-shattering. "I bet every guy in a fifty-mile radius wanted to hire you with that promising name."

"Fortunately, Aleska prevented it from getting worse."

"How long did it take you to figure out the cards were sending the wrong message?"

"Aleska got a hold of one of them. Actually, it was Imogene who thought I did it as a practical joke to freak Aleska out, and she called to tell me that my sister was sufficiently upset and on her way home to kill me. I can still hear Imogene laughing, screaming, *'Tits and Asses!'* After that incident, I promised I wouldn't make any decisions without Aleska. We didn't get all the cards back. For about six months, we kept getting calls from strange people, mostly men, asking for a list of the full services we provide."

My laughing subsides as her cheeks grow pinker. "I would have hired you, too. Hell, a personal chef who cooks naked."

"Only idiots would think that. And we did weed out the crank calls. Actually, we had to change our number."

"Priceless."

As we approach the little swath of homes in her isolated cul-de-sac, a particularly shiny, expensive Tesla parked in front of Talia's house stands out. Mila is leaning against the doorframe of her home, engaged in conversation with Adam.

"Seriously?" I mutter.

"Adam is here!" Talia exclaims in a soft, high-pitched voice. "I thought he was calling me from the city. I wonder what he's doing here."

"He's doing what he does best. He's managing people. He's managing you, and now he's managing your mother," I say, parking

154

abruptly next to his car, which is impractical for the unpaved roads in Hera.

Talia huffs in response and jumps out of the truck before I cut the engine. I'm faster. I'm out of the vehicle and by her side in a flash. At the same time, Norma comes out of her house next door, waving one arm while she leans on a metal walker.

"I need help!" she yells in a crackly voice.

Talia's mother braces her hands against her doorway and leans out to see what's wrong with Norma, but it's like an invisible force field is preventing her from stepping over the concrete threshold.

Talia, Adam, and I head quickly to Norma's home. My speed and long legs get me there faster, and I feel like a ten-year-old beating everyone else in a race. Adam is right on my heels, and the ten-year-old in me would love to trip him and watch him fall on his face. I keep my juvenile feelings in check, though, and try to push down the overprotectiveness I have toward Talia and her family. It's that old game of *I was here first*.

"Norma! Are you okay?" Talia asks, out of breath.

"It's Baby! He's escaped."

"Baby?" Adam and I say in unison.

"Norma's dog. Sometimes he breaks through the backyard fence and runs for the woods. We'll have to hunt him down." Talia leads us around the back of the house with Norma scooting her walker after us.

"How hard can it be to catch a Pekingese or a little poodle?" I say, and Adam nods in agreement.

"Poodle?" Talia looks over her shoulder at me. "Who said Baby is a poodle?"

"His name implies something sweet," Adam answers. "Please tell me Baby isn't a German shepherd."

"Baby isn't a German shepherd," she says. A rustling in the woods ahead makes us all take notice, and suddenly a huge dog comes barreling toward us. A beast, really, with loose, flying jowls and what appears to be a dopey canine smile as his girth lopes happily.

"Holy Jesus," I say, mesmerized by the dog's size and speed.

"He's a two-hundred-pound Saint Bernard," Talia adds dryly. "He's two years old and has the strength of King Kong and the speed of Usain Bolt."

"Good God, that's a whole lotta dog there," Adam says.

There's a split-second when Adam and I share a *what the hell* look.

As Baby gets closer, he quickly turns and runs in another direction, as if he's willing us to chase him. Then he charges back into the woods.

The backyard is corded off by a sagging, chain-link fence. We find the foxhole dug under the fence by a two-hundred-pound dog determined to be free.

Norma catches up to us, and all that concern for her dog turns into a bright smile for Adam and me. "Isn't he a beauty? It's so nice of you boys to come help rescue Baby."

"It's our pleasure," Adam replies. I hate his politeness. I hate that he's hired Talia. I hate that he's in this town. I hate the guy.

"What are you doing with a two-ton dog?" I ask Norma.

"When I went to the shelter to pick out a companion, Baby was the one that spoke to me. Some horrible people had abused him and abandoned him on the side of a road. His tag said his name was Capone, which proved he was unloved. So I named him Baby because everyone loves a baby."

"Nice. Now, how do we wrangle this giant baby?" I scan the horizon of dense trees.

"He always goes toward the creek. He loves to chase the fish. He thinks he's a bear and can catch them with his paws," Norma explains gleefully as she rocks back on her orthopedic shoes.

"I'll head to the creek, then. You stay with Norma," I tell Talia.

"I'll come with you," Adam says, which makes Talia smile.

If he was dressed in his business suit and Italian leather shoes, I could wave him off and make a crack about his delicate nature, but the guy is wearing running shoes, a T-shirt, and workout pants. My guess is he's using the employee gym at Blackard Designs. Fortunately, I haven't run into Adam there, and I hope I never do. The guy is invading every part of my life because there's no place to hide in this damn town.

"Fine. Let's go get the beast," I say.

We jog through the trees and find the path leading to the creek. Norma wasn't exaggerating. When we find Baby, he's knee-deep in the wide creek, pawing at something in the water. He's soaked, and even with his wet, matted fur, he looks like a small bear.

"Ah, shit. This just keeps getting worse," I grouse.

"No kidding. This is going to be messy. I'll go in the water and cover his other side," Adam says, shielding his eyes from the sun while he studies our big, sloppy perp. "You stay here and try to grab him when he runs."

"No, I'll go in the water. I'll do the dirty part."

"You really are a stubborn fuck."

"Thank you."

As I step into the water, Baby finally notices us. He freezes and perks his head up. I wade toward him, with the frigid water rising above my ankles. Baby is in deeper water, but I know he can outrun me on his turf.

"Baby," I command. "Let's not make this harder than it has to be. Come." I reach out, hoping I can grab his collar before he decides to take off again.

The dog seems amused. He tilts his head at me and wags his wet tail. Just when I think the big, dumb lug is going to let me hold his collar, he bolts, but not before dragging me facedown into the water.

Baby charges toward the bank of the stream, and Adam throws himself at the dog like a professional wrestler. I jump the dog from the back, and together we manage to hold on to Baby's collar as all three of us wrestle in the shallow water.

When we drag the unwilling dog out of the creek, Adam and I are soaked, and the aroma of wet dog is powerful. Eventually, Baby realizes we're not going to play his game. He gives in and lets us take the lead. Adam and I both hold the dog's collar and walk on either side of him.

"That was interesting," Adam says, brushing wet leaves and silt off his T-shirt.

"Why are you here anyway?"

"Excuse me?" A slight smile forms at the corner of his mouth and unsettles my nerves.

"Why were you here at Talia's place, talking to her mother?"

"I dropped off a check for the week's dinner expenses. I'm hosting a dinner for some friends next Saturday, and Talia is catering."

"Yeah, I get that. She's a caterer, I know. Why couldn't you wait to be invoiced? Aleska handles the billing, and customers pay online." *I know that much, you douche.*

Adam shrugs. "Thought it would be convenient for her to have the money upfront."

"Right."

"We both know why we're here. It's not to see sweet, old Norma or play with Baby."

"Talia doesn't date clients."

"Why are you here?" he asks, undeterred by my unfriendly tone.

"We're friends. I was giving her a ride."

"But you're interested in her."

"I'm not interested in anyone. I'm married to my job."

"Good," he says with great satisfaction. "I'm tired of being married to my job."

I want to tell him to back off Talia, but we're leaving the woods and she's running toward us. Her hand is on her chest again, and it alarms me for a minute before I remember she said getting winded is a temporary part of her recovery.

She thanks us and takes Baby's collar from me. Then she and Adam lead the dog back to his grateful owner, and I follow behind slowly, stumbling a bit, lost in thought.

I could say wrangling the dog tired me out, but the truth is, seeing Talia raise her hand to her sternum is what left me weak in the knees. For a moment there, I wanted to grab her and hold her. But that's not who we are. At least not in public, as I've been reminded.

Something is changing. I'm becoming soft and too sentimental. Maybe I've become too invested in these people, and it's making me a little too sensitive.

It's not that something is changing.

It's already changed.

17

Talia

I SPEND TOO MUCH time replaying that image of those handsome men walking toward me with that silly dog between them, and I think of how thrilled I felt.

I thought I was being brave by sleeping with Peyton. Have fun with a playboy, learn a few things about myself, and become a stronger woman. I didn't expect to *like* him so much. And he wasn't supposed to cross paths with Adam. The purpose of Peyton is to help rebuild my confidence, and Adam is supposed to be the promising one, the guy I consider pursuing. They weren't supposed to show up at the same time, rescue a dog that doesn't belong to me, and simultaneously screw up the timeline I created. Everything was supposed to happen in a linear fashion, with Peyton as my practice guy, and then, when he leaves for a big, new life, thousands of miles away from here, I'll be ready for a man like Adam, the real guy. A girl can dream.

It's a busy week for all three of us, so we don't see much of each other after the Baby drama. Swill has last-minute private events added, which keeps Peyton busy. He spends a lot of time away from the restaurant, running out to meet with new suppliers, but it doesn't prevent him from squeezing my departure times into his schedule. He's there to carry and load my delivery bags and basically make me crazy with lust.

Adam puts in long hours in the city, so he arrives late for dinner. I have his table set and dinner arranged, timed perfectly for when he walks through the front door. Being around Adam is easy, too, but I don't want to look like a woman who hangs on his every word, so I'm the one to end our conversations.

Leave them wanting more. Isn't that what we're supposed to do? Especially if there are two men involved and you have conflicting emotions? Besides, the only thing I'm sure of is that Peyton wants to sleep with me whenever possible. With Adam, I'm not sure if the connection between us is more than purely friendship.

I need time to process what I'm doing. This whole "tramp with Peyton and innocent with Adam" routine is slowly gnawing at me. Aleska has caught on and has stayed tight-lipped, but it's taking all her willpower not to grill me. At least she didn't let anything slip to my mother.

Peyton has made a few attempts to approach me at Swill over the past week, but I was usually surrounded by Bash and other kitchen staff, so he played along with my indifference.

I would steal glances his way when I thought no one would catch me, but Peyton had the same idea, and we caught each other. These fleeting incidents, amorous encounters without touching, leave me thrumming with lust. I know if I had been able to reach out to touch him or steal one kiss, it would be better than before. Somehow, I know this.

I know physically being with Peyton is something that grows in intensity over time. It's a dangerous kind of passion. He's a master at pleasure, and that's a luxury I can't afford with him, unless I'm prepared to get hurt.

Funny, I thought my clever plan with Peyton would make me feel empowered, in control of my own love life for a change. Instead, I'm questioning my sensibilities.

My mother hovers around me, cleaning rooms that are already spotless from her endless days of endless cleaning. She is dying to know the details of my daily life, the gossip and happenings at the restaurant, and the encounters with my clients. She lives for news of the world outside of our home, mostly anything pertaining to the townies and, right now, she has zeroed in on Peyton and Adam.

When they came back with the big, sopping-wet dog, both looking like they rolled around in mud, my mother did more than lift an eyebrow. She peppered me with her own theories on their gallant behavior.

"They presented that filthy dog to you, like you were their queen, completely forgetting Norma is the dog's owner, not you.

And Adam hand-delivered a check so he could see you. Did you see Peyton's face when he saw Adam here? I know jealousy when I see it, and it was rolling off Peyton like hot steam coming out of a manhole cover when it's ready to explode out of the street."

I have no response for her, except for the occasional sigh or *oh well*, and I can tell it's getting on her nerves. But her dependence on living vicariously through my social life is getting on *my* nerves. I've been leaving earlier in the morning, hopping on my bike and racing off to the restaurant so I can avoid conversations with her, and then I take my time at each client's home. I talk and visit with the older ones and hang out with the families to help corral the young kids to the table. And then, when the last meal is served, I stall and delay going home. I drive out to the old, abandoned Pickwick estate, walking around the property at night and taking in the blooming trees and wild grasses, plotting out my fantasy of remaking it into the boutique inn and restaurant I've imagined so many times.

While my mother is in the shower, I decide to call my father. I would only do this in case of an emergency. My mother's agoraphobia is an emergency, and our deadbeat dad needs to help fix what he caused.

Sometimes I wonder what it would be like to leave, completely leave everything behind and start over someplace new. My father did it. Peyton does it and will do it again.

The phone rings on my father's end, and then there are a few odd clicks before he answers.

"Starlight Motel!" my father's chipper voice exclaims.

"Dad?" I ask, confused by his greeting.

"Talia, baby!"

"I thought this was your personal number? What's the Starlight Motel?"

"I'm staying here temporarily, and the owners—a nice couple—had to step away to run some errands. I let them forward the front desk calls to me."

He must be out of work again, and whichever lady friend he was shacking up with probably kicked him out.

I picture him sitting in a crappy motel room, taking calls from strangers while he figures out his next money-making scheme. Talking to him depresses me and only reminds me of how he and my mother are both screwed up in their own ways.

"Dad, I called because Mom isn't getting any better, and I'm really worried that she'll never step foot out of the house. Aleska is having a hard time with this, too. We've tried to talk to Mom about seeing a doctor, a therapist, but she gets really upset when we bring it up."

"I know, baby, I know."

"No, Dad, you don't understand. I need you to help us with this. Aleska and I can't keep Mom here like a pet. That's exactly what her life has come to."

"I know it's hard."

"No, you don't!" I shout. "You're not here. We need you to talk to Mom. For some insane reason, you're the only adult she listens to."

"I can't just drop everything and fly up there. I've got things going on."

"Things? Is this your new job? Motel receptionist?"

"I'm doing this as a favor. I've got other things cookin'."

"Great. While they're cooking, you can hop on the next flight up here and help your kids for a change. If money is the problem, I'll pay for your flight and you can sleep on our couch. You need to take Mom to a doctor."

"Babe, I can't do it. I love your mother, but when it comes to this, she won't listen to me. This agoraphobia, or whatever she's got, is something she's not willing to let us help her with. You know that."

"If you really do care about her, you'll talk to her. You have nothing to lose by trying to help her."

"Talia," he says in an exasperated voice, ready to give me more of his excuses.

"Stop it!" I scream. "Stop making excuses. I don't care which woman you mooch off of or what you do for a living or even if you ever visit us again, but if you have an ounce of love for Mom, or us, you'll do this one thing. One thing, Dad. Call Mom and be a real friend for a change. Instead of talking about yourself and the great weather in Florida, talk to her about her problem. Help her figure out how to deal with this and encourage her to see a doctor."

My father is quiet.

"I can't talk anymore," I say. "I have to get to work."

"Talia." There's none of that pretend enthusiasm he uses on everyone. "I will talk to Mila."

I end the call and take a deep breath. I'm shaking.

"Who was that?" My mother approaches while towel-drying her hair. Her robe is a faded peach terry cloth, and my first thought is that I should run to the outlet stores today and buy her a new one. Then I feel a flash of anger. If she wants a new robe, she can go to the mall with me. Otherwise, she'll have to stick to internet shopping and all the ill-fitting clothes she has to repackage and hand back to our UPS guy.

"It was a sales person, a computer. I hung up on them." I drop my cell phone in my handbag.

Aleska bursts through the front door. "I forgot my wallet! I'm going out to lunch today with the girls."

"Aleska, what do you think about Peyton and Talia?" my mother inquires as if this has been an ongoing discussion.

"What are you talking about?" I look at my mother.

Aleska looks at me with wide eyes and shrugs.

"You and how you're trying to hide the idea that you and Peyton like each other."

"We're friends, Mom. I see the guy at work."

"I think that was him on the phone," she says, then turns to Aleska. "She thinks no one notices how much time she spends with him."

"That wasn't him on the phone. I told you; it was one of those random marketing calls."

"Oh, you two. I wish you'd start dating again. Both of you. Sometimes you just need some rough male hands all over your body to make you feel good and happy."

"Ew." Aleska cringes.

"I agree. Not something a daughter wants to hear her mother say."

"It's true. You need to date again." My mother juts her chin out. "Why don't you go out with Peyton?"

I study my mother's sharp blue eyes and damp blonde hair, and I see an older version of myself. It aggravates me.

"Why don't you go outside, period?" I ask. "Why don't you go out with the women who used to be your friends? Lois and Pam and all the others who constantly ask about you? They're afraid to come to the house because you always tell everyone you're too busy. *With your fictional projects.*"

"That's not fair," my mother says.

"Really? Why don't you start dating? Oh, that's right, because you're afraid to leave the house, and you won't let us help you. You also think you have the right to butt into our business and tell us how to live our lives."

"Talia, that's a little harsh," Aleska says softly.

"No, it isn't. Harsh is having open heart surgery and neither one of your parents is willing to be at your bedside. Harsh is letting your daughters constantly worry about you because your own pride won't let you get the medical attention you need. Harsh is imprisoning yourself in your home and depending on your kids to fulfill all your emotional needs because you won't let people who care come near you."

We're interrupted by the shrill ring of the landline in the kitchen.

I run to the wall-mounted phone and grab the receiver off the hook. "Hello?" I bark, glaring at my mother as my father talks in his even, measured, smooth voice, asking to speak to his ex-wife.

"Who is it?" my mother inquires sharply. Her face colors, her eyes darken. I can tell her alter ego, the strong-willed enforcer, is back.

"It's George Clooney. For you." I toss the receiver, which doesn't quite reach her. Instead, it hits the floor with a loud thud and begins to recoil back.

I don't wait around to see if my father tries to talk sense into her. I angrily charge out of the house.

My sister follows. I hear her start the engine of our van as I hop on my Huffy. I drop my purse into my wicker handlebar basket and pedal off toward town. With my back ramrod straight, I pedal furiously, something closely resembling the Wicked Witch of the West.

It's no accident that I bike along the route where I sometimes see Dylan run. I've only seen him occasionally, since his long treks often lead him out of town, but now that I know Peyton likes to run with him in the morning, I'm going to see if I can *coincidentally* run into them on my way to work.

About a mile before I reach the restaurant, I see two tall figures in the distance coming my way. There's a sleek, powerful synchronization to their movements, so I know it's them.

The temperature is in the fifties today, but as they approach, I can see they're stripped down to only their shorts and shoes. Dylan doesn't bother with a T-shirt, and Peyton has his draped around his neck. As they get closer, Peyton wipes his sweaty brow with his shirt, and then his eyes perk up when he recognizes me.

The empty stretch of the county road is surrounded by nothing but serene nature, and the sound of their labored breaths grows louder. Their long, lean, muscled bodies with early-season tans stand out, and anyone driving by would surely get whiplash doing double-takes to admire them.

The shoulder of the road isn't wide enough for all of us, so I maneuver my bike onto the paved road. I'm close enough to Peyton to see him look at me as if I'm the best thing he's seen in a long while. And for that single moment, I relish feeling special. It only lasts a second, though, and then he looks down at my bike and his expression changes to a grimace. He runs right in front of my bike, grabs the handlebars, and pulls my bike to an abrupt stop. Dylan stops, too, looking a little perplexed at Peyton's rough assault on my bicycle.

"Hey, Talia," Dylan says with a friendly smile. "On your way to work?"

Before I can respond, Peyton leans over the handlebars and gets in my face. "Why are you still riding this heap of junk? I told you it's unsafe."

"And I told you I need the exercise." Since he's holding the bike solidly in place, I plant my feet on the ground and stand up. "It's perfectly fine for getting to X, Y, and Z."

"But it's not safe for getting from point A to point B," Peyton says tersely.

"Whoa." Dylan chuckles. "What's with you two?"

Peyton ignores Dylan and keeps his icy glare on me. I can't say I don't appreciate his alpha male protectiveness, and I did drag my bike through some extra hilly roads just to see him, but it's also humiliating to have him talk to me like I'm a misbehaving child in front of Dylan.

"What's the problem?" Dylan asks.

"I told her not to ride this thing. It's a death trap."

"Good move. Giving a woman orders is always a brilliant idea," Dylan says.

"I like my bike. We get along fine. It gets me where I need to go."

"This bike is falling apart, and it was made for city sidewalks, not country roads. You're going to get hit by a car if you keep riding this piece of junk."

We all look over as a large truck roars by. Three men in construction gear are sitting in the bed of the truck, and it passes with a friendly wave from the driver, whistles from the men in back, and three rapid-fire, short honks like "hello, toots."

"That was for me. My great ass," I tell Peyton, pointing to my rear.

I wave to the men, whom I don't recognize.

"Nice," he says without smiling.

"It's the biking. It does wonders for my butt."

"She's got you there," Dylan says.

"We'll discuss this later." He lets go of my handlebars but then maneuvers around the front wheel and grips my bike seat so I still can't take off. "And why are you going in so early?"

"I'm catering Adam's dinner party tonight."

"That's great," Dylan chimes in. "New business. You're the rock star of shrimp puffs and Talia's tasty poppers."

"Oh, shut up," Peyton says to Dylan, then turns back to me as though he's assessing how to broach this topic.

Dylan looks between us questioningly. I can tell he's curious to know what's going on, and Peyton is doing his best not to give away the secret I shared only with him.

"I'll shuffle my schedule around tonight and put Greer on the floor so I can help you take the food and equipment to Knight's place and help you out."

Dylan cocks an eyebrow. "Dude, she has hired guns to do that. It's a catering business."

"He's right," I say. "I have a staff when I cater parties and events."

"Fine. Is Aleska going to be there?"

"No. It's not her job." I don't know where he's going with these questions. It's obvious he wants to say more, but he's guarded in front of Dylan.

"All right." His tone softens. "I'm going to finish my run. We can discuss this later." He takes off in a slow jog, and I turn back to watch him run.

Dylan gives me a shrug, then bolts, catching up to Peyton. Within seconds, they're sprinting again. They are beautiful runners to behold, but I'm really only watching Peyton's long, muscular back as he disappears around the curve.

When I finally huff and puff my way to Swill, instead of thinking of the menu preparation ahead of me, I'm rewinding my moments with Peyton and playing them over and over in my head. The kisses, the way his body enveloped mine against his chest, his strong arms wrapped around me, protective and tender. When I get to the scenes in his bed, I hit pause and replay ... what feels like thousands of times.

I've had enough partners to know what's good or bad, and most were mediocre, at best. I'm not the first almost-bride who was willing to marry a man who could rarely give her an orgasm; women always think they can work on that part once they're married and improve their sex life. Peyton doesn't need any help. My face heats thinking about those orgasms.

When I walk into the restaurant, Peyton and Dylan have beaten me back and are standing at the bar, guzzling water out of beer pitchers. I blush as if my illicit thoughts are on display.

Peyton tips his chin at me, pauses for a beat, and then gives me a wicked grin. *He knows I'm having dirty thoughts about him.*

I wave nonchalantly and keep walking toward the kitchen. There's absolutely no way I can stop and talk to them and keep a straight face.

18

Peyton

I FOLLOW HER INTO the kitchen, like the stalker of Talia I have become. Her hair has come undone from the bun she loosely twists on top of her head. The rubber tie is hanging at the end of a long strand of hair, and I snatch it off her bouncing waves.

She feels the tug and quickly turns around, so I come up short before her face can slam into my chest. There it is. Her face is flushed, like how she looked when she was in my bed. Like how she looked when I watched her walk into the restaurant moments ago with a secretive smile.

"Are you going to complain about my bike again?" She looks away as if she's suddenly shy with me. That's enough to tamp down my irrational thoughts about her interest in Adam Knight. He's not here. I am. I get to see her like this.

Whether it's only professional or she's developed some feelings for the guy, I can't say it doesn't bother me. It bothers the hell out of me. I spent months with Flora and couldn't care less if she admired another man or even what went on in that pretty head of hers. I was always more consumed with my own life. But I look at Talia and think she deserves better than what she's had. Better than her ex. Better than the Wall Street guys who spend vacation time in Hera, looking for cute ass on the side. And she deserves better than me. That's why I feel like a hypocrite. I want her cute ass, too, and I want her undivided attention, and I want a career outside of this sleepy, albeit charming, one-bar town.

Acknowledging my own hypocrisy doesn't deter me, though.

"Let's talk in my office," I urge.

Bash and his cooks don't seem to notice as Talia and I cross the kitchen to the hallway where our private offices are located.

"What's up?" she asks as I close my office door behind her. When I turn the deadbolt, she raises an eyebrow at me. "Top secret?"

Her smile disarms me ... again.

"It shouldn't be, but you seem to want it that way. I like you, Madej. You're growing on me. Since we're both busy professionals with no social life, why don't we spend more time together?"

She laughs. "More sex, you mean? I wouldn't mind that. I'll schedule you in." Our flirting is easy and natural.

"You have this sweet disposition, and then you say things like that." I move toward her and cup her chin with one hand. "I'm all for more sex, but I also want to go out with you. Not that there's any place to go to in this town, other than here or the diner. But we could go to a restaurant in Woodstock or Kingston. Maybe a movie. Something other than being at Swill all the time."

Her smile disappears and her eyes narrow. "You're serious?"

"Yes, I'm serious. Why can't we go out? Like regular people?"

"You mean like people who date? Like a couple?"

"Like people who are spending time together."

"Because we're not a couple. We're not serious about each other. We can't be. You said it yourself. You're here to get Swill up and running, and then you want to get out so you can build bigger and better restaurants."

"I'm pretty sure I didn't say it like that. I'm not talking about serious stuff. Just a movie or something." I stroke her cheek with my thumb, causing a rosy hue to wash across her face again. Her skin is soft. I tilt her chin up and lean in for a quick kiss, but once my mouth brushes against her plump lower lip, I'm a goner and a simple peck is out of the question.

I really need a shower. I'm subjecting her to my after-workout stench, but she's kissing me back.

I want more.

I snake my other hand around her waist to pull her closer as I explore her mouth with my tongue like it's a first kiss. In fact, each time I'm with her, touch her, my mind and body react as though it's the first time, the exciting moment that only happens once. Her response is just as eager, and if this kiss was happening anywhere but at work, it would go well beyond a kiss.

169

I was hard the minute she stepped into the office, but now I'm downright uncomfortable, and my gym shorts can't conceal my erection. My whole body is alert with the close proximity of this woman. Suddenly, beer production and inventory seem unimportant, at least until I can get this woman's undivided attention and have her think about me the way she's focusing on Knight's party.

I know I shouldn't be jealous of her clients. She's not jealous of the women on my staff or the female customers who flirt with me. I'm a salesman, so sometimes I flirt back. On a busy night, I make my rounds to each table and talk to everyone, lay on the charm and goodwill. Talia doesn't bat an eyelash. In this case, she has a better grasp of separating business from pleasure.

But she has this one client who has me on edge. One client out of many. One man, a guy who happens to be good-looking, rich, and available. And she may think he sees her only as a caterer, another person he hires for his expensive lifestyle among the beautiful, wealthy set, but I see the way he looks at her. I see the way his eyes lock on her and watch her move across the room. I saw the way he looked at her at Norma's house. I recognize this in him because I'm positive we share the same growing appreciation for Talia.

"Come over to my place tonight," I say as plainly as possible, the way you'd ask a friend to have a drink after work.

"I think I will, MacKenzie." She's straightforward, no coyness. Typically, I would appreciate that. It's exactly what we both signed on for, so why the fuck am I overthinking this?

"Are you all right?" She looks at me with concern.

"Fine. It's that Knight guy. He rubs me the wrong way."

"I don't understand how you could dislike the man. He's my client, and he's your customer, don't forget. And he's a nice guy. He took a mud bath helping you catch Baby."

"He was showing off for you. I don't know if I really trust him."

She throws her head back and laughs. "Trust him with what? He comes in here and drinks beer, eats food, and pays his bill."

"You know what I'm referring to. I don't trust him *with you*."

"You sound jealous."

"Maybe I am. A little. You're cooking food for *him* in *my* kitchen. You're going to be at a party, with *him*."

"I'm serving him dumplings and wine. You and I meet for sex. What you and I have is a little bit *more*, don't you think?"

"Nevertheless, watch yourself around him. He's smooth, he's clever, he's manipulative."

"Stop it." She laughs again. "Someone might think you care too much, and you can't afford that. Can you, MacKenzie?"

"Good point."

She wriggles free from my grasp and unlocks the office door. "I'll see you tonight after the party. It'll be late. Should I come by here or your house?"

"I'll be here. I'm always here."

• • •

The next four hours are nothing short of torture as Talia crosses my path multiple times in the kitchen, by the bar when we both appear to get water, and then in the walk-in fridge, where I almost lose it.

I drop the tablet with our inventory lists when she bends over to retrieve a bin of lettuce. I curse, pick up the undamaged tablet off the rubber mat, and storm out of there before she can say anything.

It should have been a relief to see her pack her van and drive off, except I know her last stop will be Adam Knight's. That's all I'm thinking about. She'll be working in his extravagant home, a home that's perfectly situated in the town she loves. *I can't offer her this*, I remind myself.

Once the woman of my hardcore sex fantasies leaves the building, my brain can finally concentrate on work issues. Before we open for dinner, I like to make the rounds to talk to the staff and do some quality checks.

As I leave my office, my sister approaches me in the hallway with a perplexed expression.

"What's wrong?"

"Maybe nothing. Remember Harmony Davis?"

An image of Harmony from high school springs to mind. Tall and beautiful, dark brown skin, and rows of long, thin braids twisted together in thick bundles. She was a reserved but confident girl whose father was a well-known music producer, and she walked around school with no concern for gossipy girls or horny jocks. She did her own thing and chose to spend time with only a few, select people who tended to be the smart intellectuals at school, the ones who lived off the radar in terms of high school popularity.

We moved in different circles, but when our paths would cross, she would always ask me interesting questions, and just when I thought she had no interest in me, she let me in.

Once.

"Harmony. I haven't seen her in about a decade. Not since high school."

"She's at the bar. Asked to see you. Alone." Greer shakes her head. "Maybe she just wants to say hello, but something about it felt odd."

"Relax. I'll go talk to her." I leave Greer and walk into the dining room.

Harmony is standing at the bar, studying her surroundings, and something niggles at me. She's still beautiful, but she looks more mature. Her long, thick hair has been replaced with a short pixie cut, which shows off her graceful neck.

Before I can say her name, she turns and looks at me with a mix of warm recognition and a certain mysteriousness that always enveloped Harmony when we were teenagers.

"Hello, Peyton," she says with a small smile. Signature Harmony, kind to everyone, an enigma to everyone.

"Harmony." I smile, and then we give each other a brief hug before stepping back. "You look the same. Except for the hair. You look great."

"Looks like you cut yours, too." She inspects me.

"It was a recent, spontaneous act. I went to the local barber, who's like a thousand years old, and he couldn't chop my hair off fast enough," I say, becoming a little nervous with her staring at me. I reach up to touch my neck.

"It's good to see you," she says. "Can we sit somewhere and talk?"

"Of course. There's more privacy back in my office, but it's a mess. Or we can sit out here? The dining room will be empty for another hour."

"I like it out here. Your restaurant is impressive."

"It's not just mine," I say, leading her to one of the four-tops by a window, far enough away from the staff and Greer who are all suddenly thirsty, appearing at the bar to pour large glasses of water.

We sit, and I make sure my back is to our audience.

Harmony is dressed in a black suit with black heels, looking more like a corporate CEO than the teenage ballerina I remember.

She crosses her long legs and relaxes against the back of her chair with perfectly straight posture.

"Last I remember, you moved to Seattle with your dad. What brought you back here?"

She looks down at the table and takes a dramatic breath. "This is tough ... I've imagined this scene a million times, and each time I would concoct a good outcome and a bad one," she says as she fiddles with the salt and pepper grinders.

My nerves tighten like twine being wound on a reel. I'm being drawn into the strange aura that has always surrounded Harmony. It's neither welcoming nor frightening. It's simply the way Harmony is—*was*—with everyone. People are drawn to her, wondering if she likes them or not.

Her serene face gives nothing away, but her hands flex and twitch as she fumbles with the salt and pepper shakers.

"Harmony, what's going on?"

She pauses, then replaces the small grinders on the table. She looks at me with resignation that is a prerequisite to a confession. "I have a son. You're his father. We have a son, Peyton."

Everything in my brain stops. I can't react or speak. Maybe it's shock. I'm conflicted, a bizarre elation coupled with disbelief and anger.

I had sex with Harmony once back in our junior year of high school that could be best described as sweet. A one-time event, an extraordinary situation where the elusive Harmony spoke to me in a private conversation, away from the rest of the party. We ignored all the usual teenage angst and drama, the never-ending gossip, and we delved right into divulging some truths about ourselves. It was an open and honest discussion about our families, our problems with our parents' expectations of us, our concerns over our impending college tours, and how tired we were of high school social politics. It was a confessional of sorts, a breaking of barriers, an aphrodisiac when you're seventeen.

Then I walked her home to the brownstone where she lived with her father. He wasn't home that evening, so Harmony invited me in. It was quiet with expensive furnishings, and it was like another world compared to my rowdy homelife with three brothers, a sister, and divorced parents.

Our teenage hormones led us to her bed for an hour of teenage passion and fumbling sex. I wasn't inexperienced, but I wasn't smooth, and the last thing on my mind was being clever in bed.

My one-track mind got what it needed, and I enjoyed Harmony's company. It seemed mutual, and I assumed we'd hook up again, maybe date. It never came to that. Harmony passed me in the school hallways with only a brief smile or a curt hello. Then, a few weeks later, she and her father moved to Seattle, and we didn't stay in contact.

"His name is Finn," she says, waiting for me to say something.

"Why didn't you tell me I have a baby?" I ask angrily. I'm picturing our baby. Does he look like Harmony with her African American traits, or does he have my features?

"He's nine. He's not a baby anymore," she says defensively.

"Right. You moved away ten years ago. You had the baby in Seattle?" I say it more calmly, but my emotions are all over the place. A son? I'm a father? She's the mother of my kid, and she didn't want to tell me for a whole decade?

How the hell can I be a parent?

"Yes. Finn was born and raised there." Harmony softens her tone as if she's trying to placate me, to help me adjust to this startling news.

"You left me in the dark for ten years? I have a kid and missed out on ten years? Nine years. Whatever. Why didn't you tell me?" Rage is coursing through my bloodstream. I need to tamp it down before I say something I'll regret.

"I'm sorry you're finding out like this." Her eyes water a bit. "I struggled with it for several days when I found out I was pregnant. I thought about not having the baby and not telling my dad. I went back and forth. Should I tell you? Should I end the pregnancy? I thought about adoption, too. I thought about all the options, and I couldn't come to a decision on my own. I didn't go to you because I didn't know you that well, and my father was all I had.

"He was everything to me. He was a strict, difficult man, but he loved me and I needed him. So I told him. He said he would take care of everything, give me and our baby everything we need. He wasn't happy about the situation, and he gave me an ultimatum. I could have the baby and never worry about money, school, and childcare expenses. If I did what my father wanted, I could finish high school in Seattle and go to college. Or I could tell you, and have you involved in the baby's life and be cut off financially from my father. I didn't want to be a homeless, teenage mother."

"Your dad ... What a—" I pound the table with my fist, and she startles.

"We were seventeen, Peyton. I was scared. If my mother had still been alive, it would have been different. I tried to reason with my dad when I told him I was pregnant. I insisted you had a right to know, and that the baby deserved a father. But it all happened so fast. My dad had us out of there a couple weeks after I told him. He rented us a house in Seattle and hired people to pack up our Brooklyn home and sell it. He relocated his whole business and sound studios."

"Finn," I say, feeling the name set between my teeth. "Why would your dad do all that just to get away from me?"

"His fear of losing me. He wasn't an easy man, and he was broken after my mother died. Other than his business reputation, I was all he had. And he thought by controlling me, he was protecting me."

"What happened? What made you come here and tell me?"

"My father died. My son—our son—keeps asking about you. So, after I settled my dad's estate three months ago, I accepted a job at Genesis Two Sigma and we moved to Westchester a month ago. We have a nice house there, and Finn is enrolled in a good school. It's ninety minutes from you on a good day."

"I'm sorry about your dad, but what he did was shitty. I'm still trying to wrap my head around this. Being a father. A father to a big kid, not a baby."

"Do you want to meet Finn?" she says timidly, as though she actually thinks I'll refuse.

"Of course. Is he here?" I look out the window, expecting to see a mini-me with a bit of an attitude sitting impatiently in a car.

"No." A smile breaks across her face. "He's at home with the sitter. He knows I'm here. I told him about you, the specifics, when I decided we would move back to the East Coast. He's very bright, very thoughtful. The main male figure in his life was my father, so his death has been hard on him. And me. But it has also given me the freedom to do what I should have done years ago. I always wanted to tell you."

"A whole decade, Harmony." I mutter a curse. "How could you wait that long? Jesus."

"I ... It's not easy to explain ... but I want you to be a part of Finn's life now. If you want that, and I hope you do. He needs a dad."

"Of course, I want to. Christ, this kid must think I'm the biggest asshole for not being there. How did you explain my absence?"

"When he was little, I would tell him that his father was far away. I didn't want to lie and tell him his dad was dead. I stretched the truth so he wouldn't be hurt and wouldn't lose hope of seeing his father someday. It was easier to keep the story murky when he was little—your dad loves you but he can't be here. He stopped accepting that excuse when he turned eight, but his grandfather wouldn't discuss it. I finally told Finn the truth, the whole story, after my dad died.

"Finn doesn't think you're a bad guy. He thinks you were cheated. And you *were* cheated, by me, by my dad. It was terrible, but I can't change how we handled it. All I can say is I'm sorry, and the beautiful reward is we have a great son. It's one thing my dad did really well. He was kind to Finn, and he was involved, and he gave me the best education so I can take care of Finn."

"At least your dad did something right." It's followed by a long, awkward pause. "So you work at Genesis Two Sigma. Impressive. It's a big pharma company, right?"

"Yes." The salt shaker she's fiddling with again shoots out of her hands and drops to the floor with a loud crack. I pick it up and place it back on the table.

"I'm nervous, too," I admit. "Being a parent isn't something I've thought about. Ever. I'm not sure if I'll live up to Finn's expectations."

"He's easier to please than you think."

"You mean the bar has been set real low?"

"No, not at all. He's read about you online; some of those interviews you've had. He's excited to meet you."

I nod along, but I'm nervous as hell. What if my own kid doesn't like me? What if I'm a lousy dad? Being a drop-in uncle is easy, but I have no idea how to rearrange my life and be a parent.

"So, you know all about me then. What about you? Tell me more about you. How did you go from ballet dancer to working in the pharmaceutical industry?" It's a stupid question, but I don't know anything about the grown-up version of Harmony.

"My father taught me to be practical. Fortunately, I discovered I love science. I'm a chemist. I completed my PhD and decided I wanted to go right into the private sector instead of academia. I work in research and development. I wanted to work at Genesis because they have a whole department devoted to developing new drugs for cancer treatment, and I want to be a part of that."

"That makes sense. We both lost our mothers to cancer."

"Yes. I was sorry to hear about your mother, Peyton."

"Sounds like a great job, Dr. Davis." I want to say something kind to offset my anger.

"It is, but I'm not doing it for the money. I actually discovered what I'm meant to do in this life. Other than being Finn's mother. The research is important to me. Genesis does pay well, but I already have a significant inheritance—my father's estate was fairly large. Finn and I are set."

"Good." I nod again. *Inadequate* is the word that comes to mind to describe my status compared to Harmony's. I'm doing well financially, but Harmony's father's net worth was in the ballpark of tens of millions. His name and production company are on the labels of some of the best music produced over the last few decades. The man won awards. The only way I can compete with that in the eyes of a nine-year-old boy is if he finds out I'm secretly an astronaut who does special missions. Or I'm suddenly recruited by the New York Rangers and we win the Stanley Cup. Or the Jets, and I bring home a Super Bowl ring. Since none of those scenarios are going to happen, I'll have to make running restaurants and bussing tables in a pinch seem more exciting.

"He's very eager to meet you," she stresses.

"Can I drive over to your place now, or do you want to bring him here?"

"I'd like to bring him here tomorrow. That will give you time to absorb all of this. Think about it tonight, and we'll come by at ten in the morning. Does that work?"

"Sure. We'll have breakfast and ..." My mind drifts to a fuzzy image of this boy. I'm excited, actually happy at the prospect of having a son, and I'm absolutely terrified I'll disappoint him.

"It will be fine." She reaches across the table and places her hand on mine.

"Sure." It comes across exactly as I feel, a mixture of fear, anger, and excitement. It's this sense of vulnerability I'm unaccustomed to.

"You haven't said what I expected," she adds, removing her hand from mine. "I thought you'd ask me to prove you're the father. I thought you'd be defensive. We can do the paternity test—whatever you need."

"Harmony, I remember what happened. One condom, two negligent teenagers who think they know it all, confident that the condom broke after the deed and not during. We were the poster children for what goes wrong when know-it-all teenagers have sex."

Harmony studies me for a moment, and I think she's going to comment on our one-night fling. Instead, she observes me with a sympathetic smile. "I have a lot of photos of Finn on my phone. I can show you. He resembles you in many ways."

"No, I want to see him for the first time in person."

She smiles. "All right."

"You seem happy, Harmony. I'm looking forward to meeting Finn. I mean that. And thank you for coming here today."

We walk to her car, and before she leaves, I hug her. The embrace is much different from the one ten years ago. This one is filled with the acceptance of knowing we are now tied to one another forever. I trust Harmony. I have no doubt I am the father of her son.

When I return to the bar, Greer and Bash are waiting for the details. I keep the information to myself, not ready to tell my family. Hell, everyone will know tomorrow when my half-grown kid walks through the door.

An urgent phone call gives me the excuse to escape to the back office alone.

"Peyton, it's Aleska."

I take her off speakerphone and pick up the receiver. "What's up? Is Talia okay?"

She laughs. She's laughing *at* me, of course. "Talia is fine. She's at Adam's house. I just got a call from her other server, Bo. He's not going to make it to Adam's. He has to pull a double shift at his day job in Woodstock. I was trying to reach Talia, but she's not answering her phone."

"Is anyone else helping her?"

"She has Marguerite there to bartend. Talia can handle the serving herself, but she was expecting Bo to carry the crate of plates from the van to the house. She can't ask the client to carry them in, and Talia can't lift something that heavy. Not yet. You know what I'm talking about, right?"

"Yes, I do." *Post-surgical pain.*

Aleska knows we slept together. She knows I've seen Talia's scar.

"Good. The thing is, I'm at The Rack with the girls, and I'm on my second beer—I'm not driving."

"I'll help her. I'll leave now."

"Thank you. Talia owes you!" Aleska bellows before disconnecting.

I'm relieved to have a reason to escape the curious stares and my probing sister. My family will find out like everyone else, tomorrow, when my loudmouthed sister-in-law is sure to broadcast the news to the whole town. I'll probably have my own social media blast thanks to Imogene. #PeytonIsADaddy would be my first guess.

It will be fine, I remind myself as I dash out the door. I have the need for my own confessional, and the only person I want to confess to is playing house with another man.

19

Talia

Adam's home was made for entertaining. I have food in the oven and chilled shot glasses with ceviche on serving platters, ready to go. Marguerite is setting up a complete bar and putting the finishing touches on the dining table centerpiece and various floral displays.

We look around the open space of the first floor and admire our handiwork as Adam comes down the stairs in jeans and a fitted shirt, his hair damp from his shower.

"Looks great down here," he says. "Let's have a drink before everyone arrives. How about it?"

"Marguerite will make you anything you want." I gesture toward the bar. "She and I will not drink, though."

"That's no fun." He reaches for a shot glass and tosses the ceviche back in one bite, as intended.

"That's one of my signature appetizers."

"It's excellent." He grins. "Let's drink."

I roll my eyes at him and signal Marguerite with a finger gun.

"Wine, or do you want one of my special drinks?" she asks.

"Surprise me," he says, then turns back to me. "Come on, Piano Girl. It's your turn"

"What?" I ask warily as he opens up the grand piano and pulls out the bench.

"Over here. Play some tunes. I've heard your covers of Bill Evans and Wynton Kelly. You're good. Start playing."

Marguerite hands him a glass with a pinkish drink and a lime. He takes a whiff.

"It has vodka. I like it already." He takes a good swig, then nods at the piano. "Now."

"Fine, but as soon as guests arrive, I'm not performing."

"Yeah, yeah, let's go, Mozart."

I plant myself on the bench, and he slides in right next to me. He smells great, a blend of musky soap and aftershave, and his arm is flush with mine. I'm not uncomfortable with his attention. I think he behaves this way with most women. It's a sweet flirtation. Charming men, including my father, all have this skill with women of any age, and it's innocent enough. Besides, I have Marguerite as a witness and chaperone.

For the next ten minutes, I slip into musician mode, performing the way my father taught me, enjoying the bluesy jazz as my fingers remember the chords by rote. This is a real treat, a luxury for me, to play such a fine piano, to play at all. Aleska may have picked up the English language faster and better than me, but I'm a natural on the piano.

I'm in the middle of "Come Rain or Come Shine" when Adam's front door swings open and Peyton barrels through with my crate of dishes. I keep playing even though my eyes are on Peyton and his are locked on mine.

"MacKenzie!" Adam raises his glass. "You're coming to the party. Good. Nice surprise." Marguerite's drinks must be strong tonight, because Adam seems especially jovial.

Peyton doesn't bother to place the heavy crate down. He walks over with it, his eyes roaming over the piano and my arms and legs sitting pretty cozily with Adam's. He takes one long, hard look at Adam, then settles on me.

"Since when do you play the piano?" he demands. "Why don't I know this?"

"I'm done." I stand up and scoot away from the bench. "We're just goofing off until the guests come. What are you doing here?"

"Filling in for Biff. He can't make it."

"You mean Bo. Well, thanks for bringing in the dishware. You can put it on the kitchen counter."

"Want a drink?" Adam asks Peyton, pointing toward Marguerite's well-equipped bar.

"Um, no. I'm here to do whatever Ben ... Biff ... Bo was going to do. I thought you needed a server."

"We have it under control. You don't have to stay." I touch his elbow and guide him and the large crate into the kitchen. Thankfully, Adam doesn't follow us.

"What the hell are you doing?" Peyton asks. He drops the crate on the counter with a large thud, making every plate clink.

"He asked me to play the piano, so I played a few tunes," I whisper-shout. "Don't make a scene here. Thank you for bringing in the dishes, but you can leave now. Go back to Swill. I'll meet you later."

"No. I'm working here tonight," he replies, lowering his voice. "I sent Greer a text. She's running the bar, and I'm working for you. What do you want me to do? Hold your sheet music while you entertain the rich playboy?"

"Ha! I don't need sheet music. I play by memories."

"You mean *by ear*."

"That, too!"

"No need to raise your voice. Give me my assignment and I'll stay out of your hair."

"My hair? What the hell would you do to my hair?"

"Your *way*." Peyton smirks, beginning to unload the dishes.

"I'll plate the appetizers, and you take the platter and walk around the room. People will help themselves. You don't have to talk or be showy. We're not here to entertain them. Just serve."

"Look who's talking, Rachmaninoff."

"Actually, I'm least skilled in his compositions—why are we talking about this? We don't have time for an argument. Here, you can start with the ceviche." I hold the tray of shot glasses filled with fresh scallops and shrimp up to Peyton.

"Shot glasses. Interesting." He takes the platter.

"It's going to have to be my amuse-bouche."

"For Adam, the amuse-douche."

"I can fire you."

"I'm a volunteer."

"If I have to, I'll call Dylan to replace you."

"Ah, I see guests are arriving. I must go amuse them." He holds the tray high and stalks off toward the living room, walking more like a man who owns the place than waitstaff.

When I return to the living room with a tray of spicy endive, the house is full. Every guest must have arrived,

Adam is in his element, surrounded by wealthy people, while Peyton is working the room like a superstar.

"Talia," Adam says as I weave through the crowd. "When you get a moment, I want to introduce you to some friends."

I nod, judging the pretty redhead next to him. I doubt she's a natural redhead. She has a glowing tan as if she just came back from a tropical vacation. I'm guessing she's a successful Wall Streeter like Adam, with a penchant for an expensive lifestyle. She's holding Adam's arm like a woman determined to keep a man to herself.

She gives me a genuine smile, and I feel a little guilty for judging her.

I check on Marguerite, who works the bar like a magician, whipping up cocktails and pouring wine so quickly no one has to wait. Our staff is known for stealthy, unobtrusive service. We wear traditional black pants and white or black shirts so we don't stand out. We barely talk above a whisper when we introduce a tray of hors d'oeuvres to guests. I'll hold out a platter and announce the food—"shrimp croquettes, steak tartare, mushrooms stuffed with savory herbs and ricotta"—and let guests serve themselves. It's impossible not to notice that Peyton has a different technique.

He's wearing those jeans that make his butt look great, and they're relaxed enough to hang from the hard edges of his slender hips. His gray T-shirt shows off his V-shaped physique. The broad shoulders swoop down to his firm pectorals in front and the hard planes of muscles in back. Peyton is comfortable in any crowd and walks with a gunslinger's swagger. He's not attempting to be invisible at all.

"Hey, you in the silver dress," he says from behind a woman with glossy black hair pulled back into a smooth bun.

I cringe. He's like a guy from a construction site, whistling to a woman walking by, minding her own business.

The elegant woman in the silver sheath turns around, and instead of being offended, her face lights up with a smile when she sees Peyton. Of course it does.

My cordial, professional Bo has been replaced with a tall, sexy guy who makes you wonder what it would be like to have him in your bed, naked and hot and heavy for you.

"Here, have a shot," Peyton says to the woman.

I roll my eyes and groan. *"Have a shot,"* I grumble to myself and go back to the kitchen for more food. This is what people mean by *bull in a china shop*. Peyton is most definitely a bull, and he has the serving skills of a WWE wrestler.

I work my way back through the crowd with a new tray for Peyton.

"Here," I say in a low voice as I take his empty platter and hand him a tray of stuffed mushrooms. "Maybe you could try to be a bit more subtle. Less talking."

"You don't like my style?" He winks. There's a group of women behind him, waiting for him. They are so obvious.

"This is Adam's party," I whisper. "Don't interfere."

"Don't worry, sunflower. I'm a professional."

When he calls me sunflower, I feel a little light-headed and giddy. Like the women waiting for him.

He turns to the group, and that sexy charm of his seduces them. They're enthralled by my rogue waiter, the man I lust for, the man I sleep with and pretend is my friend.

"Hey, pretty in pink," Peyton says to another woman in a pink blouse.

I hold my breath again, wondering how long this can go on, but the woman steps forward as though honored to be beckoned by Peyton.

"Here, have a 'shroom."

"Oh, for the love of fudge," I whisper angrily to myself.

He looks over at me and grins. He's intentionally messing with me. He knows I'm a stickler for a sense of order and decorum when it comes to party etiquette, and he likes getting away with breaking other people's rules.

"Talia." Adam's voice from behind me makes me freeze. I hope he isn't angry about Peyton's performance. I'm just getting to know him, and it's been nice. I would hate for all of it to end because of Peyton. *Because I'm sleeping with Peyton and letting him into every part of my life.*

I turn around and come face to face with the woman who has been hanging onto Adam since she arrived. She's a bit taller than me, thin, but with shapely curves in the right places—her bust, her rear. Her red hair is thick and drapes in loose curls just below her shoulders. She has lovely skin, and her bronze tan highlights her cheekbones and smoky eyes. She's very attractive, but I think I'd be more envious if she were hanging off Peyton's arm rather than Adam's. That image sticks with me, the idea that I want to keep Peyton away from these women.

"May I get you both a drink?" I ask Adam and the pretty woman. I'm always in service mode and never want to presume I can behave like a guest.

"No, everything is excellent. The food ... And Marguerite is some bartender. Her drinks have won everyone over. Seriously good stuff," Adam says.

"And where did you find that waiter?" the woman inquires.

"Peyton," I say with a sigh. "He's helping out for tonight."

"Talia, this is Chloe. She's a fund manager at another firm."

"It's a pleasure." Chloe smiles and reaches out to shake my hand. I slip the empty tray under my arm and give her a firm handshake. "You've really done a wonderful job here. I bet Adam is going to have a lot of parties."

"Oh, thank you. Adam has the perfect house for parties, and he's the perfect client," I say, trying to make up for Peyton's wild behavior—every caterer's nightmare.

"I'm not just her client," he says to Chloe. "You get to know someone when they're in your home several times a week. And that guy over there, schmoozing all the women, he's not her employee. He owns that German beer hall you drove by on the way up here."

"Interesting." Chloe follows Peyton with her eyes. "Are you dating him?"

"Dating?" I say. "No, we're not dating." *It's sort of true.* Sleeping with someone isn't the same as dating them.

Adam is watching me carefully. It's exactly what I do when I'm around him. I study him and wonder what it would be like to be with him outside of work. I look for clues to see if he's interested in me beyond the way a man checks out a woman and imagines what it would be like to have sex with her.

It's becoming a little awkward with Chloe holding his arm. I have to assume she wants a relationship with him. I've been in his home enough to know that he doesn't bring any women here. There are never extra dishes in the sink, or two used wineglasses on the counter, or objects left behind that would indicate a woman spent the evening. I imagine his New York apartment is where he takes his dates. It's a part of his life I don't want to think about.

"I was hoping you'd play the piano for us again. I told Chloe you're talented."

"No. No, thank you," I say, laughing as if I get these requests all the time.

"Peyton! Over here!" A woman is waving her empty martini glass, and then a few cheers and laughter from a group of women takes over the room.

"I think I need to get Peyton some more appetizers to serve." I'd like to talk to Adam, but I really need to pay attention to my job and the fact that I'm worried women are going to start slipping twenty dollar bills in Peyton's pants and beg him to strip.

"It's all right, Talia." Adam touches my shoulder to reassure me that he isn't upset with Peyton's intrusion. I suppose Wall Street people are used to excessive, alpha behavior.

"It was nice meeting you," I say to Chloe. "I love your hair ... and your dress! Please excuse me."

I walk away, berating myself for acting like a nervous ninny in front of Adam. He's been so nice to me, so there's no reason for me to think I don't belong. As my father would say, *the rich and beautiful have to take dumps like everyone else.* We're a family of poets.

Dumps or no dumps, I can't get to know Adam when he has a gorgeous woman at his side and I have a pretend waiter who's about to be coaxed into a *Magic Mike* performance if he keeps going along with the flirty women who find ways to touch him. Oh sure, I haven't missed a single, manicured hand that caresses his shoulder, or the woman with the husky laugh who dared to stroke his unshaven jaw. *Only I get to do that! He's my ...*

Exactly. What is Peyton to me? My lover? The word makes me gag.

When I find Peyton, his back is to me, and my instinct is to put my hand in his back pocket, right where his jeans hug his perfect ass.

He's really screwing up my catering etiquette. I'm not supposed to be having inappropriate thoughts about him while I'm working, yet somehow, it seems like it's my right to slide my hand in there and tug him toward me because we're ...

And there it is again.

We're friends? Friends really don't have sex unless you're one of those women who claim her boyfriend is also her best friend. Friends with benefits? Again, I don't believe in that. Those are people who are confused about their relationship. Either they're going to have a romantic relationship or not. Friends who have sex for the sake of sex will eventually realize it's screwing up their friendship, so the sex and the friendship both end.

But isn't that what I agreed to when Peyton and I decided to sleep together? If I continue to treat him as a sex buddy without any emotional commitment, then I can't be jealous if he is also attracted to other women. He may be used to this kind of arrangement, but I'm not.

I so desperately want to feel like the old Talia, the pre-surgery Talia who had a sense of immortality and felt secure about how she rated on the desirability chart with men. One little physical scar doesn't change all that. It's the inner, emotional scar, like a zipper from head to toe, concealing all the new insecurities and fears that have arisen from the moment the doctor said *mitral valve prolapse* and *silent killer.*

I've looked in the mirror so many times since, studying my eyes, my mouth, for any change that proves I'm an entirely different person. Even if I can't see it, it's there. Marko saw it, and seeing the change in his expression, how his eyes looked at me in a different light, I felt it. New Talia made an appearance before the surgery, with her sudden anxiety attacks over every little thing, her short temper, her frenetic behavior to stay on top of to-do lists, and her constant worries of *what-ifs.*

I've been trying to unload that New Talia since I left the hospital, but she's a hard bitch to shake.

New Talia is intent on being a workaholic, on exercising dutifully, on watching over her mother and sister like a caretaker, and on living each day with as little emotion as possible. Living joylessly for the sake of surviving life. But it's impossible to live like that and not be emotional, because I remember how much life I had inside of me, even when our family was at its lowest point. I believed in the power of my youth and my desire for more in life, my yearning to love someone and to be loved, and it terrifies me that there's a part of me trying to prevent me from having that again.

This New Talia thinks she's protecting me, but she's wrong. She's wrong about so many things, and I see that now. The thought that I could always be empty and alone is unacceptable. Letting myself go, to fall recklessly into bed with Peyton, was the first step in defying New Talia. She's in my head all the time.

He could be just like your father—all charm, all talk, seducing you with sex because there's nothing more. Marko was right. You could pass this on to your children. How selfish of you.

Yes, she is right about Peyton, and she's correct about my genetic disorder, but is it selfish if I choose to find love and choose not to have a family to spare anyone heartbreak, both literally and figuratively? I shouldn't have to live like a nun. I can make sacrifices and hold out hope that I can find love, find a man who will tell me, *you're enough, you're all I need.*

I kick New Talia out of my head and grab Peyton's elbow. "Time to refill our trays."

"Hey, you're getting a little frisky there," Peyton says, then quickly turns his attention to a woman eating a leek and goat cheese puff with amorous delight. "Puff Girl, I'll bring you some more of those."

The woman noshes and nods enthusiastically. It makes me smile.

"See? I'm doing an awesome job out there, selling your goods," he says as we make our way back to the kitchen.

"You're not selling anything. You're giving away my food."

"I'm selling sex—sexy, bite-sized food on sticks and in shot glasses. You sell sexy food, sunflower."

"I've never thought of it like that." I pause for a moment to consider a new business name. Sexy Food Catering. It's better than T & A Services, but still a disaster. "Anyway, it's time to get ready for the real deal here. We make one more round with appetizers, and then we let everyone get a little hungry while I get the main courses ready. Think you can help do a little prep work for me?"

"Give me those knives. I don't want to brag, but you're going to be so fucking impressed."

"You're not modest at all." I laugh. "You're going to be chopping—nothing exciting."

I'm wrong. Absolutely wrong. Watching Peyton chop and slice vegetables is a performance that deserves its own soundtrack. And then someone puts the Bee Gees on the sound system and cranks up "Night Fever" and everyone starts dancing.

Peyton and I get caught up in the music blasting through the kitchen speakers, dancing alongside one another while he handles the knives as part of his routine. He's fast but graceful and so sexy, coordinating his movements to the beat of the music. I mouth the words of the song as I sear the chicken breasts and the steaks. We're having our own private party in the kitchen, and the fun disco music makes it easy to cook together.

Marko couldn't make a ham sandwich. The women in his family waited on the men—

I have to stop the comparisons, but Peyton is surprising me again. He likes cooking with me. And for me, watching him prep and cook as my personal sous chef, while moving in perfect time to the dance beat, is *hot!*

After a few more dances, it's time to corral the guests for dinner, the main event.

"I'll finish the salad plates. Will you tell the guests they can make their way to the dining room?" I ask. "And can you do it without making it look like you're luring them to an orgy?"

"I think I can handle it. Pretty sure they'll do what I say."

"I think so, too. Shake your ass, and they'll pay attention."

"I don't shake anything."

"You have a certain way you *walk*. It's very sexy. At least for my business." I say this very businesslike as I arrange the last of the appetizers on a silver tray.

"I'm glad you think so." He swats my butt, and I jump, hoping no one noticed us. "I'm seriously ready for tonight."

He takes my hand, holding a leftover puff I planned on eating, and guides it to his mouth. He bites into it while staring at me. That sweet, familiar stirring in my belly and below begins to whirl and spin between my thighs. I can't take my eyes off him as he finishes off the delicate puff. He then places my empty hand against the front of his crotch so I can feel his erection. Our clandestine groping makes me wet.

We are safely hidden from the party by some well-placed, modern, concrete columns between the living room and kitchen, but even if we weren't, I need to kiss Peyton. I keep one hand on his crotch, stroking him ever so slightly while I wrap my other hand around his neck. I pull him in for a kiss, tasting and stroking with my tongue. An aggression is building in me as the kiss goes deeper. His breaths become ragged, and then he grips my backside.

Someone accidentally hits the volume control and the music screeches through all the speakers. We pull away from each other at the same time.

Is he thinking the same thing I am? Wondering if we're beginning to feel a stronger attachment to one another?

Of course he isn't. He's thinking about banging you up against the deluxe Sub-Zero fridge.

I hate New Talia.

I remove my hands, and he straightens up to his full, towering height. There's an extra beat of staring at each other, and then I have to step back farther from him. He's too enticing.

"Let's get that table set up." Peyton is disturbingly cool, as though the kiss left no lasting impression on him.

I nod, willing my professional side to be stronger than my horny one.

He successfully wrangles the guests to the dining table without incident, then rejoins me in the kitchen, where we move in tandem, working the ovens and pans with very little conversation needed.

He's behaving oddly now, and it's not my imagination. He walked into the party with gusto and good cheer and worked the crowd comfortably with his usual wit, and now it's gone.

Marguerite enters the kitchen and tells Peyton she'll serve the dinner with me. She mentions that he's too tall, and too distracting, which isn't fair to the host.

I expect Peyton to laugh, as I do, but he doesn't argue. He assigns himself to keeping the kitchen clean and orderly. Something is occupying his brain. Something struck him hard. Was it triggered by our kiss?

The dinner service is effortless. Marguerite handles the end of the table where Adam is sitting, and I serve the other half. The conversations are lively, and Adam is clearly in his element as the powerful CEO who is both entertaining and witty. He's extra polite to Marguerite and gives her his full attention when she passes by with dishes and drinks. He pays attention to everyone.

It's the long, hard looks Adam gives me that throw me off a bit.

The man is confusing me. Either he likes to always have the attention of the women around him merely because it's what he's used to, or he's interested in me and working on it as *slowly* as possible. I'm not sure why. If Adam has any interest, why is Peyton taking up so much real estate in my head?

I do what I have to do in the dining room and return to the kitchen as often as possible with dirty dishes to line up in the dishwashing queue or to retrieve new items. Peyton has his back to me, standing at the kitchen sink, doing the dishes while gazing out the window at the pastoral views visible under the full moonlight. He should be running his big, busy restaurant. Instead, he looms over the sink, cleaning my knives with care, his bare hands rinsing them in the hot water as he inspects each blade. I appreciate that about him. Nothing is beneath him. He worked his way up in the restaurant business, and as a manager, he's willing to do any lowly task.

Something is still on his mind, though. He's dwelling on it intensely as he scrubs the dishes until they are spotless, so I think better of interrupting his thoughts and give him his space.

Once the dessert dishes have been cleared and Adam and his guests are back in the grand living room, having coffee or port, depending on if they're driving, the discussion turns to who will use Adam's guest rooms and who is staying at the nearby Mohonk resort hotel in New Paltz. Naturally, these people are all from Manhattan, so they won't be driving back tonight, which is already early morning.

Marguerite and I pack leftovers and store them in Adam's refrigerator while Peyton loads all the clean dishes into their crates and carries them to the van. I've watched men I've worked with do this a million times, and it's never turned me on the way it does when Peyton handles them, showing off his physical strength. Even with the extra weight of multiple racks in his hands, he walks with a macho swagger. I can't get enough of it. Of *him*.

I do one last sweep of the living room to top off coffee cups, then turn down the lights in the kitchen. Then I give a quick wave to Adam as I slip out the front door. There are enough people surrounding him, including Chloe, to keep him trapped so I can escape a situation I can't interpret.

The cool, fresh mountain air hits me as I walk to the van. The smell of pine and something floral is uplifting.

Peyton closes the van's back doors and says goodbye to Marguerite as she drives off in her orange VW Bug that her father restored for her. A pang of envy strikes.

"My father would never think of leaving me with something practical like a decent car," I say, watching Marguerite's rear lights fade away.

"Really?" Peyton asks in a stern tone. "Does Marguerite play the piano like Scott Joplin or Beethoven?"

"You've never heard me play, really. How do you know I can play like Beethoven? He was a genius."

"While I was cleaning up, I texted your sister with a *Where the fuck did your sister learn the piano?* She's drunk, by the way, out with people who are corrupting her—Imogene. The point is, she sent me a series of texts, very detailed, about you and your dad and all those piano lessons. And how you used to perform."

"That was a long time ago. And I performed at school. I wasn't Carnegie Hall caliber."

"The point is he left you a legacy. It's better than a car. He brought out your natural talent and nurtured it."

"I don't know why you're angry at me, but if you want, we can skip tonight."

"I'm not angry at you." His tone softens. "We'll unload this stuff at Swill, and then we're going to my place."

He waits for me to get in the van and start the engine before he gets in his truck and leads the way back to Swill. The restaurant is dark and closed up for the night.

Peyton takes me by the hand and sits me at the bar with a chilled bottle of mineral water. Then he carries every crate and piece of equipment into the kitchen, not letting me lift a finger. After everything has been removed from the van, I enter the kitchen.

"I can help," I say, but Peyton is already organizing the dish crates and my pans on the shelving Bash designated for my supplies.

"I got it. I want to move some things down to the lower shelves so they're easier for you to reach. Go relax at the bar. This won't take long."

I return to my lonely seat. The dining hall is dark and ominous without people.

I jump off my stool when the door behind the bar opens, displaying a shadowy figure.

"Talia, what are you doing here?" Bash asks, stepping into the dim light from the bar mirror.

I put my hand on my chest and laugh. "God, you scared me. We brought my supplies back. Peyton's in the kitchen, messing with my stuff, and he ordered me to sit out here."

"Ah ..." Bash says with a smile.

Out of his chef's clothing, he's downright cute. Rugged and muscled in jeans and a T-shirt. A tattoo runs from the back of his neck and creeps down his arm in a spiral. I wonder if it's a snake or something Native American, but I decide not to ask. It's usually covered by his chef jacket, so it seems like something personal.

He scratches his buzz cut and chuckles. "You two have been pretty cozy lately. I was going to ask Peyton why he bolted out of here earlier after Harmony showed up, but now it makes sense. He wanted to see you."

"Harmony?" Peyton didn't mention anyone named Harmony.

"She's an old friend from high school. I guess she heard about Swill and wanted to stop by and say hi."

"Oh, well, Peyton ... and me ... it's not like that. He came to help me since I was short-staffed."

Bash fills a glass with water and drinks it all in a few gulps. He wipes his mouth with the back of his hand. "He likes you. He's been acting different. In a good way. You like him. Right?"

I do like Peyton, very much. I like everything about him, except his blind ambition. "We've become friends."

Bash chuckles again. "Oh, really? That's what you're calling it? The guy flew out of here on our busiest night to help you. I can tell you two have a thing for each other. You don't have to pretend."

"It's nothing serious."

When Peyton enters the dining room and walks over to join us, my gaze follows him the entire way.

I hear Bash snort a laugh.

"How did tonight go?" Peyton asks him.

"Good. Greer is really great at bossing people around. She enjoys it." Bash puts down his glass and looks at me, then Peyton. "How did it go with you two at the dinner party?"

Peyton smiles. "I thoroughly enjoyed myself."

"He was a little obnoxious," I add.

"Not surprised," Bash says.

"Ready to go?" Peyton asks, putting his hand on the back of my neck. He couldn't be more transparent. I thought I made it very clear there would be no public displays of affection.

This is no time to complain. You want sex.

Sex with Peyton.

I stand up. "Goodnight," I say to Bash without making eye contact.

"Have a good night, guys," Bash says without any hint of teasing.

Outside, Peyton opens the door to my van.

"Sometimes you're such a gentleman."

"Sometimes? I'm sorry. I'll step up my game." He seems distracted.

I reach up and rest my palm against his cheek, feeling the ever-present two-day-old beard, the sexy scruff. His gray eyes search my face for a moment before he leans down and kisses me. His lips are soft but demanding, and I let him in. I wish all the women at Adam's party could see how Peyton kisses me.

He chose me.

And then I feel silly for thinking that I've been singled out when it's already been established that we're having a short-term fling. I wish the kiss would change him and make him realize he's already successful and that he could live in Hera and still expand his restaurant business.

I send Aleska a text so she will tell our mother that I'm not coming home tonight. Easier to have Aleska do it. We're past the point of making up lies about my whereabouts. Aleska will say I'm with Peyton, and my mother will be fine with that, knowing I'm safe. *And because sometimes you just need a man's hands all over you.* No one needs to hear that from their mother.

Aleska: *Have fun with Peyton!*

I follow Peyton to his home and park next to him. He opens my door and eagerly pulls me out by the hand.

"Hold on," I say with a laugh.

"I've been holding on all night. I served tiny bites of food to women and men tonight, watching them plot on who's going to jump who later. All I wanted to do was take the hot chef upstairs to one of the guest bedrooms. *Knight,*" he bites down on the name, "was scoping you out all night."

"He was not. He had a date. A very beautiful date. She's smart, successful, and hot."

"He's not into her," Peyton says, leading me into his dark house.

"She hung on his arm all night. They sat next to each other at dinner. He talked to her more than anyone else."

"She's an important business contact. He respects her, and maybe they're friends, but he's not interested in her, not even for a quickie."

"How did you get all that? I didn't see that at all."

Peyton flicks on the hall light and leads me down to his bedroom. "I'm a guy. I can tell Knight isn't the type to compromise his business relationship with a colleague or investor. Besides, it was clear there was no chemistry between them."

"They talked all night. From the beginning of the party to the end."

In his bedroom, Peyton slams the door shut and pushes me onto the bed. "They were talking about books and politics, and he was looking at you."

"Oh," I say softly.

Peyton positions himself on top of me with his weight on his arms and his legs between mine. His body heat and hardness positioned between my thighs send an electric shock through me, a tingling buzz that makes my skin hypersensitive to his touch. My nipples harden, and I want to rip my own clothes off.

"*Oh* is right. Your little plan of snagging a responsible, stable guy may be working," he says with a hint of disdain.

He's going to kill the mood.

"I don't have a plan. I told you about my concerns because you and I started off as friends. And friends share, right? Oh no, are we becoming more than friends?" I joke, but I'm actually probing for a serious response.

"I like you." His face is inches from mine.

I weave my fingers into his hair, but before I can say more, he muzzles me with a kiss. It's tender, and he takes his time. Everything that felt urgent moments ago slows down, as if we're testing our own willpower to keep this sensual kiss from exploding.

His lips on the sensitive part of my neck make my skin tingle, and soon all I want is to kiss him and know what it's like to run my lips all over his body.

The arrogant, aggressive Peyton I'm used to claims my mouth gently but firmly. The way his tongue slowly navigates around my lips sets off moans I don't bother trying to contain. I kiss him back, seeking more with both the kiss and my hands. Without breaking our kiss, all clothing is removed until it's just skin against skin. I've never had this much pleasure from kissing any man.

I run my hands up and down the hard planes of his back and seek out any part of his skin I can reach. His hard cock is rubbing up and down between our bodies, so I reach for it. When I envelop his thick erection, Peyton moans into my mouth, low and guttural. I want to fill his need, to satisfy him until our hunger stops feeling like an addiction and my heart stops racing.

I break the kiss and push his chest hard so he flips onto his back. Then I straddle him as he looks up at me with wonder, panting.

My nipples are hard and my breasts feel heavy. He runs his palms over them and pinches the tight peaks, causing little tremors of pleasure in my body. I have his cock in my hand, and I want to put him inside of me to feed the tremors, but I also want to give him his gratification first. I slide down his body, greet his cock with my mouth, and stroke his balls at the same time.

"Jesus," he groans, arching upward.

I take in as much of him as I can, sucking, licking, and stroking with my tongue, applying pressure until he moans repeatedly. His hands get tangled in my hair as he pushes himself against my mouth, jutting his hips upward. He's almost thrashing, close to coming.

"Talia," he rasps. "Get up. I'm going to come."

"I can finish you off," I say, stroking him as my tongue plays across the tip of his cock.

"No, I want to be inside you." His eyelids are half-closed as he watches me pump him slowly with my hand.

With my tongue, I probe the slit in the engorged head of his impressive cock, so thick and long as it stands straight up. Peyton is about to lose control, and my body is aching for him.

I reach for a foil packet on the nightstand and quickly roll one onto his heavy length. Then I sit up on my knees and grab the headboard with one hand, using the other to guide his cock into me. I'm so wet and aroused that it's effortless. I slide my body onto him and slam down hard until he fills me completely.

"Yes," he hisses, gripping both of my butt cheeks as I begin to thrust against him.

Up and down on my knees, I've lost the tempo. It's just out-of-control fucking at this point. I need both hands on the headboard to keep steady and upright as I gyrate my hips.

I listen to Peyton groan with approval and feel like I'm about to lose my mind. His body stiffens, and the veins in his neck and chest stand out when he's on the verge of coming, so I touch myself, two fingers on either side of his cock that slide against my sensitive folds and clit. He watches me, and as I increase the tempo for my own pleasure, Peyton comes. He comes hard, his cock erect long enough for me to build up to my own sweet, delirious orgasm.

I use the headboard again for support to grind against him and wring out every last ounce of ecstasy. A shudder vibrates through my whole body when the orgasm subsides.

"Jesus," Peyton says breathlessly with his hands on my thighs. He's still fully erect. His cock is just as hard as when we started, and I'm still aroused, completely turned on and wanting more.

I take his hands and slide them up to my breasts. He begins to massage them, rubbing my nipples. Then I drop my hands to his chest where I brace myself and begin another slow dance on his hard cock. I close my eyes and thrust against him, enjoying the sensation. Soon, I feel him slip his finger into me and rub my clit to another exquisite buildup. I yell out when it explodes into another orgasm, shattering my ability to stay upright. Peyton catches me and rolls on his side with me in his arms.

I'm perfectly comfortable in his bed and ready to sleep when I feel Peyton kiss my cheek. Then the bed sags as I feel his weight shifting to the side. *Is he leaving me already?* I think dreamily, then remember it's his home. Where would he go? Sleep is pulling at me. My limbs are sore from working on my feet all day and night. But the cold emptiness filling the space next to me is stronger.

Pushing away the urge to give in to my fatigue, I open my eyes to find the hulking, dark form of Peyton on the other side of the bed. His broad back is to me, head hanging down. I reach out to touch him, but the space between us is too far, so I scoot over, dragging all the tangled sheets with me.

"Peyton." I caress his lower back. "What are you doing?"

His breathing is barely audible.

"Peyton?"

He takes a breath and exhales. "When I found out, there was only one person who came to mind," he says with his back still to me. "One person I had to tell. That's why I went to Adam's house. To tell you."

"Tell me what?" I place my hand flat against the middle of his back.

"I have a son." He turns around, but even with the moonlight coming through the window, he's nothing but a shadow.

"A son?"

He climbs into bed next to me and pulls up the sheets to cover us both. His eyes meet mine, and I recognize that look when you wonder if the person you're with is going to be repelled by your new information. It happened with Marko.

This is the moment, Peyton's way of answering my earlier question of whether or not we've become more than friends. But now I know unequivocally that the answer is *yes*.

He moves his face closer to mine, and I can make out all the details in his features—the sculpted edges roughened with unshaven scruff, the gray eyes that contrast with his dark hair and sharp brows so they sometimes shimmer like silver. I've spent enough time admiring his face when he's not looking. His beauty aside, I see him clearly, and even if it hasn't been spoken, there is affection for me in his eyes.

"Tell me everything," I say, imagining a baby or toddler version of Peyton, perhaps somewhere in Brooklyn.

"A friend from high school came by the restaurant this afternoon. We never went out; she was never a girlfriend. We hooked up one night after a party, though. She got pregnant." He sighs and closes his eyes for a moment.

"You've been a father all these years? Why haven't I ever seen your son? When do you see him?"

"No, you don't understand. I found out today. He's nine years old."

"How did you not know about him?"

"When Harmony—she's the mother—when she found out she was pregnant, she didn't tell me, or anyone ... that I know of. From what she told me today, it was her dad's decision. He didn't want me involved, so he basically held it over her head. He was very wealthy and could give her and the baby everything they needed."

"Except a dad," I say, angry on Peyton's behalf.

"I think her dad was willing to take that risk to prevent his daughter and grandson from something worse, like me—a teenage husband and father. Not that we would have gotten married. They moved to Seattle and I never heard from her again. Until today. Her father passed away recently, and she moved to the area. Westchester, actually. She came to see me, expressly in the interest of ... of my kid. So he can meet me and have a father."

"That's good." I kiss him on the mouth.

He looks stunned, at the news of his son, not from my kiss.

I kiss him again. "It's good, Peyton," I say with a shaky smile.

He chuckles nervously. "Jesus. I'm trying to wrap my head around this. I'm trying to remember every detail ... if I had any inkling that she was pregnant. I was another self-absorbed, seventeen-year-old kid who was in the middle of college tours. I didn't know a one-time hookup turned into a baby. God, I have a nine-year-old."

I pop my eyes wide with a smile, trying to lighten the mood.

He smiles for real this time. "His name is Finn."

It's heartbreaking to see his face when he says his son's name, but this also means I got ahead of myself thinking our friendship could blossom into more. Another woman has come back into Peyton's life, and she's the mother of his child. She and Peyton may have a second chance.

"Finn is a lovely name."

"Harmony is bringing him to the restaurant tomorrow—today—to meet me."

"It's exciting." I try to sound enthusiastic, but in truth, I feel like I'm losing my already precarious footing in Peyton's world.

"I think Harmony chose the restaurant because it's a neutral location—not her home, not my home. But I would like you to be there. They're coming by at ten this morning. The staff won't be in yet, but I told them we could have breakfast."

"You want me to cook breakfast for all of you?" I perk up, considering I may have a role here—to help Peyton.

"No, I don't want you to cook. I'll make some eggs and toast or something. I want you to meet Finn. And Harmony."

"Oh. Good. Yes," I say.

"Bash will be there, setting up the kitchen. I haven't told him yet. And I'm going to call Greer and ask her to be there, too."

"This is good."

He doesn't notice how deflated I sound. I got my hopes up, thinking I'm special to Peyton and he wants me to meet his son. It turns out I only made the short list of friends and family to be present on this special occasion.

"My family is so big that I think I'll have to introduce Finn to everyone else at a later date. I mean, I haven't even met him yet. What if he can't stand me?"

"You're crazy," I say with a laugh. "You're a dream father. You're energetic, and smart, and fun, but more importantly, you're good at taking care of people. He might be intimidated by you at first, but he's going to see you for who you truly are, and he's going to fall in love with you."

Peyton is about to say something but then closes his mouth and stares at me. I feel a blush warm my face. Before I accidentally reveal more of my affection for him, I throw back the covers and jump out of bed. "Let's get ready for your big day!"

"It's four. Middle of the night for us. What are you doing?" Peyton asks as I rummage in the dark for my clothes. "Talia, get back in this bed."

"I should really go home, get some rest, get cleaned up for this big event ..." I ramble it off like a grocery list.

"Hey." Peyton's voice is low and soothing again. He's out of bed and wrapping his naked body around me from behind. "I don't want you to leave. I just told you the biggest news of my life. I want you to stay here with me tonight. In the morning, you can drive back to your place and change clothes if you want, and then we can meet at Swill before Finn arrives."

I turn around in his arms and rest my hands on his narrow waist. His cock is hard and pressing against my belly, so it's fair to say this news hasn't dampened the mood or lowered his libido.

"Think about it. Does Harmony really need to meet me today? You're going to introduce me to them as your friend? Your buddy? I'm your best buddy like Bash?"

"No, you're not like Bash. Harmony knows Bash from high school, and she knows Greer, even though my sister graduated a few years ahead."

"Right, it's a reunion for all of you. So if I'm not there as the cook, how are you going to introduce me? Harmony does not want to be introduced to the woman you're sleeping with, and she definitely doesn't want her son to meet the woman you're sleeping with. You haven't thought it through. This is not how you want to start off your relationship with your son. I'll stay home and meet him later like everyone else."

"You're not exactly like everyone else." He sweeps his hand down my naked back, and his erection twitches against my belly. "Fine. You can be the cook. Pretend you're there to check on your supplies or orders for the week—whatever. It's natural that both you and Bash are in the kitchen, and then I'll ask you to come out and meet Finn. And Harmony."

"This is about you and Finn. Don't complicate it by having me there."

"I want you there," he says in a gritty, demanding tone.

"Why?"

"Because I'm nervous. I'm nervous to meet my own kid, and it would help me to have you there."

I hug him and kiss his chest. "If you think it will help you, I'll be there. Thank you for asking me."

He nuzzles my head, then pats my ass. "Get back in the bed. I'm going to ask you to do something else for me."

I laugh and push away from him. He blocks my escape and pushes me back onto the bed.

"Oh, really? And what do you want me to do?" I press my foot up against his chest. The light of dawn is streaming through the windows, so I can see that sinister gleam in his eyes. My pulse races as I anticipate being taken over by him.

He grabs one of my thighs and flings it across my body so I land on my stomach. I'm waiting for that thrilling sensation of *having a man's hands all over me*. This man's hands and everything else he will offer.

"On your knees," he says gruffly. "And hold on to the headboard."

20

Peyton

B Y THE TIME TALIA arrives at Swill, I'm a wreck. She immediately goes to the kitchen and begins preparing breakfast dishes. I fill Bash in on what's about to occur and, without a word, other than "man, oh man," he goes into the kitchen to help Talia.

I pace the restaurant, then walk behind the bar and pour some seltzer, take a few gulps, and then pace some more.

Greer comes storming through the main doors, looking disheveled. "Where is he?" she barks, looking around the empty restaurant.

"He's not supposed to arrive for another twenty minutes or so. How did you get here so fast? I called you five minutes ago and you were still in bed." My sister looks like her kids dressed her. She's clomping across the concrete floor in UGGs and only half her hair made it into the ponytail holder. She looks wild-eyed and exhausted.

"I called the sitter and promised her double the money to come in early." She stops abruptly and tosses her bag onto the bar. "I got here as fast as I could."

"You look worse than me. You could have taken your time—"

"I didn't want to miss him! My God, Peyton, this is huge!" My sister is practically hysterical.

"Do you think you can calm down before Harmony and Finn get here?"

"I'm that bad?" She looks down at her clothes, then tucks her shirt into her jeans.

"Are you wearing your nightgown?"

She hesitates, then nods. "I'm going to go see what clothes I have in my locker in back. And maybe wash my face."

"You do that." I rub her back. "Take your time."

A few minutes later, when I see Harmony's car through the front windows, I take a deep breath and walk to the entrance. I pull open the large doors and stand there, dumbstruck, watching Harmony and ... my son get out of the car.

As he walks toward me, with Harmony following, I take in his skinny limbs, his shoulder-length hair that is straight like mine, and his dark complexion from his mother. He's a blend of his Scottish and African American ancestry. I'm awestruck, stunned that this small person is somehow a part of me.

With his big brown eyes, he looks up at me with an innocent curiosity. I don't see resentment swimming behind his dark pupils. If anything, he seems delighted.

"I'm Peyton." I smile and step forward to shake his hand. I want to grab him and pull him in for a big bear hug, but I don't think I've earned that right yet.

"Yeah, I figured." He laughs. "I'm Finn."

We shake, and I squeeze his hand extra hard. I don't know what I should do in this situation.

Harmony and I exchange a polite embrace while Finn watches us.

"Come in," I say. "We can eat and get to know each other." I smile again, and it's somewhat painful, a frozen smile on the verge of tears.

I'm not a person who cries, not even at funerals, but this person standing before me is my child, and it's like seeing a new kind of wonderful beauty for the very first time. I wish my mother were here to see this, to meet him, to see me as I am now.

Logistics aside, Harmony and I have created a human being, and it's all because I was a reckless teenager who couldn't use a condom properly. I want to laugh at my stupid, good fortune. As a teenager, this scenario scared the shit out of me. As an adult, it seems Finn is the product of dumb luck, and I can't complain about winning the lottery.

Finn is wearing a Knicks T-shirt, jeans, and weathered Converse high-tops. He walks with an easy gait, and it's like watching myself from my father's old videos of us.

I notice Finn size me up, too, notating any physical attributes we may share.

We sit at a table in the deserted restaurant, and Talia and Bash approach us with pitchers of orange juice and water. I fumble with the glasses, and Talia takes them from me, pouring the pitchers around the table.

"Talia and Bash are both chefs," I announce without going into the specifics of Talia's business and her use of our kitchen.

Harmony is gracious and nods approvingly, as though I'm presenting exciting information. Finn listens but continues drinking his orange juice.

"It's good to see you, Bash," Harmony says. "It's been a long time."

"I didn't think you'd remember me."

"You look exactly the same. I'm not surprised you went into business with Peyton. You two were inseparable."

Talia silently sets the table with cloth napkins and silverware, while Bash fills Harmony in about the evolution of our business partnership. I notice Talia sneak a long look at Finn, and I really want to know what she's thinking at that moment. Then she retreats to the kitchen, and Bash soon follows.

"So, this is what I do," I tell Finn. "It doesn't look like much when it's empty, but it gets very busy at night. And we have a nice bar and grill in our old Brooklyn neighborhood where your mom and I grew up, and I also have a showy restaurant in Manhattan."

This is boring stuff to a nine-year-old, but Finn humors me with a "cool."

"Hey, Finn," my sister says as she sneaks her way into the dining hall. She's changed into clean work clothes and fixed her hair, but she walks toward us like she's tiptoeing on nails. "I'm Greer."

"My sister," I explain.

"My aunt," Finn clarifies. "Mom made a family tree for me."

Greer approaches and stares at him with a smile that's a cross between a scary grin and someone holding their mouth open for a dental procedure.

"Greer," I prompt. She's going to creep the kid out.

"I'm sorry, but I can't stop staring. You have Peyton's face ..." She starts to get emotional. I put my hand on her arm to calm her. God, I hope she doesn't start crying.

"We're just getting to know each other right now." I want my sister to take the hint that I need this time alone with Finn and Harmony.

"Of course! I'm going to go back to the office and get some work done. Leave you all alone to discuss ..." Greer's nervousness is making me anxious again.

"It's nice to see you again, Greer," Harmony says.

"Oh, you, too, Harmony. I didn't get a chance to talk with you yesterday. You look great, and *this* ... bringing Finn here ... it's so exciting."

Harmony's smallest of smiles is unreadable. She's probably dreading all the questions that will come from my family. I'll have to make sure to head them off so Harmony doesn't feel like she's being interrogated.

"Our family is going to be so thrilled to meet you," Greer says to Finn.

"Come back out before we leave," Harmony tells her. "We can make some arrangements so Finn can meet the relatives."

"Yes! I'm going to be right down the hall." She points and begins to slowly walk toward the kitchen. I can tell it's killing her not to be able to sit down with us.

"So, how do you like your new home and school? Are you settling in and making friends?" I ask.

"It's okay. I miss my friends in Seattle, but there's one kid I'm friends with at my new school. Albert. He's pretty cool. For a geek, that is."

"Albert? There's a name you don't hear anymore."

"He's smart, and we're in math club together."

"Math club?"

"Finn is very bright," Harmony says.

"I do well in every subject," Finn adds.

"He's a straight A student." Harmony beams proudly at Finn. "His favorite subjects are math and science."

"Wow, good for you. I was lousy in math and science. You got the smarts from your mom."

Finn grins. It's my face grinning back at me. The kid got the killer MacKenzie smile, the one that wins people over. I'm so relieved he got his mother's brain power.

"I think you two should spend some time alone to get to know one another," Harmony says suddenly, then stands up.

"Fine with me." Finn doesn't seem surprised, so they must have planned this.

I open my mouth to protest that maybe we shouldn't be left alone because I don't know how to entertain this kid. I don't know how I'm supposed to behave with my own son.

Harmony points over her shoulder. "I brought my workout clothes and thought I'd head over to that yoga studio down the street. And then I thought I'd grab a bite at the diner. This way you guys can have an uninterrupted hour or so together without me acting as a translator."

"Sounds good, Mom." Finn reaches for his orange juice and downs it in one gulp.

Harmony's expression softens, and behind Finn's back she mouths the words, "*You'll be fine.*"

As Harmony leaves, Talia returns with one of the large trays propped above her shoulder. She swings it down to reveal a smorgasbord of food that any growing teenage boy would love.

"We made a little of everything, but don't feel you have to eat it all. These are crème brûlée waffles," she says, putting the first plate in the middle of the table. "These are breakfast burritos. They have scrambled eggs and a spicy potato hash inside. Bash says that he and Peyton lived on these when they were growing up."

"Wow." Finn looks at me, smiling and wide-eyed.

"Sticky buns," Talia continues. "Because it's my mother's recipe, and Bash insists everyone loves these gooey things. And these are mini spinach quiches, because you need something green." Talia finishes putting more plates down until Finn and I have more than half a dozen, very rich dishes taking up most of the table.

"This is awesome," he says.

"Yeah, knock yourself out," I say.

Talia puts the large tray under her arm and turns to leave.

"Hey, Talia. Thank you."

"I hope you enjoy it, Finn," she says, glancing at me briefly, then turning all her attention on the boy who is eating a waffle with his hands.

"Really good," he says between bites.

"Shout if you need anything," she says, then leaves.

"Do you eat like this all the time?" he asks.

"No. Talia doesn't actually work for me. She's a private chef for a bunch of rich people in the area. She's using our kitchen because hers was destroyed in a fire. Bash is the chef here, and he's really good, too. He keeps me fed most of the time. Try the grilled sausages." I pass him the plate.

"So, you've got it made." He bites into a sausage, holding it with his fingers again. Another male MacKenzie trait. "You're a big-shot restaurant owner, and you're rich."

"Wait. Is that what your mother said?"

"She said you have three restaurants and that you're doing well."

"That's true, but I'm not rich. I share ownership with other investors. I'm certainly paid well to run all three, but I'm not in Bill Gates's income bracket. I'm not even close."

Finn shrugs and continues eating. "But you are the boss, and you get to eat this whenever you want."

I remember being this kid, caring only about doing my own thing, being my own boss someday, and of course, food. Boys are always hungry.

"I guess so. There's more to my job than that. I have to research an idea and a location before we can open a restaurant. It's about building an environment and a menu that people will want ... We can talk about that another time." I sense he's too young to care about market niche and food trends. "So, you're nine. What are nine-year-olds into these days?"

"I'm almost ten. I'm nine years, six months, and two days."

"Ah, yes, well, we refer to that as nine. Enjoy it while you have it. Don't be in a rush to grow up."

Jesus Christ, I sound like my father.

"So, what do you do for fun?" I ask, now sounding like my deceased grandfather.

"I create computer games. I'm good at coding, and my new school is letting me teach a coding class in the afternoons."

"You're kidding? You're teaching?" I'm astonished he's so advanced, but secretly proud he's an excellent student like Harmony.

"Yeah. The school wanted to call it *Coding for Fun*, but that's lame, so I told them to call it *Gaming for Hotshots* because then kids would show up thinking they're going to play games for two hours. They do play, but first I teach them how to write code, and they have to create their own games before they can play. I kind of tricked them into learning how to code, but it worked. The class is full. The teacher assists me, but I run the class. I'm like the boss."

"Brilliant. So you're a genius like your mom."

He shrugs and keeps chowing, having moved on to the breakfast burritos. "I'm also pretty good on the skateboard. I like basketball, but I never get chosen in pickup games. I'm not very good."

"I am." I brighten up. Finally, something I can show off. "I played in high school. I can teach you a few things. I mean, if that's something you'd like to do with me. My brother works across the street at the furniture company, and they have a hoop set up in back. There's no regulation court, but we could practice shooting a few hoops there."

Finn's head perks up. "I'd like that. Can you make me taller, too?" He laughs, not at all nervous about meeting me, it seems.

"Don't worry; you're going to have a growth spurt. Your mother is tall, and I'm tall enough."

"Six seven?" He pauses eating and looks up at me with those big brown eyes.

Ah, the hopeful ignorance of youth.

"Not quite." I laugh. "But tall men and women run in our family. You'll meet them soon." I pause too long, and Finn's eyes narrow.

I've been talking to him like I'm his old pal instead of the father who wasn't there for his birth, his first steps, his first words, his first day at school, and every day after that.

"What's wrong?" he asks.

"I'm not sure what Harmony—I mean, your mother—has told you about me. I just found out about you yesterday, and I haven't told my family yet because I wanted this moment with you alone so I could meet you first."

Finn looks down at his empty plate, then back at me with those sweet, puppy-dog eyes, and I feel like I'm letting him down. But then his mouth quirks into that grin I'm already familiar with. "I understand. Mom told me that she just dumped this on you. She told me the whole story right before we moved here. I looked you up online and thought about contacting you, but Mom made me promise not to. She said she had to do the recon first."

"She said that?" I ask. "A recon mission on me?"

"She wanted to make sure she knew everything about you before she introduced us."

"She wants to protect you. That's what mothers do."

"I thought you looked pretty interesting, and since my grandpa died, I was ready to meet you. Am I what you expected?"

I smile. "Better." This kid is going to make me fucking cry. "Isn't there anything you want to ask me? Like why I wasn't around for the first decade of your life? Do you want to yell at me or something to make you feel better?"

"No. I was really mad at my mom when she said we're moving and that I would have to leave my friends and my school, but then she told me about you. She said you didn't know I existed. I was mad at her for a while about that."

"How long did that last?"

He shrugs. "I don't know. Maybe it was a few hours. Or maybe it was ten minutes. When I was done being angry, I was excited that I have a dad, for real."

I'm relieved that he harbors no ill will toward me. At least not yet.

"It must have been a weird shock. I'm sorry about your grandfather, by the way. I didn't know him well, but it sounds like he was very good to you."

"I miss him. I know he was tough with my mom sometimes—they argued a lot because he was bossy. But he was always nice to me. We had a lot of fun together."

I watch him eat two sticky buns, and then he works his way through more courses. In between bites, he tells me more about growing up in Seattle. He likes to talk and is comfortable enough with me that he carries the whole conversation for the next half hour. He wants me to know everything about him.

"When can I meet my uncles and Grandpa Stu?" Finn asks brightly.

"I think your mom has a say since she manages your schedule, and you don't want to miss math club or something she may have planned."

"I can miss math club for this." His smile breaks me.

If I knew children caused chest pains like this, I'm not sure I ever would have voluntarily chosen to be a father. I hope it's just the circumstances, and I won't spend every day aching over every little thing he does.

"Other than school, I can do any weeknight or the weekend, and Mom won't mind."

"Let's ask her when she gets back from the yoga class."

Bash and Talia make another appearance. Bash must be feeling almost as mystified as I am about me suddenly being a father.

"Thanks for the breakfast," Finn tells them. "That was the best breakfast I have ever had in my whole life."

"Are you sure? In nine years, six months, and two days, this is the best one?" I tease.

Finn laughs. "Yeah, I'm sure."

"Thank you," Bash says, then nudges Talia. "See? Wouldn't you like to be my sous chef?"

She shakes her head.

"Everything all right?" Harmony says, surprising us all. We didn't see or hear the heavy front door open. She must have skipped the diner. Is she having second thoughts about me and had to race back here?

"We were just discussing how Talia should come work for me," Bash replies.

"I thought you were one of the cooks here," Harmony directs at Talia with a little bit of edge to her voice.

"No. I have my own catering business," Talia explains. "Peyton and Bash were kind enough to let me use their kitchen while mine is being repaired."

"Ah," Harmony says flatly. "How is everything going here, Finn?" She writes Talia off, but Talia is clearly watching Harmony.

"Great. Peyton wants me to meet the rest of his family, but he said we need to discuss this with you." Finn glances at me. I wonder if I'll ever earn the title of Dad.

"That sounds nice." Harmony puts her arm around Finn's shoulders, and I suppose it's to put me in my place, to show me she's the parent here.

Greer takes that moment to return to the dining hall. "Harmony," she declares, greeting her with a big sisterly hug. They didn't show any of this love yesterday, but you bring a kid into the picture and my sister turns on the MacKenzie family charm.

Harmony gives her a stiff hug in return.

"Greer and I could arrange a night this week," I say. "At my home, I thought. We'd get my dad and brothers and all the cousins up there so Finn could meet everyone at once."

Greer lights up. "We'll throw a party!"

"I want to go to Peyton's party," Finn says. "Can I?"

"Hold on." Harmony swirls one graceful hand into the stop signal. "First, I thought we should have Peyton come over to our house. Tonight, for dinner, if you can," Harmony says. "I think it would be nice for Finn to have you in our home, and you can get to know us better. And then we can meet the MacKenzies later."

I should have known that I'm sharing the parenting *with* Harmony. I assumed it would be like divorced parents who shuffle their kid between houses and the parents lead separate lives, but it's clear—Harmony said *we*. She's coming to the dinner at my home, and why shouldn't she? She's his mother and has to vet all these people from her past before they can get near her son. But it makes me slightly uncomfortable having this discussion in front of Talia.

The blue-eyed beauty I've become so fond of stands on the sidelines, taking all this in as if she's merely an unimportant bystander. Except she's not. I haven't told her what she means to me. I'm still figuring it out, but I know she's more than a warm body to fill my bed.

She's watching Harmony, a woman who is the mother of my son. I barely know Harmony, but I'll be connected to her forever through Finn.

"This is so exciting," Greer says. She loves family togetherness more than anyone. "Peyton, you go to their house tonight, and I'll cover you here! I'll have Cooper and Imogene watch my kids."

"Finn, it looks like I'm coming to your place tonight. Better clean your room."

"Don't worry; my mom will put me to work. But when can I see your house?"

I turn to Greer. "What's my schedule like this week?"

"Your busiest nights are Wednesday, Friday, and Saturday. The reservations are loaded, and there are private parties those nights. Sunday is your easiest, but that means waiting a week to introduce Finn to the family. No way to that."

"Then why don't you do tomorrow night?" Talia asks. "Mondays are easy for both of you to take off."

"I can manage the front and back of the house for you," Bash adds. "Seriously, you always forget I can cover you and Greer."

"And I'll cater the food," Talia says. "I've refused you as a client before, but Finn is the exception." She laughs, but the joke falls flat for Harmony.

Harmony makes an extra-long study of Talia, measuring her with her invisible standards. She doesn't show indifference, yet neither does she exude any warmth toward Talia's generous offer.

"How's tomorrow night for you, Harmony?" I draw her attention back to me.

"I think it will be fine. I know Finn is anxious to do this sooner rather than later. Why don't you come over tonight at six, and then we make tomorrow night's dinner for the same? It's a school night, so I want to get Finn back home at a reasonable hour."

"Perfect," Talia answers for me. Harmony raises an eyebrow at Talia's forwardness, but Talia doesn't seem to notice. "I'm going to go take care of the grocery list and plan out some nice dishes for all of you. Peyton, why don't you text me later with a head count, or at least an estimate? And, Harmony, if there are any food allergies or food preferences, please let me know. Or tell Peyton, and he'll let me know. I look forward to seeing you again, Finn." She smiles and gives a little wave to Finn, who returns her wave, and then she disappears into the kitchen.

I have to hand it to Talia for handling an uncomfortable situation so well. Then again, maybe it isn't awkward for her if she doesn't consider time spent with me to be a thorny issue. She still has Adam Knight on her short list of contenders, and I'm the fill-in guy. I'd be more upset about this if I weren't dazed with loony happiness over Finn.

"We should get going," Harmony says. "Finn needs to vacuum the house."

"Ha!" Finn exclaims.

"Here." Harmony hands me her business card. On the back she's written their home address and her personal phone number.

I walk them out, and as we cross the empty parking lot toward their car, we see Talia on her bike coming around the back of the restaurant. She keeps that junky thing stashed by the back door, and I'm always tempted to chuck it in the dumpster. The bike frame rattles like a tin can as she navigates across the gravel lot and onto the main road.

"I like her," Finn says.

Harmony seems to peer more closely at Talia in the distance as she steers her bike toward The General Store. Then, in usual form, she hops off the bike, and we watch the bike coast on its own and hit a wooden column in front of the store. Talia walks into the small grocery as her bike clatters to the ground.

I sigh.

We stop at Harmony's car, and it beeps when she unlocks it. I want her to stop watching Talia and judging her. What amuses me, what I find endearing about Talia, makes Harmony grimace.

"What is she doing?" Finn asks, standing at the open car door. The wheels on Talia's bike are still spinning.

"I guess she's going to buy some groceries," I reply.

"Her biking skills could use some work. She's a little reckless," Harmony adds with a sharp snort.

"She needs to learn how to brake," Finn says, his brow furrowed in concern. I feel a little rush of pride for his thoughtfulness.

"I think you're right." I put my hand on his shoulder gently.

"I can teach her," Finn adds.

"That would be nice. She doesn't listen to me."

"Honey, we have to go." Harmony gets in the car, then watches Finn settle himself in his seat and go through the steps of securing his seat belt.

She must have done this a thousand times. The diligence and protectiveness of a parent, hoping they're doing everything to keep their child safe. She's been responding to this need since Finn was a baby, but it's the first time I'm experiencing it. I bend down and tug on Finn's seat belt to make sure it's snug enough.

"It's fine," he says, slightly irritated with me for treating him like a child and slightly amused that I'm already acting like a parent.

"Good. So, then I'll see you both tonight." I smile at Finn, then meet Harmony's eyes. She exhales and relaxes her tight grip on the steering wheel a bit.

I close Finn's door and keep my hand on the open window. It's a terrible sensation, letting your child leave you. I've only been a father for five minutes and already I can't bear to watch this kid drive off.

"See ya tonight," Finn says with a thumbs-up. I realize how lucky I am that he isn't angry at his long-absent father. And it's hard for me to remain angry at Harmony when she presents me with this boy.

"I'm really looking forward to it," I say.

As they drive away, I wonder why my mother didn't tell me about this awful hole you feel in your chest during these potential tear-jerker moments. I've watched my siblings experience the gamut of emotions with kids, the happiness and the worry over any and everything. I didn't expect to be overwhelmed with simultaneous fear and worry, as if someone punched me in the gut, leaving me gasping for air. How do parents live with this?

I want to jog over to the store and pull Talia aside to talk about this, but it's public, something she doesn't want. Instead, I head back into Swill, ready for the onslaught of questions from my sister and everyone else. Undoubtedly, Greer has already alerted every family member, and the phone lines and Internet are burning up as I sneak to my office through the back entrance.

I send Talia a text, asking her to come to my place later tonight. I need to talk to her about Finn.

The rest of the workday is a blur. Somewhere in there I am acting as a restaurant manager, but mostly, I am thinking about my son.

• • •

Harmony has given Finn an almost perfect life. Their home is located in a desirable New York suburb in a bucolic neighborhood of large family homes, beautifully maintained yards, and luxury cars in two- to three-car garages. They are within biking distance from the "best" school, although Harmony informs me that all the parents drive their kids and she still has to do the dreaded car line, reminiscent of her days taking Finn to preschool. I wouldn't know what that's like, of course, but it all sounds like the American dream.

Harmony is much more relaxed in her own home and opts for jeans and bare feet. She prepares a simple dinner of roasted chicken and vegetables, but it's an excellent meal and the conversation is easy because Finn does all the talking as we sit around the formal dining table.

This kid can talk. He covers every topic: his school life, the classes he loves, his old friends, his new friends, movies he loves, movies that are lame, the Knicks because his grandfather made him swear allegiance to them despite Finn being born in Seattle, skateboarding around his new neighborhood, breaking his arm when he was seven and how it made him a rock star in second grade, and how he plans to go into science like his mother.

Harmony and I sit in amused silence as Finn entertains us. This is easy. She and I don't have to talk about the past. We don't have to talk about *us* at all. We get to enjoy our son, and Finn seems pretty thrilled to command the room and to experience what it's like to have both his parents present at the dinner table.

After dessert, we all clear the table. I offer to do dishes, but Harmony insists I spend more time with Finn while she handles the cleanup. So, I get the grand tour of the house. There are photos of Finn at every age adorning walls and shelves in almost every room. The house is opulent yet casual, a symbol of Harmony's wealth along with her goal to put Finn's comfort first. His bedroom is filled with expensive toys and gadgets, the sign of an indulgent parent who has one child and is doing it on her own.

I even get a tour of the garage. Apparently, Finn has taken a great interest in tools and building things, whether it's a science project or woodworking. He has a wall covered with a pegboard where he has started a tool collection. It makes me smile as he talks about each piece that he has acquired through birthday gifts or money he earns working for his mother. Half the board is waiting to be filled. Well, now I know what I can get him for Christmas and every other holiday.

His skateboard collection has its own designated area. Finn explains it's his main means of transportation since the moving crew in Seattle left his bike leaning against the moving truck long enough for someone to swipe it. This makes me think of Talia and her riding her heap of tin around the rough roads of Hera.

I don't want to leave Finn—I could listen to him for hours—but Harmony eventually gives me the signal that we have to call it a night. They both have to get up early for school and work, so I drive back to Hera, exceeding the speed limit because I'm excited to see Talia and because my kid has me floating on clouds.

My mind isn't thinking about daily quotas or closing numbers. I'm thinking about Finn's eyes, the sound of his voice, the way he smelled when he shook my hand goodbye. For a moment there, we were both deliberating if we should try a hug, but then he clasped my hand with both of his and gave it a firm shake. I felt like laughing at how hard he tries to act more grown up than a nine-year-old. Is this because he had to mature quicker due to not having a father around to help him? It triggers shame and regret in me over not being there for him.

But then my mind goes back to the brief moment I'm hoping means nothing. After our goodbyes, Harmony sent Finn upstairs to brush his teeth as she walked me to my truck. The neighborhood was dark and quiet, a peaceful night with the scent of a blossoming spring. It's a safe place for my son.

Harmony seems to glide alongside me, barefoot with a contented, knowing look.

I open my door and lean one arm across the top of the window frame. "Thank you."

She moves closer and gives me a kiss on the cheek, but instead of a peck, she lingers longer, then melds into my body. She hugs me.

I hesitate at first because I'm not used to touching her like this, and Talia immediately comes to mind. My discomfort isn't logical. I should be able to hug her goodbye. She's the mother of my child, and she's letting me into his life. So, I wrap my arms around her and return the hug, the same way you would give a quick embrace to an old friend you haven't seen in a long time. Except, her hug becomes firmer; becomes sexual. She presses her breasts against my chest, and through the thin fabric of my T-shirt, I can tell she's braless as her nipples harden against me. She sweeps one of her hands down my back and rests it on my hip. Her lips are wet as they brush against my cheek before placing a teasing kiss on my lips.

I'm frozen in place, not sure what to do. I want to push her away and hard. The sense of violence I feel is disturbing. I've let other women and their unsolicited hands do more to me when they were merely flirting, but this feels wrong. She feels wrong.

I gently pry her hands off me and step back. "Thank you for inviting me over tonight," I say, hoping I don't come off as a jerk who was leading her on.

The sparkle in her eyes diminishes, but she recovers quickly with that cool, casual expression of hers. "We'll see you tomorrow night." There's no hint of anger, so maybe I imagined her intentions.

As I pull into my own driveway next to Talia's bike lying in its crashed position, I can't help thinking that Harmony's touches and kisses seemed to be more than misdirected friendliness. They were an expression of ownership, a sense of entitlement because she has something I want.

21

Talia

PANTS ON FIRE. THAT'S all I can think of as Peyton comes storming into his house. I'm in his kitchen, preparing a bowl of strawberries and fresh whipped cream, hoping I can play a game of slow seduction with him before he goes all caveman and throws me on the bed.

I'm about to ask how his dinner with Finn went when he holds up his finger to shush me.

"It was a great," he says, not stopping to kiss me hello or talk. He just walks briskly down the hall. "I need a shower! It's been a long day!"

He didn't even notice I'm wearing his robe. I'm naked underneath, and I'm holding a bowl of whipped cream. I'm ready for the Peyton Olympics, and he didn't even notice.

I take the dessert, walk down to his room, and place the bowl on the nightstand. His clothes are lying in a pile next to the bed. He also didn't notice the room is lit only with candles. The bed covers have been gently folded back, and I added extra fluffed pillows to the headboard. Obviously, I staged this for a premium seduction scene, and obviously Peyton missed it. It was stupid to think he'd have anything on his mind other than the child he just discovered.

My foolish insecurity rears its ugly head again.

The bathroom door is ajar, so I push it open and walk into the steaming room. The clear, vinyl shower curtain around the large, vintage clawfoot tub is fogged up. I see Peyton's fuzzy, hulking form as he washes his arms vigorously. I want those arms around me. I missed him.

I knew he was having fun with Finn, and I'm happy for him. The boy is adorable and tender-hearted like his father. I want to tell Peyton that, and I want to tell him that I missed him. Not because I only want sex; I want to be with him.

"Hey!" I fling back the shower curtain and, once again, I have that thing where your tongue is tied or knotted, or whatever that damn expression is.

His hair is slicked back, making his high cheekbones more prominent. His wet body looks like a perfectly molded Greek sculpture from the gallery at the Met Museum. The water is running down his spectacular muscles and solid planes as he raises his arms and washes underneath, making it look like an art form. His body is a piece of art, and my body reacts in kind. A flutter in my stomach and a tingling between my legs. All I can think about is his body between my legs.

"Hey." He grins.

I loosen the belt and let the robe fall to the floor. Peyton's grin disappears as his eyes wander down from my eyes to my breasts.

I run one of my hands across a hard nipple while stroking an inner thigh. I want him, and his cock is already fully erect. I wave a condom foil in my other hand.

"I missed you," he says, sounding hoarse. "Get in here with me."

There aren't any walls to support us in a free-standing tub for shower sex. "Let's turn off the shower and run the bath," I suggest. "Do condoms work underwater?"

Peyton sends a wave of water over the edge of the tub as he rushes to grab the condom from me to put it on.

I switch the valve so the water pours out of the bath spout, and then I open the shower curtain.

When I step into the warm bathwater, Peyton pulls me into him with a possessiveness I like. He leans against the back of the large tub, and I straddle him. His lips and mouth taste like toothpaste, and I think it's funny and sweet that he felt he needed to brush his teeth and shower before seeing me.

Our kisses are aggressive, sloppy, biting, hard. Peyton is rougher than usual, squeezing my breasts and biting my nipples. He groans as I hold his cock and rub it between my legs. Then he grabs my hips and pulls me onto him so he can slam himself into me. We both yelp and grunt with each thrust. We are animals.

My planned seduction of berries and whipped cream and slow, erotic touches is nothing compared to our thrashing bodies. I hold on to the rim of the tub and slide my body up and down, fast and hard. He has his fingers between my legs, stroking me, and his mouth on my nipple, sucking and nibbling. The water is slopping over the sides of the tub, and one of us has the sense to shut off the faucet. Maybe it was me.

I throw my head back with the growing climax and push myself more forcefully on his cock.

Peyton grunts. "Oh, shit."

He comes. Of course, he comes. Guys can orgasm anywhere, anytime. *Bastards!* However, bathtub sex is not as friendly to me.

Peyton lifts me out of the tub and actually puts me on the bath rug, and he goes down on me until I'm in a euphoric state and scream.

It took work. I think my mistake was thinking I could have sex in a bathroom, when really, I find bathrooms to be very unsexy. They make me think of sick people and their germs and the most unpleasant bodily functions. Hence, Peyton put in everything he had to make me climax.

After that exhaustive effort, he has enough sense to carry me to his bed for the next round.

• • •

In the morning, Peyton wakes me up, ready for sex again. It's quicker this time, no fancy foreplay, and I don't climax. I pretend to be sated because I can tell he's distracted and needs to talk but isn't necessarily comfortable about it. I prod him anyway.

"I don't think I can adequately describe what it was like hanging out with Finn." Peyton strokes my arm, giving me goosebumps. He has a half-smile when he talks about his son, as though he can't contain his euphoria. "I can sum it up as great. Overwhelming, but great."

"You're such a guy." I laugh. "All you can say is it was *great!*"

"Well, great is good. What do you want me to say?" He tickles my skin with his fingers. When I shiver, Peyton immediately pulls the comforter up to cover my bare arms.

"You could tell me more about what you're feeling."

"Ah, hell. Feelings. Women and feelings."

"Don't be a jerk. When I was watching you with Finn, you seemed like his dad. If I had just met you and was your waitress, I would have assumed you were his father. Not because he resembles you, because he actually looks more like Harmony. It was the way you talked to him; the way Finn was looking at you. Seriously, how does it feel to be a dad?"

Peyton studies me for a moment. Even after all the personal information we've shared, this topic must be the most difficult. It's the most intimate because, unlike his relationships with women, this one with his son is special. It's permanent.

"I feel like his dad. Maybe it's because I see my mother and father in him, too, so it makes it easy to jump right in and feel comfortable with him. Maybe it's because he's an awesome kid and I want to be his dad. Whatever it is, I like it."

"Good. I'm happy for you. And I'm happy for Finn. This is good, and it's special for both of you."

"Says the woman who's pissed at her father and doesn't want to see him."

I shrug. "When things were good, my family had a good walk. Those days are gone. Nothing I can do about it."

"You had a good *run*," he says with a laugh. "And you *can* do something about it. Maybe not with your dad, but you can help your mom."

"Peyton, nothing has worked. We can't get her out of that house."

"I'll help you organize an intervention or something."

"Or something," I mumble. "Enough about my crazy family. What did you and Harmony talk about? Was it easy or awkward?"

"It was fine. Everything is fine."

"Fine? She had your baby and you didn't know for the past ten years that she was raising your son. Didn't she fill you in on more details about what it was like to have a baby when she was a teenager and raise him alone? Didn't she share what she went through or how she felt all these years?"

"That ship has sailed," he says, and of course I'm picturing a big boat leaving the dock. What a dumb expression. "We talked about Finn and what he needs. We're going to stick to that."

"How tidy. You make it sound very uncomplicated and easy."

"There's no reason for it to be difficult. We're adults now. We both want to do what's best for Finn, and that's how it's going to be." With that declaration, it's understood he's not going to discuss Harmony.

I don't know if either of them has residual feelings for the other. Maybe they were both struck with a bit of nostalgia last night; memories of raging teenage hormones reminding them of their beautiful youth and the ferocious desire young love holds over you. But then, Peyton wouldn't be here with me if he still had feelings for Harmony. I tell myself that, but is it true? Maybe he's conflicted, and whatever he felt for her long ago is still there and he's waiting for Harmony to let him back into her life.

A rush of jealousy bleeds through me. In one breath, I push it down.

Peyton and I are two battered souls who find temporary comfort in each other's arms. He tells me I'm good and deserve better than men like Marko. He makes me feel beautiful. It should be enough for what we are.

This is unlike any other friendship I have had. We can talk for hours, but we also sleep together and make love like we are the only two people in the world and our bodies and souls cannot get close enough. It's only after, when we're naked and entwined in bed, that I remember he isn't going to be more than my friend. And now with Finn and Harmony, I'm even farther down on the list of people in his life.

"Are you all right?" Peyton asks. Sitting up and cupping my chin, he turns my face toward him.

I gently remove his hand from my face and hold it. "I'm fine. I was thinking about everything you need to do to make room for Finn in your life. I can help you turn the guest room into his bedroom. We can make it special, and—"

"Let's deal with tonight first. Dinner. All those people I have to talk to. All those people who will want explanations."

I'm modestly covering my chest with the sheet, but I greedily admire his naked chest and think, if I keep seducing him, maybe I can stay in his life.

Eventually we'll have to stop sleeping together. Eventually our friendship will fade. It's inevitable. I imagine him moving to a nice, suburban home in Westchester, rekindling a love for Harmony and raising their son together.

"Tonight is going to be perfect," I reassure him.

"Can you muzzle Imogene and my family so they don't scare Finn off?" He smiles and looks down at our clasped hands.

"I'll make tonight perfect for you," I say and squeeze his hand because I do want to give this to him.

I will make my best dishes and nourish their souls. I will break the tension by filling their bellies, and Finn will fill their hearts. It will be a night for Peyton and his son, and by the end of the evening, Peyton will go to bed more at ease with being a father because all the people in the room will be people who love him.

What he fears is being judged. His family will automatically release him from any sense of blame, since they are loving and easy. It's Finn's opinion that matters the most, but my gut tells me that Finn will love Peyton without fault.

• • •

After Peyton's staff meeting, he puts Bash in charge and takes me shopping for all the ingredients I need for tonight. He's sparing no expense. Peyton wants three main courses, four side dishes, and two desserts.

I cook at the restaurant rather than his house since it has more ovens and better equipment. Peyton finds reasons to hover and watch me, so I give him taste tests of each item. When I place a prosciutto-wrapped fig in his mouth or give him a forkful of braised short ribs, he looks at me like I'm the goddess who invented food. He loves everything, and his compliments please me.

At one point, he's worried it's too much work for one person and thinks he's overtaxing my heart. He's smart enough not to use those exact words, but it's implied. I give him one bitchy look, and he drops the issue.

When we arrive at his house, Imogene and Aleska are in the middle of arranging furniture and preparing the kitchen table for my buffet.

While I set up the chafing dishes for the hot food, Peyton keeps himself busy with the makeshift bar.

"I don't know why we can't put up balloons," Imogene interjects.

Aleska shoves a couch against a wall with a grunt. "Because it isn't a kiddie party."

"It's for Peyton's kid; therefore, it is kind of kiddie-ish. Why not make it a little fun? We could put baby and childhood photos of Peyton and his family all over the walls and hanging from streamers. And we could mix in photos of Finn at every age. It would show Finn that he's a part of the family." Imogene is excited and doesn't want to let her idea go, even though Peyton is ignoring her. "I'm serious! It would be a game. Guess who's in the photo!"

"We don't have time to find and print photos, and you'd have to ask Harmony to email a bunch of photos of Finn. They're going to be here in an hour, Imogene. There's no time for decorations." Exasperated, Aleska leaves the living room to help me in the kitchen.

"Well, you people are certainly downers," Imogene says. "I guess I'll be Finn's fun aunt and the rest of you are the party poopers."

Peyton chuckles. "How about a drink for all your effort? A martini, a shot of tequila?"

"Please!"

"Go easy on the liquor," I say. "Peyton wants to impress Finn and Harmony."

Imogene raises an eyebrow. "Are you implying that I'm an obnoxious drunk?"

"Yes."

"I'm not worried," Peyton says. He has that far off look again as he uncaps a bottle and searches for a shot glass.

I hand Imogene a pair of scissors. "I left two bouquets of flowers and some Mason jars in the back of Peyton's truck. Why don't you cut the stems and arrange them someplace in here?"

"Oh, good. Decorating. Will do, right after my shot."

The buffet table is crowded with too many dishes, the ovens are warming more food, the windows are open to let in the spring breeze, and Peyton is anxiously pacing when his family members arrive. His father, Stu, and uncle Fraser are both big, grizzly bear-type men who lead the pack of MacKenzies into the house. Stu brought along his third wife, Mirabelle, and his three children from his second wife. His boys—Julian, Mason, and Toby—are roughly the same age as his grandchildren, so it's a little funny when Peyton gives his four-year-old stepbrother, Julian, a high-five and calls him "bro."

Peyton's twin brothers, Evan and Neill, also bring their children. Neil has a four-year-old son, Griffin, who looks a lot like Peyton; and Evan has twin, six-year-old girls, Casey and Bridget, who resemble their aunt Greer.

By the time Greer arrives with her twins, Nikki and Owen, the noise level in the house rises to unbelievable decibels, much like a Chuck E. Cheese that's filled to capacity with running, screaming children.

It's becoming like a private club—everyone who's related to the MacKenzie clan. They're all nice to me, but it's quite obvious I'm the outsider. Even Imogene has managed to fit in seamlessly with Peyton's large family, and not just because she married Cooper. It's how she pushes herself into their personal business and is in on all their private jokes.

The food keeps me busy. I keep checking the pans on the stove top and in the oven, then repeatedly make a sweep by the buffet table to adjust and add. I'm fidgeting, making myself look busier than I really am. Everything is done. All I have to do is refill the table once people start eating, but that doesn't stop me from acting like my mother on steroids, with all her checking and rechecking. It's nonsense, but my mind is racing.

I can't remember any of the MacKenzie kids' names once I've been introduced, and it seems strange to join in conversations that Peyton's siblings are having about Harmony. They all remember her, and I certainly don't have anything to add. As far as Peyton's family is concerned, I was brought in to cook. They have no idea we have been seeing one another. Except, we haven't been dating; we've been sleeping together. Period. Just sex.

"Are you all right?" Peyton asks, gently pulling my hand away from a platter of baguettes stuffed with a variety of sandwich fillings. "You've been running around here like you're preparing for a state dinner."

"I want everything to be nice, and I hope everyone likes the food." My response is weak, but wearing a long, white restaurant apron allows me to hide behind my job title.

"Everything is perfect. Thank you." He smiles, gliding his hand up my arm.

I pivot to shake his hand off my shoulder. "I don't think you want to do that here."

He steps closer. "What? Talk to you?"

"Your family doesn't know about us, and your son and ex-girlfriend—or whatever she was to you—are about to show up, so this thing with me will make it all the more confusing."

Peyton lets out one of his deep sighs. "Sunflower, Greer already knows about us, and I'm pretty sure everyone else does, too."

"Even Harmony and Finn?" I ask, alarmed.

"Well, no. I barely know Harmony. I haven't told her about us, and it's not something I'd discuss with Finn."

"Good. Don't. Harmony is bringing Finn here to see you and your family. She doesn't want your current playmate shoved in her face, and she definitely doesn't want her son to meet your bed buddy."

"Ah, hell," Peyton says softly.

The house becomes louder and more congested as all our friends arrive at once. They must have all decided to leave their homes at the exact time and take their five-minute caravan through town as the grand Hera entourage.

Imogene lets out a loud squeal and runs to hug Cooper because they've been separated for a mere three hours. I roll my eyes.

"The townies are here," Peyton says. "You really think they have a problem with you and me? Whatever Imogene suspects has already been blabbed to Jess. And Carson, and Emma, and Lauren. You get the picture. Don't forget Lois. Doesn't she own an actual bullhorn?"

I laugh. He knows how to pacify my anxiety with easy banter. I could get used to this.

That thought is interrupted by a commotion at the front door as Harmony and Finn walk through. Suddenly, all of Peyton's attention is on his son, and he beams with pride.

Peyton walks Finn around the room and introduces him to every cousin, uncle, aunt, and of course, his grandfather. Harmony walks alongside like a bodyguard, making small talk with the familiar people from her Brooklyn past and smiling graciously at the new faces from Hera. If Harmony had any misgivings about bringing Peyton into her son's life, they must be gone.

The seniors, Archie, Emily, Lois, and Eleanor, do a fine job of welcoming them into the Hera enclave. They look like sweet old townspeople, but they're really smooth-talking publicity reps, talking up Peyton and praising his business acumen and family relationships.

People help themselves to the buffet and scatter about the living room and kitchen, eating and talking while Aleska and I retrieve their dirty dishes and fetch fresh beverages so they don't have to leave their huddled conversations. I tend to the food and clean, gliding my way around the rooms, keeping busy, but also trying to be invisible.

Peyton makes a few attempts to get me to join him and Finn and whomever they are talking to at the moment, but I manage to beg off. I've never felt more like an outsider than I do now.

Harmony watches me with a blank expression, but underneath her cool facade is curiosity and calculating judgment. It oozes from her, and it's all centered on me. She's not a fool, and she knows how to protect her own.

I park myself at the sink and do dishes, a task that can keep me occupied for the duration of the party.

"The food was divine," Eleanor says. She hands me a dirty plate, her chunky gold bracelet clinking against the dish. She and her crew of seniors love pretending as if Hera parties are high society, comparing them to their long-ago party days in New York City. "I wish your mother were here. We'll have to work on that."

"Good luck," I quip.

"You'll have to be more positive. I think Peyton's right."

"Right about what?" I turn off the faucet and brace my hands against the sink.

"He suggested to me, and the others, that we should all plan an intervention for your mother. And we agreed."

The look on my face must convey my shock that Peyton would be discussing my mother with them or care enough to think he should help.

"Oh, don't worry, dear. We'll be gentle with her. Forceful as needed, but gentle so she doesn't run screaming from the house. But then, it wouldn't be so bad if that happens. At least she'd finally be outside."

"And what do we do if she has a screaming panic attack? Put her in the psych ward? Anyway, Aleska doesn't want to get involved. She's hoping our mother's problem will cure itself."

"Aleska agrees with me."

"Since when?" It's aggravating to think these life-altering conversations have been happening without me.

"Since she and I discussed it with Peyton."

"Wait a minute. Where did this big discussion with Peyton and Aleska, and the rest of the town, happen?"

"After a yoga class. Aleska and I were talking, and Peyton came in to borrow some towels from the spa. Those boys go through too many towels at the gym. They're always skimming towels from us."

"Unbelievable. Aleska and Peyton didn't tell me about this little talk. And they aren't boys. They're grown men who like to capitalize on their good looks and charm to get favors."

Eleanor shrugs. "It works. A handsome, sweaty, shirtless man walks into the yoga studio and a roomful of women stare. It's delightful. I also think it's good for business, and it's not like you and the other pretty women haven't traded your beauty for free drinks at a bar or extra help from men."

I sigh and strip off the rubber dish gloves. "And Aleska and Archie and everyone else just happened to be there?"

"Aleska and Lois were taking the class, and Archie and Emily stopped by to see who wanted to go for lunch. We really are the most civilized group in town. Exercise, then a long, leisurely lunch."

"It's easy to do when you're rich and have endless amounts of time. Some of us have to work, Eleanor."

"Oh, I'm teasing you, honey. You need to start coming back to yoga. We miss seeing your bright smile. It's been months."

That's because my sports bras don't cover up my scar and I don't want to have to answer a lot of questions. If I showed up in a turtleneck, it would only invite more curiosity.

"Now, isn't Finn adorable?" she says, looking off into the living room where Finn is surrounded by everyone. He's the beautiful little prince holding court.

"Yes, he is. Very cute and very sweet."

"And his mother is gorgeous," Eleanor adds.

"Yes, she is."

"Too bad for that boy that his father isn't in love with his mother," Eleanor says, scrutinizing Harmony.

"I doubt Peyton discussed that with you on his sweaty towel run through the studio."

"No, he didn't need to. He's too busy looking at you."

"Eleanor, please don't start that rumor."

"It's not a rumor if everyone knows you two are running around together."

"We're not *running around*. What does that even mean? We're not running together."

Eleanor laughs. It's bawdy and loud, and heads turn for a moment before going back to their own conversations. "I love when you do that. Honey, it's so cute."

"I wish everyone would stop saying that."

"I didn't mean running, as in literally running. We all know Peyton goes on those masochistic runs with Dylan. I meant Peyton is spending an awful lot of time with you. I can see everything from my perch at the yoga studio. Our window overlooks Swill, and I see him loading your van for you, which we know he doesn't have to do. You've been doing your own heavy lifting long before he came to town. And I know he's gone out to help you a few times, catering Adam Knight's party—wish I had been a fly on that wall—and going shopping with you for supplies. You two have gotten pretty cozy."

"We have to an extent, but it has its limits, so don't go spreading rumors, please."

"Now there's a tragic word. *Limits*. It's right up there with *flaccid*." Eleanor's face distorts in disgust.

"Ew," I scoff. "I hate when you talk about sex. I know you love drama, but there's nothing here to see."

"Ha! There's plenty. Harmony is watching you like a great white shark circling a defenseless seal."

"Are you saying I'm the defenseless seal? There's no battle here, Eleanor. Really, there's no drama to watch."

"Harmony can read the room when you and Peyton are in it. Don't fret, dear."

"I don't fret. I don't even know what that is!" It comes out as a snappish whisper.

"It's a thorny situation for sure, but it's not like people haven't been doing this for years. Raising children in separate households, mothers and fathers splitting and marrying other people."

"Stop it. I'm not a seal, and I'm not in a relationship with Peyton, And Finn ... this is about them. I have nothing to do with their father-son relationship."

"Listen, little seal. It's going to come around to you eventually, and you *will* have to deal with the great white. I've seen this before. It's a package deal, Peyton and Finn. You'll have to have some type of dialogue with Harmony, some type of agreed-upon civility to make this transition easy for Finn."

"Peyton and I are not serious."

"Oh," she says flatly. "So it all ends tonight? You and Peyton aren't going to hang out together anymore? We won't see you leaving his place early in the morning or in the middle of the night?"

I freeze in mid-gasp, my mouth hanging open.

"Hmm. That's a good idea if it's just sex and you two can call it quits without feeling anything for one another."

I look away and begin wiping down the sink.

"I'll take your silence as a sign you're conflicted about this. So, yay, there's my drama," Eleanor deadpans.

I hold on to the sink's edge with one hand and face my tormentor. "I like Peyton. That part is simple. The rest of it isn't."

"It is a tricky beast, but not impossible, dear." She pats my hand. "We'll discuss this, and your mother, at a better time."

"Because you want to help me?"

"Because you're a damn cute seal being circled by the big, scary shark, and I love the drama. And I love you, honey," she says warmly before leaving me to join the others.

Eleanor stops to say something to Lois, who then peers at me with narrowed eyes and shakes her head. I toss a towel over my shoulder and turn back to my kitchen duties.

"Talia?" a young boy says from behind me.

I'm expecting one of Peyton's nephews or stepbrothers, one of the children I confuse with one another, but when I turn around, my heart races a little to see Finn looking at me sweetly with those big MacKenzie eyes.

Harmony steps behind him and puts her hands on her son's shoulders. It's as though she's protecting him from me or letting me know he belongs to her, or both.

"Finn," I say in my best cheery voice.

"Thank you for cooking all this food. I think this was the best party I've ever had."

"You haven't had the best part. My mother made one of her special cakes for you. It's a gooey, fudgy chocolate cake. I'm going to bring it out now." I say this directly to Finn, trying to ignore Harmony's laser beam eyes doing their best to drill holes into my head. I shouldn't cast her as the villain, it's not fair to her, but I can't help sensing that she hates me.

"I'm so stuffed, but I can always eat chocolate cake!" He laughs.

"How did you know he loves chocolate cake?" Harmony asks.

"Peyton told me," I add quickly before realizing she was expecting me to volunteer this type of information. She's calculating how much time Peyton and I spend talking, which means she's calculating how much time we spend together.

Oh my God, this great white is scaring the hell out of me, and she's smart like the one in Jaws! *I need reinforcements, someone on my side.*

Peyton is in the living room, talking to his brother Neil and holding his four-year-old nephew, Griffin, upside down over his shoulder. The boy is squirming and laughing, yet Peyton is talking to Neil, acting as though they don't notice the boy, which makes Griffin laugh louder.

"Peyton!" I shout. "Cake!" I exclaim, waving my hands in the air. He raises an eyebrow at my bizarre behavior until he notices Harmony. Then he quickly rights his nephew, puts him down gently on his feet, and strides over to me.

"I'll help you," he says. "Finn, Talia's mom makes the best desserts. You're going to love it."

I would have had to climb on a chair to reach the top of the fridge where we stored the cake, but Peyton is so tall that he easily slides the large cake board off and places it on the counter. It's actually three large, thin but potent tortes made to accommodate all the guests.

"Those look good," Finn says, admiring all the chocolate before him.

Harmony gives me a slight smile; an approval of sorts of my dessert choice but hardly an approval of me.

"I'm going to put them on cake plates, and then I'll put them out on the buffet table," I say. I'm in my chef mode, the safety zone where I'm in charge and people like Harmony can't agitate me.

As I place the third cake on one of my mother's beautiful, antique cake pedestals, Peyton, without thinking, casually puts his hand on my waist as he's done many times before.

For a moment, I'm paralyzed, knowing Harmony is watching. I'm being assessed and graded. I move quickly, shaking Peyton's hand off me to dress the cake platter with fresh flower buds. I catch his expression when it dawns on him what he's done.

Harmony and Finn carry the cakes over to the buffet table, and the clusters of people move along with them, eager to get their slice of cake.

"You have to be careful," I scold Peyton in a harsh whisper. "It isn't appropriate here. You're having a party for your son ... and his mother."

"I'm sorry you've been put in this position where you think you're competing with Harmony. You're not. But I'm not sorry for innocently touching you in public, especially when we're in my own home."

I put the cake boards in the sink and stand there for a moment, contemplating what I'm doing with Peyton. He's close enough to my back that the heat from his body radiates around me. His strength and solidity are comforting and make me long for his touch even more.

He exhales slowly and wraps his hand around mine. "This is one of the best—no, it's the best night I've ever had. My son is here for everyone to see, and you're here to share it with me. I think you know how much I like you ... We haven't talked about it, but I think you feel the same way."

My fist is lost in his large hand. He squeezes it. I glance out the kitchen window above the sink. It's pitch dark, so all I can see is the reflection of my face and Peyton with his mouth close to my ear.

"We don't have to live this secret life," he says in a voice barely above a whisper. "Besides, it's apparent we're bad at keeping secrets." He chuckles softly, and my body reacts to his seductive, husky voice.

"It's true."

"What's true?"

"We're bad at keeping secrets." I look up at him. "And I like you, too. I shouldn't. But I do."

His smile reaches the corners of his eyes, and there's a mischievous glint.

More than anything, I want to stroke the scruff on his cheek and run my hands through his hair while I kiss him.

"Don't kiss me here," I demand, judging the gleam in his eye.

"All right. I won't. But just know that I want to. After everyone leaves, I want you to spend the night."

"Peyton?" Harmony inquires, and I jump a little too quickly away from Peyton. "Finn has something for you."

"Great," he says, following Harmony.

Jess enters the kitchen, juggling Scotty on her hip. "Hello, friend. I miss you. We've barely spent any time together over the last few months."

"I know." I kiss Scotty's cheek, then kiss Jess's, too.

She's always a little stunned at public displays of affection, while my family's European ways have always made me a touchy-feely person, which is ironic since I have different rules for Peyton.

"Dinner was delicious, as usual," Jess says, then cocks her head with a laugh as Scotty yanks her hair and puts a fist of her red tresses in his mouth. "Great."

"He's so cute. I want to eat him up."

"Talia," Peyton says as he returns to the kitchen. "Look what Finn gave me." He hands me a large, leather photo album with Finn's recent school picture displayed on the cover insert.

I open it up and page slowly through the photos, from Finn's birth up until present. Harmony and her father are in many of the photos, but many are the type of images only a parent could capture; the unscripted candid shots of a child with spaghetti on his head or arched over a diving board, getting up the nerve to take the plunge. Then there are professional shots of Harmony and Finn at the beach, posing and laughing at sunset, or in the photographer's studio, sitting casually on a wood floor as the natural light emphasizes their beautiful features.

"It was nice of Harmony to put this together for you." I hand it back. A sudden roar of prickliness toward her stops me from saying something unkind about too many photos that include her and how she looks too posed, too perfect.

"Yeah, I'm sure she did the work. Most nine-year-old boys would make a mess of it." Peyton looks down at the heavy album in his hands, grateful to have this small bit of history of his son.

"It was very nice of her. It's a beautiful album."

"I'm going to put it in my room. I'll be right back."

I watch him as he disappears down the hall.

"Hello?"

I turn around and face Jess, still standing in the kitchen holding her baby.

"That was interesting. You two are ... sweet together. So sweet you forgot I was here."

"It's not as sweet as you think," I scoff. "Too many complications."

Jess sighs, switching her chubby baby to her other hip. "I don't know a single couple who doesn't have complications. We all bring our own problems to a relationship. It's impossible not to."

"Some people have easier relationships. I'd like that for a change." I cross my arms and lean back against the sink.

Jess settles next to me, and together we assess the talkative crowd.

"Name one couple who's perfect," she challenges in a hushed voice.

"Imogene and Cooper," I reply flatly. "Easy one."

"Wrong."

I blink twice, surprised.

"Imogene and Cooper have been going through a rough time. They can't conceive. And I don't mean it's taking a long time and they can try other options. I mean Imogene actually cannot conceive, and it's very difficult for her to accept it. Cooper would like to move on and adopt, or at least start fostering children."

"Imogene didn't tell me any of this. She's been acting like her usual self."

"She found out sometime while you were in Florida."

Florida reminds me of my own lie and how I've kept secrets from Jess.

"She had tests done because they'd been trying for ten months. She has endometriosis and it's severe. She was so stressed out wondering why she couldn't get pregnant, and then she was devastated when she found out she really couldn't."

"Because no one is flawless," I say to myself.

"No. No one is flawless. But didn't someone famous say 'Perfect is boring'?"

"I've never heard that. It must have been you who said it."

Jess coos at her baby while I think about Imogene putting up a good cover. I never would have known.

"The good news is Cooper really is a wonderful husband, and I believe she's coming around to the idea of adoption. She's been so hard on herself thinking she damaged her body somehow and ruined Cooper's chances for biological children. It takes a toll on couples, for sure."

"What about Leo and Lauren? Their relationship doesn't look complicated at all."

"Except for Leo's irrational fear of his wife and baby dying in a tragic accident."

"What?" I whisper-shout.

"Whatever horrible thing he sees in the news, he thinks it'll happen to his family. When you were in Florida, Carson booked a vacation for both of our families at a family-friendly resort. Atlantis. Who does that with a newborn? I told Carson it would be a disaster. But Scotty wasn't the problem.

"We spent the first two days of the vacation at a Ramada by Newark Airport because Leo suddenly had a panic attack right before boarding. He made a scene, and then Lauren started crying—I mean *bawling*—because she was so exhausted from working and taking care of little Maisie that she just lost it. Carson was already on the plane with Scotty, so he was escorted off to join us and resolve the issue. The problem escalated when Carson snapped at a security guard and said, 'My baby just took a dump and I need a vacation!'" Jess's impression of Carson makes me laugh.

"Why did you have to stay in Newark?"

"After all the commotion, Lauren's crying, Leo's talk about crashing planes, and Carson holding both babies while angrily telling everyone that they have loaded diapers and need their parents to be on the plane with cocktails to make this better, I tried calming the situation down when TSA pulled us aside. Of course, we missed the plane, and I'm sure the flight attendants and passengers were relieved. We were booted.

"Eventually, everyone calmed down and Carson took care of the tickets and the hotel, but every flight was booked for two days. So, we went to the Ramada and slept, swam in the pool, and ate pizza until a flight opened up for six of us. It ended up being a good vacation after that."

"Leo and Lauren always make marriage and parenting look so easy."

"I think the pressure of being put on a pedestal by everyone made them crack. We don't always see what someone else is going through, even when it's right in front of us."

"True. Some things are easier to share than others," I say.

"I thought, perhaps there's something you want to tell me," Jess says gently. "You've been a little distant over the past two or three months. Sometimes it looks as if you're ... hiding something."

"Oh," I say in surprise. "Does everyone think this?"

"If you mean Imogene and the other women, I don't think so. I don't discuss you with them. We used to share everything, Talia. The only thing that's changed is I have a baby now. I still need my best friend."

"Me, too."

"Talking with Carson or my mother is not the same as talking to you. Carson does a lot of 'Yep, I hear ya,' and my mother keeps saying 'You worry too much.' I love them, but they aren't you."

I reach out and stroke Scotty's chubby cheek. He's slumped over Jess's shoulder, his squished face resembling her bulldog, Bert. "I want to spend more time with him and you."

"I'm not asking you to babysit. Didn't you hear what I was saying? I miss the way things were. I want to hang out with you again. I can hand Scotty off to Carson, and I will get in my car and drive and meet you anywhere. I liked hanging out with you at your old kitchen when it was just us two so we could talk while you cooked. I can't really do that in Bash's kitchen with twenty people running in and out. I'd be in the way."

"Our lives have changed quite a bit. You have a baby and my job is busier than ever. I miss talking to you, too. Sometimes I feel lonely, even when I'm surrounded by a kitchen full of people."

"Then you can talk to me, because I'm going to start visiting Swill during the day. I want to start a new series of paintings, something I know my dealer will like. I already spoke to Peyton about it. He said I'm welcome to come in and do my sketches whenever I want."

"You're ready to go back to work already?"

"I've been dabbling at home in my studio, but I miss being around people. I thought bringing in a sketchpad to Swill for a couple of hours would help me creatively, and socially."

"There's definitely plenty of room before the restaurant opens. You could have your own table, and it would give us more opportunities to talk. That would be nice." I am looking forward to seeing her more often.

"Well, this is my excited face," she says, looking very tired. "We'll be working in the same place, at least a couple days a week."

Her statement is punctuated with a long, rippling fart from Scotty, who is soundly snoring. The loud fart is followed by another, and then his sleeping face turns pink as he makes tight grunting noises and his bowels release what sounds like the world's loudest cappuccino machine. I cover my nose and laugh.

"That's a stinky one. I swear my days are broken up into periods of time each defined either by Scotty's pooping or his eating."

"I think I hear my son," Carson says from the other room. "Sounds like he's making lattes over there."

"Yeah, ha-ha," Jess says.

"Can I help?" I ask with my nose plugged.

"No. I'll go change him in the bathroom. Can you believe he sleeps through these power poops?" She grabs the diaper bag from a stool and leaves me alone in the kitchen.

I'm ready for this night to be over. When I offered to cook for everyone, it sounded easy, like another party to cater. I didn't expect it to trigger so many confusing emotions.

I finish washing the remaining dishes, listening to people giving their goodbyes to Peyton and extending their compliments to Finn and Harmony. Finn is gracious for a nine-year-old, outgoing and charming like his father. He handles Lois's and Eleanor's hugs and cheek pinches like a good sport. Uncle Fraser and Grandpa Stu both promise to take Finn on the job site where they're helping Peyton's brother, Evan, build a summer cabin someplace farther upstate. Their talk about eating sandwiches on the roof and using nail guns must be making Harmony shudder.

Harmony brings in an empty glass and places it in the sink. She has a smile that could only be described as sly.

"Dinner was good," she says.

Good? My dinner was excellent, and she knows it.

"So many courses. Peyton must be paying you a pretty penny for all this work."

So she's fishing for information, wanting to know if I'm a hired caterer or if I prepared this for free because I'm sleeping with him.

"He spares no expense when it comes to food," I say, which is true since he did pay for all the food, but vague enough so she doesn't know that I wouldn't accept payment. Not from Peyton. I'm doing this because feeding people is one of the few ways that I know how to show love.

Love?

Harmony's relentless pursuit to figure out who I am and how I fit into Peyton's life is making her more aggressive with me and definitely making me dislike her. And it's forcing me to think long and hard about my feelings for Peyton. I didn't have to reach too deep for the word *love* to pop into my head.

"Huh," Harmony says, but her stare tells me she's not satisfied with my response and will keep digging.

It's as if she's daring me to do anything, and she's ready to pounce. I'm almost afraid to reach for the tube of pink lip gloss I left on the counter so I can reapply it. I wouldn't call her a shark, but she's like a beautiful hawk, taunting her prey—me, the little chef who just wants a swipe of lip gloss. And maybe a lot more with the swashbuckling hero in the other room, who happens to be dueling with Finn and his little nieces and nephews with the toy lightsabers Greer passed out as party favors.

Harmony releases me from her death stare and calls to Finn in the next room. "Finn, honey, time to gather your things. We need to leave now."

"Ah, that sucks," Finn says, galloping into the kitchen with his saber.

"Hey," Harmony admonishes. "*Language.*"

"Are you sure you need to leave already?" Peyton asks. He's sweaty and out of breath after jumping all over the furniture with his preschool and middle school fan base. Children adore the MacKenzie men. They're all clowns. Handsome, sexy clowns.

"It's after ten, and it's a school night," Harmony replies. "We have a long drive."

"Stay here." The words are out of Peyton's mouth before I can apply my fresh coat of lip gloss.

I feel stupid. Here I was, getting ready to spend the night with him, and he invites his ex-something or other to sleep over.

Harmony purses her lips.

"I'm serious," Peyton says. "You shouldn't drive tonight. My dad and uncle aren't driving back to Brooklyn at this hour—they're staying at Cooper's place. And my brothers and their kids are crashing at Greer's, so you two should stay here. You can have the guest room, and Finn can have my bed. I'll sleep on the couch."

"Yeah, let's do that, Mom," Finn says, his eyes going wide with excitement.

"I suppose we can. But we have to get up earlier in the morning," she tells Finn. "We'll have to go by the house and get your backpack, and I'll need to change clothes for work."

"We're staying here." Finn smiles at Peyton.

"Good." Peyton ruffles Finn's hair like a father who's done it a million times before.

It doesn't take long for Harmony to settle in. She finds the guest room and inquires with me—me!—where the extra bath towels are located. I don't fall for her trap. I have Aleska show Harmony around the house and how to find what she needs, including the morning coffee. Peyton is too busy loading our van with the catering crates to notice the female dynamics at play under his roof.

I say goodbye to the last guests and walk with Imogene and Cooper to their car. Stu and Fraser MacKenzie are already in Cooper's truck, singing a Scottish tune loudly and off-key to Stu's youngest children.

"I love bringing drunks home," Imogene says. "Nothing says family love like wrangling inebriated men onto air mattresses, along with their five-year-old accomplices."

Cooper laughs. "It'll be fun. Especially when one of them pops their mattress or falls out of bed."

Imogene laughs, then whispers something in his ear.

Cooper salutes me, and then hops into the driver's side, barking at his father to take it down a notch.

She must have told him she wants a moment to talk to me.

Imogene takes my hand. This sisterly coddling is so out of character for her that I want to laugh.

"Peyton had to invite her to spend the night," Imogene says. "He's being a gentleman. He wants to be close to Finn, not her."

"I suppose so."

"I know so. He also wants to be with you. What man wouldn't want to be with a beautiful, secretive, Russian spy?"

"Great," I say dourly. "*Odpieprz się.*"

"What's that mean? Some kind of Russian code?"

"It's Polish for *fuck off.*"

As they drive away, I can still hear the raucous singing when their vehicle is out of sight, swallowed up by the dark night.

I walk around the guest cars left behind. Harmony's is the only high-end luxury one, and if I were a different person and she wasn't Finn's mother, I'd key the glossy, metallic paint. Instead, I walk over to our van where Aleska is sitting behind the wheel, checking her phone.

As Peyton slides one last crate into the back end, then closes the doors, I approach him.

"Everything's in." He takes my arm and pulls me into him. With his other hand, he holds my face firmly as he coasts his lips across my temple, cheek, and then presses them against my lips.

I yield to the familiar heat and desire he summons in me. The kiss is long and sensual and makes my soul feel owned by Peyton. He maneuvers me so my back is against the truck. He has one hand underneath my ass, the other holding my leg up, and he's positioned between my legs, his jean-clad hard-on hitting every pleasure point perfectly. This Russian spy is fantasizing about stripping and giving up all her secrets to have this man take her against a catering van.

Aleska holds down the high-pitched horn on our van, startling us. "Don't make me come back there, you two. We have to go, Talia."

She can't see us, but I'm still embarrassed.

Peyton doesn't let me go until we're both laughing.

"Actually, it's good that Aleska stopped us," I say.

"Sorry our plans for tonight changed, but I couldn't let them drive home this late. It felt wrong, and I like the idea of having Finn spend the night."

"You don't have to explain. You made him feel like a king tonight. He's very happy to be here."

"I think he's the one who makes me feel like a king."

He leans down and gently kisses me again. His tenderness opens a door where I can envision us doing this for many years to come. I see us together, raising Finn, sharing a parenting schedule with Harmony, fixing up this home together, and having family dinners where people come to us, including my mother. My mother will be well again, I'll be whole, my sister will find her way, and Peyton will be with me.

The sudden kick of the engine turning over shakes me from my unrealistic fantasy.

Peyton reluctantly releases me but takes me by the hand and walks me around to the passenger side. He even opens the door and holds my hand for support as I step up into the van. I'm getting the full boyfriend treatment, which makes Aleska snicker.

"I'll see you tomorrow, spy girl," he says, then gives me a chaste kiss on the lips right in front of my sister.

We say nothing on the short ride home, but when she parks the van in front of our house and turns off the engine, she's fidgety, wanting to say something.

"What?" I ask.

"I just hope you know what you're doing, because there are other people involved now."

"I think we're on the same page."

"You *think*? That's not very reassuring. You need to be absolutely sure. You've never been in a situation like this, Talia."

I'm not sure if my sister is accusing me of being reckless or if she's trying to protect me from a man who comes as a package deal with a son and a beautiful woman who may be my competition.

22

Peyton

I'M OFFICIALLY A MEMBER of a club I never expected to join—the Daddy Club. Once you're in, well-meaning friends and family begin to tell you what you should be doing to make your child happier, a better eater, more responsible with chores, and smarter because you're supposed to provide educational toys, software, and outings for your child. Ironically, it's a club where men like my father brag about what a great dad they are because they made hamburgers one night or they took the kids to the science museum and watched them run around for hours. When I remind him that his daughter, Greer, does this daily for her kids and manages a career while they're at school, he clams up.

It's easy to be an uncle and show up for the fun times, but the day-to-day work involved in parenting eludes me, scares me. I've never dreamed of having it, but Finn makes me desire it.

His permanent life is with Harmony, in her home, but I do want more than the occasional outing with him. I want to be a part of his routine, even if it means I only get a few hours on the weekends. I want the phone calls, the texts, and dinners together. When I brought this up with Harmony in the morning before she and Finn left my home, she surprised me with her generosity.

"Let's start with Saturdays. If you can adjust your schedule a bit so you're not out all night, you can have him then."

Her words showered down on me like I'd won the lottery. Alter my nighttime work hours for that kid? Hell, I'm the boss. I'll do anything to have more time with him.

When I arrived at work the next day, I did the unthinkable. I removed myself from our busiest night, the Saturday shift. Bash agreed to run both the dining room and kitchen since we have the most employees on staff during that time. Plus, both Greer and I live only minutes from the restaurant, so one of us can help if there's an emergency.

And then I got busy making lists.

Food. Kids need food in the house at all times.

Bedroom for Finn. Other than action figures, books, and games, what do boys need in their bedrooms?

When Talia arrived, I showed her my list and she laughed. "I'll help you with his room. We'll do a little shopping."

I loved the sound of that. More time with Talia and more time with Finn.

She pushed me away so she could cook.

I stared at my three-item list for the rest of the day until Finn got home from school and I could call him.

It was one of the most exhilarating weeks for me, the prospect of my son coming to stay with me without Harmony and being with Talia every day and night.

In between work, we squeezed in morning and night runs to Target and the outlet mall to buy bedding, games, and groceries. We settled on a light purple paint. Talia said it matched Finn's favorite T-shirt from one of the photos in the album. Then we spent Wednesday night painting the guest room.

Seeing Talia in a sports bra with paint-splattered overalls turned me on so much we had sex in the hallway because we couldn't "taint" Finn's room, according to her. And then, covered in paint, we had sex again in the garage against a dusty worktable when we were supposed to be cleaning the paint off the brushes.

Each morning, we shower and then I drive her from my home to hers so she can change clothes and we have breakfast with her sister and mother. Aleska is more reserved, but Mila is clearly happy to see us together. I milk it.

Mila craves the social connection to someone new, and missing my own mother, I soak up the attention she showers on me.

I gloat to myself. *I'm better than Marko and Adam Knight. I have Talia, and I have Finn. And I will help Mila. I'll help this family become whole again, and I'll be a part of it.*

My simplistic viewpoint is reinforced when Jess shows up at the restaurant every morning this week to sit at the bar with her art supplies and work on some sketches. She won't let anyone see her large pad of paper, but when I'm standing behind the taps, going over inventory and work lists on my laptop, Talia works on her own lists and distracts Jess with their chatty conversations enough that I can get a good look at one of her sketches.

It's *us*.

Talia is leaning on the bar, looking up from her work. I'm standing on the other side of the bar as if we're in mid-conversation. It's the way Jess captures us looking at each other. It's evident to any observer that sometimes all I see in a room of people is Talia. I've seen Jess flip a lot of pages on the pad over the last few days, so I wonder how many sketches show me mooning over Talia. *Jesus.*

For her part, Talia's generosity obliterates any woman I've ever dated. She throws herself into making Finn's room perfect, and then she organizes my home to make it Finn-friendly. She never discusses Adam Knight on the evenings she delivers his meals, and I don't ask. All I know is she doesn't linger at his place any longer than necessary, and she isn't doing this because she doesn't enjoy his company. I'm not so stupid as to think she'd suddenly find this guy to be unappealing. She's drawing a line between her business and personal life, and I know this is all for my benefit. As far as Adam Knight is concerned, I've accepted that Talia has a whole host of interesting clients, including some single men, and Knight just happens to be one of them.

I finally have Talia seeing me as a responsible adult. I can't afford to screw that up with petty jealousy.

My desire to be with her has only grown, and when we're together, I'm insatiable to the point of exhausting her. When I do finally let her sleep, my thoughts go to all the possibilities of what my life could be with her and Finn; how much easier it would be if I wasn't pursuing a career that has always come first in my life.

Saturday morning, I jump out of bed as soon as the sun rises. I've had so much energy since Talia and Finn have come into my life that I need little sleep.

"Come on, sunflower; get up," I say, pulling the covers off her.

She squints and groans. "We just went to bed." She rolls in the other direction to escape me, her face covered by a mass of tangled hair.

"It's a big day. Finn's coming, and I have a surprise for both of you."

She doesn't open her eyes but lets out a low groan, which is followed by a soft snore.

"You cannot possibly be asleep already." I drag her back to my side of the bed and hoist her over my shoulder. That wakes her up.

"What the hell are you doing?"

"We're showering, and then we're picking up Finn," I answer, carrying her into the bathroom.

"Put me down. Now."

I set her down in the tub and turn on the shower.

"Peyton!" She jumps away from the cold water. "Really? You had to soak my pajamas, too?"

I smile as I strip off my underwear and step into the tub with her.

Talia tosses her wet T-shirt and pajama bottoms on the floor, and then I pull her into me for a morning kiss. She's soft and warm and tastes like some blend of sweet and herbal. The presence of our morning breaths actually heightens my senses. I love how her hair smells, the back of her neck where she sweats when she's in the hot kitchen, and the soft white-and-pink flesh around her scar. I kiss her everywhere, letting my hands roam freely, eager for more of her.

"After this, you should get Finn while I stay here and clean the house," she says breathlessly as I leave a trail of kisses down her neck.

"No. I want you with me."

• • •

She finishes drying her hair while I get dressed. I walk back into the bathroom and watch her put on some makeup, observing herself in the mirror. Her eyes travel from her face down to the V where her top button meets her scar.

"No one can see it," I promise. Her eyes meet mine in the mirror. "And it wouldn't matter if they could."

"I know, but I don't want to encourage questions. They may be well-intentioned, but how boring would that be to have people constantly asking, 'What happened?'" She uses her best American accent, which sounds like a whiny teenager.

"You're going to get tired of hiding it. You'll see. Let people ask questions. The attention will be short-lived, and then life will go on."

"If you think so, then I officially designate you as the person to handle all inquiries."

"My pleasure. And by the way, you don't need all that makeup."

"I look a little washed out and tired because you always keep me up too late. I have bags under my eyes. A little concealer and blush are necessary."

I walk up behind her and wrap my arms around her. We both watch this in the mirror: how we look together, how we fit.

"You're beautiful without that stuff. But I'm not going to tell you what to do."

She laughs, and I feel it reverberate against my chest. "You always tell me what to do. You love telling people what to do."

I hug her tighter, bending down to kiss her cheek. I want to hold on to this image of us, and I want her to see it and feel it the way I do.

"Peyton." She turns around in my arms and faces me. "I really can't go with you to get Finn. I know you have these big ideas in that head of yours, but you're wrong about this. I can't go."

"I don't understand. I thought you were spending the day with us. I have something special planned."

"I am, but I can't go to Harmony's house. That's too much too soon. It's not fair to Harmony. She's trying to build the connection between you and Finn. She doesn't need to see me with you, not when you're at her home. And it's only going to confuse Finn. If he sees me at the restaurant or at your home occasionally, that's one thing. But he may think I'm going to be something like his stepmother or something."

"I think you're making too much out of this. Harmony and I are not rekindling a relationship that never even existed. I'm sure she's dating, and I'm sure Finn has met some of those men or boyfriends in the past."

"You don't know that."

I let her have the last word.

• • •

By the time I get to Harmony's house, Finn is bouncing a basketball outside, and his overnight bag is sitting on the front stoop. He waves as I pull into the driveway, and I think how lucky I am that I'm getting to know my kid when he's at an age where dads still seem important and ideal to them. If he were already a teenager, he would have pent-up resentment and indifference I'd have to contend with, stuff that can weaken even the sturdiest of people.

Harmony emerges from the house, dressed casually, but she still comes across as elegant as she strides toward me. "He's all set and has been ready to go since six this morning," she says and raises her eyebrows in amusement.

We watch as Finn runs to the back of my truck, opens the hatch, and throws his duffel bag inside. Then he slams it closed and runs to the front passenger side with his basketball. My heart swells as I watch him settle into his seat.

"That makes two of us," I tell Harmony. "I've been looking forward to this all week. Thank you."

Harmony regards me for a moment, then lets out a nervous exhale. "We've never really been separated, you know. Occasionally, he'd spend the night at a friend's house, but he was never more than five minutes away from me. This is different. Exciting for him. A little scary for me."

"I'll take good care of him."

"I know you will."

If you're so sure of that, why did you keep him away from me all these years?

I nod. There's nothing I can say without sounding angry. My feelings for Finn are real and easy to define. My whole being reacts when he's around or even when I think of him. It's everything any parent must have—love with a heavy dose of worry. But Harmony is another issue altogether.

Once I'm in my truck with Finn, I'm at ease again. I'm the only parent, and I'm not looking over my shoulder, wondering if Harmony is judging me.

Finn fiddles with the stereo until he finds a radio station that plays typical bubble gum music. I'm about to suggest we use playlists from my phone, but he's already enjoying the shrill voice of a teenage pop singer. It makes me feel old, but this kind of compromise is one of the many aspects of parenting, right?

"Are we going to your house or the restaurant first?" he asks.

"Someplace else, buddy. I have a surprise for you. We have to pick up Talia first. Then the big surprise."

"Is she your girlfriend?"

"Well ..." I'm at a loss as to how to explain my relationship with Talia without the X-rated version of it.

"She seems like your girlfriend."

I stare at the road ahead as I contemplate that one. I sense my mini-me watching me, waiting for my response. I give up.

How do you tell your kid about your confusing feelings for a woman who wants you for sex and whose life plan is on a different trajectory than yours? *You don't.*

"We spend a lot of time together."

"She's nice, and I bet you don't fight with her like my mom and Derek used to."

"Derek?"

"My mom's old boyfriend back in Seattle. They used to argue all the time about every little thing. It sucked."

"Really?" Harmony dating piques my interest. I wonder what kind of guy she thinks is good stepfather material for Finn.

"Yeah. Once they were arguing really loudly at a movie theater, so we all had to leave. It was my turn to pick the movie. I was really mad at them. And once, they had a huge argument at one of my favorite restaurants. They ruined my birthday dinner."

"Sorry, Finn. That does really suck. No other way to put it.

"I guess you could say Talia and I may disagree sometimes, but we don't fight like that. But then, I'm not officially her boyfriend."

"What does that mean?" He looks at me, perplexed.

"It means our expectations are lower."

Finn shakes his head, confused, and I don't bother trying to explain the inane complexities of adults.

"I wasn't really prepared for questions. I assume most kids want to see their parents together, and this has to be weird for you."

"Mom said you were never her boyfriend." His bluntness surprises me. "I already know you guys had sex once, and then I came along."

"Wow. Your mother sure didn't sugarcoat that story. Does it bother you? How we ...? How you ... happened?"

"No. I only know my mom's side, though. She got pregnant when she was a teenager—I did the math—and then she moved to Seattle with her dad. We had to live with Grandpa so Mom could go to college and raise me. She didn't tell me very much about you. Sometimes I thought about what it would be like to meet you."

I glance over at him. He's got one of those sweet, innocent expressions as if he's trying to assuage my remorse and shame. I want to apologize over and over for missing the first decade of his life.

"I'm here now. It's the best I can do, Finn. I'm here now."

The rest of the drive is what I expected—bright and sunny with not too much traffic on the interstate. I let Finn blast the stereo beyond respectable sound levels, to the point where my ears are ringing with music I would never listen to unless under court order. When we arrive at Talia's house, I've accepted the fact that I'm going to be a pushover with this kid.

"Hey!" Talia smiles as she runs out of the house to greet us. Mila waves from the doorway.

"Hi!" Finn says and follows my cue, jumping out of the truck.

"Do we have time to introduce Finn to my mom?" Talia asks as she approaches.

"We have time. I want Mila to meet him. Come on." I signal to Finn.

He half-runs, half-walks in that funny, energized way young kids move.

He indulges me when I introduce him as my "whiz kid," and Mila is delighted when he thanks her for the party cakes. I'm scoring points with the mother that I'm trying to impress the most, and it's not Harmony. Sounds shitty to say, but Harmony is stuck with me as Finn's dad, so I'm not too concerned about winning her over. Mila, on the other hand, has great influence over Talia, and I want her on my side.

Talia and her mother share an appreciative smile over Finn.

Good, but not a checkmate. Yet.

I don't know where I'm going with this. These people and this situation aren't aligned with my original goal, which I'm not about to give up. I haven't figured it out, but I'll make this work.

"Ready for an adventure?" I say when we are back at the truck.

"Yeah! You can have the front seat, Talia." Finn holds the door open for her. I have to give credit to Harmony for his good manners.

"No, no. I'm sitting in back. This is your day. You get the front." She eagerly climbs in the back, and I observe her in the rearview mirror. She has her hair in that messy bun on top of her head. A short, blue velvet jacket shows off her eyes, but it's the red lipstick that makes me stare. She could be dressed to go teach nursery school and she would look sexy as hell.

These heart-pounding, good feelings are too much. Between Talia and Finn, these two could give me a heart attack.

There it is again. When I was planning my big career move, I wasn't a parent, and I wasn't interested in any woman beyond sex. I'd be lying if I said these two people don't have an effect on me.

"I meant to ask you, Peyton." Talia leans forward between Finn and me. "I left my bike at Swill yesterday. I parked it by the back door like I always do, but when I returned after my deliveries, I couldn't find it. You don't think it was stolen, do you?"

"No, it wasn't stolen," I say dryly.

"Well, where is it? Did you move it?"

"It's in Huffy heaven."

"No! You didn't." She glares at me in the rearview mirror.

"It's not like I shot Old Yeller."

"Who?" both Talia and Finn inquire.

"He's a dog. From an old movie."

"I don't have a dog," Talia says, veering off topic in that way she has when meanings get lost in translation.

"Trust me on this one," I say as we enter the town of Woodstock. It's larger than Hera but still small and charming and certainly more famous.

Talia narrows her eyes at me in the rearview mirror. "I can't believe you got rid of my bike."

"It was a danger to you and society."

"Oh, man," Finn says when Talia playfully punches my shoulder.

"Have some patience." I smile. "I have a surprise for both of you."

"Finn, see that old building, the one with charred windows?" Talia points.

"The one with the construction guys in front?" Finn asks.

"It has a missing roof. Hard to miss," I add.

"That's the one," she says. "That's where my kitchen is—was. I'll have to call the landlord to see how the renovation is coming along." Her eyes never leave the destroyed building as we drive by.

"The roof hasn't been replaced, so I don't think they've made enough progress for you to even consider working there again." I don't want her leaving Swill, not yet.

"They'll get it done. I'll have my kitchen back ... eventually. Anyway, where are you taking us?"

"Here we are." I pull the truck over to park by an array of colorful, shiny bicycles all lined up outside the bike shop.

"A bicycle store?" Talia asks.

"Cool," Finn says, checking out the bikes on display.

"You both need new bikes." I get out of the truck and walk around to the front, where Finn excitedly meets me. Talia follows behind, a little reluctant and wary, giving the new bikes a distrustful look.

The store manager I met with the other day steps outside when he sees us. "Hey, Peyton. So these are our two new riders?"

"Talia, Finn, this is Raoul. He's going to hook you up with your new bikes."

"Wow!" Finn smiles at me.

"I'm going to bring your bikes out here. The store is kind of a tight squeeze," Raoul says before disappearing back into the shop.

"Yeah, wow," Talia mumbles, and I detect her nervousness.

"It's just a bike, sunflower. It's safer than your old one." I raise my chin toward the door where Raoul and an assistant are wheeling two new bikes out.

"Isn't this a little extravagant?" she whispers to me. "Not for Finn, but for me?"

"I wanted to get you a new bike. I'm not plying you with diamonds or anything like that. It's a bike."

"These are expensive."

"It's a gift. You're welcome."

"Thank you," she whispers, looking anxiously at the bike Raoul walks toward her.

"You get the Kona Rove," he says. "It's pretty awesome on these roads. And this one is extra special because Peyton had one of our local artists give it a coat of powder-blue paint for you."

"It's so pretty," Talia gushes. "My favorite blue." She takes the handlebars and admires her bike.

"And I get the black one?" Finn asks, hopping on the other bike.

"Yours is a Kona Process. One of the best mountain bikes around," Raoul explains. "Pretty cool, right?"

"Awesome," Finn says. He rides the bike in a circle around them. "Thanks, Peyton!"

"Wait. You have to wear the helmet every time. Got it?" I demand.

Raoul's assistant hands a black helmet to Finn, who has no trouble adjusting it and strapping it on before he's off again and pedaling on a grassy hill next to the store.

Talia is given a silver helmet. She removes her bun thing, shakes out her hair, and then slips on the new helmet. Raoul adjusts it for her, seeming to take an extra bit of time—so he can enjoy her company, I'm guessing. He even holds the bike for her as she hops up on the seat. Then I take over. Before she can take off pedaling, I put both hands on her waist. It's instinctive. I want to stop her from her wobbly start and inevitable crash, but I also feel fairly territorial.

She's mine.

Talia regards me with curious eyes. "Aren't you going to let me zoom away like Finn?"

"No. He knows what he's doing. You need a few lessons on the basics, and Raoul here is going to teach you."

"Really?" She looks disappointed. "Am I the only adult who has to take bike riding lessons?" she asks Raoul.

"Not at all. And it's going to be very easy. You'll feel more comfortable on the bike, and you'll be safer," he replies.

I walk away and settle back against the side of my truck, watching Raoul give Talia instructions on the gears. Then he has her sit on the bike and walk it along with her feet. As they move farther away toward the hilly grass, I hear her laugh.

In the meantime, Finn is tearing up the practice area with little jumps and skids on the dirt patches. A mountain bike will be perfect for him in Hera. I can take him up on the trails behind my house and give him a taste of something he can't get in the suburbs with Harmony.

A half hour later, Talia is cruising smoothly on both the grass and the gravel parking lot. She gives me a big grin as she pedals toward me. "I'm going to try braking without panicking!" she shouts.

God help me. The woman is about to plow into me. I don't want her to know I'm a little alarmed and ready to grab the bike to stop her—again—but thankfully, she veers to the left and circles around for another attempt.

"It was too soon!" she shouts. "I have to slow down sooner."

I smile, trying to look calm. She's going to crash into either me or the truck if I try to save myself.

"No rush," Raoul shouts to her. "You're doing fine."

That's easy for you to say, because she doesn't have a massive tire aimed at your dick, Raoul.

I cross my arms and legs, as if that will give me some added protection should this woman lose control again.

I have to say that she looks fucking amazing with her golden hair blowing around the helmet with a sort of halo effect.

"No panicking," Raoul says as she gets closer. "Calm breaths, stop pedaling, let it coast ... and begin braking."

She glides around us with perfect control and slows down to a gentle stop in front of me.

"I did it." She smiles broadly.

"You did." I relax my whole body and reach out to brush her cheek, grazing the soft skin with my knuckles. "Perfect."

She blushes and looks down for a moment. "This is a wonderful gift. Thank you. I love this bike."

"You're welcome." I spend a few extra seconds staring at her, because she stares back. We do it so well—this staring game. *Cue sappy, heartfelt sighing.*

We watch Finn do a few more laps around, and then I harness the bikes in the new bike rack I bought for the truck bed.

"But what about you?" Finn asks. "Don't you want a bike?"

"When I was here last week, ordering these two bikes, I bought one for myself. It's already at home in the garage."

"So we can go out riding together?"

"Definitely. We can take your bike back and forth from your mom's house to mine so you can always have it with you."

"No, I'd rather keep it at your house. I'd like something of mine at your home. And besides, Mom doesn't ride, and she'll always worry about me if I bike around the neighborhood."

"Whatever you want, buddy."

On the drive back to Hera, Finn tells us that he's going to research where all the best trails are so we can attempt them all. Talia sits quietly in the back and listens. When I catch her attention in the rearview mirror, she smirks. Oh, yes, the irony—the guy who didn't want to settle down and have kids. But who says I'm settling down? I can still have the job in Los Angeles.

We arrive back at Swill around lunchtime. Talia immediately goes to work in the kitchen and shows Finn what she's cooking and how she organizes all her deliveries. Then Finn and I sit down for a lunch prepared by Bash. We eat alone, where the waitstaff is prepping the tables for dinner and the bar staff is stocking glassware and replacing kegs.

I'm not really sure how single parents who work nights take care of their kids. Greer has a part-time nanny for the day shifts and a sitter who comes in for the evening shifts, but she always makes sure she spends less than thirty-five hours per week at the restaurant. She can handle a lot of vendor issues from home and still pick up her kids from school. As the guy running the place, I don't feel comfortable leaving during a night shift, but then I already managed to do that to help Talia at Adam's party.

I haven't figured out the weekend scheduling with Finn yet, but I'm also not going to forfeit the opportunity Harmony has given me. I'll make it work, even if it means Finn spends some time in my office doing homework and playing computer games before I cut out early so we can have some quality time at my home.

I picture us getting an early start on Saturday mornings, hitting the bike trails, and then we head into Swill for meals and whatever entertainment I can create for him there before I have to drive him back to his mother's home on Sunday morning. It's not much time together, but I hope we become close enough that it turns into daily phone calls and some weeknight and holiday stays.

As we finish our lunches, Talia delivers two slices of cheesecake she made. She waits for me to try it, so I shove a hefty bite in my mouth. The flavors hit me just right. The thick, sweet creaminess baked in the traditional New York style reminds me of Brooklyn.

Finn uses a stab-and-maul technique then grunts with approval.

"Well? Tell me what you think," she demands.

"You made it the right way," I say.

"I made it yesterday, because they always taste better after they sit in the fridge overnight. I had no idea you were buying me a bike, so this can be my thank-you. A fair trade, give or take a thousand dollars." She rolls her eyes with a laugh.

"Amazing cook, right?" I say to Finn, who nods with a mouthful of cheesecake.

"I think it's amazing how similar you two are," she says. "You have the same body moves, and you eat the same way. And your eyebrowns and eyeflashes are exactly the same."

"Our what?" Finn asks.

"Eye*browns* and eye*flashes*?" I ask. I wink, and her smile drops.

"No," she mumbles and shakes her head. "That is not what I meant ... That's an old .... mistake. Thought I corrected those with my dialect and speech lessons."

"It's all right." I hope she will laugh with us, but she doesn't.

"Your eyebrows and eyelashes are similar. That's all I meant," she says, frowning, then walks back to the kitchen.

"Did I make her mad?" Finn asks.

My son has both a huge appetite and empathy, and I approve of both.

"You didn't. She's very sensitive about her accent, and sometimes I tease her too much. Let me go talk to her."

I find her in a storage room off the kitchen. She's looking up at her thermal delivery bags on a high shelf, but she isn't moving to retrieve them. She's standing perfectly still with her back to me.

"Hey." As she turns around at the sound of my voice, I grasp each shoulder and pull her gently toward me. "You don't have to be self-conscious around me or Finn—we both like you. And I apologize for teasing you in front of him. I wasn't thinking."

"I shouldn't be making the same mistakes a five-year-old makes. Eye*browns* instead of eyebrows? I sound like an idiot in front of Finn. I don't blame you for laughing."

"It was amusing, but we weren't laughing at you. Seriously, it was cute."

"Stop saying everything I do is *cute*. I hate that."

"Okay, it was sexy, and I'd like to take you right here and now."

"In dry storage? No way. You can see me tomorrow night after Finn goes home." She gives me a brief but exciting kiss, payback for feeling taunted.

My body reacts, and I reach for more, but she pushes me away.

"Nope. Not today."

"You're cruel. You get me wound up and leave me hanging."

"That's one of many reasons why we are not made for one another," she says as she turns away and reaches for her delivery bags.

"What do you mean, *one of many*?"

"Peyton." She drops the bags on the floor and looks at me for a moment. "You and I have a lot of stuff. Luggage."

"You mean *baggage*," I say tersely.

"Yes, baggage. We both have other responsibilities. You have Finn. You're a father now, and I have to take care of my mother. We said from the beginning that this is for fun. We're already starting to go off in other directions, away from each other. So it's good we're keeping it simple."

"Great ... *other directions*. Uh-huh. Well, I'll see you tomorrow night for something fun and simple. Hopefully, you'll remember the *directions* to my house."

23

Talia

I USE SUNDAY MORNING to get to know my new bike. I find some bike-friendly roads that run along the outskirts of Hera. It's an exhausting endeavor. I'm still not in the best condition for this type of cardio, but I feel highly motivated to keep going.

The Pickwick house is the last stop before heading home. I struggle to pedal the bike up the long, dirt driveway. The house looms ahead as though it's been waiting for me.

Peyton and everyone else see a battered old estate where I see something majestic, a sanctuary that could use a good caretaker and some loving renovations. But it's there, in those good, solid bones—a fine Victorian that I would love to own and turn into my own restaurant and inn. The ideas constantly churn through my head. The farm, outfitting the kitchen, decorating a dining room, and restoring a few grand bedrooms for guests.

I take one last, longing look before I head back down the hill to my mother's home.

My mood begins to sink considerably. First, I didn't like how Peyton and I left it yesterday. I recognize his moods now, when he's pretending not to be annoyed with me or aggravated by our unconventional circumstances. We entered into this uncommitted relationship willingly with the idea of having fun, except other people are involved now and we can't carry on as we have without consequences. It's really about Finn, but I also know I'm afraid about being on the receiving end of another broken heart. I've had more than my share of physical and emotional heartbreaks, and the more time I spend with Peyton, the more I let him in. And the more I enjoy our physical intimacy, the more I fall for him. I can't fall for him.

I have to stop falling.

My mother is running on the treadmill when I arrive home. The grinding sound of the motor and feet pounding on the rubber mat have become the soundtrack for this household. It helped me recover, but I can't look at the treadmill without the imagery of surgery and home imprisonment filling my head. For my mother, it's a virtual escape from her boxed-in world, running nowhere.

As her shoes slap against the tread, my dread grows. The urge to walk out the door and find someplace else to live and breathe is powerful.

As soon as I enter the kitchen, my mother's eyes lock on me. She smiles, and I nod in return as I walk to the kitchen tap and fill a glass with tepid water. I gulp it, not realizing how dehydrated I am from biking.

"I was hoping we could spend this evening together," my mother shouts over the loud hum of the treadmill motor. "I haven't seen *The Crown*, and I'd prefer to watch it with you. And Aleska, if she's home."

I planned on spending the evening with Peyton, my escape from this maudlin world with my mother, and because I crave him.

"If you have plans with Peyton, I understand," she says, reducing her sprinting to a jog so she can talk. "But we haven't spent any time together."

This is where I want to scream at her for throwing the guilt my way, as though she's a child who needs more of her parents' attention. But she's also my mother, and she never left me, and she nursed me through a broken relationship and a broken heart. And because I love her, and daughters are not supposed to abandon their mothers.

"We can watch the show. Aleska and I have been out too much lately anyway. We could use a quiet night at home."

"Good." She smiles and keeps running. She's genuinely happy. I'm filling the void so she doesn't have another long, lonely night.

I slip into my room to call Peyton. It doesn't seem fair that I have to cancel my evening with him, since our time is finite and where I really want is to be with him. But maybe this is a good way to wean myself off him. We didn't spend the previous evening together because it was a Finn night, and now tonight is a Mila night. These are the responsibilities, and they don't mix.

If I had any dreamy thoughts that Peyton and I could have something beyond sex, it was under the assumption that his commitment to Finn would require him to turn down that business opportunity in Los Angeles. Maybe he wouldn't stay in Hera, but even if he moved back to the city or closer to Finn, Peyton wouldn't be far from me. I let myself consider that when I thought there was something growing between us. Then Mom and her ever-present neediness and care brought me back to reality. Peyton and Finn can't be saddled with my problems. No one can.

Peyton picks up on the first ring.

"Hey, sunflower. Why don't you come over to the restaurant and keep me company?" His baritone sends sweet chills through my body.

"I can't." I wilt. "My mother asked me if I'd spend the evening with her. I really wanted to say no. I want to be with you, but my mother ..."

"I know." He pauses for a beat. "I understand what you're going through. Mila is lonely, and you and Aleska are barely home. Your mom is afraid of losing you both."

"You seem to know a lot about my mother," I whisper. For some reason, I want to cry. My mother's fragility and my non-boyfriend's sincerity.

"She's a good mom. I know you've had your differences and it's tough dealing with her condition. We've talked about this—getting her friends to come in and confront her to get some type of intervention going—and I'm sorry I haven't been more help. I'm not sorry I take up your time and drag you to my bed every chance we get, but I promise to be more helpful where your mom is concerned."

He has no responsibility in this, yet his thoughtfulness to help is perhaps the sweetest offer I've ever received from any man.

"You don't have to do anything, Peyton. She's my problem."

"She's your mom, not your problem. Stop acting like you can fix this on your own. I'm going to reach out to Lois and a few others. We'll organize a friendly intervention. I don't want you stressing about this. I want you taking care of yourself, your health, your heart."

"My heart." I think about the word but realize I've said it out loud. My physical heart is near perfect, but my emotional heart is always on the verge of either bursting with feelings for Peyton or developing fissures, those tiny, hairline cracks I think will appear when my time with Peyton ends. "It's fine," I say. "It's excellent."

Does he read into the double meanings as well, or am I the only one who thinks we're digging ourselves in deeper with new layers of friendship?

"It is," he says, and I can picture him smiling. "Take care of your mother. Spend tonight with her but think about me."

"I will. I'm sorry that I won't get to stay at your house."

"I am, too."

"You'd be proud of me, though. I rode my bike around the hills and didn't fall or crash once. And I visited Pickwick, and I swear I could hear it calling out to me. *Talia, Talia.* Seriously, I belong to that place."

He laughs. "I like your ambition, sunflower. Don't ever lose that. But next time, bike over to my house and get naked in my bed so I have something to look forward to when I come home at night."

"Hmm, nice fantasy, but we both have real-world situations, don't we?"

"We do. And having you around makes it easier for me to figure out how to do real-world things. It does."

"It's nice of you to say that." *I don't necessarily believe you.*

"You have a good night with your mom. As for tomorrow, get some rest because I'm planning on you spending the night, and we're going to be busy. Bring a suitcase."

I cover my mouth to stifle a laugh. "I think your brain can only handle two things. It's either work or sex."

"Actually, you and Finn are giving me a different perspective. See you tomorrow, sunflower."

His last statement leaves me surprised. Not about Finn; but that I was included. The sentiment was more than generous and could lead any woman to believe she has Peyton's full attention. Flora must have struggled with his charm every day, thinking that maybe he could be the settle-down type.

• • •

Movie night with my mother involves pajamas, a lot of cheesy, hot appetizers, and watching five episodes of *The Crown*. We go to bed at two in the morning, bleary-eyed and bloated.

On Monday morning, I resist riding my bike to Swill to visit Peyton. Everyone else's Monday is like my Sunday. I need to learn how to use my time more wisely.

Before Peyton, I had started to visit a local shelter for the homeless. I'd volunteer in the kitchen, cooking and serving meals. I haven't stepped foot in the shelter in months.

Aleska and I drive out there and help restock the food pantry, and then we cook and serve lunch to over a hundred people, mostly vets, but there are some single mothers with young children.

"I never get used to this place," Aleska says once we're back in the van. She's going to drop me off at home before she meets her cleaning crew at a client's house. "No matter how many meals we serve, those poor people can never get ahead. They never get a break."

"I know." I stare out the window, at the flowers beginning to bloom. As we drive south toward Hera, it's more green and lush. "Do you think most of the guests at the shelter still have their dreams?"

Aleska glances at me before she turns her gaze back to the road. "You mean, like suddenly they'll get a great job and be self-sufficient?"

"Whatever they've always dreamed about—a job, a home, a family. Some of them are sick, and all of them have been beaten down. Do you think they really have any hope left? Other than hoping they score a bed at the shelter for the night?"

"I guess I try not to think about it because it's sad, and it's scary. Anyone could be in that situation. Lose your marriage and your job, then you lose your house. I want to help, but if I keep imagining myself in their position, it scares the shit out of me."

"Since Dad left, it's always on my mind. Most of us are all just one paycheck or one calamity away from ending up in that shelter."

"We're not that bad off. We have some money in the bank. Our business is doing well. What's wrong with you?"

"I'm being realistic. What if something worse than my heart surgery happens? We could lose everything, too. How would we take care of Mom?"

"You worry too much because our father put you in a horrible position when he left. But we did better than survive. We made something, Talia." She smacks the steering wheel. "Stop thinking you have to save everyone you meet. Go enjoy your day off. Go have great sex!"

"Geez." I shrink in my seat.

"What? Everyone knows you're at his house practically every night, screwing each other's brains out. You stare at each other like you're about to rip each other's clothes off with your teeth."

"Thanks for the free therapy." I slam the van door and stomp up to our house. On the front stoop, I turn around to watch my sister drive away. I hate when people leave, but I always stop to watch.

Aleska drives off at a reckless speed, leaving a cloud of dust. As she turns on the county road, another car slows down as Aleska passes. This scenario is very familiar—the car, its slow rumble toward my home, and me standing at the door, watching it approach. It's the same midnight-blue sedan I noticed a few weeks ago, but instead of slowly driving by our house as if the driver is looking for something, the driver parks in our driveway, and I see Harmony behind the wheel.

She looks at me for a moment, then gets out of the car like a woman who has business to contend with. Her expression tells me this isn't a friendly visit.

"Harmony," I say, remaining on the front stoop with my arms crossed.

"Hello." She walks toward me and stops at the bottom step. This makes me several inches taller than her, which helps my confidence, and it keeps us separated by at least two feet, which makes me feel safer.

"You were here before, weren't you? A few weeks ago, you drove by here. It was before Peyton knew about Finn. Were you spying on Peyton? On me?"

"I wasn't spying. I was checking up on him."

I scoff. "I won't ask how you tracked him to my house."

"I wasn't going to let Peyton near Finn without vetting him first."

Her condescending tone suggests I'm ignorant about parenting. Perhaps, but I also know you should vet prospective fathers of your children before you get pregnant. I keep that choice remark to myself because Harmony still intimidates the crap out of me.

"I have to get back to work, so I'll make this brief," she says. She's dressed in a pinstriped navy suit with wide-leg pants. The short, fitted jacket makes her waist look tiny. She looks like a glamorous but tough businesswoman who's ready to kick some ass. My ass, I guess.

"What's up?" I ask. *Say it fast, lady. I'm already hating this!*

"From what Finn tells me, you spend a lot of time with him when he's with Peyton. You bought new bikes yesterday, and it sounds like you and Peyton are fairly serious about each other. You work together, and the little town grapevine, which does reach Westchester, by the way, tells me that you spend many nights at his home." Harmony says all this as if she's making opening statements in a courtroom. She could easily play the pretty district attorney in an episode of *Law & Order*. Except, I haven't done anything wrong, and I shouldn't be on trial.

"Peyton and I spend time together. We're friends."

"I don't care what you call it, but I do care that you are doing this in front of Finn. I care that you are using his time with his father to be with Peyton. And I care what kind of impression this will leave on Finn." With each sentence, the anger in her inflection rises. A contained fury, at best.

"We are not doing anything inappropriate. When I'm invited to have lunch with Finn and Peyton or go out on an excursion with them, it's done as friends. I'm careful not to intrude on their family time," I say, then snap, "And I have never spent the night at Peyton's place when Finn is there!"

"Good. Finn is becoming fond of you. Let's make this easy on him. End your friendship with Peyton. I'm not going to insist you quit working with him today because I know you'll be working elsewhere soon enough. But you can't see Peyton anymore. It's sending the wrong, confusing message to my son."

"I can't see Peyton anymore? I can't go to a party in case he might be there? I can't have lunch at the restaurant because he might want to sit down and chat with me? Are you serious?"

"You're being dramatic. I know you have the same friends and it's a small town. And you're working at the restaurant until your kitchen is functioning again. I know all the details. What I'm saying is that you can't have this ... relationship that's been going on. I don't want Finn to get attached to you, and then, when you and Peyton break up—because he breaks up with every woman—Finn gets hurt."

I shake my head in disbelief. "I can't believe you think I'm the kind of person who would manipulate your son's affection and then hurt him. I'm not that kind of woman. I like Peyton, and I like Finn. I value my time with them, and I make sure to behave as a guest, not a parent, and not as Peyton's girlfriend. Which I'm not. This is a very small town, and Peyton has become one of my closest friends," I say, holding back tears. "You can't tell me to never see him again."

"I can. Because if you don't, he will lose Finn."

"What do you mean?" A tear escapes, and I wipe it angrily against my cheek.

"Peyton isn't on Finn's birth certificate. We never filed any formal papers that state Peyton is the father. I have full custody. I moved back here so Finn could establish a relationship with his father. I have been easing Finn into this slowly over the last few months, and I'm watching Peyton carefully, making sure he can handle being a father. I want this to work for both of them, for all of us, but you're not part of this picture. You'll confuse Finn's heart. I'm not going to let that unstable relationship touch my son."

"Are you hoping you and Peyton will get back together so you can raise Finn in the same home? Because I think that ship has sunk. You hurt Peyton by keeping his son a secret for ten years!"

Harmony's mouth contorts into a sneer. "You decide. You can keep sleeping with Peyton and watch him lose Finn, or you can walk away and let them have a relationship. Peyton will want Finn. You know that connection is stronger than anything you have with him."

"I agree. Peyton does love Finn more than anyone. So why are you afraid of me?"

"Blondie, I'm not afraid of you." She forces a laugh. "I have experienced enough fear on my own, raising Finn as a teenage mother. You don't know what fear is."

I don't know her fear. I only know my own.

"You'd really do this to Peyton? Prevent him from dating women until Finn is an adult? Do the same rules apply to you, too, or are you allowed to date while you threaten to take away Peyton's parental rights?"

"I'm a realist. At some point, we both may find serious partners and maybe want to marry. By then, I expect Peyton's relationship to be solidified, and we'll be in stable, long-term relationships with people who put Finn first."

"But you get to decide who Peyton sees and when he can have a relationship or you'll take his son away," I say. "He'll fight you, Harmony."

She smiles. "You think Peyton's going to fight me over you?"

"No. He won't take you to court over me, but he'll fight you tooth and ... whatever that saying is. He'll fight you as long as it takes for Finn. For *Finn*. You're doing this destructive thing, Harmony, not me."

"Good, then you'll make this easy, right? You're done playing around with Peyton because you know Finn is more important. Do we agree on this, or do you want to make this really messy and very public? Do you want Finn to see this played out in front of everyone?"

"I would never hurt Finn."

"Then I'll take that as a yes to my terms."

With her ramrod-straight posture and head held high, she walks back to her car, gets in, and slams the door as her final word on the matter. I don't watch her drive away because, for the first time, I'm not sad to see someone leave. I'm seething.

As soon as I open the front door, I hear the loud cackle of women's laughter in the kitchen. My instinct is to flee the house, bike over to Swill, and tell Peyton everything.

Harmony's ultimatum hit me in the gut. I knew it was a matter of time before Peyton and I would fizzle and end. We would part as friends who entered into this with defined terms. But each day brought me closer to understanding him, and each week brought me closer to caring about him. I'm not truly ready to end it with Peyton, but since this new deadline is being forced upon me and Finn's happiness is at stake, I don't have a choice.

Norma and one of her daily caregivers, Olga, and Lois, and my mother are sitting around the table, playing cards. Baby, the pampered Saint Bernard, is lying next to the sliding door in a pool of sunlight. He's on his back with his legs splayed in the air, letting the sun warm his belly.

This is my real life.

"Son of a bun! I'm out!" shouts Lois.

Great, my mother is playing poker with Hera's one true card shark. Lois only plays for cash pots, and she has no problem taking money off friends. In this case, my mother's spending money comes from Aleska and me. I'm enabling my agoraphobic mother and her gambling.

"Could you not clean out my mom's wallet today?" I ask Lois.

"I'm actually doing well," my mother gloats.

"It's all right, sugar," Norma chimes in. "We're only allowed to use ones."

I shake my head. "I'm no math genius, but whether my mother loses five fifties or two hundred and fifty ones, it's all the same."

"These gals are ruthless," Olga says, shooting me a concerned look. "I can't afford this job."

"Oh, shut up. I'll give you a pay raise to keep playing," Norma says.

I open the fridge and grab a Snapple. Then I head down to my room for some quiet contemplation and more self-loathing. I get a swig of sugary tea and a two-minute face-plant on my bed when a simple knock on my door turns into an aggressive assault.

"It's open!" I yell.

"It's me," Lois says as she enters, then closes the door securely behind her.

"It *is* you." I roll over on my side. "What do *you* want?"

"First of all," she says, scrunching her nose and looking around the room, "I gotta say this room is depressingly bland. I've seen generic hotel rooms that are more exciting than this."

"I just sleep here." *And I hadn't planned on spending my life in my mother's home.*

"We'll talk decorating another day. I'm here to tell you that Peyton spoke to me about the intervention you two have discussed."

"He did? Already?" I sit up, more alert, my mind racing. With all he has going on in his life, Peyton's actually ready to follow through on the enormous challenge of my mother?

"Yes, and I have to say I agree, and I'm on board with Mission Getting Mila the Hell Out of the House."

"I doubt Peyton called it that."

"No, I came up with MGM THOOTH, and I have been discussing it discreetly with all parties."

"All parties? You make it sound like the UN is involved."

Lois gives a casual shrug. "With your mother, this is more like negotiating an international arms deal. She is stubborn! I'm this close"—she illustrates with her thumb and pointer finger—"to slipping Valium in her coffee and dragging her to the nearest lockdown unit for some tough love and a good kick in the ass."

"Lois, you know that would never work. If she doesn't have the will to help herself, we can do interventions every week and they'll all fail."

"Don't I know that. I've had enough friends battle addiction and other issues to know what works and what doesn't, but that doesn't mean sometimes I just want to slap your mother silly."

"You and me both. But when I say it, I sound like an ungrateful daughter."

"You aren't. You and Aleska are both fabulous, and any mother would be proud of you. Let me take the reins from here. I'll organize this with Peyton."

It doesn't seem right to drag him into my family's problems when I'm about to break everything off with him.

"What's wrong? You look like you're about to cry. Sweetie, it's all going to work out. Don't worry about your mother. It really will be fine."

I let her believe all my grief is for my mother. "Why do you need to involve Peyton? I think he has enough things on his dishes."

"On his plate?" Lois chuckles. "Yes, he does, but he also really likes you and wants to help. And he's big and strong, and I may need him to put the straitjacket on your mother and shove her in my car."

I smile faintly, trying to mask my misery. "Let's hope my mother has the same sense of humor about this when all her well-intentioned friends invade her home and insist that she get a life."

"Now that's the spirit." Lois shakes her fist. "This is your day off! Why don't you go see that handsome fella and share an ice cream sundae?"

"Ice cream sundae?"

"I was being polite. Ice cream sundae is code for hot, sweaty sex. Somebody in this house should be having some, and it's not going to be your mother anytime soon."

"I never would have broken that code."

"Talia, dear, you cannot spend your day off here in this house when there's a nice man who would love to see you."

Despite Lois's prodding, I don't run out to see Peyton and hang around the restaurant while he works, soaking up his lusty attention. Instead, I learn how to lose at poker and bridge, and I think about what I'm going to say to Peyton. I have to end a friendship with a man who has become the best lover I've ever had.

I thought a carefree relationship with him would be easy. I thought terms like *fling* and *casual* meant that people could come and go from these relationships without consequences. Maybe other people, not me. This was not designed for me.

After my last losing round of cards, I drive over to Peyton's house. He texted me at nine and said he was on his way home since Bash is handling the closing.

I let myself in with the key Peyton slipped into my hand a few weeks ago, which seems like years now. I put my purse on his kitchen counter, but I leave my jean jacket on since I don't think I'll be staying long.

"Hey," he says with a grin as he comes padding down the hall, barefoot and shirtless, wearing loose-fitting sweatpants that hang low on his narrow hips. He finger-combs his wet hair roughly. "Needed a quick shower. Got blasted by the stout tap tonight."

I inhale his damp, musky scent as he cups my head and gives me a quick but thorough kiss.

I have one hand resting on my purse as though I'm prepared to promptly leave once I've said what needs to be said and, with my other hand, I'm clutching my cell phone so I don't touch him and slide my hand down his bare back, which is what I really want to do.

"Take off your jacket and shoes and get comfortable."

Before I can respond, my phone rings.

Peyton watches me as I let it ring several times and go to voice mail.

"Are you not taking calls tonight?" He looks at me quizzically. I haven't spoken a word yet.

"No. It's not important."

"Come here," he says, pulling me by the waist. He wraps his arms around me and nestles me against his warm, freshly showered skin.

I let go of my purse, but I still grasp my phone as I circle my arms around his waist. I love the way he smells and feels. Everything about him is sensual. I long for this, for him, as he looks at me with a steady gaze. Then I remember what I came here to do. It's about Finn. It's about me moving on to something more stable and permanent.

He kisses me again, and then my phone rings. We keep kissing until the ringtone becomes annoying.

"Please answer it. I won't be offended."

"I can talk to them later," I say as the last ring ends.

He sighs and shakes his head. "Give me your phone." He releases me and puts out his hand. "At least listen to the messages in case it's an emergency. It might be your mother."

"She doesn't go anywhere or do anything; what kind of emergency could she have? She can't find the TV remote?"

"Be nice. You've been getting awfully crabby about your mom. Unlock this," he demands, holding the face of the phone in front of me.

I tap in my code, and then he takes the phone back to scroll through the recent messages.

"Here." He stabs at the phone with his finger to play a message, and Adam's strong voice fills the room.

"Talia, I was wondering if I could take you out to dinner this Friday when I'm back in town. I thought you could take a break from cooking for me. And I really would like to sit down and have a social dinner with you. It doesn't have to be a date if this message is making you nervous. Call me."

Peyton angrily ends the message, cutting off Adam's chuckle. He glares at the offending phone in his hand. "No, she's not going out to dinner with you. You fucking … fuckwad," he growls. "She's busy!"

"Give me the phone."

"Did you know about this? Did you know he wanted to ask you out?"

"He said it doesn't have to be a date. And no, I didn't know, but maybe he wants to be friends the way you and I are friends."

Peyton holds my phone away from me. "The way you and I are friends? Sex? Are you trying to be funny?"

"No, not sex. He's a friend I talk to, not a sleeping-with type of friend. Oh my God, I can't even keep these definitions straight. It's a confusing mess."

"Has he kissed you?"

"Are you asking me, or is this an interrogation? No, of course he hasn't kissed me. I haven't done anything with Adam. He's just being nice. Now give me my phone."

"Being nice," he mumbles. "Let's see who else called." He stabs my phone with a finger, and then the next message plays.

I groan when Marko's voice comes to life.

"Nat, I miss you. I don't know what else to say, but I'm sorry. I really want to see you. Will you please call me back? It's Marko, in case you forgot."

He sounds sad. Marko is not someone who readily admits he's wrong, and hearing his voice reminds me of a time when I thought I was happy, when I thought I could love only him.

"Jesus fucking Christ," Peyton says. "No, she can't call you, asshole!"

His possessiveness is touching and pretty sexy in an angry alpha way, but it's also nuts. He's supposed to save this kind of territorial rage for some other woman who will own his commitment, someday in the faraway future, if it ever happens.

"Jesus, Talia, what's going on here?"

"I don't know. They just happened to call me at the same time. I had no idea either one would want to ask me out. I think Marko probably wants to make the air clearer and apologize in person."

"And do you feel you need to *clear the air* with him? Do you think you two left things unresolved? And what if he thinks this is an opportunity for him to get back together with you?"

Peyton stands before me, large and towering, and half-naked. He's gorgeous and sexy and so very irate. There's a distinct pleasure in watching a man like Peyton exhibit jealousy. I would enjoy this moment more if this were the beginning of us and not the end.

"I have no interest in getting back together with Marko. Maybe I'll forgive him, but I'll never forget, and I can't be with a man like him."

"What about Knight?"

"Adam is different than Marko, but none of this should matter to you. You're acting jealous, and you shouldn't. Everything has gone your way. Your restaurant is a success, you found out you have an amazing son, and we've had some fun together. But we need to end this thing we have going on."

"What?" he asks sharply.

"We have to stop sleeping together. We have to stop hanging out together, because it leads to sex. That's all it's been, and I've had my fun, and you helped me get back in the game—see, I remembered that line—and now I'm done. You have two major things in your life. Your son and your restaurant. Finn doesn't need to see you running around with me, and I don't want to be the other woman."

"The *other* woman? What the hell are you talking about? You're the only woman."

"For now, but we hooked up for sex. That's how this started, and we said from the beginning we both have different agendas. Your big picture is about your career, and you'll have to move someplace else to be near Finn. And that's the right thing to do,

My big picture is smaller. It's all in Hera, and I want to settle down here with someone who wants the same thing. I want a permanent relationship with a man who feels I'm enough and Hera is enough."

The light and happy sparkle I saw in his eyes when I arrived is gone. His expression darkens as he regards me with suspicion.

I justify my deceitfulness and unkind words by reminding myself this is in Finn's best interest. I can't tell Peyton that Harmony basically threatened me—well, him. It would cause terrible friction between them, and it would impact Finn. I have to put aside my growing affection for Peyton and obey Harmony's demands for the boy's sake.

Peyton hands me my phone. There's a painful stillness between us.

"Some people would say we're in a relationship, Natalia." I don't like hearing him say my full name with such sternness. "Most would say this wasn't a hookup, it's not just sex. You sleep over, but we also spend our days together. You have a nightstand in my home full of personal things. You have a toothbrush and your favorite blue towel in my bathroom. I talk to you more than anyone else, and I think it's the same for you."

"This worked for us because we had an understanding. You always planned to leave Hera to join some corporation," I say, flustered. "You want the excitement, the popularity, the money, and the challenge in the big cities. And I don't want those things. Our hookup or affair was perfect to fill the time." I am convincing myself with my almost perfect logic.

"We were filling the time," Peyton repeats softly.

"We could do what we're doing because our situation was temporary. But Finn changed that. For the better! You have to stay near him, whether it's back in New York City or you move out to his suburb ... I don't know where you'll live ... but I can't be a part of this. I don't want my presence in your life to confuse Finn."

"So this is all about Finn?"

"You're a parent. Everything you do affects him. I don't want to be in the middle of you and him, and Harmony."

I'm not good at expressing what I'm thinking. I can't tell him how my attraction to him has grown into real affection and I'm beginning to care deeply for him, and how the thought of being in a serious relationship with Peyton and Finn is actually desirable. I can't tell him the truth because Harmony holds all the power.

My statements come across as mean and selfish and maybe it's best to end it this way. He can feel relieved I'm out of his life rather than let down.

"In other words, I have too much baggage," he says.

"We both have baggage. I can barely handle my own," I say, hating the taste of those hurtful words in my mouth. My stomach is in knots. Right now, I hate myself.

"Finn isn't baggage; he's my son," he says carefully with a hint of anger.

This is good. You want him to be angry with you, to dislike you enough to no longer care. A broken friendship will make it easier to walk away, and Harmony will be satisfied.

"He is your son, and you're both lucky to have each other," I say. Inside, a part of me is dying for sounding so cruel, for being disingenuous. "I think I should find a new kitchen to use until I can move back to my old place. It would be better for both of us if I'm not at Swill."

"No. We have a contract. I stand by my agreements. You can use the kitchen at Swill until the renovation on your other kitchen is finished."

"You don't have to do that."

"You should go, Talia," he says, utterly composed, without a flicker of emotion.

I take my purse and walk out of his home.

As I drive away, the front lights he always leaves on for me shut off, blanketing his house and my car in the cover of night.

I've left a few items at his home that will either be boxed and delivered to me later or thrown away. They were only important when I used them in Peyton's home. After this, they are sad trinkets, symbolic of an ending.

24

Peyton

CANCELING HER LEASE AGREEMENT with her landlord in Woodstock is easy. Several times on my way over there, I ask myself why I'm compelled to keep Talia in my life when she has no interest in seeing me anymore. I tell myself I'm saving her thousands of dollars in rent, money she can put toward her dream. I'm hoping it will make me a hero. I'll do anything to repair this loss.

For the past three weeks, there's been a deep freeze of silence between us. When she's in the kitchen at Swill, I make a point to work in the back office or in Zander's office hidden in the brewery. I reappear when Talia leaves for her deliveries—the only time I can work in the dining room or the kitchen without feeling sick.

The kitchen renovation is almost complete and having her gone from Swill could make my life easier, assuming I get over her. So, why cancel her business lease? *Because I don't believe her.*

When we hooked up, as she so eloquently put it, I had no intention of getting serious with her. Or so I thought. However, Talia moved my whole being in another direction, as did Finn. That kid changed everything. Whatever I thought I knew about love and ambition, Finn redirected every circuit in my brain and made me care about two main things, two people: Finn and Talia. Somehow, they are supposed to go hand in hand.

I'm not one for destiny and fate—I think life is a series of random events, and it's our job to navigate and adapt—but sometimes we get gifts along the way, and if we don't recognize them, we lose them. Most likely, I've unintentionally squandered opportunities and people, as well. Not this time. I'm going to be sensible and give Talia her space and the chance for her to see that Adam Knight isn't the guy for her.

I walked through the renovation of Talia's rented kitchen with Mr. Ricci. He showed me the progress and how he was updating equipment. I assured him that it would be easy to find another chef to pick up Talia's lease on such a well-designed commercial kitchen. Then, as I brushed drywall dust off my jeans, I made calls to a couple of Swill's vendors. One offered the name of a local pastry chef who needs a kitchen to expand his business. He was there within ten minutes and gratefully signed a long-term lease for Talia's kitchen. They both thanked me. I felt like I had done a good deed.

Talia might think it's revenge, except I'm not that kind of guy. She broke up with me, and while I'm ticked off, I'm not vengeful. I have a plan to win her over and getting her out of that forty thousand dollar debt she signed on for years is a start. If I'm right, if I really believe in my intuition, she'll eventually realize I'm what she's looking for. How she fits in with my LA plans, though, I haven't gotten that far.

Back at Swill, clouds of construction dust keep billowing from my jeans, so I head to my office for some clean clothes. As I change, I congratulate myself on how I'm making an adult decision and putting Talia's needs first. I have a head for this business, and I can do more than relieve her biggest debt. I can help with financing for her dream business—the Purple Peach or whatever she wanted to call it. I'm on board, and I'm going to be her biggest fan.

I'm thinking of Talia as the office door swings open and her eyes go wide as I finish zipping up my jeans.

"Sorry," she says. "I thought you were out. I came in to get a pen. I'm doing inventory ... Needed a ..."

I reach for a clean T-shirt I have stashed in the desk drawer, but I take my time. I'll play it up—anything to see her look at me the way she used to.

"A pen," I complete her sentence, plucking one off my desk and handing it to her.

She makes that exasperated fish face with pursed lips and puffed cheeks—that I love—and narrows her eyes. "Nice beef cock."

"Sometimes, I think you're verbally molesting me." I slip on the T-shirt. "You don't have to sneak up on me. Just ask if you want to see some beef*cake*."

"Huh." She thinks about that for a minute, and I want to laugh for the first time since she broke things off between us. "Cake doesn't make any sense. It should be cock."

"You might want to think about that one for a while. You're missing the point of the analogy—a naked body being as desirable as cake."

She looks up to the ceiling as if she's actually contemplating the meaning.

"Hey, I'll be your beef cock if that's what you want." I walk over to her and rest my hand on the edge of the door high above her head, inching it closer to her.

"Peyton." She finally smiles. I missed that smile. Then she steps back toward the hallway to put a safe distance between us. "The dirty-minded fiend is back."

"I never left."

"Are you speaking to me now?"

"I never stopped speaking to you. You're the one who made the new rules. I'd be lying if I said it didn't bother me." *It was like you took my heart in your fist and squeezed it as fucking hard as you could to see how resilient I am.*

"How is Finn? He hasn't been in here in a while." She is genuinely curious about him, and I know she cares.

"He's good. Thanks for asking. He's been helping me set up a new home theater and sound system at the house, and we've been hitting the bike trails every weekend. And we're constructing something in the garage for his school science fair. I don't know jack about science, but I'm giving it my best shot. Harmony and I have worked out a deal where he gets to spend one or two weeknights with me. I get to be more involved with his school stuff and it gives her some personal time. I'm trying not to be the father who drags his kid to work with him and pretends it's fun for the kid."

"I noticed you're working fewer nights, and Bash is doing a good job covering. But this place *is* different when you're not around."

"Nice to hear. Thanks. And what about your work? Are any guys giving you problems?"

She smiles. "You mean Adam and Marko?"

"Are there more assholes in the vicinity other than those two?"

"I told Marko to stop calling. But Adam is still my client. I got out of that Friday night date with him because I'm not ready to date him or anyone. I used the *I can't date clients* rule."

"But you're still interested in him," I say, trying to sound reasonable. *Stay calm, be agreeable.*

"Let's not talk about Adam. Let's agree not to discuss who we're dating or sleeping with."

I flinch, thinking of her rolling around naked in bed with Adam or some faceless guy. "Are you sleeping with someone? Seriously, you didn't date me either, but you had no problem sleeping with me."

"God, no." She smacks my arm. "I just said I'm not ready to date anyone. That doesn't mean I'm jumping into bed with any guy for sex."

I give her a pointed look.

"You were the exception."

"You forgot to say I was also exceptional."

"We can't do this flirty stuff. We're not doing this."

"I'm changing the subject. Mr. Ricci called and left word that the renovation hit a snag and the timeline on your kitchen will be delayed by another three months or so." *Or as long as it takes me to convince you to come back to me.*

"Oh no. Why didn't he call my cell phone and let me know?"

I shrug innocently. "Maybe he tried and couldn't reach you, so he called here. Anyway, I told him I'd relay the info to you."

"I was counting on moving back next month, at the latest. I thought the work was going quickly."

"They have a delay on parts and some problems with permit inspections," I add, thinking of some more bullshit I can toss in. "You can stay here as long as you need."

"Thank you. I don't know what I would have done if you weren't here."

I hope you remember this, sunflower, because I plan on breaking your new rules.

25

Talia

INITIATED BY LOIS AND followed up by Peyton, a series of texts is sent to everyone, informing them of when to be at my house. The intervention will happen right after eleven in the morning, when my mother will most likely be working around the house with her cleaning caddy in hand. My job is to text her and say I'm coming home for lunch.

I'm amazed the first text goes off to her without me blowing our cover. It also makes me laugh with a bit of hysteria at the fact my housebound mother has a cell phone. Aleska bought it for her last week, thinking it would help edge her out the front door and start walking around a bit with the comfort and safety of a cell phone at hand. So far, she only uses it when she doesn't want to leave the treadmill to suse the landline.

I'm unconvincing as a spy, and right away, I'm afraid my nervousness is about to sabotage our plan. I have to make sure my mother is either in the family room or the living room when everyone else arrives. We have to keep her away from the bathroom or bedrooms where she could lock herself in if she panics.

At first, I send too many texts to the group, questioning my ability to "position" my mother, and then I send off several texts questioning the effectiveness of a plan that really should be run by medical professionals and not a disorganized group of neighbors.

**Imogene to group: *Shut up and get your ass over there! Give us the signal when the coast is clear!*
Talia to group: *Coast?***

Peyton to group: *You'll do fine. Tell your mom you're on your way. Notify us when she's relaxed. Make her sit down. Keep her there.*

Lois to group: *We've been over this!*

Archie to group: *Is this my group? Can you hear me?*

Jess to group: *Archie, yes, we see you.*

Archie to group: *I'm having trouble following these messages. Why can't we have a conference call? Smiley face.*

Imogene to group: *Because it's not 1992 and you don't need to type smiley face! Emoji or emoticons, Archie! They're on your damn phone!*

Archie to group: *Is this Imogene speaking to me? Dear, I have no idea what these science-fiction words mean. I feel like we're in Logan's Run!*

Emma to group: *Who's Logan?*

Cooper to group: *What nut let my wife create this group? Cross her at your own peril. I cannot save any of you.*

Imogene to group: *Oh, shut up <3*

Dylan to group: *I feel the love here. This is the perfect group to do an untrained intervention on a perfectly nice, unsuspecting human being. Perfect group to serve Satan.*

Talia to group: *I'm on my way home now. I'll let my mom know.*

Archie to group: *Talia, you're great! We will all be there to support Mila. LOL!*

Talia to group: *LOL? I'm scared.*

Imogene to group: *GOOD GOD, ARCH! What's with the LOL?*

Archie to group: *I'm sending Talia our love! Lots of love, dear!*

Imogene to group: *THAT'S LAUGHING OUT LOUD! We've been over this! Remember the debacle in the email chain for Mr. Harigrove's emergency brain surgery? You were LOL'ing all over that thing.*

Archie to group: *I forgot. Sad Face.*

Eleanor to group: *Reading this hurts my head. Should I bring booze to this event?*

Jess to group: *Alcohol at an intervention? Seriously?*

Eleanor to group: *We're not intervening because she's a drunk. We're intervening because she needs to get out more and booze it up.*

Dylan to group: *Yeah, that's why we're doing this. Mila needs to drink more. You should bring your bong while you're at it. Mila could use some of your flashbacks to the 60s.*

Lois to group: *Not a bad idea! Pot is medicinal. Mila could use it!*

Aleska to group: *Someone pray for us. My mother bites. I've seen her do it! Tequila shots might subdue her.*

Lauren to group: *I just got caught up on the texts and I'm very concerned that some people are missing the point of what we're doing today. This is not funny! Peyton, would you please explain the mission?*

Peyton to group: *Please don't drag me into this texting circus. I'll go help Talia with the setup. I will send out the signal "NOW" when we need you to head to Mila's house. Walk in all at once.*

Imogene to group: *It's like we're getting ready to nab a unicorn!*

Leo to group: *What's the plan?*

Imogene to group: *OMG, LEO! If I see you, I'm going to run you over with my car! Drink a Red Bull and get with the program!*

Carson to group: *Can you delete me from this group? My back pocket is pinging with all these notifications. Everyone at work is staring at me like I've got a bomb strapped to my ass.*

Jess to group: *Carson, don't you dare mute your phone. If you don't show up on time, I will paint our house pink.*

Talia to Mila: *I'm on my way home.*

Mila to Talia: *I made chicken salad sandwiches. Love you.*
Peyton to Talia: *I'm on my way.*
Talia to Peyton: *Great! I love you.*

What? What? No, no, no, no.

I stare at the message intended for my mother. I told Peyton I love him?

I pedal home fast, a little out of breath. Before I get to our driveway, I see Peyton's truck parked on the shoulder of the road. He flags me down as if I could actually miss him of all people, on an empty road.

"Hey," he says, holding my handlebars as I come to a stop. "I didn't want my truck to tip off your mother in case she's looking out the window, so I'll walk in with you, okay?"

"Good. I am nervous."

The breeze picks up his natural, musky scent, and all at once I am enveloped in Peyton's exquisite protective maleness. I look around as if Harmony has private investigators following me.

He takes my bike from me and walks it to the house. The bike is between us, so I tell myself I'm not breaking my agreement with Harmony. And I'm not going to feel guilty about his involvement in this farce of an intervention. There's nothing romantic about it. A dozen neighbors showing up to coerce my mother isn't what anyone could categorize as seducing a man.

"Well?" He looks at me with a sideways glance. "Your hot text? To me?"

I love you.

"It was an accident!" I blurt out. "I was talking to my mom. I sent it to you by mistake."

"I figured," he says. "But some people say there are no accidents."

"Some people are stupid."

"Fair enough."

As we approach my front door, I realize I miss this with him—being a team, the strong feelings I can't ignore when we're together. Our eyes meet, and there's a second when I foolishly hope he's thinking the same thing.

Peyton props my bike by a large concrete planter that bears the dead stalks of perennials that haven't been cared for in years.

When we first moved into the home, my mother gardened with a vengeance, beautifying the front yard and squaring off a plot in the backyard for vegetables. Now Aleska and I take care of the lawn and trim the hedges, but our limited efforts don't camouflage the abundance of dead vegetation. It gives the outward appearance of something sad happening inside the home. Considering our hundred-year-old neighbor has hopeful blooms popping up all around her yard, thanks to a pricey landscaping service, they make our home look that much shabbier.

I reach for the doorknob and hesitate. "All of a sudden, I have no idea what I'm going to say to her." I search Peyton's face for an answer. "How am I going to start this conversation? Maybe I should let Lois—"

"You'll talk to her as her daughter. You love her, and she knows it." He puts his hand on my shoulder for a few seconds then removes it. "Open the door."

The front door opens right into the living room, and my mother is there in her short bathrobe, a thick terry cloth that swaddles her body like a heavy blanket, but it only reaches midthigh. She has her back, or I should say butt, to us as she bends over the coffee table to put out two plates with sandwiches and chips.

"I thought it would be nice to sit out here," she says, assuming she's talking to just me. When she stands and turns around and sees Peyton next to me, she does some sort of backward bunny hop and quack. "Ack!"

"Hi, Mom."

"Why didn't you tell me you were bringing company? I just got out of the shower!" She touches her wet hair and tugs at the hem of her robe as though she can cover her legs.

"Hello, Mila," Peyton says. "Sorry if it seems like I'm barging in at a bad time." He walks right by her to the entrance of the hallway that leads to our kitchen and the rest of the house. He's going to block the hall and any escape routes to other rooms with doors that lock.

"We're here!" Imogene says, walking through the front door, which is still wide open.

"What are you doing?" The panic in my voice is evident.

"Talia, what's going on?" My mother looks at me, then turns sharply to see what Peyton is doing.

"What the hell? I didn't send you the signal," Peyton says to Imogene.

Imogene brushes by me, followed by everyone else. They parade in like a herd; Jess and Emma first, followed by Lois and Eleanor, who push by us to claim seats on the couch. Then Archie and Emily both shuffle in with their walking canes in hand and perch themselves next to one of our two armchairs. Leo and Lauren walk in holding hands. Cooper, Carson, and Dylan enter with mumbled greetings to my mother, who stands there, clutching her robe closed around her neck, wearing an expression of petrified rage. Aleska saunters in and is about to close the door when Norma pushes her way in with her walker.

"I saw all the people and got over here as fast as I could," Norma says with a huff as she leans on her walker.

"Good to see you, Norma." Imogene then turns to address Peyton. "We got a little confused on the timing. So we all drove over, and when we saw your truck on the side of the road, we parked there, too. Then we stood around and decided we should start walking toward the house."

"I told you all to wait for me. Jesus." Peyton looks at them in disbelief.

"It happened so fast!" Imogene says.

"We couldn't help ourselves," Lois adds, not at all sorry for her untimely arrival. "We're givers. It's why we're here."

"Aleska? Would you care to explain what this is about since your sister won't?" our mother huffs. "Can you tell me why fifteen people are crammed into my living room?"

"This is an intervention," Aleska replies with a sigh, plopping herself into one of the empty armchairs.

"Mila, have a seat. Please," Peyton says.

My mother lets him guide her to the couch where he puts her between Lois and Eleanor. Then he reaches behind her for the hand-crocheted throw on the back of the couch and gently drapes it over her lap so she feels less exposed. Honestly, the robe covers a lot more than the string bikini my mother used to sunbathe in before she became the town hermit. But when you have a room full of unexpected guests and you're only wearing a ratty, short robe that shows off your naked legs, it must feel a little risqué.

Lois claps her hands to get everyone's attention. "Let's leave the bullshit at the door! We're here in love. And now Talia has the floor."

I gape. I don't know how to follow that introduction.

"Talia," my mother snaps. She crosses her arms. "Start talking!"

"Hey," Peyton says as he makes his way to me. "Talia's not the bad guy here. There is no bad guy. She's trying to start a dialogue to help this situation. She wants to help you, Mila." He snakes his arm protectively around my back.

"You know why we're here, Mom. This has gone on too long. You've been living like a recluse in this house for four years. You're too young to waste your life like this. We're all here to help you get out of this situation, whatever it takes, so you can live again. Really live."

"This is my life," my mother says, directing her anger at me. "I don't tell you how to live. It's no one's business." Her eyes flare.

I've seen her angry before, but this is something new. She's got crazy eyes, as if she's possessed.

Aleska shakes her head at me with that *this is going to be impossible* look.

Everyone's eyes are on me. Sure, none of them can speak up and tell the angry lady in the bathrobe that she's two seconds away from crazy town. They're waiting for me to impart great words of wisdom that will magically inspire my mother to address her illness?

"Fine," I growl. "You want to argue instead of agree, then let me tell you that it's my life, too. And it's Aleska's life!"

The old Talia comes alive. She's been lurking underneath all these months, beaten down by a shitty ex-boyfriend and a deceptively cruel heart. I've walked the line gingerly with too much care, pretending that certain men don't affect me and carrying on with a family charade of normalcy. There's nothing normal about my family or me, which is fine, as long as we can talk about it. And now I'm going to talk about it to half the town in the middle of our living room, which feels very much like a public square at the moment.

"I'm tired of pretending that this is okay," I start. "Our life is not okay. Having my mother chained to her house out of fear is not okay with me or Aleska, or any of your friends. And this shouldn't be okay with you. You should fix this and have a life again."

My mother stares at me with a face of stone.

"Stop looking at me like that!" I shout, and she twitches. "Of course, this is our business. Our lives revolve around you and this house. We are grown women with our own business, but we're afraid to move out because we have to take care of you. We're the only ones who see you every day, so we have to make sure you're safe. We love you, so of course we're going to support you, but giving you shelter and food isn't enough. You are completely dependent on us, and I know that makes you unhappy. This is not living. You're just existing and pretending, like the rest of us, that we can continue to be happy with expecting so little. You are an educated, outgoing woman. This cannot be enough for you."

"I have my online support group," my mother exclaims, and the others in the room look around at each other, wondering what to do with that information.

"They aren't your support group!" I shout. "They are anonymous commenters! You could be talking to a rapist or a murderer who's pretending to be agoraphobic!"

"That's silly." My mother rolls her eyes. "A murderer needs to be out among people in order to murder them. He doesn't have time to be agoraphobic."

"Do you hear yourself?"

Aleska sighs forcefully. "You have to get out of this damn house, Mom. You need to work again and be with people. You need to feel productive, and you need to socialize and have fun again. Talia is right. This isn't okay. Not at all. And you haven't seen a doctor in years! You need yearly checkups! You are wasting your life!"

"Do you think my time here is wasted?" My mother shoots her scary eyes at me again. "I'm the one who nursed you back to health. Every hour of every day."

Once again, the attention in the room shifts to me. Everyone's confusion is apparent.

I feel pressure from Peyton's hand on my lower back, and then he squeezes my side. The place most women hate to be touched, the extra fat that taunts us, but now I know why they're called love handles. Through my cotton blouse, I feel the heat and comfort of Peyton's touch, and for once I'm thankful I have a little extra flesh there.

"I took care of you because I'm your mother. I wasn't wasting my time taking care of you after your surgery. I am the person who kept track of all your medication and proper dosages, and I'm the one who made you stay on top of all your physical therapy exercises. I think I was very productive, and I thought my help was important to you."

"Of course, it was, and I have told you how much I appreciated having you take care of me. Do not treat me or Aleska as if we're being unkind. This intervention is hell because you're making this all about you. This is about all of us. Your condition affects all of us."

"Wait. Stop." Imogene raises her hand in the air. "What are you two talking about?"

"Exactly," Eleanor adds. "What's going on? I thought this was about Mila's agoraphobia. What family secret have we stumbled on? Please share."

"Ah, shit." Peyton crosses his arms.

"Great," I mutter.

"What did you expect!" Aleska slouches back into the armchair and puts her legs up on the armrest. "She's not going down without a fight."

"Talia," Peyton says to get my attention. "Talia, you have to tell them. It's time."

"Yes, Talia. You have to tell us," Jess says. She's the best friend I have pushed aside for many months, and her knowing look tells me she expects an explanation.

"Lordy, this is going to be good," Lois declares. "Come on, sugar; give it to us straight."

"Tell them," my mother prods. "You've kept it a secret from them for months, and I went along with it. Tell the truth, and I'll go outside. Do we have a deal?"

"You'll go outside? If I tell them, you'll go outside?"

"Yes. I will," my mother challenges.

I open two buttons on my blouse and pull the collar tips wide to reveal the scar that slices down my chest under my bra. After a whispered chorus of "oh," I button my blouse up again.

"I had surgery. I was going to tell all of you ... eventually."

"Surgery? That's all you can say?" Jess asks. She looks like a little kid who just found out there's no Santa Claus.

"Your brevity is appreciated." Peyton smiles. "But you kinda have to give them more than that."

I've been holding myself so stiffly, but his beautiful smile cracks my tension-filled limbs, and I give in and share a brief laugh with him.

"I had surgery to repair a defective heart valve. I'm perfectly healthy now."

"You had open heart surgery and didn't think to tell us? I'm your best friend. How could you not tell me?" Jess asks.

"Take it easy," Carson says. "Talia doesn't need an inquisition."

"I'm sorry. When I was diagnosed, things moved quickly, and it coincided with Scotty's birth. I was seeing so many doctors and specialists in the city, and whenever I came home, I just wanted to not talk about it. I didn't want to put my stress on you while you were pregnant."

"Wow. Heart surgery," Lauren says. "That's huge. What were your symptoms? I can't believe all of us missed the signs."

"I didn't have symptoms other than a cold that wouldn't go away. A doctor detected a heart murmur. Another doctor diagnosed me with mitral valve prolapse. A leaky heart is what they call it."

"A leaky valve? Those things can kill you," Cooper says.

"That's why I got busy, seeing the best surgeon, getting the pre-surgery testing done. Jess went into labor, and then I went in for surgery soon after Scotty was born."

"I knew it!" Jess says. "I knew you couldn't possibly spend two months in Florida with your father—you barely speak to the man. You were in the hospital, right?"

"I was only in the hospital for one week. I spent two months here, recovering."

"You've been here this whole time, and we all thought you were in Florida? I could have been here with you. I could have helped with whatever it was you needed. I was home all day with a baby, and I had no idea my best friend was two minutes away. I thought you were two thousand miles away."

"Jess, this isn't about you," Imogene says. "Sorry, I know you're emotional about your friend not telling you some very big news, but she had her reasons. People are in a lot of pain after surgery. They can't lift anything, certainly not babies, and they need quiet time with rest, not squealing babies, no matter how cute they are."

"You're right. It's not about me." Jess exhibits a marked sadness.

My omission has damaged our friendship, and it's a reminder of another relationship I need to repair. "I wanted to tell you more than anyone, but it was an overwhelming period for both of us. You were pregnant and scared, and I was scared about dying. I didn't have any energy left to be a friend to anyone."

"Your reasons are justified," Emily speaks up, and Archie agrees.

"Well, this is why my mother is angry at me today. She and Aleska got me through this tough time and kept our business going. My mom did all the cooking for my clients, as you know. She's hoping by divulging my health crisis—which has been resolved—she can deflect from what we're doing today.

"This is an intervention, Mom. No one is questioning your devotion to us as our mother. Even when we disagree or argue, I will say you are an excellent mother. But you're also very sick. You deserve more than this, and so do we."

"That was lovely," Lois says. "You have such smart, loving daughters, Mila. Not every parent can say that."

"It's true. It's so true," Eleanor says, holding my mother's soft, unlined, alabaster hand with her wrinkled, tan one. Perhaps the only benefit to being housebound is my mother doesn't have any sun damage and looks much younger than her age. Sitting between the two older mavens with their frosted and styled, silver hair, my mother looks like she could be my older sister. "We're not here to harass you. The scary part is over; we're all talking about this in the open. No more denial. We just want you to see a doctor."

My mother pushes Eleanor's hand aside and abruptly stands up, holding the lapels of the robe tightly. She actually steps onto the coffee table and hops off the other side, which is the fastest route to the front door.

Did I mention my mother is fast?

She's fast.

And clever. She must have figured out Peyton's job was to keep her contained in the living room and prevent her from running to another part of the house. She fooled us. She slithered between Imogene and Jess, as far away as she could from Peyton and me, so we couldn't grab her. We definitely didn't expect her to run out the front door.

The door hangs open as we all move to the entryway and watch her jog down the front walk, hugging her robe as she takes each barefooted step.

"Uh, should we chase her?" Leo asks.

"Go, Mom! Look at her! She did it!" Aleska exclaims, stepping onto the front stoop.

"Don't do that. Don't encourage her to run," I say. "This is crazy. I didn't expect her to actually run outside. What are we supposed to do now?"

"Let her wear herself out?" Lois asks. "Why not? Let her run."

"Do we have a Plan B? Are we just going to stand here and watch her?" Carson asks. Like everyone else, he can't take his eyes off the runaway, peach-colored robe.

"Move!" Peyton barks as he pushes people aside and heads out the door after her.

I'm right behind him, jogging a little to keep up.

"What are we going to do?" I ask.

He begins jogging, and I have to start sprinting to keep up.

"We'll try to reason with her."

He catches up to my mother and returns to a comfortable gait. I stay on his other side because I think any attempt that I make to talk my mother through her breakdown will only enrage her further.

I glance behind us and see our friends following like a slow-moving herd of confused cows. My family is the center of this public comedy. Even Norma is making her way behind everyone else, clomping her walker down the sidewalk.

We reach our roadside mailbox, and my mother suddenly wraps her arms around the battered tin box like a shipwreck survivor who finds a lone buoy in the middle of the ocean.

"You did it," Peyton says. "Can I walk you back inside now?"

My mother looks terrified, wild-eyed, and her face has contorted into someone else entirely. Someone who looks lost.

I put my arm around her. "You're safe, Mom. Let's go back inside," I say, trying to be as comforting as I can to make up for my less-than-gentle manner from before.

"Mom!" Aleska reaches us. "That was awesome! You did great!"

"We need to get her back inside," I say.

"What? Are you nuts?" Aleska puts her hands on her hips with indignation. "She needs to keep going."

"She's not even dressed! Her hair is wet, and she looks crazy!" I snap.

She needs a soft-spoken therapist to urge her back to her senses. Obviously, I'm not that person. Lately, whatever my mother does or says grates on my nerves, and I can't cheer her on while she parades down the street in her robe. And parade she does. She lets go of the mailbox and begins her march toward town. She follows the shoulder of the county road, which is rocky. The crushed gravel must be killing the soft skin on her bare feet. Fortunately, there's never much traffic on this road, maybe one to two cars per hour. We have this vast, open road to ourselves, with the rest of the circus following. We're like carnival people without the fun costumes.

"This isn't safe, Mila," Peyton says. "You're going to hurt your feet. Let me get you back home."

"No! No, I said I'd go outside. That was the deal, and now I'm outside and I might as well go to Bonnie's Diner for a cup of coffee." She walks faster and moves off the shoulder to walk on the paved asphalt.

"You're going to town in your robe? Really? We didn't ask you to do this, Mom," I say.

Peyton and Aleska flank her sides so she can easily ignore me.

"Arguing with her is not helping," Peyton says.

"Walking half-naked to town isn't exactly the way she should be introduced back into society," I say sharply.

"Hey, she's out of the house. You've been begging her to get out and she's out," Aleska barks back.

"Can't you see she's having a breakdown?" I shout.

"Mila, what do you want us to do for you?" Peyton asks gently. His voice is full of kindness, a distinct contrast to her squabbling daughters. "I can get my truck and drive you back home. It's your call."

My mother doesn't respond. She keeps walking angrily in the direction of town. She releases her tight grip on the robe and begins pumping her arms furiously as if we're all in a walk race.

The sound of a car slowing down behind us makes all four of us turn our heads. It's the sheriff.

My mother scoffs and looks away, walking with intention.

The sheriff is in the proper lane that heads into Hera, and we're walking illegally in the middle of the opposite lane, so he's able to cruise right next to my mother.

He leans an elbow out of his window as he drives and smiles at us. "I got a call that a band of gypsies are heading into town."

"Oh great, the fuzz!" Lois says loudly from behind us.

The sheriff looks back at Lois and sighs. She has that effect on everyone.

"Norma called me," he says.

"Sheriff," Peyton says. "We're trying—"

"Sheriff!" my mother interrupts. "I'd like to report a home invasion. A dozen people showed up at my home and forced me out." She uses a haughty voice without looking at the sheriff and keeps walking. And we keep following.

"Mom!"

Aleska laughs. "I wish I had brought my phone so I could film this."

"These are her daughters," Peyton explains to the sheriff. "Her friends and family staged an intervention. And she's angry with us, so she decided to leave, and …"

"I know," the sheriff says. "Norma told me that part, too. You must be Mila. I'm Sheriff Doyle. Everyone calls me Gavin."

My mother finally gives him the courtesy of her attention.

"Norma said I should arrest you and take you to the hospital."

"I haven't done anything wrong! There's no law that says you can't leave your home in your bathrobe!"

The sheriff smiles. He has a rugged face with a nice smile. He's maybe a few years older than my mother. I wonder if he gets calls like this all the time—dealing with wacky locals who do odd things like taking their horse into the grocery store with them. It happened!

"Sweetheart!" Eleanor shouts from the herd. "Let Gavin take you to the hospital. My therapist is there and ready to see you. They will give you fantastic drugs to knock you out and make you feel good, and then we can all discuss this rationally!"

"I'm not going to arrest you, Mila," says Sheriff *Gavin*. "But I'd be happy to drive you wherever you want to go."

"Maybe I want to go home and just make sticky buns," my mother snipes.

"I like sticky buns," he says. *Oh, this man is a pro with crazy people.* "How about I pull up ahead on the side of the road and you get in and we can talk? I can't in good conscience let you walk barefoot, especially if you're going to cover a few more miles."

"I could talk." My mother lifts her chin and shrugs. Now she's cool and collected. Whatever happened to "it takes a village?" How about "it takes a man?" I guess sometimes it takes the attention of one person who can affect you.

I notice the sheriff doesn't wear a wedding ring. I wonder if he's single and looking for a challenging woman with enough baggage that would sink a boat, but who happens to make great sticky buns.

"This could be very good," Peyton says to me, a little smile dancing across his lips as we watch the sheriff park on the side of the road, and my mother almost skips over to his car. Then she gets in on the passenger side, leaving the rest of us standing awkwardly in the road.

The others start to walk back to my house, but Peyton and I stand where we are as if we're both hoping for a private moment together.

"For a guy who says he doesn't want to settle down and have a family, you sure know how to insert yourself into other people's lives." Confident that Harmony is not in the vicinity and none of my friends would spy for her, I playfully punch his shoulder.

For the first time, I witness him blush. He looks down and smiles, and there's a sweetness that covers up those rough, sometimes arrogant edges of his.

"It must be this town, and Finn. Hard to be the same person when my circumstances have changed."

And then I remember Harmony's words, warning me about what will happen if I choose to maintain a close friendship with Peyton.

He will lose Finn.

I can't jeopardize Peyton's new family.

"You have everything you want," I say. "I'm happy for you."

"Not everything. So, why don't we grab dinner together someplace? I can give you dating advice."

"Very funny, but I can't. Anyway, thank you for today. My mother doesn't know it yet, but she thanks you, too." I step away from him, feeling reluctant but sure it's the right thing to do. "It's all going to work out. Right?"

"It's a big question." He studies my face, and for a brief, dreamy moment, it seems like we're both back in Carson's SUV, driving a baby through the wooded hills, laughing and flirting and experiencing that first real flicker of attraction.

And now I'm left with *longing.*

"I hope it all works out," he says. "For both of us."

26

Peyton

"**D**O YOU HAVE TO be so obvious?" Bash asks, plating some new entrees he's trying out. He wipes the rims of the plates with a towel, then places them on the main worktable so the servers can sample them.

"What do you mean?" I ask, noticing Talia's delivery bags are loaded and stacked, but she's nowhere in sight. The cooks and servers are on a short beverage break in the bar while Bash sets up the menu tasting, so we're alone and I can speak freely.

"She's in the cooler getting some extra parsley for her garnishes," Bash says.

"Huh. So, what are you serving here?"

"Get off it, dude. You didn't come in here to eat the same food I had you sample two hours ago. You're in here to see Talia, and I know it. The staff knows it, and Talia knows it, which makes me wonder why she's taking so long in the damn cooler. First you two were barely talking to each other, then you were always together, showing up together, leaving together. Then it went back to not talking. What the hell happened?"

"I had a kid, I guess."

"He's a great kid, and Talia really likes him. That's not the problem."

"The kid comes with a very intense mother, and I suppose my career choice isn't exactly ideal for a woman who wants a normal life. Same issues I had with Flora."

"No, these aren't the same issues you had with Flora. Number one, you weren't in love with Flora."

"I never said I'm in love with … anyone."

"Fuck that, dude. You are so into Talia. And why not? She's great. And she works in the same business as you—there's no way your career is a problem for her. She likes working in our kitchen, and we like having her here. So do you. And everything between you two was falling into place perfectly. When you found out about Finn, Talia didn't judge you. This is light years ahead of what you had with Flora or any other woman. So what the fuck are you doing to screw this up?"

"I don't know. I honestly don't know. Talia just decided we had to end anything beyond friendship. She claims we both have a lot of baggage and somehow we're not right for each other."

I haven't spoken to anyone about this, and Bash and Greer are usually the first people I turn to when I have a problem.

Over the few months we've known each other, something about my relationship with Talia gave me a sense of great accomplishment, as though I'd become a better person, the man I had been striving to be. I felt like I was transforming into someone else, hopefully someone good, but that feeling faltered when Talia ended it.

"Adam Knight is interested in her, and I don't know whether it's genuine or if he's playing her. She knows what she wants. She has long-term plans carved in stone when it comes to her personal and professional life. So maybe she's playing along with Knight, maybe it's just sex, maybe it's more. I'm fucking clueless because she won't tell me a damn thing. But believe me; it's pissing me off."

"Because you're in love with that fiery little blonde."

"Stop exaggerating. I never said that."

"So, why are you jealous of Adam? Because you don't want her to fall for the dude. Shit, even I can see that."

Talia enters the kitchen, so I swallow my next remark.

"Hey," I say to her.

"Hey there," she returns, carrying a bouquet of parsley over to her delivery packages. "Well, I'm taking off."

"You're leaving early today?" I ask. I could kick myself because, yes, I'm so obvious. I even know the woman's delivery schedule.

"I have a light load tonight, so I want to get the dinner service done early. Norma's my last delivery, and I promised her that I'd stay for a game of cards. She wants to talk about my mom."

"Good. And your mom is doing well? Lois told me your mom has made a couple of visits to a doctor."

"Yes, it's very exciting," Talia laughs in a high lilt. "Thanks to Sheriff *Gavin*. He comes by the house every day and has coffee with my mom. He's the one who takes her to her appointments. He's designated himself as her driver and assistant for the next month, according to our calendar on the fridge. You were right when you said he could be a very good thing for my mother. I think they like each other."

"I told you I know something about men."

"Oh, Christ," Bash says. "Talia, can you hang on while we taste these new dishes? I want your feedback."

The staff break has ended and everyone is filing into the kitchen and milling around the new plates of food Bash has on display.

"Gather round," Bash says.

"Yes, Chef!" the staff sings out in unison.

As Bash explains the dishes, their titles and descriptions, so the servers can pitch them to customers, everyone grabs a clean fork and takes a few bites from each plate. I check the iPad I'm carrying and review the reservations and any important notes Greer may have added. I also watch Talia out of the corner of my eye, tasting the food and complimenting Bash.

"Everyone, listen up," I say. "We have some very special guests tonight, so I want you to be in top form. I know you give it your best, so tonight shouldn't be any different, but be aware of the special company we have this evening."

I give these pre-evening meetings before we open, and Talia is sometimes here, but this time, I'm suddenly more self-conscious as she watches me.

With the weight of her gaze upon me, I'm humbled. And I'm neither a humble man, nor am I known for being philanthropic, but Talia looks at me in a way that suggests I am a man worth knowing. It is a lofty feeling. If I was meeting her for the first time, I would simply think she's checking me out—because that's who I used to be. However, after months of being with her every day, I know more about Talia than any other person. I have memorized her, all of her, down to the smallest details to capture her essence.

I scroll through my tablet. "Tonight we have Major Schmidt with us. He's an old friend of Bash's family and served in Iraq and Afghanistan. I hold a special place for people like him. Make him feel welcome, please. We're seating him and his guest at table eleven."

Talia smiles at me. It throws me off for a moment, and then I remember to read off the rest of the VIP reservations.

"We also have Joley Casper joining us tonight. As most of you know, she's a popular food blogger in New York City. She has a huge Twitter following, so she'll be watching and tweeting while she's here. God help us. She'll be here at seven, and we're putting her at table five. Let's give her something to rave about."

"I love her tweets!" Sunny chimes in. "She's hilarious!"

"And ruthless." Wayne, one of our more aggressive servers, pumps his fist. "She's the perfect woman for me. She loves food, and she's mean."

"I'll make sure you are not her server," I say, and everyone laughs. "Also, we have Jenny's parents here tonight." There are a few *ahhs*, and Jenny smiles. "They flew in from Indiana to see her, so let's wow them. Greer will be stopping by all those particular tables to visit, and for those special people, we're comping everything, so don't let the bill touch their table."

"It's going to be a full house tonight, with the first turnover estimated at six thirty," Bash adds. "I want this kitchen running smoothly."

"Yes, Chef!" the servers and cooks chant.

"If you see food come up, I want you to run it, even if it's not your check," Bash continues. "And when you're coming back into the kitchen, don't walk by a dirty table. If the customers have left the table, pick up some dishes and bring them with you back to the dishwasher. We need everyone pitching in because we're short a busboy tonight."

"Yes, Chef!" Everyone laughs.

"Talia," I say, and she looks surprised. "Why don't you tell the staff what you think is the most important part of the service experience?"

She shrugs and casually says, "Turn off your vibrators."

My laughter is the loudest above the others.

She grimaces. "I meant, set your phones to vibrate. I hate when I see a server looking at their phone or you hear it ringing in their apron when they're standing next to a table. It makes the customer feel unimportant."

"You hear that?" I say to the group. "No phones. I don't want to see or hear them on the floor. And we're all bussing tonight, and we're all moving food. If I'm not here plating trays, Greer will be. You've all been doing a great job with customers and making things run smoothly. But tonight will be extra busy, and we're short-staffed—the customers can't suffer. It needs to run like clockwork in the kitchen, but the dining room needs to feel relaxed and casual. So keep your panic attacks contained to the back of the house."

"Yes, sir!" Wayne salutes and clicks his heels together.

"Get out of here," I say, chuckling with the others.

"You're such a nice boss," Talia comments, lifting one of her delivery bags and propping it on her hip.

"Shouldn't you be getting on the road?"

"I'm leaving, but I'm glad I didn't miss the pregame show. You're like a god."

"Not funny."

"It wasn't meant to be."

I pick up her other delivery bags and carry a tower of them on my shoulder, following my dream girl out of the kitchen. We head through the dining room toward Greer, who is talking to a group of businessmen by the hostess station. One of the well-dressed men turns around. It's Danny Bourdain.

"Peyton! Just the man I'm looking for."

Talia glances back at me. There's no mistaking her anger.

"Good to see you, Danny. I'm gonna run this stuff outside, and then we can catch up."

"Hey, I'm not going anywhere. I came here to see you." Danny gives one of those big *I'm going to make you an offer you can't refuse* smiles.

Talia slams open the front door and holds it for me. "After you." She glowers at me, fuming as I carry her bags to her van. "Why are they here?" she demands, taking one thermal bag at a time from me and placing them strategically inside the van.

"We're going to have a conversation about working together."

"In LA? Really? You're still considering this? You would move there? What about Finn?"

"I'm not abandoning Finn. More than anything, I'm doing this because of him. This is a chance for Bash and me to be part of a national brand."

"It's all about you. God, Peyton, I actually started to believe you were different. When Finn came into your life, I thought, here's a good man. He's going to be a good dad. He's going to put his kid first before his own needs. I can't believe you're going to screw this up for you and Finn."

"I'm not screwing up. I'm weighing my options." It's difficult not to sound defensive. "This would be great for developing our brand, and that's money in the bank for Finn. I'm building something I can pass on to him."

She slams the van doors closed. "I can't believe you! You can't take Finn with you to LA, because his mother is here, which means you'll be traveling, gone for months at a time. This will go on for years. While you build up your brand, and your fame, and your bank account, Finn will grow up without a dad. Again! It's like that old song 'Cats in the Crib,' when the dad finally realizes he missed his kid's whole childhood because he put work first. I'm so disappointed in you."

"In me? First of all, the song is 'Cat's in the Cradle,' and I am not the dad in that sad song. Give me a break. Second, you're the one who decided I wasn't good enough to be with you. Don't you think I'm disappointed *in you* and how you're judging me? And I wouldn't be leaving Finn. I would have to do a bit of traveling at first, a West Coast, East Coast thing, but I wouldn't abandon him."

"Right, that's what they all say. Before you know it, Finn will be eighteen and off to college. You already missed the first half of his childhood. This is it. Do you really think you're going to get another chance with him? If you choose Danny Bourdain over your own son, I will lose all respect for you."

"I thought we had some kind of connection," I say, floored by her response. "We were starting to get pretty close, and I thought you of all people understood how I feel about Finn and how important it is for me to do right by him. I can't believe you have such a shitty opinion of me."

"I didn't, until I saw those guys in there."

"You have misinterpreted this whole thing, Talia. I'm not meeting with them to serve my own needs. I'm doing this because I have some great ideas and these guys can help make them happen. It's about creating something bigger and better, and it all comes back to Finn and ..."

"And what?"

The distrust in her eyes makes me wonder if I was wrong. Maybe I'm the one who misinterpreted what I thought was happening between the two of us. Perhaps I was nothing more than a convenient lothario for her.

Until Talia, I was never confused about women, any woman. Either I was interested in being with them for a while, or I wasn't. There were no gray areas in between that made me question my feelings for them or where I stood. Because I never had these feelings. I never cared. Until this Polish chef and her hotheaded opinions about men made me care about her.

"This opportunity is important to me, but it will also allow me to offer more to Finn."

"Harmony is rich. Finn is already taken care of financially, so don't use money as an excuse."

"I don't want Harmony to foot all the big expenses: his private school, college—all of it. Kids are expensive. Finn needs to see me as an equal contributor."

She snickers. "Right. Same thing my dad used to say about needing more money. Look how that turned out."

• • •

The meeting with Danny Bourdain and his business partners goes well, but there isn't a moment when I'm not thinking about Talia and the fury directed my way. Her rage makes me want to prove myself to her.

I give these guys the grand tour and have no problem revisiting my restaurant ideas for their recently acquired Las Vegas and Malibu locations. My arrogance is full throttle, the kind of cockiness that helps sell me and all that is me. Bash is the reserved one. He joins us for a good, long meeting, but as he talks about different menus and themes, my mind wanders back to Talia.

I imagine her out on her deliveries, thinking about me, furious with me, wishing I would change. *Adam Knight is trapped on his toilet with a painful call from nature so he can't flirt with her—it's my fantasy—so Talia sets up his dinner without him and promptly leaves his home. Attagirl. Then she's back in her van, driving and thinking about me and how I am her type more than any other man.*

I have family in Hera, a business in Hera, and now I have a son who roots me to this place she calls home. Those are the practical items on her checklist, and then there's the chemistry between us. When we're in the same room, our emotions get knocked up a few levels. We're hormonally charged when we're together, whether we're going over inventory lists in a fully staffed kitchen or arguing on the street. There isn't a moment when I don't want her, and there isn't a moment when I don't want her to care about me more.

When she left me standing in front of Swill as she drove off, I was on shaky ground, thinking I'd really blown it with her. Then the meeting with the Bourdain-Torrance guys made me all cocky again. After a few hours of talking, and after we watched Swill fill to capacity with customers and energized waitstaff, we agreed we wanted to move forward with a partnership. I was feeling good about my business and feeling confident that I could still win Talia over. It'd require some explaining to knock some sense into that stubborn head of hers, but she wouldn't be so emotional about this if she didn't care. That thought is what keeps me going.

I walk Danny and his colleagues out to their cars, the only Maserati and Aston Martin in the full parking lot, and they do look preposterous among the dust-covered trucks and SUVs. I do a quick once-over to make sure Talia didn't key their cars while they were inside schmoozing me. Then we say our goodbyes with plans for upcoming meetings with more executives from Bourdain-Torrance. I'm confident Bash and I will get everything we ask for and more.

My grandiose thoughts are interrupted by the vibration of my phone in my back pocket. It's Talia. She probably thought of more ways to yell at me.

"Talia," I say, thankful she can't see my smile and how smug I'm feeling at the moment.

"I need you here ... She's dead!"

She's crying and explaining what happened as my truck tears out of the parking lot.

27

Peyton

I<small>T'S DARK WHEN</small> I arrive at her house, but the lights from the ambulance and the sheriff's patrol car light up the night. I park a good distance away so I don't block the emergency vehicles, and then I jog toward the commotion.

The EMTs are at the back of the ambulance with a stretcher. The covered figure is lifeless. I glance up at the front door of Talia's home and see the sheriff, Gavin, consoling Mila. To the left, standing in the open doorway of Norma's home, Talia is watching the EMTs and crying. Through the flashing lights and with the backdrop noise of crackling voices on the ambulance radio, it's like swimming against a chaotic tide to reach her. I grip her arms and pull her against me. I'm too rough. It's the charged atmosphere of death and fear. I hold her more tightly as if this will make a difference and change the outcome. Her head down, buried against my chest, she keeps crying.

"I'm sorry," I say. No matter how heartfelt those two words are, they feel useless.

"She was very old," she says between sobs. "She knew—we all knew—it was going to happen soon. She wasn't really eating for the last two weeks."

"Still. It's hell to lose someone you love. Was her nurse here?"

"No. Norma was alone. I found her. She died all alone." She cries harder, gulping sobs.

I lift her chin so I can see her face. Her eyes are puffy and red, and she sorely needs a box of tissues.

"She wasn't alone. You and your family spent time with her every day. She was not a lonely woman. Norma was loved, and she was happy."

Talia stops crying and wipes her eyes and runny nose with the hem of her shirt. "I walked in like I always do, to deliver a hot meal to her. I don't know which nurse was on duty today, but Norma likes to let them go home early. She was sitting at the kitchen table. Her forehead was resting on it. I thought she fell asleep in the middle of the Sudoku puzzle she was working on." Talia shakes her head. "I knew, though. I think I felt it before I walked in the house. The air, something ... it all felt different, like something was missing. It felt like something was gone. Even when I called her name, I knew she was dead. If people do have souls, Norma's was not in that room. Maybe I was imagining it. The absence of energy."

"You've never been through this, have you?"

"No. I've been to wakes and funerals, but I've never been there when someone close to me dies. I wish I could have been holding her hand when she took her last breath. I wish she could have been comforted."

"If it helps, I don't think Norma was scared of dying. She's lived longer than most people, and right until the end, her mind was sharp. It's possible she let her nurse go home so she could be alone and enjoy her puzzle, because she knew this was her last day."

"She generally got what she wanted."

"She was strong. And you're strong, and you're going to help your mom through this, too." We both look over at Gavin and Mila. "Someone needs to contact Norma's relatives, if she has any, and help with arrangements. You'd be better at this than your mother."

"Me?" Talia looks up at me, scared. "I don't know how to do this, and I'm a wreck like my mother. Look at me. I'm a mess."

"You're not a mess. You're sad, but your mom is more fragile than you. She was starting to make progress, but Norma's death may set her back."

"Talia!" Aleska waves at us. The ambulance driver says something to her, and then she runs over to us.

"Where were you?" Talia asks.

"We were running behind at work. Marguerite just dropped me off. When I saw the ambulance, I thought something happened to Mom. Then I saw Norma. They covered her face when I got closer."

I push Talia toward her sister. They hug, and then they both begin crying again.

"She was so old. We should be celebrating her long life," Aleska says through her bawling.

"I hate when people say things like that," Talia says through her choking sobs. "Peyton says I should be the one to call her family."

"He's right. You need to call her niece. She's in Arizona or Guatemala, or someplace like that."

"Those are two very different places," I remark. This crying and hugging could go on for a while.

"She lives someplace south, very far away," Talia adds. "Lois will know how to reach her."

"Yes, Lois will know. She knows everything. And Norma knew everything," Aleska says, and then she and Talia look at each other and watch each other cry as if it's a competition.

"I'm sorry." I gently tug them apart. "Aleska, could you please go comfort your mother? I'm pretty sure the sheriff needs to get back to work and deal with Norma's ... situation."

Aleska wipes her eyes. "Who's going to watch over Mom now that Norma's gone?" There's a pause, and then Aleska takes off running toward her mother.

"That's what I'm worried about, too," Talia tells me. "You'd think my mother was the one checking in on an old woman every day, but it was Norma checking in on her. I could leave the house each day knowing my mother had Norma. And one of Norma's nurses was usually around."

"Your mother doesn't need a babysitter. Stop thinking like a parent. You're not her mother. She'll be fine."

"No, nothing is fine. I assumed Norma would live another ten years, at least. She was part of my five-year plan, because I kept forgetting how old she was. Who makes plans for the future that include a hundred-year-old woman?"

"It shows how important Norma was to your family."

"She's my ... She was my biggest cheerleader. She's the one who believed in my dream for the Pickwick house. She was encouraging and never once made me think it would be a financial disaster. Like you did."

"I never said your Pickwick thing would be a disaster. I'm a businessman. I look at all sides."

"And I'm not a businesswoman? I wish Norma were here to put you in your place."

"I wish she were here, too."

As we walk across the lawn to her home, I slip my arm across her shoulders. All the emergency vehicles and people are gone. We watch Gavin get in his car and follow the ambulance. Mila and Aleska retreat inside their house. We're alone, and I catch myself kissing the top of her head. Talia stops walking.

"What are you doing?" she asks.

"Sorry. Habit. I forgot I'm not allowed to do that."

28

Peyton

THE LINE FOR VIEWING the casket is out the door. Everyone knew Hera's oldest resident. It's the kind of event that closes down businesses for the day.

I'm wearing a black suit, and I got a cut and a shave at the barbershop since I've been requested by Eleanor to be a pallbearer. Norma had her will written sometime back when she was in her sixties, at least forty years ago. It's baffling that she didn't amend the will to update the pallbearers, but she must have had her reasons, sentimental or otherwise.

At the time, she liked the idea of having her former kindergarten students be her pallbearers. They were listed by name in her will. Unfortunately, if you live to be a hundred, you're probably going to outlive your six-year-old students who would now be in their eighties. Norma outlived all but one of them, which is why Eleanor called me and the other guys to fill in.

It's my turn to have Finn, but I asked him if he would stay with his mom today. He was very understanding.

Mila is the most distraught. I'm not going to lie and say I'm not also hoping to spend some time with the bereaved daughter and comfort her, too.

The minute I park my truck, Lois flags me down from the church door, yelling my name and telling me to jump the line.

As I put on my suit coat and brush some lint off my sleeves, I hear murmurs, women remarking on my appearance. It's awkward considering the circumstances. Sometimes this whole town makes me feel like I'm on display.

I stride quickly past the line to Eleanor, receiving a few whistles along the way. Who does that at a funeral?

I look back at the culprits, a group of senior women who run the town knitting club.

Eleanor and Lois hustle me up to Norma's open casket while I scan the church for Talia.

"This is a trip, isn't it?" Cooper says as he approaches me with Carson and Dylan. They're also dressed in suits, so I don't feel completely out of place among this crowd in summer casual wear.

"Very different than Mom's funeral. This almost seems like a party," I say.

"It is," Carson says, edging his way past us to see Norma. "Norma wanted this to be a fun day."

"Nothing says fun like putting someone six feet under," Dylan remarks.

"Oh hush, you boys," Lois says.

I get in line behind them as we approach Norma's casket. When she comes into view, I'm taken aback for a second, and then I'm amused. This funeral has Norma's handiwork all over it.

The casket is white. The interior is a light pink satin. Norma is laid out in a bright pink gown with sequins and long, white gloves that reach to her elbows. I've never seen anything like this and can't stop staring at the tiny woman who looks like she was a Vegas showgirl in a former life. I can't stop myself from smiling. I'm positive this is what Norma intended all along. To make people smile, to make them feel good.

"Oh, Norma, honey. You look fabulous. Doesn't she look fabulous?" Eleanor asks of those circling her casket.

"She looks like she was dressed by Bob Mackie," Lois says.

"Who's that?" I ask.

That was a mistake. I get a long-winded lecture on Sonny and Cher, Carol Burnett, and TV variety shows from the 1970s.

"You had to ask," Carson mutters.

The viewing line is long, and if the priest is ever going to be able to start the service, they need to get the people in their seats to clear the aisle. Others will have to stand in back and outside, listening on the outdoor speaker system that's been set up.

Lois and Eleanor usher the pallbearers to the pews available to us, and that's when I spot Talia sitting with her family. Mila is between her daughters with Aleska on the aisle. I nudge my way through the bottleneck of people, trying to get to them. Aleska smiles when she sees me and immediately nudges Mila and Talia to their right so I can sit down.

"Thanks," I say to Aleska. Then I lean over so I can see Mila and Talia. "This is like being at the hottest show in town. I think I had an easier time getting tickets to *Hamilton*."

Aleska giggles. Talia shakes her head and doesn't look at me.

I reach over Aleska and put my hand on Mila's arm. "How are you doing? I know this is really difficult for you, and it wasn't easy for you to come here either."

Mila covers my hand with hers. "I didn't think I could do this, but you were so helpful. Thank you for what you told Gavin."

Talia snaps her head in my direction. "What did Peyton do?" She glares at me. "Gavin drove you here. He's the one you should thank."

"I did thank him. Gavin said Peyton told him what to say to convince me to come here today. When Gavin stopped by our house last night to talk to me—after I said I couldn't go through with this—he used Peyton's words to convince me."

"You didn't tell me that," Talia hisses.

"I don't tell you everything," Mila replies.

"In either case, I'm glad you're here," I say.

"On our way over, we got to ride in the sheriff's patrol car. Talia and I had to sit in back like we were perps." Aleska grins. "It gave Talia flashbacks."

"Shut up." Talia promptly crosses her arms like a petulant child with a pursed mouth and stares straight ahead.

I want to know more about Aleska's remark, but the priest begins speaking and a general hush falls over the congregation. I steal one more glance at Talia. She's wearing a fitted black dress and simple, tiny gold hoops in those dainty earlobes of hers. Her crossed legs are bare, and she lets one of her black pumps dangle from her toes. I get a good look at those legs. I know how smooth the skin is and how they feel wrapped around me. The last place I need to get an erection is in church, at a funeral, so I put that salacious thought aside.

Her hair is swept up into a twist, and there's no way not to notice her beautiful profile and her blue eyes against her black dress. At the moment, she looks like an angry young widow.

I'm told the priest, Father Pat, flew back from Disney World, where he was vacationing with his sister's family, so he could preside over the funeral of Hera's oldest resident. He launches into humorous tales about Norma, and the whole event starts to resemble a celebrity roast. Norma's quest to begin her worldwide travels in Thailand at age ninety get a few laughs, and her philanthropic efforts in Hera summon up cheers and applause. There are plenty of hilarious Norma stories, including one about her chaining herself to a rollercoaster because the attendant and the park officials felt she was too old to ride it at the age of ninety-four. I feel guilty for laughing at that one since Talia and Mila sit in stony silence like two doomsday sentries.

When I'm given the signal from Eleanor, I stand and mentally prepare myself to perform my pallbearer duties.

"Go get 'em," Aleska says.

Talia keeps her attention riveted to the front of the church.

Cooper and the other pallbearers stand, as well, and make their way to the aisle.

Eleanor filled me in that the old man sitting at the front of the church is Jasper, one of Norma's former students. He struggles to stand up from his pew, then looks around, worried he's not capable of the task at hand. He has at least fifty years on us. When he sees me and my brother, though, followed by the other men much taller and much younger than himself, he looks positively relieved.

"Thank God," he says. "There's no way I could lift this thing, even if I was twenty years younger and they gave me a forklift." His rheumy eyes look apologetic.

Eleanor jumps out of the front pew with her gauzy turquoise top flowing around like fairy wings and begins maneuvering all of us into position around the casket. She moves me up front, along with Jasper, the idea being that I will carry the weight while he will be seen as the one with seniority. Cooper and Leo are behind me, and then Dylan and Carson are behind Jasper, reassuring the old man that he doesn't have to do anything except pretend he's carrying the casket.

"Don't shoulder it," I tell Jasper.

He raises his hands and puts his fingers on the bottom rim of the casket for show. He's almost a foot shorter than me.

Our walk down the aisle is excruciatingly slow due to Jasper's slide-and-shuffle gait. The organist begins playing the score to Cher's "If I Could Turn Back Time," which I certainly wasn't expecting, but then these are not traditional people, and Norma loved a good show.

The church has a festive vibe as people watch us carry the casket. This is nothing like the crying, grieving group of mourners at my mother's funeral, where I didn't think I could survive the service.

It's only a ten-minute drive to the cemetery, but it takes another hour to get all the cars parked. Like one giant tailgate party. Lois even brings out a bullhorn and shouts at people to get to the grave site.

I seem even more out of place among the large crowd, which looks as if they are sporting the new summer collection from Old Navy. Inexpensive floral shirts and dresses and a lot of flowy outfits like Eleanor's get up. It must be a Hera thing—these oddball characters and their nutty customs.

I catch Talia observing me, mentally judging me for judging her people, I suppose. I give her a quick smile, then take my place behind her and other people who knew Norma best.

I lean over Eleanor's shoulder and whisper, "I feel overdressed."

"Nonsense," she whispers back. "You look dapper. Exactly as a pallbearer should."

"Then why is Talia and her family in black and the rest of the town look like a psychedelic acid trip?"

"Mila is traditional. She has those old-country ways. If they could wear black veils, they would. But here in Hera, if you live to be a hundred, it's a day to celebrate."

"Hush," Talia whispers to both of us.

I wink at her, and she bunches up her angry mouth and looks forward again.

In the distance, I see Gavin leaning next to his patrol car. I'm assuming he's waiting to drive Mila home. The other patrol car next to him is the one that led the procession, and I suppose he's hanging around in case someone causes trouble. Something like moonshine or bathtub gin being passed around comes to mind. I laugh to myself a little too loudly and heads turn. People think I'm laughing at the priest's witty sermon.

"It's not that funny," Lois says from my other side. She's wearing long, dangling, silver earrings that jingle like bells when she moves her head. Her jewelry certainly goes with the billowy, red clown pants she's wearing.

"It's kind of funny," I say. "This whole place is just plain weird sometimes."

"You love us," Eleanor comments as she fluffs her head of fresh silver curls.

Talia turns around and looks at me again before granting me a brief smirk. I smile in return. It's good to be in this position again, where being near her, even at a funeral, makes my whole day.

We have to stand in the hot sun quite a bit longer as dozens of people come forward to tell their personal stories about Norma, all trying to outdo one another with the funniest Norma story or Norma quote. Each of them places a flower bouquet on her casket. Soon, the pile of flowers is so high I can't see the people on the other side of the grave.

"This is interesting," I say into Talia's ear.

She swings a foot back and a sharply placed pointy heel hits me squarely in the shin. I grunt and lurch in pain.

"You can't escape," she whispers with her back to me.

"I don't want to escape. I'm exactly where I want to be."

Talia is motionless, but Jess and Imogene turn around and look at me. Jess raises an eyebrow.

• • •

Gavin appears by Mila's side, puts out his arm for her to hold on to, and walks her to his car. He seems to have the right touch with a woman who is a bundle of nerves and anxious to be back in her little house.

I want to ask Mila how it feels to be outside and have the sunshine on her face, but her solemn expression and eagerness to have Gavin steal her away say everything. Then I watch Talia and Aleska for a while, talking to a few people and passing out free hugs. Talia is warm and animated with others while she's been putting up walls with me. This new resistance is beguiling and only serves to make the pursuit more enticing. When she gives old Jasper a hug and says she'll see him at the house, I make my approach.

"Can I give you a lift back? I know it's not as exciting as riding in the sheriff's car, but I bet I have a better playlist."

She looks around as if she's thinking of a reason that she can't be in the same car with me.

"It's just a ride," I say with a bit of annoyance.

She gives me a hard look. "I suppose I can't avoid you completely. Too small of a town, right?"

"Precisely. And I'm simply being a good neighbor."

Her plump, pink lips form a little smile, but her eyes look wary. "I'm only saying yes because Aleska has offered to drive the band in our van. Their truck broke down, so Aleska is racing out to get their equipment and drive them back to the house before the guests—"

"Band? What band?"

"The Frankies."

I laugh. "The who?"

"The Frankies. Norma requested they sing at her party. She saw them perform at The Rack a couple of years ago, so she put it in her funeral instructions to have them play. Although, I don't think she considered how small our house is and how big her audience will be."

"I'm still stuck on the first part. The Rack is a biker bar. What was Norma doing there?"

"She was meeting us girls for beers. Norma liked to have fun."

"I'll say. So I'm assuming The Frankies are hard rock?"

"No, they sing all Frank Sinatra songs. Duh."

"You're joking."

"Why would I joke about that? Norma loved Frank Sinatra, and the lead singer looks like Sinatra from the 1940s. The whole band dresses in those suits and hats men wore from that time period. They reminded Norma of when she was young."

"I can't wait." I move past her to open my truck door for her. I support her elbow as she climbs up into the cab and get a good, long look at her smooth, bare legs.

She adjusts herself in the seat and crosses her legs. I admire the whole picture of her and take a swift breath to keep the naked images of her in my bed away. No such luck. She's gorgeous and sexy and doing nothing but fueling my desire for her.

"Jesus," I mumble as I hand her the shoulder strap to buckle in. "Being your neighbor is tricky."

"Poor baby. Drive fast. People come early when they know there's going to be good food."

"Yes, ma'am. We don't want to miss the first batch of sticky buns and The Frankies' opening number."

The party has already started when we arrive. Mila is rushing around, putting out dishes of food on the kitchen table and the card tables set up around the living room and family room. People park their cars and trucks on the lawn, and visitors push slowly through the house. The front and back doors are left open to keep the oxygen flowing and people moving.

The Frankies are set up in the backyard, right off the kitchen deck. There are four of them; I suppose to symbolize the famous Rat Pack. They are young, maybe late twenties, tops, and look more like rockabillies and a mix of Buddy Holly and Elvis Presley, yet they croon like Sinatra and Dean Martin. The music has everyone bopping their heads, and some of the older people have taken off their shoes so they can dance on the piece of linoleum that has been laid out on the grass for this purpose. I see Archie and Emily do a slow waltz around the others in their stocking feet. They all look a little silly, but I'm tempted to grab Talia's hand and take her out there and dance to "New York, New York."

As if she can sense what I'm scheming, she dodges through the crowd to help Mila in the kitchen.

"This is nuts," I say when I find Imogene and Cooper.

"Nothing like Mom's funeral; that's for sure," Cooper says. "These people know how to have fun."

"In Hera, we like to celebrate a person's life," Imogene says. "I need another tequila sunrise."

"They're serving those?" I stupidly ask as Imogene slurps the remains of a big, pinkish-orange concoction.

"Of course! It was Norma's favorite drink." Imogene says, then tips her glass to get the very last sludgy, neon remains. "Actually, that's not true. Norma loved cocktails. Period. Any retro drink would do. We went with tequila sunrises because Eleanor loves them, too, and she makes them really strong."

"I'm going to find Talia," I say to no one in particular as Carson and the rest of our friends approach with more orange drinks in hand.

The crowd in the house finally starts to thin out as people choose to take their food and drinks outside, filling the front and backyards. Talia is taking her hosting duties seriously, zipping around, clearing and serving. When I reach her, she is talking to a short woman who looks to be in her seventies.

"Hey," I say to Talia, and then I greet the woman with a hello. It is a cocktail party, after all.

"This is Norma's niece, Doris," Talia explains. "She flew in from Alabama."

"Oh, so you're not from Arizona or South America."

"Ha-ha," Talia says. "So Aleska and I were off by a few thousand miles."

When Doris smiles, she resembles Norma.

"It's a pleasure to meet you. I'm Peyton. Your aunt was an amazing woman."

"It's nice to meet you, too. I wish I could have lived closer to Aunt Norma, but my work kept me in Alabama. I'm comforted knowing she had all of you and this lovely town to look over her. I really want to thank you for everything you've done, honey." She grasps Talia's hands.

"No, thank you! Really, I love doing this!" Talia says exuberantly with a big smile.

Her hyperness and odd statement startle Doris. And me. Talia blushes with embarrassment at her outburst.

"It's all right, honey," Doris says. "I'm going to go visit with Lois and Eleanor a bit and get one of those pretty drinks."

As Doris disappears into the kitchen crowd, Talia whips her head in my direction. "How crazy did I just sound? Because I sound crazy to myself. Did I just thank her for Norma's death? What was that?"

I laugh. "This is normal. You're having mixed feelings of sadness and joy over Norma. I have to say that serving cocktails and having a dance band adds to the confusion. Don't worry about it. No one thinks your enthusiasm for bereavement cooking is odd at all." I rub her back, enjoying how the black silk picks up the heat from her skin, and then that moment is punctuated by the lead singer of The Frankies belting out an oldie but goodie with the words *psycho killer* in it.

Talia makes a face. "Is that Frank Sinatra?"

"No. Talking Heads." I laugh. "Sorry, but their timing is perfect."

"Because I sound psychotic? And stop touching me like that." She shakes my hand off. "It confuses me. It's not the funeral. It's you. You confuse me. When you touch me like that, I can't tell if you're treating me like a child or like another one of your conquests."

"I'm treating you like a friend who's in distress."

"Talia!" a woman interrupts. She pulls a middle-aged man alongside her who I assume is her husband. "You did such a nice job with Norma's arrangements. She would have loved this."

"Thank you, Bev. It's good to see you, too, Rupert. This is Peyton MacKenzie. He owns Swill, the—"

"Oh, man, we love that place," Rupert gushes and shakes my hand.

Then Bev's eyes tear up a bit, and she dabs at them with a heavily worn tissue balled up in her hand. "I'm going to miss our old gal."

Talia hugs her. "Me, too. So much."

"Anyway, we have to get home and let the dogs out." Rupert claps his hands together.

I look at them and Talia, waiting for a punch line to the pop reference.

"They really do have to let the dogs out," Talia tells me. "They own a kennel."

Right. This is country life, where bands play Sinatra and Talking Heads at funerals and we have to let the dogs out.

"Makes sense," I say as they depart.

"Thanks for coming!" Talia calls loudly. "Let's do this again!" She grimaces. "Not this. I'm sorry. You know I was referring to seeing you two again."

Bev waves at her.

Again, I should be allowed to laugh.

"What the hell is wrong with me today?" she whispers. "I sound like an idiot every time someone tries to talk to me. These inappropriate things fly out of my mouth."

"You don't sound like an idiot when you're talking to me, and you look fantastic. You're perfectly fuckable. Now maybe that's inappropriate to say here, but it's true. I'd do you right here with The Frankies singing 'Burning Down the House.'"

Talia pauses and listens to the lyrics. "I think Lois changed the song list. That is definitely a Lois song."

"You should add funeral parties to your business card for T & A Services."

"You shut up," she smarts back, but she also laughs, and finally her real smile comes out.

This is us.

I want to tell her to look at us. We're great together.

29

Talia

"ALL I SEE ARE SQUIGGLY lines," I say, looking at the monitor next to me. I'm lying on the examination table with my shirt pulled up and electrodes stuck to my chest.

My cardiologist moves the sticky pads around, under and over my breasts. The pads are cold and gooey, but his hands are warm as he fusses with the pads and wires.

"Beautiful squiggly lines are what we want," he says. "Your heart looks excellent. It's perfect."

I leave his office reassured and less harried than when Aleska dropped me off.

I need to call my sister for a ride home, but first I stop at the nurses' station to schedule my next six-month checkup. Then I walk in a daze, relieved at my results. I'm a little less afraid of my heart malfunctioning, and I think I'm actually starting to believe my doctor when he says my heart is perfect.

Despite losing Norma, there's something in the air that feels right. That thought lingers with me as I walk through the hospital lobby and the sliding glass doors at the entrance—and right into Peyton.

"Are you all right?" he demands.

I'm surprised to see him. "Yes. I was here for a checkup. I'm fine. Nothing serious. What are you doing here?"

"Checkups *are* serious." He looks me over. "I ran into Aleska at the gym, and she said you were here. Surprise, I'm your ride. What's this stuff on your chest?"

He brushes my collar aside and picks some of the sticky residue left over from the electrode pad adhesives.

"The doctor put those there for my echocardiogram. He removes them after my echo, but I usually find the stray ones when I take a shower. I don't think he is comfortable peeling the ones off my boobs."

"Well, I'm perfectly comfortable removing them." That's exactly what he does as we stand in the entrance passageway with people coming and going. Peyton peels two pads off my chest and rips an errant pad that was hiding partially under my bra.

"Ow. Careful. How did you even see that one?"

"If you let me feel you up in public like this, I can find anything."

"For this mauling, you should at least buy me lunch."

"That was my intention all along."

Our suggestive conversation gets a glare from a woman passing by with a walker. "Not in my day!" she exclaims, shuffling away in a huff.

"I don't mean to be braggadocious," I say, "but my heart is pumping like a pro, and my doctor even showed me a photo from the surgery! My heart doesn't look red at all. It's purple and black and gooey. No one tells you how slimy everything looks." I'm so excited after seeing that photo that I had to tell someone, and Peyton happens to be the one here.

"That's hot. Sign me up."

"Oh, you."

Harmony's threat and my decision to stop spending time with Peyton seems like a long time ago ... I'm not giving either much thought. This is turning into a great day, so I let myself get swept away by Peyton's presence and accept his lunch offer.

He takes me to a sandwich shop in Woodstock that I like, and we get our food to go. Without me asking, he drives us to the Pickwick estate. This is Peyton being attentive and caring, and I soak it up. I am selfish, eager to be with him, knowing I'm breaking Harmony's demand and sending mixed messages to Peyton. It's not like I chased after him. He's the one who hunted me down at the hospital. I'm good at rationalizing my behavior.

We sit on the grassy hill overlooking the grand home and farmland that is growing wild with tall, flowering grasses and weeds everywhere. Peyton found us a flat patch of grass and covered it with a beach towel that Finn left inside the truck's extended cab.

They've been exploring lake beaches and streams, just as fathers and sons should do. I wish I could have been with them.

I know they don't take Harmony with them, but sometimes I envy her just the same. To be the mother of Peyton's child, to share this boy with him, sounds wonderful.

I fill him in on every single renovation I would do to the house, and how I'd add in the restaurant to the first floor with glassed-in sunroom extensions. I go on and on about the wood restoration, the kitchen makeover essentials, and the fixtures and furniture I would put in the guest rooms. Peyton listens, not a single joke, so I continue with explaining the variety of lettuces and vegetables I would grow. This is the part where Marko was visibly absent from our conversations, and I could tell his mind was elsewhere when I was talking, but Peyton is a captive audience.

I expect him to lecture me about the challenges or make fun of the goats I want to raise and the artisanal cheeses I'd like to serve and sell. It's the first time I've been able to talk openly to another person, other than Norma, about my dreams without getting the friendly pushback of negativity.

"This is nice," I say, pushing the paper lunch bags aside and steal a glance at Peyton. He looks delicious in faded jeans that hug his long, muscular legs in all the right places.

He leans back on his elbows and surveys the picturesque scenery, the hills in the distance and the valley below. "It's very nice." He puts his hands behind his head and gazes up at the sky.

I'm entranced by his strong, tan arms. I know those arms so well—how they feel to the touch, how they feel around me.

"You're staring." He slowly turns his head toward me.

"You're nice to look at. I never said you weren't."

He glances at my mouth, then back up at my eyes. The fire in his eyes is everything I'm feeling inside. Lust. I can't hide what my body and brain are saying.

I stare longingly at his thick thighs and his groin where the denim is so faded and soft from hundreds of washings that I know what it would feel like if I put my palm on it and feel him grow hard underneath. His T-shirt inches up from his waistband so I can see his taut, flat abdomen and a hint of what's beneath the zipper.

I feel like breaking rules. I want to be with Peyton for this hour or for however long it will last, and I'm willing to defy Harmony.

He looks as if he's reading my thoughts. *He knows.*

The urge to touch him, to run my hand over his hard groin and across his chest is giving me a rush of pulsating heat between my legs. The image of slipping my fingers beneath the waistband of his jeans and feeling him get turned on is making me think the kind of dirty thoughts that will get me in trouble if this keeps up. My brain and body don't care. I've convinced myself that I'm not doing anything that could possibly harm Finn, because no one knows Peyton and I are here.

This friendly picnic lunch is too much for my libido. I'm past the point of trying to hide this blatant wantonness. My nipples are hard peaks through my bra and white blouse, and Peyton knows it.

He's up in a beat, pulling my head to his mouth while slowly guiding me down to my back. Then he has my blouse open and my bra unclasped, his hands on my breasts as a warm breeze caresses my half-naked body. He shifts his weight to cover me as he undoes his jeans, and I wiggle out of mine.

My hands are greedily groping him. They don't know where to go first. They want to be everywhere, gripping his broad shoulders, sliding up his torso so I can feel the curve and firmness of every muscle. But my hands go right to his underwear. I tug it down aggressively as if it offends me. He keeps kissing me deeply through all of our urgent maneuverings.

When I stroke him, there's a low rumbling from deep within his chest, like an animal awakening. He growls. I return his ferocious kisses, biting his lip and stroking him hard. That low, guttural sound is the only language he's capable of at the moment. I understand that language. It controls us.

Peyton moves one of my legs up onto his shoulder and perches himself above me as I rub the tip of his cock between my legs. I taunt him with the wetness, going in circles, then rubbing up and down as he struggles to open a condom package.

He rips the foil with his teeth then slides the condom on quickly. He jerks my hand away so he can thrust into me fast and hard. I've lost my position of power.

My legs are thrown back, propped up against Peyton's arms, as he continues to thrust forcefully into me. There are more aggressive kisses and love bites, but he's concentrating on fucking me like a wild animal, speaking his own language of starved, furious need.

His face changes fluidly through emotions, of man and beast, anger and desire, longing and hunger. As he gets control of himself and finds his rhythm, his eyes soften when he looks at me.

I run my fingertips over his lips, and he bites them. Still an animal. Still not talking, no words about me giving in to him and breaking my will to stay away from him. *I am a hypocrite.*

My breath catches when a streak of sunlight crosses his face, making his gray eyes glitter like silver. I am hopelessly weak when I'm with him.

He's thrusting harder and faster, and all I can think is that I don't want him to leave Hera to expand his career in Los Angeles. I don't want him to leave me.

His expression alters from a frantic need to the tense-filled moment of a climax, and finally to a state of euphoria. I'm entranced by his ever-changing façade and how beautiful he looks. It's only then I notice how hard I'm gripping him, digging into his back so he won't leave.

"You didn't come," he says.

"It's all right."

"No, it isn't."

He pulls out of me and slips his fingers in, stroking until I let a moan escape. He increases the tempo and pressure as he dips his head down to my breasts, working his tongue over my nipples, teasing them with firm and gentle sucks, sending rippling waves of arousal throughout my body. I let my arms fall to my sides and enjoy this man pleasuring every part of me.

When he begins a well-choreographed dance between my legs with his tongue, I lose the ability to move. I'm suspended in the oblivion of my own climax. I hear a deep moan of satisfaction. It's me.

He doesn't let me orgasm slowly. He works his thumb and tongue together until I'm in an internal frenzy, on the brink of madness. When I reach that wonderful place of surrender, my body shudders with a ferocious gratification and my mind fills with all the romantic and lustful images of Peyton. I smile and lie quietly, spent, enjoying the potent aftershocks of our lovemaking, and I can feel that stupid grin plastered on my face.

Peyton chuckles and kisses my cheek.

I open my eyes to his splendid smile.

"Wouldn't it be nice to wake up like this every morning?" he asks.

"I would die. Literally. If we did this every morning, I'd never make it to work. I'd lose my clients, my career. I'd go broke and starve to death."

"Nice try, but it's an unbelievably lame excuse."

"Excuse for what?"

"Excuse for not saying what you really want. For not admitting that I'm the man you want to be with. Not that Marko piece of shit you were trying to mold into a fiancé, and not Adam Knight."

"I've never denied that we have a great physical connection. But we've been through this. You're not an option for me because my life is here, in this town, and you've made your career opportunity with Boudoir Enterprises your priority."

"*Bourdain*. And that one was intentional."

"I'm not going to tell you how to live your life, because you have Finn to consider. I can say that your idea and mine of doing what's best are not the same. We're not even in the same ball game."

"Ballpark," he snaps.

"Or ball game! Like we're on opposing teams instead of both playing for the Mets."

"Yankees! Christ, if you're going to put us on a New York team, it has to be the Yankees."

"You're being ridiculous."

"No, I'm being pissed off. I know what you're trying to say, but you're wrong about me. You're wrong about us."

We get dressed in silence.

Peyton guzzles the remains of his water, then slams the bottle down on the hood of his truck. The plastic doesn't have the same effect as if it were an empty whiskey bottle, and it seems to bother him that he has nothing else to throw, break, or kick to show his anger.

I stuff our paper wrappers and garbage in the takeout bags and toss them in the back of his truck.

Pickwick, ever-present in my heart, stands silent. I take one last look, lovingly imagining it as mine, renovated to its magnificent glory with a grand porch full of guests enjoying the sunset and mingling with each other over cocktails. Peyton is in that image. No matter how unrealistic it is to put him in my fantasy, he's there, admiring the views of the lush farmland and green hilltops with me.

I'm pulled from my daydream when a car comes speeding up the long road to the estate. It's Harmony. Even her car looks angry as it grinds its way over the dirt road, spewing gravel and pebbles in its path and producing plumes of dust billowing from behind.

"Shit," Peyton mutters.

Harmony parks next to his truck and jumps out of the car, walking toward us with a purposeful stride she owns so well.

"What are you doing here?" he asks with irritation.

"Looking for you!" Her eyes flit to mine for a second, and I'm pretty sure I see her irises turn a solid black, a distinct tell of a demon. If looks could kill, this would be the one to do me in. I'm just glad we're fully clothed and the beach towel and all evidence of our sex picnic are out of sight.

"You found me," Peyton says. "How did you even know I was up here? And where is Finn? I thought you were taking him to my house."

"I did. You weren't there—"

"He has a key. We had an agreement. He gets to stay alone for an hour in the afternoon at my house the same way he does at yours when you're at work. And then I leave work early and meet him."

"Except you're not at work! And I can't find Finn! I thought, as a new father, you'd be more enthusiastic and make a bigger effort to be there!"

"What the hell are you saying?" Peyton shouts. "How can you not know where he is if you just dropped him off? I'll go there now. I had no idea you were going to drop him off this early."

He takes out his phone and calls Finn.

"Don't yell at me!" Harmony shakes her fists like she's ready for a fight. Then she turns toward me. "You broke our deal!"

I may be intimidated by Harmony, but I'm not going to stand by and let her talk down to me like I'm a child. She just said she lost her son; shouldn't that be the discussion here?

"Dammit," Peyton says, clearly frustrated that Finn isn't answering his phone. Then he shouts, "What deal?" looking at me, then at Harmony.

"I don't want your girlfriend du jour hanging around Finn. He has enough going on in his life with losing his grandfather and trying to get to know you."

"Don't talk about Talia like that," Peyton says, taking a step closer to Harmony. "You're being hysterical. Finn is a street-smart kid, who's somewhere around my house. You just came up here to give Talia a hard time."

"Firstly," I chime in, "Peyton, don't belittle her by calling her hysterical. I hate when men say things like that to mothers who are worried about their kids. It's sexist."

Both Peyton and Harmony look surprised by my statement.

"And secondly," I continue, "I'm not hanging out with Finn and Peyton. Not since you gave me your little notice. We were here having lunch, discussing business and about to leave. I'm not a homewrecker. It was an innocent lunch."

My little lie gets a single, raised eyebrow from Peyton.

"I don't know what the fuck you said to Talia," Peyton says to Harmony angrily. "Did Finn have his keys with him?"

"Yes, of course. I watched him go inside. Do you really think I'd drop him off anywhere and just drive away?"

"It's not anywhere; it's my home, and it's his home, too. Now, let's be a little more civil about this. Leave Talia out of it and don't talk to her behind my back. Did you threaten her?" he demands as he tries to call Finn again.

"No," I volunteer.

Harmony's eyes leave mine and look at Peyton's phone. Is she feeling shame for what she said to me and guilt for not knowing where her son is?

Peyton studies me for a moment, torn between defending me and locating Finn. "I'm going to go check on Finn now. I'm sure he's playing a video game and has headphones on so he can't hear his phone. You're coming with me," he tells me. "Once we know Finn's okay, we'll head to Swill."

"Really?" Harmony asks. "Are you her chauffeur now?"

"Today? Yes, I am. I picked her up from the hospital and drove her here, so I'm her ride. Do you have a problem with that? Do you really want me to insist she walk the four miles to the restaurant?"

Peyton's anger silences Harmony. She gets in her car and follows his truck.

Thankfully, it's a short drive to Peyton's house because the sudden coldness between Peyton and me is a painful contrast to what we were doing thirty minutes ago.

"I'll wait here," I say as he pulls to a hard stop in front of his house.

"This isn't over. We're going to talk about what was said at lunch, and I want to know what Harmony said to you—this *deal* business. I'll be right back. I'm sure I'll find a nine-year-old boy zoned out in front of a computer game."

I exhale in relief when he exits the truck and watch him unlock the front door to let Harmony enter first. Within thirty seconds, Peyton is running out of the house, looking frantically around the property, behind the shed and near the creek. Harmony follows him with fear exposing her vulnerability.

Alarmed, I jump out of the truck and run toward them. "Where's Finn?"

Peyton looks at me, panicked. "He's gone."

30

Peyton

HARMONY IS CRYING AND trying to explain something while my mind is racing, thinking of where Finn could be. I'm trying to get in the head of a nine-year-old again, thinking of the time I spent away from home exploring new places. But I was a city kid, and we traveled in packs. This is rural territory, and Finn is out there somewhere, alone.

I'm dialing Finn's number again when I see Talia bolt right by me. Her bright telephone bag, that comical possession she takes everywhere, is slung across her body as she runs toward the woods behind my house. I want to yell at her to stop, but Harmony is crying and shouting at the same time. She's a mother who has lost control of the situation.

When Talia is out of sight, I turn my attention back to Harmony. "How did this happen, Harmony? You dropped him off and then what?"

"I dropped him off an hour ago. He wanted to come early and hang out at your place. I thought it would be nice for me to cut my workday short and go shopping at the outlet malls after I dropped him off. I did see him go into the house, and he waved goodbye before he closed the door. And he knows to always lock up."

"Don't you have a GPS tracker on his phone?"

"Yes, it says he's here. I was at the mall and kept calling to check on him, and the tracker shows he's at your house, but ... but he wasn't answering. I've called more than a dozen times."

I walk back to the house and pull her with me. She rambles on about how she wanted to pick up some of his favorite snacks

321

and junk food and drop them off since he said I don't keep a lot of food at the house. *Yeah, not since Talia dumped me and stopped leaving homemade meals and pastries stocked in my kitchen.*

Tears are streaming down Harmony's cheeks as we move from room to room, calling out Finn's name. Harmony's fear is contagious. I keep thinking he's injured or unconscious somewhere.

"What the hell?" I pull out my phone again and call Finn. We hear the phone ringing in the den off the kitchen. Of course, we already checked the room, but this time we see Finn's cell phone wedged between two couch cushions.

"Oh my God," Harmony says when I retrieve Finn's phone. "He knows I gave him the phone for emergencies. He knows he's supposed to take it with him *always.*"

"This doesn't mean something bad happened to him. It means he forgot his phone. At least we know why he wasn't answering our calls."

"That doesn't make me feel any better about this!" she screams.

"Panicking won't help us. Hera is a safe town, and Finn is a smart kid. We'll find him."

"But he always takes his phone!" she shrieks. "Where could he go? You live in the middle of nowhere!"

"The woods," I say, doing my best to think like Finn. "He likes the woods and trails here."

I run to the door that leads from the den to the garage, with Harmony right behind me. I flip the switch for the overhead lights. Even in the dim light, I can see that Finn's bike is missing from the wall rack.

"What are you doing?" she asks.

"His bike is gone. That's a good sign. He's out riding."

"Hey, Peyton!" Cooper shouts from outside the garage.

"I texted him and your sister when I was at the mall to see if they had heard from Finn," Harmony says.

"Good call. They can help us look for him."

We meet Cooper and Imogene outside.

"What the hell is going on?" Cooper asks. "We tried calling you to tell you we haven't seen Finn. It kept going to your voice mail."

"We've been looking for Finn," I say. "Harmony dropped him off early while I was out, and he wasn't answering her texts or calls so she came back and looked for me."

"I know they like going to the old house," Harmony says. "The Pickwicker-something. Finn said they'd ride their bikes out there sometimes. I was hoping he was there with Peyton. I googled it, and my GPS got me there."

It's true Finn and I sometimes bike there. The place makes me think of Talia. I had no idea that Finn discussed so many details with his mother.

"He left his phone in the house, but his bike is gone," I explain to Cooper. "I think he's out on the trails by himself. That explains why Talia took off running toward the woods. She figured it out before I did."

"Good. She got a head start on us," Cooper says. "I alerted everyone else. Sent out a group text telling them to call if they spot Finn."

"It's going to be fine. We'll find him," Imogene says in an uncharacteristically sweet voice, putting her arm around a sniffling Harmony.

"Okay, so we think our little guy is on the trails." Cooper looks up at the hills looming behind my home with the same concern as me. There is a myriad of trails from easy to advanced to downright deadly, and they cover miles upon miles of rough, hilly, forest terrain.

"That's my guess. I don't know which one he took. We've done at least five of the ones that are directly behind my house, but there are three that are definitely off-limits because they're too dangerous, and he knows it."

"Which means he's probably on one of those off-limits trails," Cooper comments. He always speaks with a measured, authoritative tone, a leftover trait from his FBI days.

"I hope he's not attempting Satan's Lair," Imogene says.

"What?" Harmony asks. "Does this town really have a trail called Satan's Lair? Are you serious?"

"No. It's Harper's Lair," I say.

"Stop scaring her," Cooper tells Imogene.

"I'm not trying to. When we were kids, we called it Satan's Lair because of the gnarled trees that would force us to bike on the edge of the drop-off."

"There's a drop-off?" Harmony asks. "Like a cliff? What the hell kind of town is this that lets kids bike on dangerous trails?"

"The kind of town that puts up *Do Not Enter* and *No Trespassing* signs on the illegal trails to keep people out," Cooper explains. "The teenagers and older bikers go in there anyway. It's part of the thrill."

"Does Finn know about this trail?" Harmony asks me angrily.

"Yes. Every biker does. We rode by the entrance when we were biking the Peak Trail."

"Should we assume our little Finn-meister is defying his parents and working his way through Harper's Lair?" Cooper asks. "If we go directly there, it will save us checking all the other nearby trails."

Harmony gives me the kind of look that says she's sure this is all my fault for buying Finn the bike and living in a place where kids try to compete with nature instead of playing on a good old-fashioned, asphalt playground.

"You stay here in case he comes back," I tell her. "I'll check out the trail."

"Like hell. He's my son. I'm going with you."

A crying Harmony is one thing. A pissed-off mother is another. I'm not going to argue with her.

"Then I can't take my bike. We'll have to go on foot and move fast. Your shoes are going to be a problem."

She looks down at the flat, canvas slip-ons she's wearing over her sockless feet.

"Don't worry about my shoes. I'm going."

"I'll go with you two, and Imogene can wait here at the house in case Finn beats us back." Cooper types on his phone. "And I'm texting Carson to have everyone else search the trails, too. Leo is fast on his bike. We'll send him to the other difficult trails."

I break into a jog toward the woods and scan the hills for any sign that would tell me which direction Finn went. There's nothing but dense trees, and they aren't speaking. I wonder if Talia is closer to finding Finn than we are. Her sudden reaction, bolting toward the woods, venturing out on her own to find my son, gives me hope.

I don't show Harmony how this fear of losing Finn is searing through me, or that the thought of Talia out there trying to save him is maybe the only thing keeping me from falling apart.

Cooper and I jog at a brisk pace, following the narrow footpath created by some outdoor adventurers decades ago. Harmony lags about thirty yards behind us. She's less nimble in her soft, flexible shoes that provide little support, but she has a hard, determined look, so I know she doesn't mind the pebbles and twigs that must be stabbing the soles of her feet.

Only someone who is acquainted with the old house I live in and the land it inhabits would know about this private trail that leads through jungle-like terrain before merging into a road that is the access to public parkland and trails for hikers and the illegal, hidden trails made by rogue bikers.

A lot of brush brought down by the last storm still covers the path, so we have to climb over some high obstacles. On one of the branches crossing our path is a light blue scrap of paper. On closer inspection, I notice it's a heavy-duty cardstock with some numbers printed on it and a partial address: *Hera, NY.*

The paper is freshly torn and doesn't show any wear from the elements, which means it was placed there recently. I shove it in my pocket and keep moving.

"How could he have gotten his bike through this?" Harmony asks, catching up to us.

"He wouldn't," I say. "On bike, you ride a half mile down the road from my house and take the public access road up to the park's information station. From there, he can hop on any legal or illegal trail. This is the shortcut if you're on foot."

"There's the road." Cooper points.

We pick up our pace to a full-on sprint. I hear Harmony stumble and curse behind me, but she's soon emerging from the trees.

We look in both directions of the road—no cars—and ahead to the artery of dirt roads marked with state park signs for visitors.

As we reach the middle of the road, I see another flash of blue paper in the distance, lying against the base of the largest signpost for the state park. It's another torn piece of the same cardstock. I pick it up and see *T & A Services* printed on it.

Cooper peers over my shoulder. "Damn. That's one of Talia's old business cards. T & A Services." He laughs. "She's leaving us a trail."

"Smart woman." I'm proud of her.

"How do you know she's on the right trail?" Harmony asks.

"I don't. But I trust her to know what she's doing."

We proceed farther on the public path and find another piece of one of Talia's business cards along the way. Then we stumble upon a crucial clue—a whole business card at the entrance of a blocked trail with warning signs. It's Harper's Lair.

Harmony retrieves Talia's card before I can and reads it out loud. "That's certainly a poor choice for a business name," she says matter-of-factly.

It irritates me that she wants to take the time to criticize Talia when our purpose here is finding Finn. He could be in jeopardy, and Harmony is being petty.

"Yeah, that name was quickly abandoned," Cooper says, helping Harmony over the metal pole blocking the dirt path.

"We're lucky she still has those cards," I say. "Her little breadcrumb trail is saving us time from guessing where to go."

"Or we could be going the wrong way and wasting time already," Harmony adds.

"What's wrong with you?" I shout. "Talia is helping us because *you* fucked up! You're the one who dropped him off too early when you knew I wasn't home yet!"

"You were the one who bought him that expensive bike and showed him where all these death trap trails are! I didn't know it was too enticing and that he'd leave your house! He always follows the rules at *my* house!"

"Settle down, you two!" Cooper shouts.

I barge ahead of him and start running as soon as I see fresh bike tire marks. There's a set of fresh footprints next to them, too. Small feet. A woman's feet. Talia's Adidas treads.

I keep running, and Cooper keeps up, but Harmony is falling behind again. Part of me is glad, wanting to get to Finn first and be declared the better parent. My own pettiness agitates me.

"Have you ever biked this trail?" I ask Cooper.

"No." He slightly pants as we run up a steep incline. "I've hiked it and know this is where it gets tricky. I've seen guys carry their bikes up this part to get to the top. You'll see. It's where they ride their bikes downhill like a giant slalom. They have to take a sharp turn at the bottom. Only the daredevils, the ones trying to outdo the others, will do it."

We reach the top of the hill and wait for Harmony to catch up. It's a biker's paradise, a slalom that has been molded perfectly over the years by relentless mountain bikers. My gaze follows the thousands of dusty tire prints; mostly disintegrated tracks, some smoothed over by water and wind, but two stand out. Finn's bike tread and Talia's footprints.

Running down a steep hill is stupid, but my dad gene just kicked into overdrive and all I can think is that I have to save my kid. I make it down the course without falling and breaking my neck as I stumble into a nearby tree to slow down just as I reach the deadly sharp curve. Finn's bike tracks disappear over the edge, and Talia's footprints vanish with them. And right in front of me, suspended in two large shrubs growing out of the side of the cliff, is Finn's bike, wedged sideways. I have an image of him hitting the curve, his bike getting caught in the shrubs, and Finn goes flying off it. He's somewhere below.

Panic bubbles up in my chest. *Please be alive.*

"Shit!" Cooper says when he sees Finn's bike. He grabs onto another tree and leans over the cliff to look down.

I get down on my stomach and perch over the edge where the bike tracks disappear. When we hear a rustling sound directly below, Cooper and I exchange a hopeful look.

"That's Finn's bike!" Harmony shouts when she catches up. She's out of breath, and her pants, hands, and feet are covered in trail dust. She must have fallen when we weren't looking, but that doesn't stop her from throwing herself on the ground next to me to see over the cliff's edge into the tangled jungle of trees below.

"Finn!" I shout into the abyss.

The trees are so dense we can't see through them, but we hear a murmur. Two voices.

"Dad?" Finn's voice cries out weakly.

Dad. He called me Dad.

"I'm here," I yell. "I can't see you, though."

"I got him," Talia says.

I can't see her either, but my body exhales with relief that Finn isn't alone.

"I think his arm is broken," Talia shouts. Her blonde head appears out of some leaves along with a flash of Finn's arm. "I'm holding Finn. He's on my back."

"They must be standing on a ridge. Those can give way at any moment. We need to do this fast," Cooper says in a low voice.

"Hold tight. We're going to pull you up."

We hear rustling as Talia struggles to push through some brush. She emerges with Finn holding on to her piggyback style. He has one arm wrapped around her neck and the other hanging limply. At least he has his helmet on—*thank you.* They're both covered in debris, their faces smudged with dirt. Talia's long hair is tangled with leaves and twigs. She's gripping two, thin tree branches that grow out of the side of the cliff like vines. She looks up, searching for us, and then her eyes go wide when she sees me, and there's a visceral change in her face from terror to courage.

"I think Finn also injured a foot or an ankle. He can't stand," she says. "He can't put weight on his feet, so I can't let go of him."

"Hold on, baby," Harmony says to Finn, trying to keep the tremor in her voice at bay.

"Don't move." I look directly at Talia. "Don't try to climb with Finn on your back. I'm going to pull him up first and then you. You just hold on to those branches as tight as you can."

"I understand." Talia trusts me to do this right.

I look over at Cooper, and he nods. He grabs another tree next to me, then wraps an arm around my waist. I move my upper body over the drop. Harmony grabs hold of my ankles to help weigh me down and keep me in place as I hang over the cliff, closer to Talia but not close enough to touch. I find one of the twisted branches and shake it to make sure it's secure enough to use as leverage. Then I stretch my other arm and attempt to grasp Finn's good arm. My reach is too short, so Cooper and Harmony help me scoot farther over the edge to the point that if they lose their grip on me, I'll fall headfirst to the next flat surface thirty feet below.

I reach Finn, and I grip his bicep, knowing that I could very well break his one good arm with what I'm about to do.

"Finn, you have to let go of Talia now and hold on to my arm really tight."

Finn hesitates.

Talia's knuckles are turning white, and I don't know how much longer she can hold on to the tree with a hundred-pound kid on her back.

"Now!" I urge Finn.

He lets go of Talia's neck, and my grip on his bicep tightens. He yelps in pain as I pull him up with all the force I can muster. I'm worried I'll snap his bone, but arms can be fixed.

It happens quickly. I yank hard, and Finn is launched up and over my head. Harmony catches him, and I release him.

My arms feel like they were stretched in a torture device, but I immediately turn back to Talia to pull her up. With only Cooper holding me now, I reach for her with both of my hands.

She doesn't hesitate, letting go of the tree with one hand and grasping one of my hands before she lets her other hand go. We're in sync, no commands necessary.

She holds on to me, and I jerk her up fast, using her weight as momentum so she can clear the cliff edge. Cooper pulls my whole body back hard and fast so we're on solid ground, and then I have to twist and roll onto my back while I pull her. She crash-lands on top of me, her elbows and head colliding into my ribs. The muscles in my arms and back scream with agony.

"Jesus," I say, out of breath. Another sharp pain shoots through my back, and my arms fall to my sides.

Talia immediately rolls off me and collapses onto her back. Harmony is sitting on the ground at my feet, holding Finn in her lap. Cooper is on his knees, looking as if he's about to throw up from the sheer physical and emotional intensity of the situation.

I raise my head and look at Finn. "Are you okay?"

He holds his injured arm and nods with tears pricking the corners of his eyes. I look at all their dazed faces and let my head fall back on the hard, cold dirt. The pain in my body and my racing heart tells me this was a close call.

"I take it back. This is Satan's Lair." Cooper holds his head and takes a deep breath. "Don't tell Imogene I said that."

"Let's not do this again," I say.

"Amen, brother," Cooper replies.

• • •

One sling, one air cast, and three hours later, we leave the hospital in Kingston. Finn is asleep, sprawled in the back seat of my truck, and Harmony is sitting up front. In the emergency room, we talked privately and both agreed not to fight or place blame, that we should just be thankful that Finn is all right.

After we all witnessed Talia's heroic efforts, Harmony was fairly quiet, except for questioning Finn. Apparently, he was overly excited to be at my place on his own and didn't think a little bike ride would get him in trouble. In his excitement, he forgot to take his phone and, as we expected, when he passed the blocked entrance to Harper's Lair, the lure of the infamous trail was too tempting to our nine-year-old mini-me.

I predict a future filled with many long lectures.

Once we all knew Finn was going to be fine, it hit me hard what extremes Talia had gone to in order to save him. He took the curve too fast and was thrown off his bike and over the cliff. He said he couldn't see anything but felt his shirt get tangled in tree branches, which is what stopped his fall.

He had his one good foot on a rock ledge and used his uninjured arm to hold one of those branches that curled like a jungle vine. Then he waited, because he realized he didn't feel the weight of his phone in his jeans pocket. He estimated he had been hanging on to the tree and ledge for about twenty minutes before he heard footsteps approach.

It was Talia's good instincts to take that trail, and when she spotted Finn's overturned bike, she carefully climbed down and found him. He admitted that, when she told him she would give him a pig ride up, he cried because he was so relieved an adult was there for him, and because he had no idea what a pig ride was until Talia explained. I laughed loudly in the hospital emergency room when he told us that.

"Anything you want to say?" I ask Harmony, who's leaning against the passenger window with exhaustion.

"I was thinking we're lucky. It could have been very bad. And I was thinking I've been a little too hard on you, this town, and other people."

"Other people? You mean Talia?"

"Maybe."

"You have to agree that her trail of business cards was good."

"It was clever. More clever than offering T & A services."

"That's one of the things I like about her." I smile to myself. "There's a certain naïveté, but she always means well."

Harmony gazes out the window.

"I'm still pissed at you," I say, lowering my voice so Finn doesn't hear this or wake up. Harmony turns to look at me. "Did you threaten Talia?"

"I told her to stay away from you."

"Why?"

"At first, it was because I resented her. I resented you, I guess," she says, barely above a whisper. "It was a reminder that I'm a single parent."

"Is that what ...?" I look back to make sure Finn is still sleeping. "The first time I was at your house ... when I was leaving, you hugged me in a way ... Were you hoping we'd get back together?"

"Yes. I suppose I was thinking it was a possibility. But it didn't feel right. I'm sorry about that."

"Whatever was there when we were seventeen is gone. And we didn't really have anything beyond that one night together."

"I know. It was scary for me to leave Seattle. I know it was the right thing for Finn. And me. I'd like to have a co-parent. And a friend. Weeks ago, I felt threatened by Talia. I wasn't ready for another woman in Finn's life. I wasn't ready for your girlfriend to be someone Finn likes being with. It was all too much for me, and I reacted badly."

"What exactly did you tell her?"

"I told her you'd lose Finn if she didn't stay away."

"Jesus Christ, Harmony." I want to yell at her, but I have to be a responsible parent and think of the kid in my truck.

"I'm sorry. Finn told me things have been frosty between you and her. Now you know why. She was keeping her distance because of me."

"I can't believe you did that, and I can't believe she didn't tell me."

"At least you know she was doing it for you and Finn. She was putting you two first."

I scoff angrily and shake my head.

"I am sorry, Peyton. Sharing Finn with you is still new to me. I've made some mistakes. I'm sorry."

"I believe you. I do."

"I did find you and Talia together today, so perhaps she realizes my threat was unfair and wanted to see you anyway."

"No, it was a fluke. She needed a ride to work, and we took a detour to look at that house she likes. That's all."

"Oh. It seemed like more."

"I was just her ride."

Harmony is watching me. I don't want to discuss Talia with her and attempt to be the type of friends who talk about romantic relationships. I was so sure that I could have it all, that I could arrange all the people I want in my life and carry on any which way I want. I have enough stuff to work out without sharing everything with Harmony.

"Are we good?" I ask.

She looks at me with her classic Mona Lisa smile. "Parenting is never-ending. We'll undoubtedly have more disagreements."

I don't let Harmony's vague comment bother me. I care more about getting Finn settled in his bedroom, which I do, and I'm still thinking about Talia and what she did for us.

Cooper and I carried Finn back to the public access road, where Imogene met us with my truck, and then Carson showed up with his truck. I drove Finn and Harmony to the hospital, and Talia, stubborn Talia, refused to go. I wanted her to have the ER staff look over her bruises and do the usual tests, but she said she wasn't going back to the hospital that she had just checked herself out of. I didn't want to keep arguing with her after what she'd been through, so Carson took her, Cooper, and Imogene back.

With Finn safe in bed and asleep, my mind reverts back to the woman I can't let go of. Other than giving Finn a light hug goodbye before driving off to the ER, she left without saying anything to me.

We shared another intense, powerful experience, and it's like she keeps walking out of my life when we get to the good part of a movie. The part where everyone survives and gets to be happy.

31

Talia

"YOU LOOK DESTROYED," Imogene says.

"I'm *exhaustipated*," I reply.

"That's not a real word," Jess adds.

Imogene shakes her head. "You really do not look your best."

I give her a pointed look. "Don't you have to go stir your cauldron?"

We're huddled at a corner table in Swill while Lois and Kimberly finish setting up the dining hall for tonight's big auction benefit. They're hoping to raise enough funds to renovate one of the historic houses on the main street and turn it into a public library. As a director and archival specialist in the county library system, Kimberly came up with the idea for a small library in our town's busiest area for both the growing student population and the adult literacy programs she's cultivating. She's counting on the new, wealthy residents to donate heavily.

"It's been a rough week," I say. "On top of that, I can't believe I have a giant Saint Bernard running around our house. Baby truly *is* a giant baby, and he leaves giant craps all over the backyard, which I have to clean up because it's killing the grass. He's a handful."

"And you saved a boy dangling from a cliff. Don't forget that one," Imogene says with a straight face. "No biggie."

"I happened to be in the right place at the right time. That's all."

"You *reacted*," Jess says. "You *handled* it. Most people could not have done what you did."

"I agree," Imogene says. "Stop selling yourself short. You're a goddamn hero. Own it."

Across the room, Peyton is talking to the waitstaff for their pre-dinner meeting.

I've thought of nothing else but him and Finn and that scary incident out on Harper's Lair. I was trying to be brave for Finn, but my insides were roiling with a terror that was comparable to or worse than when I was being wheeled into surgery.

When Peyton was hanging over the edge of the cliff and holding me with both hands, it was only then that I thought I had a chance at surviving. Once we were all safe, I could barely speak. I was so shaken up and uncomfortable with Harmony watching me.

I'd broken a sacred pact, the one where I should abide by a mother's wish to protect her child, even though I never agreed to her terms.

"I know my adorable, idiotic brother-in-law can't stop gushing about what you did," Imogene says.

"I love that." Jess smiles. "I like Peyton. And you deserve to be treated like a superstar."

"He was talking about me?"

Imogene grins. "Ask him yourself. Here he comes."

"Hey," Peyton says, appearing by my side. I missed his sexy swagger as he crossed the room. He just materialized before me.

"Hello," I reply. "I saw the online ads for the auction tonight. Aren't you excited to host a big town benefit at Swill?"

"Not really, no. It's Kim's event, but Lois is micromanaging her. She's already made Kim cry. Lois is brutal, and she's been bossing my staff around all day for this fucking thing. The whole staff took a vote and want me to ban her from Swill for life."

Imogene and I laugh, while Jess is too busy studying the dynamic between Peyton and me, looking for clues—she's working so hard at it.

"How are those wrists of yours?" He takes both my hands and turns them over to inspect the scratches and fading bruises.

"They work well enough." I pull them away from his gentle touch. "How is Finn recuperating?"

"He loves lounging on my couch, watching TV all day. Eleanor's with him during the day, feeding him all the junk food he could want, and she has him hooked on *Judge Judy* and *Dexter*. She's a terrible influence. Fortunately, he'll be back at school on Monday and can take the air cast off. He's decided he'd like to wear it for a while to help with the highly embellished story he's manufactured to tell his friends."

"He is such a great kid, and he promised to include me in his story," Imogene says. "I'm going to be his brilliant aunt who rushed into action like MacGyver."

"You weren't even there," Jess says accusingly. "You stayed at the house. Talia was the one who jumped into action."

"I said she was the hero." Imogene shrugs. "But the hero always needs backup. That's me."

Peyton looks at me with a twinkle in his eye.

"I don't want the kid to tell everyone I was sitting at Peyton's house, eating Cheetos and texting people," Imogene says, and Peyton and I laugh.

"Because that's exactly what you were doing," Jess quips.

"I did find some orange fingerprints on the cupboards and the remotes," Peyton says, playing along.

"I needed sustenance," Imogene defends. "I'd rather go back to talking about Talia's big, farting dog."

"Have you ever had a pet? A dog?" Peyton asks me.

"Yes. We once had an adorable dog for three days. I loved him, but my dad gave him to a neighbor because the dog would bark at every pedestrian or car that passed by the apartment building. He drove my father insane."

"That's terrible. You fell in love with your new dog and your dad gave him away? Must have scarred you for life," Peyton says.

I wonder if he's hinting at something bigger. My father leaving? Marko leaving? My screwed-up relationships with men, including him? No, it's not possible a dog I hardly knew could symbolize that much meaning. I'm reading way too much into Peyton's words.

"To be fair, we were all kind of scared of the dog," I say.

"Was he really big like Baby?" Jess asks.

"No, he was a Chihuahua. His name was Zeus. He looked so cute, but he terrorized everyone who lived in our apartment building."

As the others laugh and make a few sarcastic comments, I think about little Zeus and how he was simply trying to find his place in the world. We didn't give him a chance.

"Peyton, we need you in the kitchen!" Greer shouts as she runs to answer the phone at the hostess stand.

"Guess I need to help run this place." He takes an extra moment, looking as if he wants to say something to me. Then he glances at Jess and Imogene and seems to decide against it. "You're sticking around for tonight, right?"

"Are you kidding? I don't have a choice. Lois is putting my cooking services up for bid. She hasn't even told me the details, but she has threatened all of us if we don't show or if we try to leave early. I don't need a public shaming from the meanest yogi in the universe."

His smile reaches his eyes. It seems specially created for me. I'm lost in that smile until Greer barks his name again.

"I'll talk to you later." He touches my hand, his fingers lingering for an extra beat. Then he's striding across the restaurant, employees buzzing around him.

"Hmm, nice," Jess says approvingly. "He likes you."

"Did I tell you Baby has diarrhea and has accidents in every room of our house?" I attempt to change the subject.

"You are a bounty of fun topics," Imogene says.

"She doesn't want us to talk about Peyton," Jess states the obvious.

"It's easier for me if we don't."

"Let's talk about why you can't talk about it. Him. Peyton," Imogene urges.

"Not now," I say firmly.

Imogene lets out an exasperated groan.

"A new topic it is," Jess confirms. "Did Norma leave your mother and Aleska anything in her will?"

"Another fun topic," Imogene mutters.

"My mother received vintage Halston dresses with instructions that she's supposed to wear them to cocktail parties. And Aleska got all of Norma's vintage Chanel suits. A dozen in perfect condition."

"Halston and Chanel, pretty sweet," Imogene says with more interest.

"How could Norma afford those clothes?" Jess asks. "She was a kindergarten teacher."

"A hundred years ago," Imogene adds. "She and her husband were also good at investing. They were Depression kids, people who knew how to stretch a dollar. Seriously though, they knew how to buy stocks and hold on to them long-term through all the bad times. They weren't frugal, but in those days, people didn't renovate houses or worry about having designer kitchens or driving expensive cars. They were the Buick and Oldsmobile crowd. The World War II survivors. They believed in the cocktail hour, smoking Pall Malls, and eating at supper clubs with friends. They lived simply, but they had big lives."

"You make it sound like such a romantic time. Except for the Depression and the war part. Sometimes I think I was born in the wrong era," I say, thinking of how I learned to play the music from that era on the piano. Some was melancholic; some was made for dreamers.

"You can always take up smoking," Imogene says.

"Don't listen to her, Talia." Jess touches my hand. "I think Norma had a very romantic life too. Look at what she lived through, and she never gave up on love. I think she left Baby to you because he's something for you to love. Leaving him in your care means she trusted you. I think she's giving you a sign of things to come."

"Lord, I hope the signs point to more than canine love," I say. "Why can't I have Baby while wearing a black Halston halter dress?"

"I think Norma was very deliberate," Jess explains. "The dresses signify your mother's need to liberate herself and socialize in the real world. The expensive Chanel suits are Norma's way of preparing Aleska for her future business career. She isn't studying accounting and finance in night school so she can keep cleaning other people's toilets. She's either going to help you expand your business or start something new. Aleska definitely has a head for numbers and business."

"I have a business, and I don't wear Chanel suits," Imogene says, chewing on a soft Bavarian pretzel.

"You work in a shed. A nice jewelry studio, but it's still a shed," Jess says. "We're talking about Talia now." She snaps her fingers multiple times in front of Imogene's pouty face that's bulging with a mouthful of pretzel dough.

"All of these expensive symbolic gifts, and I get a dog. Does that mean I'm destined to be a dog walker?"

"No. You have a career, too. It's a growing career with a lot of potential," Jess says. "And Archie said Norma's estate isn't settled yet, so I expect some money may be coming your way, too. But I do think you're blind to what's in front of you. You have someone to love. I'm referring to a certain man. Baby really signifies settling down and making commitments." Jess sounds so sure of her analysis.

"As much as I hate listening to Socrates over here and her *symbolism*"—Imogene flashes air quotes and rolls her eyes—"I have to agree with her on this one."

"Ladies," Peyton says as he passes by us. "A table has been set up for you and your friends over there." He points to one of the extra-long tables in the center of the room and keeps walking, too busy to stop and chat this time. He's got Lois on his back about auction displays.

He makes my heart flutter, and when it feels like it's slamming against my rib cage, I have to redirect my brain to non-Peyton thoughts, such as peeling potatoes for the massive amounts of garlic mashed potatoes I make for the Lopez family every week, or the nasty surprises Baby keeps leaving in various corners of our home. There are plenty of ways to distract me from thinking of Peyton, but they never last.

The restaurant has officially opened for the evening and customers are starting to pour in, hoping to get a good table near the stage. I'm not sure why, since there won't be a band or entertainment, unless they consider Lois a one-woman show worth paying seventy-five dollars a head to have emcee.

I'm listening to Jess and Imogene ruminate about me, but I'm watching Peyton in my peripheral vision, and then Adam walks in with two men. Greer greets them and escorts them to their reserved seating. No doubt Lois made sure to have the richest man in Hera seated near the stage so she can cajole him into excessive bidding.

I'm torn, watching and silently mooning over Peyton, and feeling excited that Adam is here, too. I don't know what kind of woman that makes me, other than simply a confused one.

"He's handsome," Jess says, looking over at Adam.

"A lot of good-looking men here," Imogene adds. "But who is the hottest in the land?"

"I'm partial to Carson," Jess says.

"Choosing your husband is always a safe response. I suppose I have to go with Cooper. What about you, Talia? You're a single woman. Out of all the men here, who do you think is the most handsome? Who do you lust over? Is it more than one man?"

"I'm taking the first amendment on this."

"Oh, honey," Jess laughs. "It's the fifth amendment that gives you the right to not speak in a court of law. You're taking the fifth."

"Not answering the question speaks volumes," Imogene says. "You're unsure."

"I've been there." Jess picks up her big hobo bag that is overstuffed with extra diapers and hoists it on her shoulder. "How about we go sit at our reserved table? You've been hiding back here long enough, Talia."

"Sometimes I like being in the background. Lurking. Observing."

"Move it," Imogene demands.

The three of us get up and wind our way slowly around the restaurant, saying hello to friends and neighbors. I socialize without really listening to anyone. It's difficult. On one side of the room, I see Adam fully engaged with his friends, talking, smiling, taking long swigs from the pilsner glass in front of him, and then there's Peyton, walking around the restaurant, greeting the pretty florist, Kris, and helping the waitstaff carry the extraordinary centerpieces to every table. Peyton isn't the kind of guy to have flowers in his restaurant; he prefers masculine minimalism. Another piece of information I've acquired since I started sleeping with the man who is wrong for me in every way.

I wish I could simply turn off the desire like a water spigot, and then give it fully to a man who could be Mr. Right. I want to find the right man the same way Jess and Imogene did. They found their perfect matches in Carson and Cooper, but Peyton is nothing like those men. Peyton wouldn't be satisfied if his career lived and breathed in Hera. Plus, for all the kind things he does for me and the sweet things he says, it's only a matter of time before the tension and stress in his life drives him into the arms of another woman who crosses his path.

I can't blame him for seeking attention from women who satisfy a basic need. After all, that's what he and I have been doing until I find someone who isn't as nomadic as Peyton or doesn't have more emotional baggage than me. In some ways, Peyton is too similar to my father—the charm, the handsome playboy good looks, the absentee dad. I am a tough critic, but I need someone who is the exact opposite of my father.

As we approach the large table where my friends' husbands are already toasting with beers, and other people are paired off in couples. I suddenly feel the need to escape their domestic compatibility.

I tell Jess and Imogene I'm going to talk to some friends, and I'll meet up at our table later.

A few tables away, I spot people I know and slip into one of the two vacant chairs at their table. They are a couple, too, but Hoyt is so antisocial that he couldn't care less about my dating life. He doesn't even stop eating to say hello.

"Look who's here." Ian, the nicer one, puts his phone down and smiles.

"I haven't seen you in a while. Thought I'd stop over for a visit."

"Hoyt. Put down the roll and say hello." Ian picks up the salt shaker and holds it over Hoyt's plate. "I will dump salt all over your plate if you don't stop for a minute and show some civility."

Hoyt sighs and puts the roll down. "Hello, Talia. Nice weather we're having. I recommend the currywurst, and the herb chicken is especially good. How's that?"

I'm used to Hoyt's abrasiveness. He intimidates most people, since he's at least six-five and built like a bear, and he wears a full beard like a lumberjack.

"As you can see, my husband is repelling everyone in town. We have to sit at the children's table because Hoyt is a big, crabby baby." Ian's remark is rewarded with a grunt from Hoyt.

Hoyt looks at me and pulls his plate closer to him. "I'm not sharing, in case you're wondering."

"You're delightful," I say.

"Isn't he? I'm a lucky man!" Ian shouts to the whole boisterous dining hall.

"Don't worry, Hoyt. I'm not here to mooch off your plate. I'm here every day, so I get plenty of free scraps from the kitchen."

"Good," Hoyt says as he gnaws through half a chicken with his big hands.

"For God's sake, use your flatware." Ian stabs a cherry tomato from his own salad.

Hoyt is unfazed by Ian's complaints. "You're here for something. What do you need?"

"Love that you don't engage in small talk. I'm fine. Thanks for asking."

"Lord." Ian gives Hoyt a disapproving look.

"I just want to eat and get out. Is that too much to ask?" Hoyt puts the chicken carcass down and picks up a sausage with his fingers.

Ian mumbles a curse.

"Way to be part of the community," I say. "Aren't you going to bid on anything? The library needs the money, and you love food, so you should bid on my donation. Lois promised she'd jazz it up. All I know is I'll be cooking a gourmet meal for the lucky winner. That could be you."

"Get to your point, woman. What do you want?"

"Can't you feel the love rolling off him?" Ian says.

"Here's the thing," I explain to Hoyt. "I want to sit here and be chummy with you. Pretend you're really into me. I'm trying to get Adam Knight to notice me."

"Honey," Ian brightens. "I'm sure he's noticed you. I've already checked everyone out in this room, and I'm sure he has, too. He's already scoped out all the attractive women, just like I've already scoped out all the attractive men in case I need a replacement husband." Ian takes another dainty bite of salad.

"Yes, but I want more than the *hello* dude-head-nod. He's one of my clients, and I don't know if I'm mistaking our flirting banter for something else. I'm trying to figure out if he's actually interested in me or if it's his mo."

"God, what is mo? Does he have some rare disease?" Ian asks.

"His mo. You know, his modus operandi. Maybe it's his mo with all women."

Ian laughs. "His MO. Got it. That was a good one."

Exasperated with laughs at my expense, I nab a cherry tomato off his plate and chomp on it. "Done laughing? I'd like to get Adam's attention, and I need an accomplice, a *date*. And Hoyt stands out."

"Right, encouraging jealousy by creating a fake boyfriend with a gay dude is always a solid plan," Hoyt deadpans.

"Oh, this is good." Ian picks up his phone. "Let me take a photo of my grumpy-ass husband and his pretty new girlfriend." He snaps a photo. "This is a keeper!"

Hoyt points at Ian. "You better not post that anywhere, or I'll smash that fucking phone with my fist."

Ian sighs dramatically, puts the phone on the table, and then holds his hands up in surrender.

"You two are an anemone."

"You mean an anomaly," Ian corrects. "But I like your word better. Shows you can't help who you fall in love with. I wanted Tom Ford and sharp suits. Instead, I got Grizzly Adams and flannel."

I'm pleased I happen to recognize that old TV reference.

Hoyt breaks into one of his rare smiles, and it makes me smile, too.

"Come on, Brokeback Hoyt. Step up and be her stud. It's just for show."

"And you don't see the conflict here?" Hoyt directs at me.

"No. You're so elusive and introverted that Adam doesn't know you're gay."

"Or married," Ian adds.

"Or married," I confirm. "He may get a little jealous in a good way when he sees me with you. Instead of asking me to have dinner with him because I'm the only woman available, he may pursue me. Or not. But it's worth a try."

"So he's already asked you to dinner?" Ian sounds seriously intrigued.

"I didn't accept. I kept thinking he was just looking for some company when he's in town. The rest of the time, he's in the city, surrounded by women. I don't want to be the Hera dinner mate."

"No, of course not. He should be asking you to have dinner with him in Manhattan, four courses and nothing less. Or at least Woodstock. It's not a real date unless he drives you at least ten miles." Ian is adamant.

"Who is this joker you're trying to impress, and why do you want me involved?" Hoyt asks.

"Why do you think I married you? Because you're a sexy mountain man who makes men and women drool, you fool. Own it."

"You're both very attractive men, but—"

"But Hoyt stops traffic. When he stands up to go to the restroom, all heads will turn," Ian chimes in.

"That's because I'm tall."

"It's because you belong on a show like *Outlander*, or at least on a roll of paper towels," I say. "That's why I chose you for my devious man-trap plan."

"And as your fake boyfriend, what would you need me to do?" His tone is softer and kinder. Underneath the perpetual grimace, the beard, and his massive bulk, the man is really a gentle giant.

I scoot my chair next to him to make sure we're in Adam's line of vision. "Pretend I'm your favorite person, and you adore me."

Hoyt turns his head to look for Adam.

"Don't look!" I pull his bearded jaw back.

"I can't look? I don't even know who he is."

"That's perfect. Just be flirty," I say.

Ian bursts out laughing. "He doesn't know how to flirt. On our first date, he thought it would be romantic to take me to a furniture convention at the Javitz Center. Then he bought me a beer at some filthy bar in the Village where my shoes literally stuck to the floor."

"I bought you a steak, too. Porterhouse."

"It was a whole side of beef. I needed a chainsaw to eat that thing."

I put my arm around Hoyt's shoulder, which is a little awkward. He's too tall and wide. So I settle my arm on his back with my cheek against his arm. "While Ian teases you, I'll dote on you. We make a great couple."

"Can I at least finish my food?" Hoyt asks.

"How about I feed you a few bites, like we're crazy for each other?"

"Hell no. I'm not that kind of guy."

"Fine. Eat." I glance behind Hoyt's back to see if Adam is paying attention and get caught in the act.

He smiles at me with the dude-head-nod. I smile and wave back. Here we go again with the smiling and waving.

"This is nice," Ian says. "I feel like we're in middle school, where tweens play peekaboo with their crushes in the cafeteria. And I have to say that that Adam man is hot. I remember him coming into the shop. He spent a fortune on furniture. Hoyt, are you sure he didn't see you there?"

"So what if he did? He doesn't know me. I thought we all established that."

"Take off your wedding ring." Ian quickly reaches across the table and tugs on Hoyt's ring. "I can't get this thing off your beefy finger. It's like a damn kielbasa." Ian keeps tugging.

"You have to take that ring off, Hoyt," I say. "I don't want him to walk by our table and think I'm an adulterer."

"This is ridiculous." Hoyt pulls the large gold band off his finger and slips it in his shirt pocket. "I can't believe you're going along with this silly charade."

Ian shrugs. "I think it's fun."

"Then let's do this right." Hoyt throws a big, heavy arm around my shoulders and pulls me in for a side hug that feels like he's crushing my rib cage. I press my hand against my heart to catch my breath.

Ian winces. "Flirt with her. Don't smother her." Then he snaps a photo of us.

"Just be you," I say to Hoyt.

"This is me. I'll even buy you a beer."

"Now you got him, Talia. Wait until the big romantic tells you about the new table saw he set up in our garage."

Hoyt's eyes light up, and for the next twenty minutes, he tells me all about their new home workshop, describing in detail the new equipment right down to the special nails made by Trappist monks or some guys who live in tents and forge their own steel goods.

"Why aren't you at the table I reserved for you?" Peyton's voice comes from behind us. He comes around the table and studies Hoyt's arm around my shoulders, then looks down at me with a raised eyebrow.

"Don't give me the eyebrow treatment," I reply. "I'm visiting with my friends, Hoyt and Ian."

"I *know* Hoyt and Ian," Peyton says dryly.

"We're playing a game," Ian adds, and I shoot him a dirty look.

"What game?" Peyton asks me. There's no humor in his tone.

"We're trying to see who can convince Hoyt to drink a strawberry daiquiri," I reply, thinking of the fruitiest red drink that Hoyt would never have.

"Are we serving daiquiris now? And frozen margaritas?" Sunny, the most effervescent waitress, asks excitedly as she overhears.

"No, we're not," Peyton replies. "Never."

"Why not?" Sunny whines. "I have a whole table from the senior center who always ask when we'll start serving fun, frozen drinks."

"No," Peyton says.

"Now I'm thirsty for a frozen margarita," Ian says.

"No, you're not," Peyton says, irritated.

"Why are you so down on frozen drinks?" Sunny asks. I give her credit for not backing down against Peyton.

"Because this is a German beer hall, not a TGI Fridays. And because blender drinks are pathetic concoctions of sugar and ice. And I hate the noise!" Peyton shouts over the sudden, piercing screech of Lois's microphone that she's testing on the stage.

Sunny sighs with exasperation. "Peyton MacKenzie, I am determined to break you until you embrace delectable, fruity beverages that are frothy, frozen, colorful treats to people everywhere." She marches back to the kitchen, and I laugh at Peyton's obvious frustration.

He turns to me. "You know these two are still newlyweds, right? You're like the third wheel here. There's room for you over at the other table. Your sister is there."

"Like I don't see enough of my sister." I roll my eyes. "At that other table, I'm the third wheel to at least four different couples."

Peyton sighs and stalks off toward the kitchen.

The microphone starts shrieking again, and Lois attempts to talk over it. All conversations cease and all eyes turn to the stage.

"I can help with the mic!" Kimberly is giddy. She eagerly jumps up from her chair and circles her way around tables to get to the stage. "I'd like to say a few words, too!" She nabs the cordless mic right out of Lois's hand and fiddles with it. She doesn't look like she knows any more about it than Lois. Then Kimberly whacks the mic on her thigh a couple of times and repeats the words "testing, testing" a few times. The audience laughs. The indignation on Lois's face is priceless when Kimberly thwarts Lois's attempts to retrieve the microphone again.

"I want to thank everyone for coming out tonight for this great cause," Kimberly shouts into the microphone. Her voice is amplified so loudly that people cover their ears. "And I want to thank Peyton and Bash for letting us use Swill. And a super big thank you to Bash for the fantastic food. Oh, I forgot to introduce myself. I'm Kimberly Baker. Most of you know I'm the head librarian and also a specialist in archival history for the county. And we're here tonight to make Hera's own little library a reality! Let's hear it for libraries!"

There's some errant clapping, but Kimberly doesn't pause long enough for applause. "I'm just so excited about this fundraiser, and that everyone wants to help! I love my town! Let's hear it for Hera!"

The applause comes on stronger this time now that Kimberly has warmed the crowd up, but it's cut short when Lois causes another scene, yanking the microphone away from Kimberly.

"And that's enough of that!" Lois barks, and the audience roars with laughter. "You go sit down and let me handle this."

"Oh, Lois!" Kimberly stomps her foot before going back to her table.

"Ladies and gentlemen, a round of applause for Kim, *the librarian*," Lois says mockingly.

Everyone claps extra hard for Kimberly since we've all been the recipient of Lois's humiliation tactics. Hoyt's high-pitched whistle almost renders me deaf.

"I love when Lois hosts these things," Ian says. "It's amazing we allow this. It's like putting Stalin in charge of a preschool. It's a wonder Lois isn't advocating for a town jail, a single cell that she'd get to be in charge of."

I laugh too loudly and get *the look* from Lois.

"She scares me," Hoyt whispers. The weight of his heavy, muscled arm is making me hunch. With pain. I doubt we look like a romantic couple, but I try to keep up the appearance since I see Adam glancing my way.

For the next hour, Lois rattles off services and items up for bid and makes sure the winning bidders overpay excessively. A private yoga session with Anima-Christi, Lois's top yogi, goes for eight hundred dollars after Lois taunts the bidders with insults. A funky, psychedelic blanket knitted by Hera's own local knitting guild, appropriately called the Knockout Knitters, sells for eighteen hundred dollars after Lois screams at a bidder, "You can do better than that!"

Ian and I exchange a look. We may all be afraid of Lois, but we're all secretly impressed at the results of her ability to coerce money out of innocent participants.

"I bet she worked for the CIA or Mossad," Hoyt whispers. "That woman was trained professionally somewhere. I'm not buying her yogi act one bit."

I watch Lois shoo another person away from the stage and tell some tall man sitting down front that he needs to move because he's blocking people from seeing her.

"When she says *namaste* to people on the street, they always glance over their shoulder and duck as if they expect to be hit by a bullet," I say.

Ian and Hoyt laugh, again too loudly.

"Shut up, please," Lois says, singling out our table. "You're *next*." It sounds like a threat.

"*Oh shit!*" Ian mouths to me.

I know I'm about to be humiliated. I never know how Lois will do it, but I always know it's coming.

"Next up is a gourmet meal prepared by Hera's own award-winning, professional chef, Talia Madej!" Lois announces it like an Oscar presentation, which is embarrassing in itself. And I've never won an award, unless Lois is referring to the Quiet As A Mouse award my sixth-grade teacher gave me at the end of the school year when I didn't qualify for any of the academic awards all the other students earned. But, if Lois thinks she can wrangle more money for my donation with false advertising, I'm not going to be the one to argue with her.

Peyton and Bash walk out of the kitchen and stand off to the side of my table, so I have Lois, Peyton, and Adam in my line of view.

"She is a highly coveted personal chef," Lois continues.

Ian smiles and mouths a, "*Wow.*"

I cringe.

"She's in such great demand that she can't take on new clients"—*great, she's killing my business*—"so this is an opportunity for those of you who have never experienced the incredible culinary delights of Talia."

"She makes it sound like I perform sex acts," I whisper.

"It's awesome," Ian says gleefully.

"The winning bidder will receive a six-course meal cooked and delivered by Talia. Not only that, she will dine with you!"

"What?" I snap and look at Lois, who pretends not to hear me.

"Whoa," Ian says. "She's setting you up, honey. She's going after the single men with money, and you're the bait."

Peyton turns toward me, his poker face giving way to displeasure.

I shrug. It's not my fault Lois is auctioning me off to the highest bidder.

"I'm opening the bidding at five hundred!" Lois shouts. "That's cheap, people. I expect to see all your paddles go up!"

All the paddles do go up, along with a chorus of cheers, some of which come from Imogene, Dylan, and Jess.

I shrink back into Hoyt to hide, but he removes his arm from me so he can start eating the Linzer torte and pretzel bread pudding Sunny just delivered to our table.

"One thousand," Adam says loudly, raising his red auction paddle.

"Two thousand!" Peyton says firmly, holding up a paddle he must have produced out of thin air.

"This is getting good," Ian says with relish. He pushes his chair back to get a better view.

"Very nice, Peyton," Lois says, narrowing her eyes like a wicked witch or evil queen in every Disney movie ever made. "Any other takers? What do you say, Adam?"

The audience quiets down, clearly captivated.

"Three thousand," Adam replies and gives onlookers a confident smile that says he's got plenty of time and money to play this game. The same smile that puts him on the cover of magazines.

"Four thousand," Peyton says. He looks right at Adam and crosses his arms.

"Things are heating up in here," Lois says, fanning herself with an auction paddle.

I agree. The intensity radiating off Peyton is both exhilarating and infuriating. Exhilarating because he's so damn sexy. Infuriating because I find him so damn sexy, and because he's trying to sabotage my chance with Adam.

"Ten thousand," Adam says, calmly, like a man who knows he owns this.

It's a game that only Adam can win. He's rich, and I hate to see Peyton throw his money at this, thinking he can prove some misguided point to me. Harmony would be furious if she were here to witness this.

I cross my arms and give Peyton one of his own death stares.

He scoffs and looks back at Lois. "Fifteen thousand."

Bash looks uncomfortable and utters a very audible, "Shit."

Lois hoots and the audience cheers, egging the men on. Yes, I used to think that meant throwing eggs at people.

"Talia, I think you'll have to put out for this," Ian says.

"Shut up," Hoyt growls. "I don't like this. Not one bit."

"Hey, it's fine. I'm only having dinner with one of them. Peyton and Adam aren't strangers. It's a perfectly safe transaction."

"Lordy," Ian says.

"Yeah, I get how that sounded."

"You can always bring one of our dogs with you." Hoyt is serious.

"Hades. He's the wolfhound," Ian says.

"His name is *Al*." Hoyt shoots Ian a look.

"Best guard dog," Ian adds, holding up a photo of Al on his phone. The dog is taller than me.

"This has to end with the next bid," I say. The atmosphere in the room is no longer fun. It's hostile, and I'm starting to feel anxious.

Adam studies Peyton for a few seconds, overtly sizing up his competition. *There could be blood.* Then he smiles, showing off his blazing white teeth. "Fifty thousand."

"Oh my God!" Kimberly shouts and jumps up from her table. She begins to cry and laugh, jumping like a game show contestant. "Thank you so much! We're going to have a library in this town!"

Lois shushes the cheering crowd. "Hold on, folks. Peyton, do you have a counterbid?"

I'm in disbelief at Adam's bid, and I'm angry that Peyton is trying to compete with money he doesn't have. A flicker of rage passes between us. Then he puts down his paddle.

"No," he says emphatically to Lois. He retreats to the kitchen, followed by Bash.

Hoyt shakes his head. "Poor guy."

"Are you kidding? He just saved himself over fifty thousand dollars!" Ian exclaims. "No offense, Talia, but that's an expensive dinner, even for Richard Branson. Or Idris Elba, if anyone is keeping lists of successful hot men. Now you get to go out with Mr. Hedge Fund Hottie."

"Will you be sympathetic for a moment?" Hoyt doesn't like to see someone lose. "It's easy for that other guy to throw money around. Peyton didn't do this on a whim."

I let that sink in. Peyton can be impetuous and crave attention like anyone else. I think back to last year when he was the center of attention at Cooper and Imogene's wedding reception, and then his more recent behavior at Adam's dinner party. Peyton was gregarious and easy-going with the women, even if he was there to help me. He has been there for me these past few months.

Maybe it was a mistake to sleep with him knowing how easy it is to fall for him. I don't regret it, though. If anything, Peyton has confirmed my ideology about men and commitments. I know what I want, and it's not playing house with Peyton. The blind, heady passion that ignited between us is nothing like I've ever experienced with anyone else, but who's to say I can't have that again with someone new?

Like Adam.

Seeing Peyton retreat to the kitchen, his posture and broad shoulders showing no sign of defeat as he leaves the room, is like a knife digging slowly into my back, precariously close to my heart.

"Excuse me," I say to Ian and Hoyt. "I have to go thank Adam."

"Men will gladly accept blow jobs as a thank you," Ian says.

"Don't listen to him," Hoyt says gruffly. "I don't know what's going on between you and Peyton, and I don't know what that other guy is thinking spending that kind of dough for a dinner, but I can tell you that you deserve to be treated the way you want. It doesn't matter how much he spent. He paid for a meal, nothing more."

Ian snorts. "Thanks for the uplifting speech, Dad."

"You're a sweetheart." I kiss my fake boyfriend on the cheek. "We were great while it lasted, Grizzly." I'm off to find the hedge fund hottie.

Adam is surrounded by his friends and two waitresses who are enjoying their good luck of having a table of wealthy, attractive men. Their night will end with a very generous tip.

As I make my way over to him, he smiles and ignores the activity at his table. He stands up to reach for me, gently cupping my elbow. Everything about Adam tells me he is a gentleman.

"Now you have to have dinner with me." He smiles. "I won."

"You won. I'm arrogant enough to know I'm one of the best chefs around. However, not a single one of my dishes is worth fifty thousand dollars. You're crazy."

"Not crazy at all. I happen to be a big proponent of libraries. Also, you're worth it."

My face heats with a savage blush.

"I'm looking forward to this," he says.

"Me, too." Though, I'm torn. I want to stay at his table and bask in his attention, and I want to check on Peyton because I feel responsible for what happened tonight. "Um, will you excuse me for a minute? I need to check on something in the kitchen."

Adam isn't fooled by my weak excuse. We both know who's in the kitchen. The man who lost.

I want to find out why it matters to me. I should stay here and be with Adam as his prospective date and not as his home chef. How often does this happen to me? *Never!* I'm angry with Peyton for ruining the moment, and I'm angry with myself for caring what Peyton thinks.

Adam is gracious and says we can discuss plans later, and then I storm through the dining hall. A blind rage, which I've aptly titled Hurricane Peyton, is filling my blood stream.

"Where is he?" I yell when I enter the kitchen.

Bash hands a skillet off to his sous chef. "I sent him out back. He's mad as hell and was getting in the way here. If you're going to yell at me, I'm going to have to send you outside, too."

"Don't bother! I'm on my way!"

As I charge through the kitchen, every cook with a hot pan or plate quickly moves aside to let me through. I surprise Ray, a new hire, who's so startled by my violent presence that he drops a rack of barware onto the conveyer belt of the dishwasher.

I push the back door open too hard and it slams against the building, wedging itself into a wooden post.

"Great. You broke my door," Peyton says sharply. He's twenty feet away, holding a baseball bat. There's a pile of empty cans at his feet. He picks one up, tosses it in the air, and swings his bat, slamming the can into the open dumpster.

I turn around and take hold of the door handle while bracing my foot against the building and pull as hard as I can. It won't budge.

"Ha!" Peyton gives a sinister laugh, then resumes batting the tin cans.

Another attempt at unjamming the door causes me to lose my grip, and I fall on my rear end.

"Christ," Peyton mutters. He drops the baseball bat and stalks toward the door. He yanks it free with one hand and slams it closed hard enough to shake the ground. Then he reaches a hand down to me. I take it, and he pulls me up with so much force I'm surprised he doesn't dislocate my shoulder.

"Why did you do that?" I ask.

"Because you fell on your ass."

"Not that. Why did you bid against Adam? I don't understand what you're doing, and why you're bidding with money you don't have."

"I have it."

I must react with an incredulous look because he sneers.

"Really? You think I'm a shitty businessman? The kind who would be buried in debt?"

Yes, I did think he was carrying huge loans on his restaurants, especially Swill. He gets a lot of press as a much-talked-about up-and-coming restaurateur and entrepreneur, but those are words I always associate with "borrowed money." It never occurred to me that someone so young in this business has more assets than liabilities.

"I'm not a fool. I can afford to bid against Knight."

"I've never considered you a fool. I was shocked by how aggressively you bid against him." I don't ask him why he stopped bidding.

Peyton slowly circles me. In the darkness, with only the dim light fixture by the door illuminating his shape, he resembles a sexy vampire or someone more dangerous. He's contemplating, orchestrating his words, thinking before speaking. I'm not used to him holding back, but this is who we've become. Two ill-matched people driven by physical impulses and torn by separate needs and ambition.

"It was a good experiment," he says.

"I don't understand."

"Knight showed he's very interested in you. That's good. That's what you wanted all along."

"He donated a lot of money to the library fundraiser because he's generous. He gets dinner with me as a token gratuity." I try to downplay the monetary significance. I don't necessarily believe it's because Adam is overly fond of me. It's a paltry sum compared to his net worth. The bidding against Peyton was Adam's game. The power play is what he enjoyed. I have many clients similar to Adam; I've seen this before.

"Don't undervalue yourself, sunflower. You're worth more. I wanted to make sure Knight knows that you're the best he could ever have."

I stare at him for a moment, not sure why it feels like he's breaking my heart. *I wanted this, right?* Then why does a wave of sadness wash over me, as though he's letting me fall off a cliff?

I take a step toward him, and he steps backward, away from me, a signal of finality.

"You should probably get back to Knight and reassure him that you're not going to renege on this very expensive date." He's talking to me like a friend, the way Cooper would toss me advice. It's blunt without all the urgent, sexually charged emotions between us that usually punctuate every sentence.

I've lost my ability to respond, so I go for the door, wanting to leave this miserable sensation surrounding us. I pull the heavy steel door to the kitchen open.

"Hey, sunflower." His voice is smooth and the words roll out slowly like he took a swig of whiskey before speaking.

I look over my shoulder at his handsome face, grave and perfectly complementing his posture—akimbo, like a thief in the night.

"You chose well."

32

Talia

"Lilies! Everywhere, lilies!" Greer announces to everyone in the kitchen where I'm prepping twelve deliveries for tonight and simultaneously pretending not to keep track of Peyton's every move.

"We didn't order flowers," Peyton says in a bored tone as he exits the dry storage room with a stack of invoices in his hand. He glances at me for only a millisecond, easy for the untrained eye to miss, but not for this highly trained Russian spy who is overly sensitive to his presence.

"They're for you, Talia." Greer smiles at me. "Come see."

I put down my knife, brush my parsley-covered fingertips off on my apron, and follow her into the dining hall. Magnificent stalks with vivid blooms of red, orange, pink, and yellow are arranged in large bouquets on all the largest tables. I've never seen so many daylilies in one place.

The rest of the kitchen staff joins us to see the floral arrangements that have overtaken the whole dining room. I sense Peyton approach on my right as we all observe the outlandish display. They aren't your typical, store-bought bouquets either. These look as if someone went out and cut hundreds of tall stalks of lilies moments ago and put them, splayed wildly, in matching, tall, heavy, clear glass urns.

"There are a dozen vases. All of these are for you." Greer hands me a small, white envelope with my name handwritten on it in black ink. I recognize Adam's handwriting from the notes and work-related scribblings he's left on his kitchen counters.

"They're from Adam," I say, putting the unopened envelope into my apron pocket.

"Why twelve vases?" Greer asks. "Is that number significant?"

I shrug. "I once mentioned it would be more romantic for a man to send twelve bouquets of colorful lilies to a woman than one bouquet of red roses. It was because of a silly article in a women's magazine that showed his photo with a list of romantic gestures you can expect from him. He said the reporter made everything up, and I said that's good because giving women red roses is too predictable. I was just teasing him."

Greer laughs. "He certainly called you on it."

Peyton gives a disapproving grunt. "This is overkill. He's just showing off for you. It's not like he picked them himself. How hard is it to call a florist and place an order over the phone with a credit card?"

Greer glares at her brother. "You're being obnoxious."

"You're being easily impressed," Peyton says to me.

"I wasn't expecting something like this. Yes, it's impressive."

"Peyton," Greer says. "Some men are romantics. I've never known you to give any woman flowers. Except Mom. You used to hunt through every cheap bodega and flower stand in Brooklyn to get her sunflowers. But your mother doesn't count."

Peyton grumbles something about the dining room smelling like a funeral home, then herds the staff back into the kitchen.

"Sunflowers?" I ask Greer as she fingers the stem of a red lily and admires it.

He calls me sunflower.

"Oh, yes. Sunflowers. They were our mother's favorite. She said they are the biggest and happiest flower. Peyton loved to make her happy. He was definitely the baby in the family. I don't care what he says, he was a mama's boy. He'd do anything to put a smile on her face. I think he thought he could make everything better. Fix every bad day my mother had at work, especially when she hit the corporate glass ceiling. Peyton was really young at that time, and he thought our mother was actually hitting her head on a ceiling made of glass. It was precious. And I suppose a ten-year-old Peyton thought the sunflowers would make her happy enough that she'd fix her marriage with our dad.

"Peyton would ride his bike all over Brooklyn neighborhoods, always coming home with those giant sunflowers. He looked so proud when he'd present her with another one. Back then, he was just as tenacious, but he was also an optimist." Greer pauses. "Now he seems so ruthless with women."

"He's not that bad," I say, looking at the enormous sprays of lilies. The best way to describe it is that they make me feel *positive* when I think of Adam, and a little sad when Peyton flashes in my mind, which he does constantly.

Am I gaining something or losing something?

"Do you think Peyton will mind if I leave them here? I don't have room for these at home."

"The dining room is my jurisdiction, so I don't care what he thinks. These big vases work well on the large tables. They're lovely, and you can come visit them when you're confused about Peyton and need to be reminded that Adam is pretty fantastic."

"I don't know what you're talking about." A smile creeps across my face, and Greer laughs.

"Sure you don't. I'm Peyton's sister. I see everything he does. I can practically read his mind, and since this place opened, his mind has been on Finn, naturally, and you."

"We're over."

"I see," she says more seriously. "And you have a big date with Adam. I love my brother, but he's even worse at relationships than I am."

"We were never in a *real* relationship."

"Ah, yes. Defining a relationship is really tricky." She departs with a friendly smile, leaving me alone with my flowers and her lingering sarcasm.

• • •

I'm packing meals in the delivery bags when Peyton makes an appearance. After three months of working in his kitchen, I'm used to blending in with the staff, and the cooks and servers are used to working around my little area of the worktable. Sometimes I have them try my new dishes when Bash holds their afternoon tastings, and I like to participate in their daily chatter, which is usually gossip. It has given me good insight into the men and women working for Peyton, and undoubtedly, most of them, like Greer, have a fairly good grasp of what has been, or was, going on between Peyton and me. You can't really keep secrets in a restaurant. Something about the environment makes everyone's life naked to anyone employed there.

When Peyton begins talking to Bash, there's an obvious shift in the room. I am invisible. He blatantly ignores me now. I used to at least get a cursory glance if we'd been arguing. His eyes would meet mine at some point, and I felt like a lucky recipient of one of his hardened glares or his mirthful stares, both of which I welcomed. I could never get enough of his eyes, and there's nothing wrong with feeling your insides puddle, a little weak with a schoolgirl crush.

That's done. He's decided to treat me as if I'm not even here, and I don't like it. Calling off our trysts, whatever they should be called, is one thing. Pretending I don't exist is plain mean.

"You can stop going over all your little lists with me," Bash says. "I know everything. I can run this place without you."

"You wish," Peyton says.

"Go see some palm trees and swim in the ocean. Really, we can manage without you."

"Screw you. I'll call you when we check into the hotel."

I stop tugging at a zipper on one of my delivery bags and look directly at Peyton. I can't keep up the charade of nonchalantly eavesdropping. "Where are you going?" I demand.

He looks my way and regards me with a slight tilt of his head that suggests I'm making an inquiry into something that's none of my business. "LA, of course."

"You're going to see the Bourdain people?" I'm astounded. After everything he went through with Finn, he's still willing to break up his family to follow money and fame?

"Yes, I'm going to meet with them."

"I can't believe how selfish you are!" I give up on the bag's zipper and storm out toward the van.

"Hey!" Peyton follows me outside with my other two bags. "Do you think you can keep your opinions to yourself?" He arranges my bags in the back of the van and slams the doors closed.

"I thought my opinions mattered to you. I thought you took my advice seriously and you realized how lucky you are to have Finn. You set up your house here for him. You said you wanted to give him a stable life!"

"I'm going to LA to see what Bourdain can offer. Finn is going with me. Tomorrow night."

"Oh." It's like my last breath is being sucked out of me. "Harmony agreed to this?"

"She understands this is a big opportunity for my career."

"But she moved across the country so her son, your son, could be with his father. Why would she ever consider letting you take him to LA? She would give up custody?"

"No one ever said anything about giving up custody," he says with so much disdain I shrink back.

My cluttered thoughts render me speechless.

"Harmony is going with me."

I never saw that one coming. I feel sick.

"There's something I need to tell you." He pauses, not meeting my eyes.

Can this get any worse? Is he trying to make me hate him? Are he and Harmony a couple now?

"You don't have to tell me—you don't owe me anything."

"I do."

He steps back and rocks on his feet, bothered, hesitating. Then he kicks a rock and walks around in a circle, cursing to himself and kicking more rocks. He's beginning to make me nervous.

"I owe you some objectivity, and to make amends," he says. "I've made this whole thing between us difficult. I'm sorry. We agreed it would be casual, but I kept trying to convince you to accept less than what you deserve. You should be with the person who's best for you."

This is what I wanted, right?

I acknowledge his statement with nothing more than a nod and get into the van and leave.

• • •

I couldn't sleep last night. By three in the morning, I was so tired of being consumed with Peyton's news that I walked on the dreaded treadmill for an hour, conjuring happy thoughts about tonight's dinner with Adam. I'll be on a dinner date while Peyton is flying to Los Angeles. With his new family.

I finish packing the six-course meal. It's too much food for two people. Too rich, too much butter, and the meal will end with a flourless chocolate torte, so if the butter and fat don't kill us, the sugar will put us in a nice coma. I cooked the meal at home rather than at Swill under the watchful eyes of the staff.

Adam said he would send someone to pick up the food since it won't fit in his car, and then he'll pick me up at five. I'm surprised he wants to eat at such an early hour, but then, maybe he has plans to crush my soul by topping Peyton's news. Soul-crushing dates take extra time so all the harsh words can get out and the disappointment can be fully digested.

After a young man in a truck came by to get the food, I received another text from Adam, informing me to dress in jeans and wear comfortable shoes.

"I don't know, Talia." Aleska is sitting on my bed, watching me select a casual outfit. "A five o'clock dinner? Jeans and sneakers? It sounds like two seniors going for the early bird special at a diner."

"I think we're eating outside. He said he wants to beat the mosquitos." I observe myself in the full-length mirror. I'm wearing skinny jeans with a sleeveless, pink wrap blouse and a pair of white Toms slip-ons. "Should I wear my hair up or down?"

"Down," she says in a bored tone as she flips through a magazine. "That way he can run his fingers through your hair when he kisses you."

"What's wrong? You're acting like this is a bad idea. You're the one who kept saying how fabulous Adam is and wouldn't it be great to date a man like him."

She tosses the magazine on the floor and looks at me in the mirror. "You look very pretty. He'll think so, too."

"So, why are you so gloomy?"

"I guess I'm a little sad that, after all you and Peyton have been through together, you're tossing him aside so you can go out with Adam."

I turn away from the mirror and face my sister. "I didn't toss Peyton anywhere. He's leaving for Los Angeles tonight, and he's taking Harmony and Finn with him. He's practically a married man!" I pick the magazine off the floor and throw it at her head.

"Hey! Don't get mad at me. You asked me, and I told you. Adam seems terrific, but I don't think you and Peyton are over each other."

"We were never supposed to be into each other. I slept with him to prove to myself that not every man will reject me like Marko did. Peyton and I had an understanding that we were friends who slept together. I did it to make myself feel better after ..."

"After the surgery, and the depressing recovery ... and you wanted to feel good again."

"Yes, that's it exactly. I wouldn't have gotten involved with Peyton if I had known about Finn."

"So you and Peyton haven't slept together since he met Finn?"

"Well ... no ... that's not true. I wasn't going to continue with the sleepovers, but we got carried away a few times."

"Is that what we're calling it now? Sleepovers? And getting carried away?" Aleska chuckles. "I think you two are crazy about each other. And no matter how charming and nice Adam is, you're not going to be into him as long as you have feelings for Peyton."

"Sometimes feelings aren't enough. Sometimes you have to put them aside and move on."

"But, why would you? Peyton is a great guy. So he has a kid, and there's an ex-girlfriend in the picture. It's a little complicated, but you guys were working that out so well, and Finn really likes you."

"Peyton is seriously considering a big job opportunity in LA. It's thousands of miles away from me. He has Finn. And Harmony. He has a ready-made family. When Harmony and Finn came into his life, in the back of my mind, I always knew it was a possibility that they would come together as a family."

My sister frowns. "I can't picture Peyton and Harmony together."

"Let's drop it. I have a date to get ready for. And if you see any evidence in Adam's home that he has any ex-wives or children living in other states or countries, would you please tell me?"

"Adam has been too busy climbing the corporate ladder to get married or have kids. He's at that age, though. He's looking now."

"He said that to you?"

"He doesn't have to. A single man doesn't buy a home made for a family in a town like Hera unless he's thinking about settling down."

• • •

Adam picks me up in an expensive-looking red convertible. He's wearing jeans and a gray polo shirt, and he looks dashing with his Ray-Bans and early summer tan.

"Where's your Tesla?" I ask as he holds the passenger door open for me.

"At home. I thought we'd take out my new toy. It's a Bugatti."

"I don't know anything about cars. It sounds like an Italian dessert."

He grins. "You look very beautiful. As always."

"And you always say the right thing." I get in the car, feeling light and hopeful.

We zoom along the back roads, and I point out areas of interest. They are only areas of interest to me because I like old farms with rusted-out trucks planted by the front of their driveways as if they died before reaching the home and the owner decided it wasn't worth the bother to have it towed.

Adam turns onto a dirt road designated as *Private*.

"We can't drive here; it's private land," I explain.

"I know. I have permission to use it." He shifts into low gear as we take the uphill road slowly.

"Where are we going?" I brush my windblown hair out of my face. It keeps sticking to my lip gloss. Not the look I was going for, so I hold it back with my hand.

"You'll see. A friend owns this property. He's going to build a house up here, but we're the only ones here today."

The road opens into a wide-open hilltop with a three hundred and sixty degree view like I have never seen.

"We're not alone," I point out.

In the clearing where I assume the house will be built is a table set for two and a woman dressed in black with a black apron retrieving my food from the truck that came by my home earlier. A few feet from the table is a quartet taking their seats on wooden, fold-out chairs. I watch as the cellist positions her instrument against her long, flowing skirt, then adjusts the sheet music on the stand in front of her.

"Pretend they're not here."

"You didn't have to do all this. I would have been happy to serve the food myself at your house. You don't have to try so hard to impress me."

"Are you impressed?" He parks the car on the grass and gives me a moment to take it all in.

"Yes. You're good at this. Must have had *a lot* of practice."

"If you're implying I've dated many women, I suppose I have. However, I consider myself a gentleman, not a womanizer."

"Did your mother advise you to use that line?"

"My father." He cheerily gets out of the car and comes around to assist me before my foot even touches the ground.

We walk arm in arm to the table, which has been set with real silver, a small vase of wildflowers, and rose petals scattered across the white tablecloth. There's fine china with sterling food covers over the plates, and crystal goblets for the wine, which has already been decanted. My mother's pastries and my chocolate torte are arranged on a three-tiered, glass platter. The pieces all look like authentic antiques. Adam went all out, down to every last detail.

"Thank you, Sasha," Adam says to the woman handling the food. "I'll take care of the rest."

Sasha nods, then leaves in the truck.

"A string quartet," I say with admiration. "Mozart. Number fourteen. G major." They are far enough away from the table that we can still talk without raising our voices.

"You know your music." There's a gleam of appreciation.

"I know some. I never played the violin, though."

"I decided against having a pianist tonight because bringing a piano up here would have been a mother of a job. Also, because no one can top you."

I laugh. "Oh, heavens, nice save."

"Really, I'm not this smooth. I've never done this." He waves his hands at the extravagant setup. "Other people came up with the idea. I'm not that creative."

"Where did you find Sasha? And this china? This didn't come from your home."

"Sasha works at Mohonk. And, no, I didn't date her. The musicians perform in the area and came recommended by a friend. The china is on loan from a friend, too."

"You have nice friends."

"It was Lois. She gave me the phone numbers. She loaned me the china."

"I take it back. You don't have nice friends."

Adam laughs. "She's a tough one, that woman."

I walk over to inspect the china. "I should have recognized this. I've seen it displayed in one of the hutches at her home. Once, I took a plate out to look at the pattern more closely and Lois actually told me to put it back. *Gently*!" I say in Lois's gravelly voice. "I hope my food lives up to your expectations."

He pulls out a chair for me. "Honestly, we could have hot dogs and potato chips, and this would still be perfect." His mouth quirks into a brief smile, and I'm touched by his statement.

Once we start drinking the wine, the conversation flows easily and we're both back to our usual banter. My initial concern over trying to live up to a fifty thousand dollar date doesn't hang over my head like I thought it would. Adam is funny and quite open about his work and his life. Behind the good looks of the rich CEO facade, he's really just a small-town boy from Ohio who grew up in an average, middle-class American family with its share of drama and comedy. I like the way he can make fun of his family members in a loving way and can put aside work. He's different than both Marko and Peyton in that regard.

The musicians play throughout the meal, and when we finish the desserts and the cheese plate, Adam dismisses them. They pack all their instruments into the trunk of a fairly small car, and when they get in the car and drive away, it makes me think of circus clowns packed in a tiny car. Now it's just the two of us.

Adam looks very handsome, even more so in the orange hues from the sunset. This is the moment I've been waiting for. I'm eager at the prospect of being alone with him here, unlike being alone with him when I'm working as his chef.

"More wine?" he asks, holding up an unopened bottle of claret.

I shake my head.

He stands and reaches his hand across the table to me. I take it and stand, too.

"Let's stretch our legs and take a walk."

Holding his hand, I step around the table closer to him. We both stop and look at each other, experiencing the final buildup from all those moments together in his kitchen, wondering if there could be more than talking. Adam doesn't waste this chance.

With his free hand, he gently wraps it around the back of my neck and pulls me in for a kiss. His lips are firm but tender. I'm elated that he's finally kissing me, but then something malfunctions. My brain must have missed a signal, because I'm waiting for my body to catch up with my racy thoughts. I respond to the kiss, trying to be an active participant, but nothing seems to come naturally. I must have fried my brain circuitry overthinking this for so long that now I'm ruining the kiss.

This is work! I'm thinking about each step like a checklist. *Lips. Tongue. Grope. Touch. Lips. God, no, this can't be happening.*

He deepens the kiss, and I want to reciprocate, but I feel wooden, like this is one-sided. Adam is doing all the kissing, and I'm just standing there, moving my lips like a robot. Maybe he's thinking the same thing, because he becomes a bit more aggressive, and it gets to the point where our kissing starts to feel like we're attacking each other.

We stop. *Thank God.*

How could this not work with Adam? I feel stupid that I failed at kissing him, at seduction with this incredible man.

I look at the ground. I can't meet his eyes.

"Oh," Adam utters. "Shit."

I look up at him, dreading this.

"You didn't feel anything," he says.

"It was a nice kiss."

"That's a horrible thing to say. If it doesn't make you lose your mind, it's not a kiss worth having."

"I'm sorry. I didn't … We didn't have those chemical things." I motion with my arms in a circle like I'm imitating a blender.

"We didn't have any chemistry with that kiss." He sighs. He worked so hard to create the perfect date, and I'm the part that fizzled.

"I tried. We were trying so hard."

Adam barks a laugh. "I'm sorry, but the way you said that was funny."

I relax and smile, too. "I hear that a lot."

"I'm really surprised. I assumed this would be easy and perfect with you."

"I thought the same thing. We have this—something—between us." I motion with my arms again like it's an actual thing, and it makes him laugh more. "No, really, there was something between us whenever we saw each other."

"There was. There is. But it's not there now. Not after I kissed you. That kiss didn't do anything for you, did it?"

"No," I admit reluctantly. "I don't think it was the biggest turn-on for you either."

"Oh, I thought I was turned on until I realized the fire went out. I don't understand what happened. We've been dancing around this for a while. Every time I was around you, there were these little fireworks, like we were building up to something big. What the hell happened?"

"I think I'm your safe choice, not what you really want."

His smile turns into a frown. "How so?"

"You came to Hera and bought your own castle, and you're looking for a woman who is more like Hera than Manhattan."

He studies me.

"Think about it," I say. "The type of woman you want … she's independent and has her own goals, and she's someone you're so comfortable with that you enjoy her company. You thought that woman was me because I feed you. I remind you of something good and safe, and when we're together, it feels natural and easy. We both mistook it for something more than friendship."

"Sounds like you have it all figured out."

"In theory, this should have worked. You're perfect for me in so many ways. You're smart and charming, and I could talk to you for hours. And you're so handsome!"

He chuckles. "You don't have to let me down easy."

I shrug. "I'm sorry."

"There's nothing to be sorry about. Guess I'm no substitute for Peyton. It was dumb of me to think I could swoop in and steal you."

I'm surprised he even considered Peyton as competition.

I'm humbled by his honesty, and he's right. I did think he'd be the guy to make me forget about Peyton.

"So Peyton is the lucky guy."

"I never said that."

"You didn't have to. I've seen what passes between you two. I thought I could break it."

"I'm not with Peyton."

Adam looks at me quizzically. "I'm used to dating any woman I'm interested in. That makes me sound like a complete jackass, but the truth is that a lot of women do fall for the superficial aspects of my life. My money, my high profile. I've always used that to my advantage in dating. I'm ready for something more, and when I met you, I knew you were different than the other women I've been with."

"I am different than the women you date. I don't come from the world of finance. I usually wear steel-toed work boots, not heels. And I've been told my English sucks. Don't worry; you're going to find the right woman, and you're going to have all those … chemical … things."

Adam gives another hearty laugh.

"Chemistry!" I shout over his laughing. "You're going to have explosive chemistry with the right woman."

"You think so? Will I find her in Hera? Because I'm tired of the New York social scene."

"My crystal ball is broken. Obviously, look at me. You shouldn't worry, though. She's going to be the one who loves being in that big house with you. You'll have those long talks and both forget about work because all you'll care about is being with each other. You'll both be madly in love in your very own modern castle. That's how it's supposed to work. That's the real-life fairy tale."

"This is good to know. I'll be on the lookout for her."

"Do you want Aleska to start bringing your meals to the house so it isn't weird being around me?"

"No. That's absurd. I still want to see you. We're friends, right? I look forward to those nights when I get a great meal and good conversation with you."

"Good. And when you meet Miss Right and she starts staying at your house, I'm going to have to double your fees since I'll be cooking for two."

"Wouldn't have it any other way."

• • •

Another night of misery. I only fall asleep these days after exhaustive crying. Tears soak my sheets as I bury my head in my pillow.

Peyton is in Los Angeles, but every reminder of him is all around me. I can taste and smell him in the air. My memory is playing tricks on me, hurting me so I feel the pain of separation from him.

"What can I do?" my mother asks from my bedroom doorway.

I wipe my eyes with my sleeve. My face feels swollen and heavy, the tight puffiness that comes with too much crying. I can't see through my soggy lashes. My mother is nothing but a blurry image.

"I was so wrong." I fumble with the tissue box on my nightstand. The empty box falls to the floor.

"We often are."

"I've been duplicitous, carrying on with Peyton and pursuing Adam at the same time, and now I'm paying the price."

"No, honey, you're not being punished. I should have said something when I saw what was happening between you and Peyton. You were both falling in love, and I don't know why, but you seemed to be in denial about the whole thing. What can I do to help?"

"There's nothing you can do. I let myself fall for Peyton. He's just another man who's all tied up in himself. I always find the man who is the most difficult in every way. There is something fundamentally wrong with me."

"I don't think we choose who we love. You didn't love Marko. Not really. You thought it was more important to be with someone— even if that someone was wrong for you—rather than face life's challenges on your own. You and I are alike in that way, but I've changed. So have you. We're stronger. We're better than before."

"I don't feel stronger or better. I feel awful. Like something in me has died."

I have two hearts, and they both betrayed me before. The heart that keeps my blood pumping needed to be repaired, and I thought it would kill me. The heart that's supposed to fill me with love led me to an *impossible* love, and it, too, feels like it will kill me.

I love Peyton. It's not incremental based on a single scenario I've experienced with him. It's an all-encompassing love. There's not a part of him I don't love. If only I could find a nugget of hatred or resentment to carry me through this heartache, this broken heart. But I can't. There's not an ounce of animosity. Just undying love.

Stupid, hideous love.

33

Peyton

AFTER LEAVING TETERBORO AIRPORT in New Jersey, we are soon entranced with the endless trays of food and cocktails pushed on us. Flying courtesy of Danny Bourdain involves a complete kitchen staff with a gourmet chef and servers anticipating your every need as you sink back into the plush surroundings that make you forget you're on a personal jet.

When he isn't drilling the pilots with questions, Finn is curled up in a king-size, leather seat, playing computer games and watching movies. The flight attendants dote on him with sweet and salty treats. It makes me uneasy. I don't want him to get used to this.

Is this who I am? The man who wants all of these luxuries? I definitely don't want my son to expect his life to be this easy.

Harmony sits in another seating area, reading biomedical research papers and other work-related documents. Occasionally, she glances my way with one of her pointed eye rolls when some decadent tray of caviar is passed around, or a bottle of 1986 Chateau Margaux is uncorked for us.

I sit with Merrick, Danny Bourdain's second-in-command, the brains behind the whole business enterprise. Danny is the famous French-American chef and face of his chain of restaurants, and Merrick is the soft-spoken, behind-the-scenes CFO who likes organization and efficiency and who knows how to turn profits.

Many people compare me to Danny—either it's our personalities, our ability to talk to everyone, or the attention I'm getting as a young restaurateur on the rise. But I would argue that I'm more like Merrick, except a little louder. Like him, I pay attention to detail, and I know every employee by name and their weaknesses and strengths in a restaurant. I want Danny's success, but living large, owning homes in several countries, flying on personal jets, and dating a revolving door of women are things that don't appeal to me.

When we land in Los Angeles, an SUV limo chauffeurs us to Danny's main home in Malibu, where he's waiting to make me an offer I can't possibly refuse, as he put it. When someone as famous as Danny Bourdain goes out of their way to court you, it's impossible not to be flattered, but the devil's advocate on my shoulder remarks on all the decadent waste.

My personal devil must be talking to Talia on a regular basis, because I keep feeling a slight repulsion and disappointment at how much money is being spent to entertain me and to amuse the Bourdain-Torrance Enterprise executives.

At Danny's lavish Malibu home, which was recently featured in *Architectural Digest*, Danny himself greets us at the car. He's barefoot and dressed in loose-fitting, linen pants and a simple, cotton T-shirt. In his late fifties, with his wet hair slicked back, he looks like a very fit surfer. Then he tells us he actually spent the morning surfing with his kids. So maybe there is a part of his life I would like—having more time with my kid.

Danny's three daughters, ranging in age from ten to seventeen, take Finn under their wing. They gear him up in a wetsuit and outfit him with a surfboard, after trying to determine which size to start him with, and then they march down to the beach, a mere fifteen steps from the deck off the back of the house. We're assured Finn is in good hands. Danny's children are all experienced swimmers and competitive surfers. Nevertheless, Harmony stands watch on the deck with a flute of some fresh fruit and alcohol-infused concoction someone from the household staff hands her.

Danny takes me and Merrick to his private library on the second floor that overlooks the Pacific with a 180-degree view. My son's red wetsuit is visible in the distance. He's clinging to a surfboard after falling off. I relax a bit and take in the comfortable surroundings of Danny's personal room.

Unlike the rest of the house, which is modern minimalist that screams money, his library is wall-to-wall bookcases mixed in with expensive art and Danny's awards. Worn leather couches and oversize armchairs, restaurant and wine magazines tossed everywhere, and a general ambience of lazy comfort.

Danny notices me slowly taking in all the accoutrements. Candid shots of his children and ex-wife are everywhere, too. I know his ex-wife lives down the street in her own ostentatious home, but she and Danny remain close and have family dinners with the kids at least twice a week.

It was clever to bring me to his home first rather than going straight to the hotel. Danny wants to give me a taste of what I could have. He's showing me that, in any business, we project what we sell, the image or persona needed for the face of the company. The lifestyle and the appearances in the media don't mean I can't carve out my own private place where I can be myself and not the showman.

I wonder if I could have the same set-up with Harmony living nearby, or would she expect us all to live in the same house, convinced it's best for Finn? Our conversations have gotten as far as agreeing we need to support each other's careers, and we need to be more than civil for Finn's sake. We are working on friendship, but we haven't delved into the deeper logistics of living arrangements. It starts to complicate things, and although I'm entertaining the idea of having us all live in one big, platonic house for practical reasons, when do the lines get blurred? Can Harmony and I walk freely around the house in our underwear without confusing Finn? Is he going to think his parents are eventually going to get married? And what if we blow it, drink too much one evening, and decide a quick hop in the sack won't hurt? Of course, I don't want that to happen, but I'm also still reeling from losing Talia. Who knows what dumbass thing I will do, thinking it will distract me from missing her? I can easily imagine all the different ways I can screw this up.

"It's a pretty great place to raise a family," Merrick says before taking a swig of scotch.

I like that about him. He's direct; no pretense. He has enough money for him and his future generations to retire today, but he likes working and likes wearing jeans and a basic, white dress shirt that says he probably shops online and doesn't have a personal shopper in New York or Milan on standby. I think Merrick is whom I always wanted to be. I just didn't know it until I met him in person.

After three days of touring all of Bourdain-Torrance's Los Angeles restaurant operations and inspecting new land and building acquisitions I would oversee for development, I'm sold.

It's light years away from Hera. The land, the air, the people are so different here. The separation is palpable, made worse because of Talia. If only that small-town woman had no effect on me. If only I had never gotten to know her. If only she didn't exist.

That little fucking devil lurking underneath my conscience tells me I'm too weak to be like Merrick or aspire to Danny Bourdain's success as long as I pine for Talia. And that's exactly what I'm doing.

Putting thousands of miles between us and restructuring my life with a more stressful career and a ready-made family isn't lessening the mild torture I feel from missing her.

While I visit the restaurants and meet with other principals in the company, Harmony and Finn are given the white-glove treatment with a personal chauffeur and a realtor who works for the company. They tour a half-dozen homes for sale in various neighborhoods and in different price ranges, depending on proximity to the ocean or the sections Harmony selected from her online research. Everything is in the seven figures, but I'm not concerned since Merrick and Danny boosted my generous salary and annual bonus package with a housing bonus that would be paid up front.

They're pretty much throwing money at me to make me say yes. I'm not sure how I got to be so lucky to be the chosen one, to be targeted and courted by Danny when there are plenty of other people out there like me who are just as driven and experienced, yet young enough to be pliable and molded into Danny's protégé. I like to think I'm actually talented in this business, and I've paid my dues and worked my way up doing the grunt work. My own restaurants show my ability to manage a business and recognize talent and customers.

A sour feeling tells me it's not at all what I think. An offhand whisper from Merrick one day—"like a son to Danny"—sticks with me. I know from years of following Danny's career that his first child, a son, died at the age of twenty after battling bone cancer for three years. Maybe I'm his replacement son. Maybe I do represent the idealized version of Danny himself and who he thought his son would have grown up to be if he hadn't been dealt a lousy hand of terminal illness. I don't know whether to feel special for being taken in with open arms and given carte blanche to Danny's world, or if I'm more than slightly concerned that I'm feeding into Danny's illusions. The old me wouldn't care about *why*. He'd grab the holy grail with both hands and embrace the opportunity. The me today has more questions. Not necessarily about Danny's business offer, which is solid, but about myself.

My instinct is to turn around and look over my shoulder for Talia, thinking I will see her nearby so I can discuss these concerns with her. I could just as well share these ideas with Harmony, shore up our developing friendship, but I don't.

Harmony is reserved throughout our stay. She appreciates the lavish hotel and the five-star service, but she isn't dazzled the way Finn is. She takes notes on the houses she visits and asks detailed questions about the public and private schools in the particular areas. Then she insists I accompany them to see a home for sale in a prestigious neighborhood the realtor is aggressively encouraging.

It has five bedrooms, a swimming pool, an outdoor kitchen for parties, and too many rooms for three people, along with a seven million dollar price tag. It's a renovated showplace, and I'd buy it on the spot, but Harmony gives a firm "No, we need to discuss this." I don't get excited about houses, or worse, renovating them. Nevertheless, I do see Finn's reaction, and it adds to my motivation. I would like to be a parent who can give him this if it will make him happy.

Am I threatened by Harmony's wealth and the fact that she has provided Finn with a high standard of living? Probably. Because she also has full custody of Finn. How do I compete with that? By becoming a superstar with Bourdain-Torrance and raking in the big bucks.

Back at the hotel, over fast-food bags since we decided we were all tired of delicately designed dishes and heavy cream sauces, Harmony shares her notes with me.

"What were you thinking? You almost made an offer on that house." she says in the living room portion of the suite. Finn is out of earshot in the master bedroom, watching a movie and feasting on fish tacos.

"It's a great house. Good school district. I thought it had all the things we need."

"Need? No one needs a seven million dollar home."

"If it's the money, it would come from my sign-on bonus."

"I have enough money to buy four of those houses!" she whisper-shouts angrily.

"You do?"

"Peyton! It's not the money. It's the idea of living in that home. Did you think we'd all live there together? Because I don't see that happening."

"Oh, right. I'm jumping the gun. I don't really know what you want, but that house seemed like a good start."

"Really? You think that little enclave of homes we saw is the perfect place for Finn? You picked the most expensive home out of all the ones Finn and I have seen. You also picked the neighborhood where we didn't see a single person of color. Except for the gardeners. This isn't like Brooklyn. We keep seeing homes in the least diverse parts of the city."

"You moved Finn to Westchester. It's not as diverse as Brooklyn either."

"Our neighborhood is, and so is his school there."

"Shit, don't be so pissed off. I'm sorry I liked the house. It won't happen again. You choose the house and the school. I'll go along with whatever you think is best for Finn."

"I thought that's what I was doing when I moved him back to New York. I thought living near you and letting him get to know his cousins and family in Hera and Brooklyn was the best thing for Finn. I agreed to this trip because I thought you were networking, building your relationship with Danny. I didn't believe for a minute that you'd drop everything in New York and move here. But the longer we're here, the crazier you seem."

I shove aside my unfinished tacos. "How so?"

"I don't recognize you." She shakes her head. "I thought it was a good decision to move to New York, so Finn could have a relationship with you and your huge family. It's everything he wants. It wasn't easy to reach out to you. It felt like a great risk. I didn't know what kind of person you'd be now, but after some research on you, I had to take that risk, for Finn's sake."

"Oh, that's right. You were spying on me. And Talia."

"I was doing what anyone in my position would do—making sure you were fit to be a parent. Making sure I wasn't putting Finn or me in danger."

"Danger?"

"I didn't know you, Peyton. You could have changed completely since high school. You could have been a hotheaded prick who wanted nothing to do with a kid. And I have money. My father made a point of teaching me how to protect it. It's also why he didn't let me inherit a dime until I was finished with graduate school."

"You thought I'd go after your money?" I raise my voice.

"I wouldn't have moved to New York if I thought that, but it was something to consider. You were already doing well on your own, so it wasn't really a concern. But I'm a safety girl now. I was so young when I had Finn, and I was completely dependent on my father. I never want to be in such a vulnerable position again. I wasn't going to put Finn or myself at risk."

"And neither of you are at risk," I snap. Suddenly, I feel like she's the nagging wife I never wanted. "I haven't changed. I haven't done anything wrong. You're the one who kept Finn from me for a decade!"

"We're not going to have a fight over the past. I already admitted I was complicit when I went along with my father's demands to keep you away from Finn. But this LA thing is all on you! It's a stupid idea!"

"Stop fighting!" Finn shouts from the doorway of the bedroom suite.

Harmony raises her hand to her mouth and looks at him apologetically. "Honey, we're sorry. We're having a little disagreement. Everything is fine, though."

Finn's face is bunched up in anger, and he looks like he's about to cry. "The best place for me to live is where you two don't fight!" With that, he runs back to the bedroom.

I move to stand up, wanting to go after him.

"No." Harmony points furiously at me to sit back down. Then she closes the French doors to the bedroom with a gentle click. "Let him be alone. We'll talk to him when he's ready."

"You pick the neighborhood and house. I'll let you choose."

"No. Dammit, Peyton!" she whispers. "You've been walking around LA with your head full of dollar signs. You've been looking at this from your point of view. It's all about your success."

"You agreed to come. You knew I was being offered a job here." I keep my voice lower than hers. She has the advantage; Finn has been with her and on her side for his whole existence.

Harmony looks back at the bedroom doors to make sure Finn can't hear. Then she sits on the chair opposite me with the coffee table between us. She huddles down with her elbows on her knees and fidgets with her bracelets. "Do you realize you haven't smiled once on this trip?" she asks. "Danny and Merrick have shown you this glamorous lifestyle, beautiful houses, expensive restaurants, and they make it look easy, as if everyone lives on the beach and has time to surf all day. I don't believe all the hype they're dumping on you. I think the work would be long hours, and you know better than anyone that this business requires a relentless devotion and the expectation that many things will go wrong."

"You don't need to tell me how my business works. I've been doing this since I was a teenager, and I work my ass off."

"Yes, you do. But what I took away from the last few days is that you never once looked happy. You never cracked a smile, Peyton. Not even when we took Finn skateboarding at Venice Beach or when he was learning how to surf at Danny's place. If that doesn't make you smile ... I have to question why you're doing this."

Hearing her say these things makes me feel hollow inside. She thinks I'm shallow and selfish. How can she not see I'm doing all this for Finn? He's the only thing making me feel rooted to anything substantial. Whatever I had in New York, aside from the family business, I lost.

"I'm doing this for Finn. For all of us. This position with Bourdain-Torrance will make my career skyrocket. I'll have the means to provide Finn with every opportunity."

"You already have the means to provide well for Finn. You're already a success. More money and fame won't make you a better father. If you're worried about your father and uncle—I know about the money problems with their first business—you are solid enough to take care of them as well."

"So, what are you saying?"

"I don't want to move here. This isn't the best place for Finn. He's better off in New York, where all his family lives. He wants to get to know his cousins and aunts and uncles better. He wants the fishing trips with Grandpa Stu, the sleepovers with the cousins, the family dinners with you and your siblings. He goes to a great school, and he's made friends. If you take this job, you're going to make Finn start all over again, and no matter how many new friends he makes here, he won't have his family. They'll be thousands of miles away.

"And just because my dad left me money doesn't mean I don't want to work. My career is important to me, too. I didn't spend all those years in college and graduate school to spend my days at the beach. I'd have to get a new job, too. It's not just about you, Peyton."

"Why didn't you say this before we flew out here?"

"Because I didn't think you'd actually want to go through with this. I thought this trip would be a nice little vacation with Finn, and you'd come to your senses and realize you've got it made in Hera."

"Finn can see my family anytime. We'll have the use of Bourdain's company jet to fly back and forth every month if we want, so Finn will see plenty of the MacKenzies. And I'll have the means to fly them out here for extended stays with us."

"God, you are infuriating." Her nostrils flare, and I picture us arguing like this for many years to come.

"Career-wise, I can't do much more in Hera. I'm not a small-town guy, and our restaurants in New York are running fine without me. Career opportunities like Bourdain's are unicorns, and this is a huge one. I'd be a fool to turn it down. This has been a dream, a goal of mine."

"Goal? Who gives a flying fuck about goals? I'm not moving Finn to LA for your *goals*."

"What do you want me to say?" I ask, defeated.

"I want you to admit it's better for Finn, for you, for all of us to stay in New York. I want you to turn down this job."

"I can't. I already accepted Danny's offer."

34

Peyton

Harmony takes Finn back to Westchester and says she'll call in the next few days to talk. She was still giving me the silent treatment when we landed at Newark airport—on our commercial flight since Harmony refused the Bourdain jet this time. Finn was still unhappy with the tension between his parents. We haven't told him that I accepted the job and that we won't be going there together.

I remember what it's like to be a little soldier between two fighting parents. I went through something similar when my mother had an affair, then my father had his own, and then they divorced. I survived the deep freeze between them, but only because they decided to live in houses directly across the street from one another so their five children could keep their own lives and friends intact. We could sleep at either home, and I would run back and forth between each house throughout the day to raid the better-stocked kitchen or to find a television or computer that was free. It became even easier and almost normal when my parents became friends again. Unfortunately, Finn doesn't have siblings he can share his parents' drama with, and I've only been part of his life for a few months. His devotion is to his mother.

Going back to Hera is daunting.

Aleska's team kept my home spotless while I was gone. I walk around the house and assess how long it will take to pack up my personal belongings for a move. Fifteen minutes by my estimate. That's how little I've invested here, other than Finn's room.

I approach his bedroom with hesitation. I haven't convinced myself that I can change Harmony's mind, and even if I can, I may have damaged my relationship with Finn forever.

As I enter, a flood of emotions assaults me. The happy memories this room brings settle into a mixture of remorse, darkened by uncertainty. It's the most personal room in the house. I think back to when Talia helped me paint it and turn it into a special place fit for a curious young boy.

As I sit on the bed, a horrible sensation strikes me. This room is like visiting the grave of the son I've lost.

I bolt from the room, jump in my truck, and drive to Swill.

Adam Knight is the first person I see. His back is to me, and as I pull into a parking spot next to his car, I see Talia looking up at him, smiling.

I get out of my truck and look through the cab at them.

Adam turns when I slam my door. "Hey, MacKenzie. How was LA? Productive?"

A long strand of Talia's hair blows across her face. She tucks it behind her ear as she looks at me, too.

"It was good," I reply. I should head inside the restaurant, but seeing them together unnerves me. I don't like it. I want to know what they're discussing. Another date? Is she spending nights at his place now? I hate how I feel and sound when I see them together, but I don't do the wise thing and move on. "What are you up to?" I fake nonchalance.

"I'm giving Talia advice on her plan to develop that old Pickwick estate."

"Jesus, you're really pursuing that money pit?" I say to her. I hear how condescending I sound. Nothing like Adam's upbeat, supportive optimism. No wonder she's more interested in him.

"It's actually a great idea, and the financials are workable," Adam explains. He looks like Mr. Cool Diplomacy. He's got on a pair of those expensive designer jeans that are overly distressed to make rich dudes look like they do hard labor, and a T-shirt that shows off his gym body. Sunglasses are perched on his head, and he's sporting a tan, either from driving his convertible or maybe taking long weekends in tropical locations. Normally, I don't notice these things about other men, but I notice every detail about Adam, because he is with the only woman whom I'm interested in. He is exactly what Talia is looking for, and I'm an idiot to think I could have ever competed with him.

Talia glares at me, challenging me to make more disparaging remarks to pop her fantasy bubble about her dream farm and inn.

I end the uncomfortable situation by tossing my keys and catching them in my fist. "Well, I need to get to work."

Talia turns to Adam. "I have to get going, too. A lot of deliveries tonight. But thank you for the information."

"Make my place your last stop. I can throw together some spreadsheets for you before you get there, and we can go over them. Over dinner. Sound good?"

"Really? You have time for that?"

"Absolutely. It's no problem. I'll call Archie and get the numbers on the cost of the estate. I want to know what the property taxes are, and then I'll put together some estimates for you on what the total buildout would be, and the operating costs, and what you can expect as a profit margin—assuming the numbers work in your favor. But I'll make them work."

I can't listen to this guy's sales pitch anymore. What a bunch of bullshit.

I throw open the front door to Swill. My boots pound on the floor, echoing throughout the empty dining hall. *I'll make them work*. Like he's some fucking financial wizard. He may run a hedge fund, but that doesn't make him a fucking money god. Even Wall Street gurus have taken major stumbles in the market.

"Hello to you, too. You look like someone shit on your Froot Loops," Bash says when I enter the kitchen.

"Hi," I grumble. My phone rings, and I reach in the back pocket and check the display. It's Danny. He doesn't waste time.

"Hey, Danny," I say and throw Bash a look that says this call is the most important thing in my life.

Bash shakes his head and grabs a crate of fresh vegetables, which he takes to the walk-in fridge.

"I emailed you the details on the Vegas property, and I want to know if you could fly out next week to do a walk-through with the real estate agent," Danny asks.

Bash emerges from the fridge, studying me with nothing short of contempt. When did we become this? He's been my best friend since we were kids. Out of everyone I know, Bash has always been on my side. He's supposed to be behind me, *us*, one hundred percent on this big move and career change.

"Yeah, I can be there. Next Wednesday. And then I want to go back to the other Santa Monica property. I think we need to move fast and make an offer on it soon. I could have shovels in the ground on the Vegas lot in less than six months, but Santa Monica has more red tape involved."

Bash rests his palms on the worktable separating us. He leans his weight into it and stares at me as I finish the call with Danny.

I shove my phone back in my pocket. "How have things been around here?"

"Perfect. Said I could handle it, and I did." His lips form a thin, tight line. He wants to say more.

I can tell when Bash is holding back his temper. When we were kids, he couldn't control it and would be the first to jump on any guy who tried to mess with us at school or bullied him personally with racial slurs. He heard every derogatory remark about Native Americans, but by his twenties, he moved on from physical altercations and started using his knowledge about his Lenape heritage to put racist commenters in their place.

"Good. And how's Greer doing running the front?"

"Get to the point. From the sound of that phone call, it sure sounds like you're working for Bourdain. When did you decide this?"

"Why are you so angry? This was our plan. He made an exceptional offer, and I accepted while I was there. They have a very good package on the table for you, too. I'd like you to fly to LA with me next Wednesday so you can see for yourself."

"What about your businesses here? You can't just dump everything on your dad and Greer. There needs to be a transition period to turn over the management and financials. You know that."

"Flora will expedite the paperwork for us. Greer can manage here. My dad and uncle already handle Brooklyn and Manhattan full time. Everything is under control. You and Greer can discuss who will become head chef at Swill. Other than that, when we go out next week, Danny already has a company-paid apartment that you can live in until you find your own place. And these are not cheap rentals, my friend. Danny goes all out. Top-of-the-line housing."

"So you have all this figured out? Harmony is on board with this, too?"

"She will be."

"I'm surprised she'd drop everything here."

"This is what you and I talked about for years. This is what we wanted."

"I don't want it, Peyton."

"I don't understand. You've opened three restaurants with me. You were the one reluctant to move to Hera temporarily. You kept saying you needed to be in a city. We're going to open two places in Los Angeles and one in Las Vegas to start, and a fourth is in the works. You're going to oversee the kitchen designs and the menus. That's just the beginning, Bash. Bourdain has so much more for us."

"I don't want it. I don't want to work for a conglomerate. I like being our own bosses. I like Hera. I like what we created here. Swill is something unique, and I put a lot of work into this place and the staff. It's the right fit for me."

"Are you serious? You're the guy who thought Brooklyn was too small for you—population over two million—but you're settling into Hera, where you're resident number nine hundred and two?"

"I didn't know it when Swill was a blueprint, but working in this kitchen for the last few months has been great. And living in this town has shown me what I want. I'm with someone I like."

I must have made a strange face, because he grimaces. I cannot for the life of me figure out whom he is talking about.

"Kim," he says.

"Kim Baker? Kim the librarian? I thought you two just hooked up once. I didn't know it was serious."

"We didn't hook up. We went out on actual dates, and we've been seeing each other for over a month. I want to see where it goes because I've got something good here. She's great."

"I don't know what to say." I feel defeated again. I can't seem to win with anyone. It's bad enough I'm losing the battle with Harmony, but if Bash doesn't move across the country with me either, I'm really starting over on my own. Without my son. Without anyone I love.

"I'm taking Kim to Lake Placid next week. I need a vacation, and I want to spend it with her. I'm staying in Hera, Peyton. If you won't let me retain part ownership in Swill, I'll work for Greer if I have to. I'm not going to LA with you, though."

"Jesus, we've been a team for years. Are you really going to give up your career for a woman?"

"Don't go there. You sound like an ass. Are you really going to give up a woman you're in love with for a job?"

Talia. Her name grabs me by the throat. I'm not good enough for her. I'm not good enough for my son. I'm not worthy of any of them, including Bash. He deserves to have what he wants.

The kitchen crew returns from the employee break room, where they were having a staff meeting. Their chatter dies down when they sense the tense atmosphere. Bash and I are having a stare-down.

"Fuck!" I slam my fist against the stainless steel table.

The room goes completely silent as I storm out of the kitchen.

35

Peyton

I F YOU LOSE LOVE and family, how much is career ambition worth? That thought haunts me as I pull into Harmony's driveway and park my truck.

Finn is shooting hoops, so I don't want to crowd his court space. He glances my way as I kill the engine, but then he goes back to taking his shot.

When I step out of the car, he lobs the ball fast and hard at my chest. I catch it before it knocks the wind out of me.

So my son is still angry with me for yelling at his mother and, like me, instead of using words to express this, he's exerting violence against inanimate objects. MacKenzies are famous for this. Just ask my dad about the four couches my mom had to replace because of her rambunctious, fist-wielding sons.

I take the shot from my car, wanting to show off some of my basketball skills from my days of high school fame. I shoot long and smooth. The ball sails effortlessly and torpedoes through the hoop with a mere swoosh of the net.

"Not bad." Finn catches the ball and dribbles it away from me.

"Not bad? That was at least two hundred feet away," I say, trying to break the ice with him.

"More like thirty feet."

"Hey, come on. That shot was awesome."

Finn hitches the ball against his hip, looks at me, and snickers. "Yeah, whatever you say." He looks around, avoiding eye contact with me for as long as he has to. "Mom said you're going to move to Los Angeles. You took that job."

"I didn't know she told you. What do you think about it?"

"She said we're not going with you."

My heart sinks. I was hoping Harmony would have changed her mind over the last few days and present good news to me tonight.

I approach him, cautious about physical affection. I want to give him a pat on the back and kiss his head. I don't. He steps back a bit from me.

Finn is testing me or himself, as though he's already invested enough in me and can't give me any more since I broke the emotional trust developing between us.

"Anyway, you're late. Mom said dinner was ready twenty minutes ago."

"I lost track of time. Got here as fast as I could."

Finn looks discouraged. *This shows how little you care about other people. You can't even be on time.*

I follow him into the house and drag the oppressive cloak of guilt with me.

"You're late," Harmony says. She places a basket of bread next to the lasagna pan on the dining table and looks at me, waiting for an acceptable excuse.

"Sorry. I really am."

"Wash up. Both of you," she demands.

Finn and I wash our hands at the kitchen sink, then return to the dining room. Finn slams himself into a chair, looking grim and fed up. I take the seat across from him.

"I was actually driving around, wondering what the hell I'm doing, other than making everyone angry at me."

"At least you're thinking about it," Harmony says. "That's a start." She slices and shovels large rectangles of lasagna onto our plates. "Well?" she asks, holding the spatula in the air as if she's ready to smack me with it.

"Well ... I spoke to Danny. Said I'd fly out there next Wednesday. I was hoping Bash would go with me." I fidget with my fork.

"Did Bash accept their offer, too? Is he going with you?" she asks in a clipped tone as she sits down.

"No. Apparently, he likes his life here too much to leave."

"Imagine that." She takes a bite of her salad and watches Finn shove a forkful of lasagna into his mouth.

"I was hoping you had changed your mind and we could—"

"No, I haven't. I've explained to Finn why it would be a bad idea for us to move out there."

"What about a new schedule with me? I could fly Finn out every other weekend. I could fly here, and fly with him to LA, and bring him back."

Finn looks between us.

"That's not going to happen." Harmony shakes her head, then takes a sip from her water glass.

She's made it clear that there's no room for negotiation where Finn is concerned, and I'm not surprised. If I had full custody of my kid, I doubt I'd go along with a stupid plan of putting him on a cross-country flight twice a month. It's unnatural. But I'm the jerk who's coming up with these terrible ideas because I don't know how to handle my own life.

Harmony takes another bite of salad and chews it delicately as she watches me, waiting for me to say something reasonable. I have a sudden flash to high school and watching Harmony eat her lunch slowly, refusing to be rushed by school bells. She took her time eating and talking and always looked so cool and calm.

Why isn't she yelling at me? I'm about to fuck up her kid's life. Again.

I make a few, half-hearted attempts at my brick-size piece of lasagna, but I've lost my appetite. The fear of losing Finn is becoming a reality. I was so sure Harmony would appreciate this once-in-a-lifetime opportunity I've been given, and that it would be my chance to give back to Finn in a big way. It's also the fear of staying here. Even if I were to move back to the city or to Westchester to be closer to Finn, the geography and the close proximity to Talia would kill me. I would be one of those fucking *sad dads*. Those single dads I see moping around bars because they can't get their shit together. If I stay anywhere near Hera, I would be an awful person to be around, and Finn would get sick of me.

"Finn, I don't want to go without you." I want to make it clear I'm here for him, but I leave it there because every other step is a potential time bomb.

"We discussed this," Harmony says to her son. "We already packed up our lives and moved across the country to be here, closer to your father and closer to all of your relatives. We can't move across the country and start all over again because your father doesn't know what he wants."

That last line surprises me.

They both look at me.

"I want to work for Bourdain, and I want Finn in my life."

"No. That's not going to happen," she says. "Not in a meaningful way, not if you're living in California and he's living in New York."

Finn stops eating and puts his fork down.

"Harmony, I thought you invited me here to work something out."

"I invited you here because Finn needs his dad, and you need him. You think you're here to sell me on Los Angeles? You think you need more money? Being richer isn't going to make you happier. I should know."

"May I be excused and go back outside?" Finn asks Harmony. She nods.

What crosses between them is a mother looking sympathetically at her son who's discovered his father *is* a selfish, *sad dad*.

He doesn't say anything to me, and I don't offer any encouraging words as he trudges out the front door. Soon, we hear his basketball thumping on the driveway.

"Shit," I whisper, looking at my plate of uneaten food.

"Peyton!"

I look up as a whole baguette whacks me in the head.

Harmony's cool façade has been replaced with her full-on rage mode. "You are breaking that boy's heart!"

"I don't want to hurt him! It's my heart, too!"

She takes a deep breath, then exhales sharply. She closes her eyes and breathes slowly for a minute or so.

I pick the baguette off the floor.

When Harmony opens her eyes, I quickly scan the objects closest to her, preparing myself for another assault. It's the sharp lasagna knife sitting a few inches from her throwing hand that concerns me.

"There. No more yelling," she says calmly. "The problem is you don't understand how rich you are because you've taken your wealth for granted. You've always had this wonderful, big family looking out for you. I envied your family. I envied the confidence it gave you to be who you wanted to be. I envy that you followed your passion and built an amazing career at such a young age. You have everything here, Peyton. Your family, your business, your friends, and your son. What could possibly compel you to give any of that up? And what about Talia? At first, I wasn't thrilled about her, but I know you've been seeing each other. How does she feel about you moving to LA?"

"We ... She broke it off. She's not an issue."

There's an edge to the way Harmony looks at me in disbelief. "Okay, I see what's going on. You are really screwed up on so many levels, so let me help you here. You need to get your priorities straight, Peyton." She points her fork at me. "You need to grow up and get your shit together. Stop using money as an excuse, because you have plenty. Stop talking about opportunities thousands of miles away when you have all the opportunities you need right here in New York. Here are your priorities." She begins to tick them off on her fingers. "Finn, your family, your business, that woman whose name I'm tired of mentioning ..."

Her last comment forces me to smile. "You're on fire."

"I have my moments when I like to give back. To be a mentor for those who behave like ..."

"I've been an asshole." I toss my napkin on the table.

"Yes. You have. So how are you going to fix this?"

• • •

I shoot a few hoops with Finn.

"I don't want to do this anymore." He drops the ball and kicks it to the side of the driveway.

"Want to talk?" I reach out to him, but he shrugs my hand off his shoulder and plants himself on the steps of the front stoop.

I sit next to him, giving him enough space between us.

"You don't have to pretend anymore if that's what you've been doing with me," he says, not looking at me, watching the cars cruising down his street.

"I haven't been pretending with you. I love being with you. Did you think I was faking this with you?"

"I don't know anymore. I thought we were having fun together."

"We were. We are. Look at me, Finn."

He slowly yet reluctantly turns his head toward me. I've seen that face, that expression of pure disappointment. That was me when my parents were fighting all the time and when they announced their marriage was over.

"Mom and I did fine before I met you," he says. "I didn't know much about you. I wanted to hate you. I told myself that I don't need a dad. Then I met you, and I wanted to keep you." His eyes expose a sheen of unshed tears glistening in the front porch light. Then a single tear slides out of the corner of my eye. I wipe it with the heel of my hand.

What kind of father does this to a kid?

"Ah, hell, Finn. I'm sorry I hurt you. This whole job thing I've been bragging about wasn't about punishing you or your mother in any way. I thought it would make me better. I thought I'd be a kickass dad. I hope you can forgive me."

"People can be forgiven." He bumps his leg affectionately against my mine, and then he leans in. "I think you like me a lot."

It's a relief to laugh. I hug him close. "I'm pretty sure I love you." I kiss the top of his head and squeeze him harder against me.

"Please don't move away from me, Dad," Finn whispers against my chest.

Dad.

I love when he says that.

36

Peyton

HARMONY AND I HAVE worked out what I need to do. It knocks my ego down a thousand notches, which apparently is what was required. It's better this way. I'll have Finn in my life and that won't change.

I've made the right decision, but I still can't sleep. I've turned all my energy back to obsessing about Talia, wondering if she's at Adam's house at this moment. In his bed.

At three a.m., I search the Internet and find the movie Talia said was her favorite. *Eat Drink Man Woman.* I stream it and begin to watch, thinking I'm doomed. It's in subtitles and looks like an artsy, philosophical flick, the kind of film that's difficult for me to sit still through.

However, I'm mesmerized by it. The family drama, the cooking scenes, the widower father, a chef trying to hold his family together, the family rituals, the love, loss, sorrow, and happiness. It has everything. This Chinese family could just as easily be a family in Brooklyn or Hera. It could be Talia's family. It could be mine.

I watch the film again. My heart connects with the father and the sisters. They each have love interests, the outliers, and even on the second time around, I wonder if the outliers will upset the family dynamic or strengthen it.

That's my problem. I think of myself as an outlier to Talia and her family instead of someone who deserves to be a part of her family, someone who truly can strengthen what she has.

You're not an outlier. You love her. You love her family. You belong with them just as much as you belong with Finn.

It's not about having separate circles of people. It's about bringing them all together.

I watch the sun come up. I still haven't slept, but I feel like I could run a marathon.

Los Angeles is three hours behind, too early to call Danny Bourdain. Instead, I text Dylan.

Fifteen minutes later, he's in front of my house in his running gear. He lets me set the course, and I guide us on a seven-mile loop through town and up around the Pickwick estate.

We have long stretches of silence when we're pushing our muscles to the maximum on the hills, and then we have long periods along roads or fields where I talk, volunteering information about my relationship with Talia, Finn, and what transpired with Danny Bourdain. Dylan doesn't weigh in with his opinions. He doesn't prod me with questions about LA or Talia, which is one of the things I like about Dylan. He's a good listener. Maybe it's from all his hours of therapy, or maybe it's instinctual for him. He grunts or says *Ah* throughout, but he lets me essentially unload every thought in my head.

When we arrive back at my home as the early summer heat sets in, we drink out of the kitchen faucet and wipe off the sweat with a roll of paper towels.

"You have a big day ahead of you," Dylan says. "Some apologies to make."

"You think?"

"Probably some groveling, too."

"Think it will work?"

"Yeah, it should. First, you need to repair your friendship with Bash and get that business shit straightened out. That should be easy. Talia could take a lot more effort, though. Just say the right things."

"What the hell is the right thing?"

"Dude, that's the great fucking mystery. But you know what you need to do first."

I'm standing there with a wet kitchen towel compress around my neck, waiting for him to elaborate and give me detailed advice.

"Good run. I'll see ya later, dude," he says as he heads out the front door.

I know what I need to do. It rings through my brain. And I do know.

"Are you sure?" Danny Bourdain asks.

"Yes, I'm sure. Thank you for everything," I reply and end the call.

After Danny, I have a brief chat with Harmony to confirm what she and I discussed the night before. She says she has always believed I would do the right thing and not make the grave mistake of putting a job before Finn or the people who matter to me. It's nice to hear her say this, that she has faith in me. Then she puts Finn on the phone so I can tell him the news.

He isn't letting me have any part of the good-natured Finn. He says, "*What*?" as if I am an annoying interruption. Then I give him the full story of how I got blindsided by the glamour of the job opportunity, and I end it with an apology like I've never given before.

I get choked up thinking about him at the other end of the line. A boy who has been waiting for his father to come into his life, and then I enter with a bang and almost ruin all of our lives with my grandiose agenda.

"I love you, Finn. Don't doubt that."

"I know," he says in a voice so small I can barely hear him.

Bash is the next call. Then I shove my phone in my back pocket and head to Blackard Designs to see my brother.

Cooper is usually in the factory part of the shop, working the big ovens they use to age and weather some of the wood before it's crafted into furniture. I walk around the noisy factory in a hard hat, looking for him and trying to stay out of everyone's way until Daisy, the receptionist, physically removes me. She shoves me out of the factory and walks me past the woodworking studios until we reach Carson's office.

"Can you handle your brother?" Daisy says to Cooper. "He's a nuisance on the floor!"

"He's a nuisance, period," Cooper adds.

Carson is sitting back in his desk chair with his dirty boots up on his desk, and Cooper is sitting in front of it. The desk is strewn with burgers and fries from Bonnie's Diner. They laugh as Daisy pushes me into the room and closes the door.

"Ten is a little early for lunch," I comment, putting my hard hat on the desk and sitting in the chair next to Cooper.

"We started work at five this morning," Carson says. "Have to load a huge order in an hour."

"What's up?" Cooper asks me.

"Do you have a number for a hit man?"

Cooper laughs. "Need a problem to go away?"

"Adam Fucking Knight. You don't have to kill him, just maim him where it counts, like his dick."

"Hell, Imogene can take care of that for you."

"Seriously, use your connections to find out what you can on the guy. Please."

"Back up, dude. Is this about Talia?" Cooper asks.

I nod. "I need to know what I'm dealing with. Who I'm competing with."

"Settle down, Corleone. You're the guy who's been putting everything and everyone else aside for Danny Bourdain. What's going on with Los Angeles? You've been really cagey about it and avoiding my questions for the past two weeks." Cooper gives me the hard-nosed MacKenzie look, the one perfected by my father when one of his kids was in trouble.

"I'm not going. I'm staying in New York."

"Really?" Cooper says with a smile. "Glad to hear it."

"That's great," Carson says. "It'll be nice having you here. Are you going to keep living in Hera or move back to the city?"

"Hera."

"What went down with Bourdain?" Cooper asks. "I was pretty sure he had brainwashed my little brother and was going to have you moved out there in a matter of days."

"It came pretty damn close to that. I was ready to go."

"And what about Bash? He must be relieved," Carson adds.

"I think I've saved our friendship. How did you know Bash didn't want to go?"

Cooper sighs. "If you hadn't been so caught up in your own drama, the restaurant, and chasing Talia, you would have known that Bash has a sweet little crush on Kimberly, my favorite librarian."

"I haven't been paying attention. I guess it's getting serious. Funny, I thought I was evolving, with Finn and all. It took a good reaming from his mother to wake me up."

"Good," Cooper says. "What's going on with Talia? Have you spoken to her?"

"No. We've managed to dodge each other at the restaurant. I don't know how serious she is about Adam. Bash doesn't know any more than me. His head is in the clouds over Kim. He said Talia hasn't mentioned anything out of the ordinary. But I know her. She'd keep it quiet."

"Why can't you just ask her directly? What's with this covert operation of getting intel from other people?" Carson asks.

"Like I said, I want to know what I'm dealing with before I talk to her."

Cooper chuckles. "You think I'll find the smoking gun on Adam, and you can use it in a case for yourself to persuade Talia not to see the guy?"

"I'm feeling kind of desperate. I'll try anything." I stand to leave.

"I know that feeling. It's not good. It leads you down a rabbit hole of guessing games and wasted time." Carson points a french fry at me. "Don't go there. Talk to her."

"It's not that simple. I said something ... Jesus, I actually encouraged her to go out with Knight. Thought I was being big about it."

"Well, aren't you a fuckwad." Cooper sits up and leans toward me. "I'm going to pull in some favors and get that information on Adam for you. I expect it to come back clean. Let me be clear, Peyton, you have a kid who needs you, so you need to know exactly what you're doing for his sake. If Talia is this important to you, make sure you're not playing some game just because you like the competition with Adam Knight. You're either all in or you're out."

"I'm all in. I'm staying in Hera, and I'm going to be a full-time father to Finn, and I'm going to run Swill."

"Who wants a shot of scotch?" Carson pulls the bottle of Macallan out of his desk drawer.

"Me," Cooper and I say in unison.

37

Talia

GREER IS HOSTING THE girls' night at her home. Her twins spent the day with their father, and then he dropped them off, stomachs full of fast food, and hands gripping bags of candy as the women started arriving. Imogene helped Greer get the kids in bed, and by eight, they were asleep and we were in the kitchen, mixing cocktails.

I brought appetizers I made at home and uncover them so the eating can commence. Jess gives Greer a belated housewarming gift—cases of margarita glasses, martini glasses, champagne flutes, and wineglasses for reds and whites. Emma unwraps a tray of antipasto that Dylan artfully assembled, and Lauren and Kim both produce bags of Doritos and Lay's potato chips because everyone will want something crunchy and greasy.

"My God, I can't remember the last time I did this," Greer squeals as she sits on her new sectional couch. She's out of her work uniform of designer blouses and high-heeled boots, and cozied up in slouchy sweats. "My ex installed the new TV last week. It was a gift! Can you believe it? He thought my thirty-inch TV was kind of sad, so he surprised me with this sixty-inch monstrosity. I have to say, he's so much more thoughtful as a husband and father now that we're divorced."

"Maybe he's found some new woman and feels guilty," Imogene says, planting herself in the middle of the couch so she faces the center of the big screen.

"Imogene, you always manage to turn something nice into something ugly," Jess says.

"Hear, hear," Lauren says. She and Kim arrange all the food on the oversize, square coffee table in front of us so we don't have to exert extra energy to walk to the kitchen for snacks.

"Oh, I don't know," Kim says. "I think it's great that you and your ex-husband get along so well. I think it's sweet he's doing these extra nice things for you. He must see how hard it is to be a single parent when he has them for weekend outings.

"I saw him at Swill the other night when he brought the kids in for dinner while you were working. He kept his cool during Owen's meltdown and Nikki's refusal to eat. He must appreciate what you do every day."

"Are you always this sunny?" Imogene asks Kim. "I've known you forever. When does bitterness and cynicism kick in like it did for the rest of us?"

"Kim is a naturally happy person," Lauren says. "She chooses to see the glass as half-full, and you choose to see it as perpetually empty."

"She's in love," I say, and Kim's face turns a lovely shade of pink.

"It's Bash," Greer says to the others. "Talia and I have watched that little relationship blossom over the last few weeks. They are so cute together. It reminds me of that blind young love you have in high school. Except without the stupid teenage behavior."

"I'd like to have a strong drink first if I'm going to be hearing about teenage love," Imogene grouses.

Kim laughs. "I'm sorry, Imogene, but the DVDs I brought tonight are *Pretty in Pink* and *The Breakfast Club*. Classics. Teenage Love."

"Are you kidding me?" Imogene shouts. "Those are my mother's favorite movies. Why aren't we streaming *Black Mirror* or *Mindhunter?*"

"Because I won't have my cable or Internet until next week," Greer explains. "I got a DVD player with the TV. That's why I asked Kim to bring some videos from the library."

"Well, congratulations," Imogene says to Kim and raises her martini glass. "A toast to Kim and Bash. And may we all have a lifetime of hormonal teenage love like every character Molly Ringwald ever played."

"Yes!" Lauren says. "I love those movies."

"I've never seen them, so I don't have a clue," Jess says. She's sipping the very strong drink Imogene made her and takes a moment to realize all eyes are on her. "What?"

"Where did you grow up to have such a deprived childhood?" asks Greer.

"I missed out on the whole high school teenage experience. I watched movies my parents chose. Oldies like *Stalag 17. The Queen.*"

"Goodness," Greer says.

"They're good movies," Jess says defensively. "Not romance. No romance with my parents. Definitely no hot guys."

Kim starts us with *The Breakfast Club*, and there's an audible swoon from Lauren and Emma when Judd Nelson appears, which I don't get at all.

Greer scoots over on the couch, closer to me. "Are you going to tell us about your date with Adam Knight?"

"It was nice. We're becoming good friends, I think."

Imogene overhears our whispering and pulls her gaze away from the movie. "Really? Nothing is going to happen with Adam? You looked happy when you came back from your date. I see you two talking all the time—at the diner, in front of yoga class. I thought for sure you two had planned that."

"Nope. Just friends. He's been putting together a business plan for me, helping me out."

"Helping you out with Pickwick?" Imogene asks, alarmed. "Is he buying it? Is he buying it for you?"

"No, nothing like that. He's teaching me some basics on land acquisition and developing a property. Looking for investors. That kind of thing. Now, can we watch the movie?"

Greer looks a bit reflective. I'm sure she's dying to know if I have feelings for her brother.

"Peyton has always been something of a closed book with me when it comes to women," she whispers so only I can hear. "I liked seeing you two together, sneaking around. It was sweet. Have you spoken to him since he got back?"

"No. We said everything we could possibly say before he left on his trip. It was kind of ugly. And honestly, I can't do this anymore with Peyton. We shouldn't talk to each other. Ever. It's hurtful."

"I'm sorry to hear that." Greer's face falls. "I was hoping his trip would give him more perspective on why he's better off being his own boss here."

"I can't talk about it with him anymore. We have completely different views on the subject. I really want to get back into my own kitchen. Today, I heard from another tenant that the renovations are complete, so I'm going to talk to my landlord to see how soon I can get back in there."

"I'll miss seeing you at Swill. I really will," Greer says.

I smile. "We'll still have that sadistic yoga class together."

Greer looks like she wants to say more on the subject of her baby brother, but then she just pats my leg and we finish watching the first movie.

"These films make teenagers believe in fairy tales," Greer says. "It sure didn't work out for me. I was divorced before my twins turned three. Movies like this are kind of masochistic, if you ask me."

"Same here," I say. "Men don't live up to my expectations."

"I was you once!" Imogene points an empty vodka bottle at me. "But then I found that there are more men. They're everywhere!"

"That's helpful," I say.

"She's drunk, but she's right," Kim says. "Over the last three years, I only had two dates. Then I met Bash, and I'm crazy about him. I'm so happy he's not moving to Los Angeles with Peyton."

"Bash didn't tell me that," Greer says softly, looking worried.

"Oh, I think I wasn't supposed to tell anyone," Kim says, swaying a bit with a drink in her hand. "Bash told me after he spoke to Peyton, but Bash hasn't told anyone else. I think I just spilled his beans."

"It's all right. We were going to find out soon enough," Greer says. "It's just that Bash and Peyton have always worked together. If they're dissolving their business partnership, it means Peyton really is leaving all of this behind. It makes me sad. I love working with him."

"Aw ... It's making me sad to see you sad." Kim pops open the other DVD case. "Time for another movie to distract us."

I don't think there's any movie that could possibly distract me from thinking about Peyton. I talk like I'm confident and not at all upset over Peyton. I'm faking it. All of it.

The thought of not being with Peyton hurts beyond anything I have ever experienced. The thought I may never see him—him leaving Hera altogether—pains me beyond belief. The only other person in the room who seems to be experiencing a similar grief is

Greer. She thinks she's losing her brother, the sibling who helped her get her life back on track after her divorce.

Maybe everyone thinks I'm losing a short-term lover, but lover isn't adequate enough to describe what Peyton has been to me. He was my true friend, my love. *Love.* He gave me love and showed me how to love myself when I could only see a flawed self, a flawed family, and a flawed future.

38

Peyton

"THIS IS FANTASTIC NEWS! I'm so happy for Finn. And you. And I'm happy for me! My God, I had no idea how hard this would be on me. I knew you wanted to work for Danny Bourdain, but I don't think I ever really considered the consequences until I heard you were going and Bash was staying." Greer smiles and sighs with relief.

"I didn't realize the impact it would have on Finn or me. Which is an understatement."

"I've never told you how much I appreciate everything you've done for me and the kids. Giving me this job, this new career, this new life in this town—I owe you so much gratitude. I have loved working with you. And when you convinced me to leave Brooklyn, I was doubtful, but you were right. The thought of not working side by side with you didn't really hit me until a few days ago, and I can't tell you how sad I've been over this. Have you told Talia?"

"I'm talking to people in a specific order so the town isn't buzzing with gossip. I don't want her to hear a twisted version. But I'm struggling with how to approach her ... what to say. I was in bad form the last time we saw each other. Now you know why I haven't been going in to Swill before four—afraid to face her."

"About that. Heads-up, Talia is a bit jaded about you. Men, in general."

This is hardly new information, except it's worse hearing my sister confirm it.

"She's torn, and supposedly she and Adam are not a thing."

399

"Supposedly," I say skeptically.

• • •

I head over to the Blackard factory again to see if Cooper has any damning evidence on Adam that I can use when I go begging to Talia.

That's what it will come to. At some point, I'll have to beg for her forgiveness for my behavior—anything for her to choose me.

I've timed it so Cooper and Carson are having lunch again in Carson's office, eating sushi. It always comes as a shock to tourists that Hera has fresh sushi at The General Store. They employ a real sushi chef, Daniel Takahashi, who left a high-end Manhattan restaurant to park his sushi station in the town's small grocery. He dubbed himself early on as Sushi Dan and built a loyal following among Hera's residents and people in the surrounding towns with the help of daily Instagram posts by him and his fans.

"What have you got for me?" I ask, closing Carson's office door.

"We have extra sashimi. It's excellent," Carson says, pointing a chopstick at it.

"Not food. I want to know what you found out about Adam. Did you run a background check?" I ask Cooper.

"Jesus, you're really worried about this guy."

"He's the only thing that stands between me and Talia."

Cooper eyes me with concern. "You sure? You don't think that jerking her around for months has anything to do with her seeing other people?"

"Seeing other people?" I raise my voice. "Who the fuck else is she seeing?"

"Calm down," Carson says. "You're ruining my lunch. Coop, tell him about Adam."

"Yeah, tell me about Adam." I sit down and slam my fists against my thighs. "Tell me he has SEC violations or any kind of infractions on his record—something to show he's committed fraud or done unsavory things to get to the top."

"Can't," Cooper says. "I called in favors with a few people I know, and there's nothing on Adam. He's clean. The guy is legit. He runs a clean house."

"I can't believe it. No one gets to where he is without stepping on people. I was hoping there would be reports of sexual misconduct. You checked all his firms, starting with his first job out of college?"

"My information is so complete that I know his income down to the penny from all his investments. Hell, I can give you itemized lists of his lunch expenses and when he buys new socks and underwear. Your nemesis is an upstanding citizen."

"Fuck," I mutter.

"However, I did acquire some interesting information I think you'll find delightful."

"Delightful? About Adam?"

"No. Like I said, Adam is clean. But Talia has an interesting juvie record. A good friend has access."

"Talia?" I try to wrap my head around the sweet woman I know committing a crime. "Let me guess, she was caught with pot in her backpack at fifteen like half the kids in our school."

"No. Grand theft auto. She was thirteen when she stole her neighbor's Cadillac and took it for a spin. This was when her family lived in Queens."

"What? The woman can barely ride a bicycle, and you're telling me she stole a car?" I look at them both in disbelief.

"I know the story." Carson smiles, finishing his last bite of a handroll.

"You didn't think to tell us?" Cooper asks.

Carson laughs. "You were FBI. How did you not know?"

"This wasn't my area, and it never occurred to me to dig deeper into Talia's records when I met her. She's a personal chef with glowing testimonials," Cooper explains. "How do you know?"

"She told me," Carson says. "When I interviewed her years ago. I needed a housekeeper. She was nervous during the interview. Said she wanted me to know that she had once *borrowed* a neighbor's car when she was thirteen, but he didn't press charges, and she has never stolen anything. She said I could trust her in my home. I thought it was funny. Brave of her to volunteer the information."

"I can't believe she could steal a car. And actually drive a Cadillac. I can totally see her explaining it's not the same as stealing." I picture a slight, thirteen-year-old girl with a long ponytail swinging back and forth as she drives down her neighborhood street, trying to see over the dashboard. "How did she steal the car? Did she know how to hotwire the transmission?"

"According to the official police report," Cooper reads from his phone, "*Subject says: Mr. Richardson always leaves his car keys tucked in the visor, and I know how to get into the garage through the back door. The door has a doggy panel big enough for me to squeeze through. When asked why she stole the car, Subject says: It's so pretty. It's my favorite color. Baby blue. I couldn't resist. Subject is very apologetic. Mr. Richardson is not pressing charges."*

Cooper and Carson are laughing. That's Talia. All those sweet, silly things she says, they make my heart shudder with affection.

"She did tell me that, even though her neighbor was very proud of her careful driving, she did accidentally knock down two of his garbage cans when she backed out of the driveway. The judge required her to show up to a hearing, and the charges were dropped," Carson says. "I love the part about her *careful* driving."

"That's my funny girl."

Cooper and Carson both pause and look at me.

"Oh. I said that out loud."

"Yep," Cooper says.

Carson begins clearing the food containers. "Instead of talking to us, you should be talking to her."

"I will. I have to be careful with her. There's a lot at stake."

"That's bullshit. If you're too careful, she's going to think you're still playing games. Be direct. Get in her face and tell her the truth," Cooper says.

"How about we hit the gym?" Carson stands and stretches. "I could use a workout."

"Join us." Cooper puts his arm around me as we head down the hall toward the front of the shop.

Blackard Designs faces the main street of Hera, and I can see part of Swill across the street. As Carson asks Daisy about new messages, I stare out the front window, pleasantly surprised to see Talia coming from the direction of Swill. She's pedaling her bike at a leisurely pace—the baby blue bicycle I gave her—heading in the direction that will take her out of town toward Woodstock.

"You're looking at her like a lovesick little boy," Cooper says. "She is a pretty woman."

"She's luminous," I say, watching her figure disappear from sight.

"You're whipped."

"Don't I know it."

402

39

Talia

"WHAT DO YOU MEAN, it's not my kitchen anymore?" I ask angrily.

We're standing in the beautifully renovated kitchen that shows no signs of fire damage. The counters, flooring, and several of the appliances are brand-new. And there's another chef in my space, baking cakes!

Mr. Ricci, my landlord, looks at me in confusion. "Talia, you canceled your lease over a month ago. I have people on a waitlist who want these kitchens. This man here paid his deposit and a full year's rent in advance and signed a two-year lease."

The baker looks up nervously from the cake he's painting flowers on with a pastry bag, as if I may suddenly destroy his sugary masterpiece with my fist.

"I never canceled my lease," I say through gritted teeth.

"Your boss ... the boyfriend, he came by and told me you didn't need the kitchen anymore."

"Who are you talking about!"

"The tall man. Let's see ..." Mr. Ricci thinks slowly.

"Was it a Mr. Peyton MacKenzie? Tall, good hair, sadistic eyes, and a really big chip on his shoulder?"

"Yes, that's him! He said he could speak for you and that you were happy in your new kitchen."

"You let him break my lease? I didn't agree to that, and you didn't get my signature!" I shout angrily.

"I thought he was your boyfriend and some kind of business partner. He was very convincing!" Mr. Ricci's brows knit into a single, fuzzy, gray caterpillar. "Oh, no."

I look back at the baker, and then at Mr. Ricci. "This is my kitchen."

"I'm sorry, Talia. Things haven't been the same since my wife got sick. She handled the books and all the leases. The paperwork." He throws his hands up in anguish. "I'm taking care of her, but the paperwork has gotten a little messy."

His sad, round face pierces my forgiving side. I could call Archie Bixby and get this legally untangled in my favor, but I don't want to put Mr. Ricci under more duress.

"Are you going to sue me?" he asks shakily.

"No. Mistakes like this happen. They happen all the time to me."

"I can put you at the front of the waitlist. Would that help?"

"Thank you."

"And maybe things with Mr. MacKenzie will sort themselves out and you'll stay in his kitchen," he says brightly.

• • •

He's not at Swill. I search his office and the brewery, the two places he's been hiding in since he returned from LA.

Bash turns from the grill when I march through the kitchen. "He's at the gym," he says, reading my murderous mind.

"Thank you. Did you know that bastard canceled my lease at my kitchen?"

"No, I didn't. Listen, I know it's easy to be pissed off at Peyton, but he always finds a way to make it up to people."

"Arghhh!" I storm out of the kitchen and grab my bike, riding it across the street to the side entrance of Blackard Designs.

When I throw open the door to the gym, there are no men. However, Jess is running on the treadmill, and Imogene is talking while Lauren does bench presses.

"Wow, you look mad," Imogene says.

"Where is he?" I demand.

"Locker room," she says. There's no doubt who I'm searching for.

I walk toward the men's locker room. A perverse giddiness takes over as I zero in on my target.

"They're all in there!" Imogene yells to my back.

"I don't care!" I swing open the door to the men's locker room and am assaulted by a wall of steam with a pungent, funky odor of male sweat—body stench mixed with Parmesan cheese and the beer that must be oozing from their pores.

There are more than a dozen men in all different states of undress. Leo is closest to the door, and he wraps his towel around his skinny, naked torso when he sees me.

"You can't be in here!" His voice goes up three octaves, practically a squeal. His glasses steam up, and he wipes the lenses with his fingers.

"Oh, please. Who's going to stop me? Not like I haven't seen any of this before!" I walk on the rubber mat that runs down the middle of the locker room.

"Hey!" Carson says when he notices me. He's completely naked. He grabs his towel off the bench and holds it in front of his crotch.

"Like I haven't seen that before. I walked in on you and Jess going at it like rabbits. Besides, I have no interest in your pecker."

"*Hey,*" is all Carson can manage again.

Cooper laughs. "She looks mighty pissed off." He has his towel fully secured around his waist while he swipes on some deodorant.

"Fuck!" Hoyt shouts when he struts out of the shower room and runs right into me. His waist is already covered with a towel, but he pulls it tightly to him as if he thinks I'm going to wrestle it off him.

"Relax," I say. "I'm not here for you. Your precious cock and balls are safe."

"We could have you arrested!" He looks like a big, wet, furry bear hugging his tiny towel to his waist.

"So call the cops."

Dylan and Cooper both laugh. They have no inhibitions. Dylan is buck naked. His ass is literally on display as he casually rifles through his gym bag.

"Don't we have any privacy rules around here?" Hoyt shouts to the room. "If I walked into the women's locker room, Imogene would slit my throat."

"No, first she'd cut your dick off, and then she'd slit your throat," I say as I keep walking through the steamy room, heading for my prey.

"When did you become mean?" Hoyt looks indignant as he covers himself head to toe with more towels.

"When I was deceived by this giant prick over here," I say as I approach Peyton who's completely naked with a big Cheshire cat grin on his face.

I don't fall for his sexy smile, and I sure as hell don't look down past his abs.

With one foot propped up on a bench, he finishes wrapping a towel around his waist then leans his other elbow down on his bent knee so we are face to face.

"Are you here to see me, sunflower?" He chuckles. "You sure know how to make an entrance. Got all the guys taking cover." His grin grows wider. He's challenging me to look him up and down, especially down.

I resist the challenge and the urge. It's not hard to sense what's between us, under his towel. His erection. I cannot fathom how men are always turned on. A room full of his naked friends doesn't diminish his basic urges.

"Don't get cute with me. I am so fucking angry with you! You fucked over my business, Peyton! I could sue you for this! False identity, assuming my identity, identity theft ... I don't know what it's called, but I know what you did has to be illegal!"

"I did it to help you." He raises his voice. "I'm saving you thousands of dollars in rent and insurance. You get my kitchen for free." He's still smiling like he's Prince Charming saving the ungrateful woman.

"I didn't ask you to do that! You know how much I love my kitchen! I planned on moving back in there this week, but today I found out that you went behind my back and canceled my lease a month ago! My landlord already rented it out to another chef. I'm screwed, you asshole!"

"Guys, come on; settle down," Carson says, walking over, fully clothed now. "Let's take this outside and talk about it. We can get it all sorted out. Let's just leave all the naked guys to some privacy."

"Never mind," I spit out. "I'm leaving." I turn around and stomp my work boots on my walk out, but they don't have the desired dramatic effect I was hoping for, just a squishy, slurpy sound as my boots strike the wet rubber mat.

"Talia! Wait!" Peyton shouts.

I don't look back. Outside, I stride to my fancy new bike that always makes me think of Peyton.

"Talia!" Peyton says, running up to me, holding the towel tightly around his waist. A miniskirt would cover more. They really need bigger towels at the gym.

He holds the towel closed with one hand and grabs my handlebars with the other.

"Let go," I say.

"Not until you listen to me." He's no longer grinning, and he doesn't look smug. He looks scared. "I would never sabotage your business or hurt you."

"You already did."

Imogene and a few others come out to watch the spectacle. Carson is trying to usher them back inside. Greer is taking her gym bag from her car and stops to watch us.

"Look at me," he says gently.

"Kind of hard to do when you don't take me seriously." I look off in the distance of Hera's little main street. "This is all so humorous to you. It's all so easy for you—playing games with people." I fight back the tears. He has committed the unthinkable.

"Please, look at me."

I give him a dead stare.

"I'm sorry I canceled your lease without telling you. It happened in a moment of jealousy. There was Adam. And I really wanted to do something for you, give you a gift that meant something. It was a spur-of-the-moment idea, a gift."

"Fuck you and your gift!" I shout, and Greer flinches.

Peyton is stunned. Speechless for once. *Good.*

"You don't get it!" I continue. "You've always had this come easy to you, but I've never had control over my life as much as I did when I signed that lease and opened my own kitchen. I started my catering business *without* the help of my dad, *without* the help of Marko, *without* the help of any man. It is the only power I have had over my career, and I just found out that *you* took it all away."

"But you have free rein in my kitchen," he stammers.

"Exactly. *Your* kitchen. I get to be the recipient of your generosity, which makes me dependent on you. You don't understand why this is a big deal to me because you don't really understand me and what I've been through. It took me months in my own kitchen before I felt like my own boss. That kitchen was the only place that was mine. I don't have my own home like you do. I don't have my own building like you do. I don't even have my own car! That kitchen was the only place I could escape to and actually be alone. It was mine, and I felt safe there. You took it away! Do you not understand that?"

Peyton looks too panicked to speak.

My anger rises when I start crying. "You hurt me in probably the worst way possible. You took away something I love, and you brush it off like it's no big deal. The fact that you don't understand the damage you've done is just as hurtful. I thought I knew you. I thought of you as a good person, too good to do something like this, especially to me."

"You make it sound like I committed a crime. I was only trying to help you." He sounds and looks unsure.

"You were helping you. Making yourself feel good by supporting someone like me. I don't know if I can forgive you. I don't know if I can ever trust you again, and I don't need more untrustworthy people in my life. It's good you're leaving—"

"I'm not," he says firmly. "Honestly, Talia, I really was trying to do something good for you. I'll make this up to you. If I have to buy the baker out of his lease, I will pay double, triple. I'll make an offer he can't refuse. Whatever it takes to get your kitchen back. Had I known all this—the significance of that kitchen—I wouldn't have broken that lease. My intention was to take some financial pressure off you."

"I don't want you paying an obscene sum to buy the baker off. That would make me feel horrible, too." I wipe my face free of all stray tears. "If I stay at Swill, what about long-term? I'm not an employee, so what if you sell it someday and the new owners want me out? Or what if—"

"I'm the owner. I'm not going anywhere. I said I'm not leaving, and I'm not."

Images of him flying across the country with Harmony and of him in flashy Bourdain-Torrance restaurants swim around my mind.

"I'm staying here. In Hera. Because of Finn, my family, and because ..." He trails off, and I wait for him to finish.

I straddle the bike because he still has a tight grip on the handlebars.

"I'm staying in Hera. I turned down Danny Bourdain's offer. I'm going to stay on at Swill."

I imagine this is a lot for him to give up. Peyton doesn't give up opportunities like this.

"For how long?" I ask.

He thinks I would be relieved? The anger is bubbling up inside of me. He's acting, saying all the things he thinks I want to hear, except this isn't who he is. He's a risk-taker. He dreams big. He never intended to stay here. He's always put himself first, like my father, like Marko.

He lets go of my bike and crosses his arms, more of a defense against the women who have stepped outside of shops to get a view of him and a chance to add to the gossip about us that will follow later over burgers and cherry pie at Bonnie's Diner or over German drafts at Swill. "I'm staying for *good*."

"In the immortal words of Nancy Sinatra, you're *lying* when you should be *truthing.*" I can't remember the actual verse—from one of Norma's vintage albums—but this will do.

"Seriously?" he scoffs. "Not sure those are immortal words. And how do I know you didn't mangle them?"

"Nice. Now you make fun of me. I guess the truth does hurt."

"Talia," he whispers urgently and glances around at the people who are popping out of stores to witness our little spectacle. "Can we go somewhere privately to discuss this? Let me finish getting dressed and we can go to my place."

"Go to your place?" I glare. "For a quickie?"

"No, I wasn't suggesting that. Jesus. I want to talk because I fucked up with you, and I just made a major life decision ... and I need to talk to you."

"Wow, Peyton MacKenzie made a life decision. Everyone gather 'round. Let's all talk about him and his amazing future."

"Talia." If I wasn't angry, I would think he was saying my name with reverence. "I said I'm sorry about the lease, and it's fixable."

"Not everything is fixable. How can I believe you? You tell me you're staying because it's good for Finn, Bash, your family ... Sure, it would be if it were true. But I don't think it will last. I think you're playing everyone, and I honestly think you have no idea. Because this is your MO—yeah, I got that one right this time. It's just a matter of time before this little town drives you crazy, and you'll regret turning down Danny Bourdain. No matter who loves you, whether it's Finn, or ... it doesn't matter who loves you, it will never be enough. It happened with my father. It happened with Marko." I cover my mouth. I never wanted to say that out loud.

He stares at me as I step down hard on the pedal to get good traction on the gravel. Then I take off. I feel my back wheel bump over something with substance and hear Peyton say "*Shit!*" That was his bare foot I rode over.

"I did not intend to do that!" I say, glancing back at him as I ride away.

He's crouched down, holding his foot and looking up at me in pain and confusion.

"Sorry!" I shout again so the whole town can hear.

I pedal back to Swill as fast as I can with plans to barricade myself in the walk-in cooler.

40

Peyton

I WATCH HER PEDAL away. My injured foot burns, but nothing like the ache in my chest.

I hear a crunch on the gravel and turn toward the parked cars. Greer is standing next to her open car door, holding a case of paper towels and her gym gear. I'm expecting sympathy from my sister, but her expression says otherwise. She stares at me, not quite comparable to Talia's angry glare but pretty damn close. She must have heard the whole altercation.

She tosses the paper towels into the car, slams the door, and then walks toward me, looking mad enough to take a swing at me with her gym bag. "I can't believe you did that. I'm so glad Mom wasn't here to see you behave this way toward a woman."

"Didn't you hear my apology to Talia? I was trying to offer her … everything. I was not trying to undermine or hurt her business. I was trying to save her money. Thousands of dollars. It's just sound business practice. Why are you angry at me, too?"

"Do you hear yourself, Peyton?" Her eyes and nose flare. "You are a man, a very entitled man, with a powerful position. Imagine if someone just took that away from you? You took away the only power Talia had. She told you that in those exact words, and you still don't get it.

"You think I'm angry? I'm *furious* with you! You of all people, you were raised by a strong, independent mother. How could you be so cavalier about this and do something so damaging to another person you're supposed to care about and still try to justify it?"

411

"Because I didn't see it the same way, obviously."

"You need to accept what she's saying. You've never been in her position. You've never had a parent leave you. You never had a fiancé leave you. And you didn't take care of a sick parent. You entertained and loved our mother while she was dying, but the rest of us were the ones who were with her day in and day out, managing the worst parts of her illness. Talia is doing all that, and she's running her own business without the wealthy investors you have always benefitted from."

"I get that, Greer."

"No, you really don't. But I hope you do soon. Talia is a young woman in a very precarious situation, in a very competitive world, and she secured that kitchen by herself. You took—"

"I took it all away," I finish. It's hitting me harder now. My destructive *good deed* is coming into focus. My mother would indeed be horrified by my actions. "What do I do? I've lost all credibility with her. She doesn't believe me. She doesn't trust me."

"Then you have a lot of work to do. You'll have to figure out how to make it up to her and earn her trust back. I don't know, Peyton. This may have been a deal-breaker."

• • •

She thinks I'm like her father? Like that asshole ex-boyfriend? After all this time, my reputation with her is right down there in the cesspool of parasites.

"What are you muttering about over there?" Imogene asks as I walk into my house and toss my keys on the kitchen counter.

Finn is working on a poster for social studies, a project he had researched thoroughly before he asked me to take him to purchase the art supplies—a hefty sum that shocked even me.

"So, what happened with Talia after I left?" Imogene asks, pulling pink glitter tubes out of a package I don't recognize buying. "Are you limping?"

Like I want to repeat this to another woman. I'm thankful I have Finn here as a buffer.

"No pink. No glitter," Finn says. "I appreciate your help, Imogene, but I can do this."

"I don't think you understand presentation." Imogene looks dejected when Finn moves his board and art supplies to the other side of the table, away from her.

"What are you doing here?" I ask Imogene. "Did Harmony ask you to cover for me?"

"No," Finn says. "Mom dropped me off as usual, and then Imogene showed up."

"I came over to help my nephew with his project! I brought my best decorating stuff. And also because I want to know what happened with Talia. After work, I looked for you at Swill, but they said you took the whole day off. Talia was there, working, but she wasn't saying a word about you. I got worried."

"Right. You got worried." I need to get my sister-in-law out of here so I can sulk in peace.

"Hey, I'm not leaving until you tell me what that gym incident was about."

"I can't repeat it. I screwed up big-time. Call Greer. She'll tell you everything, and then you can take her side, and Talia's side."

"All right." Imogene takes out her cell phone. She begins talking to my sister and grimaces at me before she takes the call outside.

"What did you do?" Finn asks while he continues to work on his poster.

"I did something that was hurtful to Talia. I thought I was doing her a favor."

"Sounds like you're in trouble."

"With Talia, always."

While I ice my foot and watch Finn design his board, we listen to Imogene screaming outside.

"*I can't believe he did that!*" she shouts a thousand times.

Finn gives me a few worried looks.

A half hour later, after Imogene has heard every juicy detail from Greer, she returns in a huff. "You're lucky I cooled down!" she whisper-shouts.

"You don't look cooled down," Finn states.

She covers his ears. "Peyton, I love you, but I could kill you for what you did."

"I can hear you," Finn says.

Imogene removes her hands from his head. "Your father really screwed up. Talia lost her commercial kitchen because of *your dad*."

I sigh and put my boot back on.

"He told me." Finn pushes his completed poster aside.

"Please don't repeat the whole argument. Finn doesn't need to hear all that," I say to Imogene.

"I won't. I think Talia and Greer gave it to you good." She points to my foot. "I wish I had seen that. Greer said it was hilarious when Talia rode over your foot. I can't believe she apologized to you for that."

"I deserved it. I don't know what else to do. I said I'm sorry, and I offered to buy out the other chef. She didn't like anything I said."

"Oh, you poor baby," Imogene mocks. "A woman has turned you down. What will you do?"

"Can you be my sister-in-law for a minute and not Judge Judy? Before this debacle, Greer had mentioned or implied that Talia wasn't seeing Adam. Do you know if that's true? I'm not sure Talia would divulge something that personal to Greer."

"Oh, she did. We had a little party while you were gone. Girls' night. Talia said she and Adam don't have any chemistry. They had a nice date—just dinner—and I guess they agreed that they're better off as friends."

"Really?" My voice pitches too high.

Finn gives me a quizzical look. "Dude, what's wrong with you?"

"A lot, according to Talia. She compared me to her dad and her ex ... former ... the jerk she was going to marry." I wince as I walk to the fridge. My foot feels like it has a nail in it.

"Marko was a douche—" Imogene clams up, remembering Finn is listening to our every word.

"Douchebag?" Finn says.

"I'm supposed to be *monitoring* your language, according to your mother." I reach into the fridge for a bottle of mineral water.

"Oops." He grins.

"You are not like Talia's father," Imogene says. "He left his family. They divorced long-distance, and he doesn't send alimony. And you're not like Marko. He was controlling and cruel. He fooled all of us. If Talia hadn't had heart surgery when she did, those two would have gotten married. And where would she be now? Those are two horrible men, and you are nothing like them, Peyton."

"You need to tell Talia she's wrong," Finn says innocently.

Aunt Imogene has to hold back her sharp tongue.

"Right, Talia would love for me to tell her she's wrong," I say.

"It's not about telling her she's wrong. It's about changing her mind, winning her over," Imogene clarifies.

"Yeah, that's super easy. Thanks. I think, all this time, in the back of my mind, I heard that little voice telling me I wasn't good enough for her. I wasn't worthy of her standards. But I never associated myself with that type of guy—the way she describes her dad or her ex with so much acrimony. No wonder she likes Adam. And I encouraged her to choose him. Then she did. Of course, she'd pick a guy like Adam. He's so different than me. I just didn't realize I was put in the same category as the two men she despises the most."

"You're not that different than Adam," Imogene says. "Successful, single, never married, attractive."

"Father of a ten-year-old," Finn adds.

"You're nine, and I don't consider being your father to be a mark against me."

"That's right," Imogene says. "If anything, you should get points for having such a great kid and being a great dad. And having such an awesome sister-in-law everyone wants to be friends with."

"I was a no-show dad for ten years. Nine. Whatever. I look bad."

"Talia likes me," Finn states. "You have to give her a bigger apology. A really good one."

"Such a smart kid. You're lucky your mother is a brainiac," I say. "I tried to win Talia over before. Then I made the mistake of giving up. Now she's not interested."

"Maybe you're doing it wrong," Finn says. "I have an idea. I have great ideas."

"Let's hear it. Give it your best shot." I perch myself on the table next to him and listen.

Finn does have a plan. The kind of plan a kid would come up with if they were building a tree fort with glue and Styrofoam or planning some harebrained mission with like-minded, sugar-fueled kids. When he's done giving us his grand plan and produces a sheet of paper with a drawing that he made to make it easier for the dumb adults in the room, Imogene actually claps. It's not something I want to do, but this is my kid, and there's no way in hell I'm going to disappoint him again.

I turn to Imogene. "So, do you have a person who can make these today?" I ask, holding up Finn's visual aid.

"Oh, I have a guy who can do this." She's thrilled. "I have a guy for everything."

"Of course, you do. I guess we're in business, then. Let's do this." I give Finn a fist bump.

I'm fairly certain I'm setting myself up to be the punchline tonight. I may not win the girl, but I'm going to score a lot of points with my son.

41

Talia

I'M ASSEMBLING THE REST of the pomegranate and goat cheese for the toasted baguette when I look out Adam's kitchen window and see Peyton leading more than a half dozen of our friends up the hill. They're all wearing white T-shirts with text on them that I can't read from this distance. It reminds me of the intervention we attempted with my mother, except this time I know they're coming for me.

I glance behind me where Adam has assembled some of his employees that he invited up for a dinner meeting to strategize. He explained the portfolio and various market shares, all of which went over my head. His work seems very dry to me, but he and the others in his living room seem enthusiastic and animated about some new fund they've started. I have to make sure Peyton and his posse don't make a scene and embarrass me in front of Adam's guests.

Since our uneventful kiss, it actually hasn't been awkward between Adam and me. We've gone about with our regular routine. I serve him dinner several times a week, and if anything, our conversations are easier. We know each other better and have become closer as friends without the pressure to be anything but ourselves.

"Excuse me," I say to Adam. "I see a delivery guy coming, so I'll go handle it. You continue with your discussion, and then we'll have dinner shortly." I keep my tone breezy.

"Sure, thanks," Adam says, looking a little befuddled. I'm sure he knows he doesn't get Saturday evening deliveries out in this country house hidden on a dirt road that has no name marker.

I bolt out the front door, wiping my buttery fingers on my apron.

Peyton looks like he's leading a gang of misfits, his tall, hulking figure taking long strides toward me. His T-shirt says *TEAM TALIA* in big letters.

Finn pulls up next to him, and behind them are Imogene, Jess, Emma, Lauren, and their husbands, laughing but obviously doing their part in this exhibition.

Kim and Bash are holding hands, striding alongside with smiles on their faces. They are in love. Greer is holding her children's hands. Owen and Nikki are waving at me, excited to get my attention. The older crowd, Archie and Emily with Lois and Eleanor following, and the last two people are my mother and Gavin.

A little gasp escapes my mouth when I see my mother. She's not smiling. She's holding Gavin's hand, looking stoic. Everyone is wearing a stupid *TEAM TALIA* T-shirt.

I'm touched by Peyton's demonstration. I also sense my body tightening in refusal as I watch him approach. Our eyes meet, and it strengthens his tenacity. I can tell he's not going to walk away without *something*. He's going to try to make me see everything *his* way. But I can't.

"What are you doing here?" I whisper to him.

"What does it look like?" he asks, not smiling. "You wouldn't talk to me back at the gym. I wanted to explain, to tell you that I am incredibly sorry for what I did to you. I'm not leaving this town, and you're one of the reasons why. I'm wearing this ridiculous T-shirt to show you—"

"Hey, they aren't ridiculous," Finn says. "This was my idea." He points his thumb at himself.

"Thank you," I say to Finn as the others catch up and gather around.

Dylan holds his hands clasped above his head like a prize fighter and dances in a circle. The back of the T-shirt says *SONS OF HERA*.

"They all did this for me," Peyton says, then lowers his voice. "And I did this for you. I'm not beneath public humiliation to show you how I feel. Let me buy back your lease and fix this for you."

"I told you *no*. You'd pay a ludicrous amount of money. I don't want to be a part of that."

Adam and his guests come out and huddle around the front door behind me. Peyton looks frustrated.

"The T-shirts are adorable," I tell Finn.

He smiles at me, then looks between me and his father.

"You guys can't be here," I direct to Peyton. "I'm working."

I'm confused about him; a heady rush of love riding on a surge of anger. I've been in this position before, and it ended badly.

I've had three important men in my life. One abandoned me, one hurt me, and one fixed me. The fixer, the heart surgeon, is the only one I'm grateful for. But now I need a fourth and final man to love me. It can't be Peyton. No matter how much I would love him to be the one, he can't be that man. He's already betrayed me.

He will stay in Hera for Finn and his business, but his work will be unfulfilling, and it will nag him until he has no choice but to follow his ambition. Maybe he'll take Finn with him or he'll wait until Finn goes off to college, but it will happen.

Peyton will leave someday.

"Hurry," Finn says. "Everyone is here. Say it in front of everyone."

Peyton takes a breath as he registers the size of his audience.

"No, I'm sorry. You really can't be here," I say.

"Don't stop on our account," Adam chimes in. "This is so much better than our meeting. Let's go, MacKenzie. Give it your best shot. Make this good."

Peyton gives me a tender look. He's building up to say something, but I can't stand the thought of falling for what he has to say and thinking I'm safe.

"Please don't say it," I whisper, interrupting his train of thought.

He looks crushed.

"Don't. I mean it."

Peyton is not used to this much resistance from anyone. Finn looks just as confused and slightly hurt.

"Well, this sucks," Imogene gripes.

"Shut up," Jess says.

Everyone is silent, waiting for me to make my next move. The initial laughs and smiles upon seeing the *TEAM TALIA* T-shirts have quieted into murmuring frowns.

Peyton steps closer to me. "I'm sorry I didn't execute this the right way. I'm sorry I've upset you. And I'm not trying to be a dick toward Adam."

"No problem here," Adam says, looking sympathetically at Peyton.

"Tonight," Peyton affirms. "Let me see you tonight."

I want to say no again, but all these people are watching us so expectantly, and I don't want to be the person to let Finn down. His eager face crumples when my mouth forms another no.

"I'm going to stop by your house tonight," Peyton says.

"Fine." I shake my head in exasperation.

He puts his arm around Finn and directs him back the way they came. My friends don't say anything, with the exception of a few audible grumbles from Dylan and Imogene. Even Lois goes quietly back down the hill to her car.

Adam's guests go back inside while I watch Peyton's caravan drive away.

"He seems pretty serious to me," Adam says as he steps next to me.

"Peyton likes winning. He's serious about winning, but then he moves on to his next conquest."

Adam shakes his head. "Didn't look like that to me. I think he's serious about you, and he's intent on proving that."

"I hope not."

"You're just afraid he'll prove you wrong." He walks back into the house and leaves me alone.

• • •

At nine o'clock, there is a firm knock on the front door. A look passes between Aleska and my mother, who are watching some inane TV show that I can't follow because my mind is on Peyton.

I leave them in the family room and walk down the hall to the front door. The longest walk of my life, with so much doubt on the other side. I take a deep breath and open the door.

Just like hundreds of times before, he never fails to make me feel gobsmacked, in awe of his beautiful face. And then it's his eyes. Those stupid, gorgeous eyes trap me in place.

"Hi," he says with a tentative smile.

420

"Hi." I gaze at him a moment too long. *I can't live like this!* "Let's sit outside. My house is too small, and there are too many ears."

"Sounds good." He steps off the front stoop and pulls up two upturned, Adirondack chairs sitting by a patch of dead grass. He places the chairs next to each other and brushes off their seats. "Please." He points to the chair for me.

I sit down, keeping my arms wrapped around me as if I'm holding in all my tightly wound nerves and emotions. The weathered wood creaks loudly as Peyton settles his weight into the other chair.

"I wanted to see you as soon as I got back from Los Angeles. I was waiting for the right time to talk to you. Little did I know I would make everything worse instead of better. I'm pretty sure I only have one shot left with you."

"You thought going to Adam's home in those T-shirts was your shining moment?"

"That was Finn's idea. I felt I had to do it to show him I value his input on this. And I had to do it to show you I could put myself in the position of looking ridiculous and humiliated ... for you."

"I was still angry at you. I was flattered, too. It was funny to see you coming up the hill dressed like that. And Adam's guests found it very entertaining, too."

"Entertaining Adam is always important to me."

"You like to cut him down, but you two are similar in some ways."

"Except one very important way."

So earnest. Not a word I would have used to describe Peyton in the past, but here he is, being earnest and putting his vulnerability on display for me. My breath catches.

"Talia, you don't think of Adam in the same way you think of me."

"I guess you heard about my date with him."

"I heard. I'm also not making any assumptions about you and me, because I know you don't forgive people. Your dad and Marko come to mind. I'm hoping I'm the exception and you'll believe I'm sincere when I say I want to be with you. Only you. On your terms."

"My terms? I have no idea what you're talking about. You and I have never discussed—"

"We've discussed plenty. At work, at my home, in my bed, we've discussed the important things in life. What's important to us. You've revealed everything about yourself. You also thought I was too self-absorbed to listen to you, to pay attention to the details and what you were saying between the lines. I heard every word you said, Talia."

"You think you know me so well?" I laugh half-heartedly and steady my shaky hands in my lap, trying to wrestle my nervous, gurgling stomach with calming thoughts. Having hot and sweaty sex with Peyton is easy, it's when my libido takes over. But this is hard. Revealing true feelings and taking an emotional risk with him is terrifying.

"I know you," he says. "I watched *Eat Drink Man Woman*. Your favorite movie."

I can't hide my surprise that he remembered.

"Yeah, I remembered," he says. "Of course, you didn't pick something common like *Titanic*. I had to hunt the movie down, but I found it. I wasn't going to quit until I saw the movie that made Talia Madej declare it the best movie ever."

"Wow." A flush of heat warms my skin. I'm thankful it's too dark outside. "Did you like it?"

"I did. Very much. I've been trying to figure out which character is most like you."

"No, you haven't. That's not how you spend your waking hours."

"Wanna bet? I've been a little obsessed with its relevance to you. I want to know what you're thinking when you watch it. At first, I assumed it was all the cooking scenes that appealed to you, but it's not that simple. That would be too obvious. It's much more than that, isn't it?"

"You're right. It's more than the complicated cooking scenes. Although I like the part where the oldest daughter is upset with the neighbors' late-night karaoke singing, and then the middle daughter says, 'We communicate by eating. They communicate by singing.'"

"Because you use cooking and feeding people as your way of showing your love for people. I know that, too, Talia."

"Yes."

"Every scene and every character in that movie made me think of you."

"I'm like the eldest daughter. My heart was broken by a man—Marko—and I assume I'll be taking care of my mother forever so

Aleska can move out and have a real life of her own. But I'm also like the middle daughter. She wants a career, and she thinks she may be in love with a man who's not available."

"I'm available."

"I'm not finished. That daughter chose instead to have a friendship with that man, in case you weren't paying attention."

"I was paying attention. You're not her."

"Okay, well, I'm also like the youngest daughter, because I did play a manipulation game with you when I shouldn't have."

"You're not like the youngest daughter either. She needed a shotgun wedding. You're not like the timid, oldest daughter, and you're not like the middle daughter who casts off a jerk boyfriend but settles for friendship with a married man. You're like Master Chu, their father. He holds everyone together."

"I'm like a seventy-year-old man?"

"In theory. He says, 'Worry is what makes us a family.' You worry a lot, sunflower."

"I do. If I'm going to worry so much about everything, I'd rather be surrounded by a big family, like Master Chu."

"You want some payback or reward for all the worrying you invest in other people," Peyton says. "You want your own family … and the father in the story had a heart condition. Like you, it was both physical and emotional."

"Not exactly like me. He's an old man, Peyton. I love that movie, but you're reading too much into it, and you're not a psychiatrist."

"I'm not finished. The father is in love and wants more in his life than cooking grand dinners for other people and all the family drama that surrounds him. He can't put his life on hold, so he proposes to the woman he's in love with, a much younger woman."

"I don't have a much younger man, and I'm definitely not proposing to anyone."

"You have me, and I'm not going anywhere."

I quickly stand up. I've been in this situation before. A man I thought I would love forever used an opportunity similar to this to propose to me, and I said yes. Fear begins to creep in, along with a cold sensation. I want to believe everything Peyton is saying, but I cannot be hurt again.

"This is too much, too soon. I think I should go inside." I take a step away from my chair, but Peyton stands and pulls me toward him.

"We're right together."

"I used you, knowing you were going to leave Hera."

"But now I'm not leaving."

"But look at all the baggage I come with. This ... us... was never a possibility. Look at me and my life. I'm a mess, and I can't fathom combining my life with yours. You are a restless, ambitious man, and I'm a worried, stay-put kind of woman. Oil and water, right?"

"Wrong. Opposites attract," he says gently, then kisses me on the cheek. So chaste. "Think about what I said. Take your time."

"No pressure, right? I only have to work in your kitchen every day."

"I'm not holding that over your head. Regardless of what happens between us, it's your kitchen, too."

"Nice in theory, but not realistic." I pull away from his grasp. "Last time I made a decision like this—to be serious with a man—it blew up in my face. This is too fast, Peyton."

"No, it's not. You have some concerns, and that's understandable. I can be patient and wait for you."

"Some concerns," I scoff.

"I'm in love with you," he says effortlessly. "And you're in love with me, sunflower."

I put my hand up to stop him from saying anything further. "It's also possible that this isn't love at all. We could be under the influence of our own extreme emotions. In my case, my surgery was fairly traumatizing to me. And you became a parent overnight, and it's made you more emotional. And don't forget you encouraged me to pursue Adam because you were only in this thing with me for sex. Then you got jealous toward Adam. Maybe you and I aren't fit for a serious relationship because we're scared and indecisive. Did you ever think of that?"

"I'm not scared now. I've made a decision," he says coolly.

"I'm scared, Peyton. I'm scared."

The headlights of a car turning into our driveway temporarily blind us. As the driver cuts the lights, Peyton and I are blanketed in a dark silence. The sunset came and went, and I never noticed.

"Hi, guys," Gavin says as he approaches. He's nothing but a black silhouette until he's within a foot from us and I can make out his face in the moonlight.

"Hi," Peyton and I say in unison.

Gavin senses the delicate air between us. "Well, you don't want to stand out here too long. The mosquitos are pretty thick these days."

The light above the front door switches on, and then my mother appears on the threshold, smiling warmly at Gavin. "Hello."

Aleska appears behind her, but her eyes are on me and Peyton.

"Why don't we invite these two to join us in a movie or a game of Monopoly?" Gavin says. It's evident he wants to be with my mother and leave the two sullen people on the front lawn.

"No!" I interject. "Peyton was just leaving, and I have … stuff to do."

Peyton's face falls and he exhales sharply.

"I made you dinner, and I just took a pie out of the oven." My mother is cheerful as she holds the door for Gavin.

"You don't have to keep feeding me," Gavin says politely, but you can hear the appreciation in his voice at the thought of one of my mother's late-night feasts.

"Yes, we do," my mother, Aleska, and I all say together.

Then Peyton and I are alone again.

"So, I'll leave," he says.

"Yeah, and I'm going—"

"And then I'll try on another day." He tips his head at me, then walks across the lawn to where he parked his truck on the side of the road.

I don't want to be caught watching him walk away. I definitely don't want to think about how he just looked at me. *With those goddamn gorgeous eyes gazing upon me like I'm his future.*

42

Talia

WE AGREE TO MEET. His text arrived early in the morning, and I spent a half hour wondering what more we could possibly talk about before I decided to respond. And why did he pick such a public place?

I park my bike in front of Bonnie's Diner and survey the street for anyone who may notice me. The diner is only steps away from Blackard Designs, and across the street I can see Swill and its parking lot. Anyone could spot me heading into the diner, the busiest gossip hub in town. I only hope none of my friends are inside there now.

I take my purse out of my bike basket, checking its meager contents as a means to stall. The sun is beating down on my face. Standing here sweating isn't going to make this situation any easier. I just have to go inside and face the consequences of my decision.

I'm greeted with a swoosh of cold air conditioning as I open the diner door to a cacophony of a sizzling grill, conversations among the tables, percolating coffee, and silverware clinking against dishes. All familiar, comforting sounds.

Imogene's mother, Pam, who is also the owner, waves hello to me. I wave back, then quickly move through the crowded diner, glancing at all the occupied tables, looking for that one face.

He's sitting in a booth in the farthest corner from the door. I wonder how early he got here to snag that somewhat private spot. Though nothing in this diner is very private. Maybe that's why he chose it. The diner is the primary source of all community information in Hera. It's also the location where a person is least likely to yell or argue publicly if they don't want to be the subject of dinnertime gossip. So maybe that's why he chose this spot to meet. He wants me calm and rational and hopes the setting will prevent me from creating a scene.

As I approach the booth, he steps out and stands, puffing his chest up a bit. He looks like he wants to hug me, but I don't want to move closer and make it easy for him.

He puts one hand gingerly on my shoulder and gives me a hesitant smile. "Talia," he says with a hint of relief.

"Hi, Marko."

I haven't seen him in more than seven months. The rage that consumed me is gone. And there's not even a whispered trace of the marital fantasies I used to have daily.

He looks exactly the same. The same bulky physique from his gym routine. The same rugged, yet clean-shaven face that gives him a tough-guy persona. I used to think it made him look sexy. I'm sure it still does to many women. His deep tan is the result of doing roofing jobs shirtless. I know him so well. His ego was always seeking out female admirers, and I was foolish enough to care about that because I thought it said something that he chose me over the other women who fawned over him. His jeans and polo shirt are a little too snug for my taste. Too showy, too much machismo.

He gives me a peck on the cheek as if that's the safe thing to do. "You look beautiful. Thank you for coming."

A bit of my residual grudge hovers near the surface, but I want to prove to him that I'm healthy and strong and doing just fine without him. I actually curled my hair for him—his favorite look. But it's not for him. It's for me, and I want to show him what he's missing. I also wore a blouse with a bit of cleavage so he can see my scar.

"Thanks. I feel great. You look good, too." I step away from him and slip into the booth.

He eases his large frame into the other side, and then the waitress appears with two cups of coffee and menus. Marko gives her his familiar smile-wink combo. I hate it, and in that split second, I hate him.

He turns back to me and just stares.

"What?" I ask tersely.

His eyes dip from my face to my chest then back. "I'm sorry." He reaches across the table and takes my hand. I let him. The feel of his rough fingertips brings back memories.

On the outside, Marko looks like a caricature of a TV assassin. On the inside, he can be warm and tender, when he isn't being a clichéd ass. I forgot about his nice side. In all the months I was scared for myself, I didn't stop to ask him if he was afraid I could die. I knew his concerns about birth defects, and passing on my faulty genetics to future generations, but I never really knew if my possible death crossed his mind.

"I'm sorry I wasn't around when you needed me most. I didn't want to disappear. You have to believe me. I've always loved you. I didn't know how to reassure you, and I saw how weak I was."

"Are you asking me to forgive you? I don't understand why you're here."

"I want to apologize and to ask for your forgiveness. You deserve more than an apology. You went through something very difficult, and I didn't live up to my part as your fiancé. I don't blame you if you hate me."

"I don't hate you. I was angry with you. I was hurt by you. Then I had to stop thinking about you and take care of myself. I had to stop caring about you so I could get on with my life."

"Have you stopped caring about me?"

"I spent months wondering why my fiancé would leave me when I needed him most. I accepted that this must have been a test of our love. My illness showed me a different side of you. And me."

"But I'm here now."

"Marko." I shake my head. "I was so sad. So broken. At the hospital and during my recovery. It was only when I stopped being angry at you that I could make any progress. You leaving taught me how to be strong on my own."

"I should have told you how scared I was for you. I wasn't taught how to be that kind of person. My family—"

"Your family believes in taking the blows. Acting tough. Never, ever talking about things like fear or feeling helpless," I say, and Marko looks a bit ashamed.

"I can't blame my family for my bad behavior, though. What I did was all my fault." He squeezes my hand.

I really want my hand back.

Our two untouched coffees are no longer emitting steam, and neither of us touches the large, laminated menus. Perusing the entrees and deliberating over what to eat would suggest we're dining together, about to linger over a long meal, perhaps as two people trying to make amends and rebuild our relationship.

The waitress doesn't return to take our order. She and every other person in the diner are aware of the ex-engagement drama going on in booth twenty-four.

"I've had plenty of time to think about how I let you down." He pauses for a moment, and I see the old Marko energy, the arrogance making a resurgence. He bites his lower lip and looks at our clasped hands. Hope is making him brave. He can see a way to win this.

"I've also thought about us. I had plenty of time when I was flat on my back in the hospital bed and at home. Pain makes you reflect on everything in a very succinct manner. It gives you a window of opportunity where you have clarity and no doubt."

Marko smiles. His desire for what he wants is obviously muddling his ability to understand what I'm saying. "I want another chance, Talia. I'll make this up to you. I still love you, and I still want you to marry me. And I think you met me today because you still love me. I've always been in love with you."

Always? Even when you looked disgusted when we received my diagnosis? Even when you chose not to visit me during my recovery?

"This isn't fair," I say. "You don't get to come back. You can ask for forgiveness—that's one thing—but asking me to step back into our relationship, which was nothing but a phony ... a charade, it's not even a remote possibility."

I search my memory for a time when I may have ever resisted or blatantly disagreed with Marko, and nothing formidable comes to mind. I was such an agreeable, passive girlfriend. Until now, I didn't see myself as that type of person.

Marko is unaffected by my resistance. "I understand I hurt you," he says as if he's speaking to a child. "But I never let go of the idea of us being married someday. I didn't see other women. Never considered it."

"Too bad. I did. I mean, not women, but I saw other men. Well, one man." I pull my hand away from his grasp.

"You're already dating?" His incredulous expression, as if I couldn't possibly be dating if he wasn't, angers me. "Aren't you still ... healing?"

"Healing? Do you mean from my surgery or from your jackassery?" I'll have to thank Peyton for that choice word.

Marko blinks, startled by my strong language.

I sigh. I really was a passive, good girl type with him. He's expecting the compliant, submissive side of me.

"Health-wise, I'm in great shape. And emotionally, I'm over you. I'm a different person."

"What are you doing here?" the familiar, deep voice demands from behind me.

"Oh, for fuck's sake," I mumble.

Marko looks shocked at my response. Then he steps out of the booth and stands to his full height, six feet of puffed-up muscles, which is actually a few inches shorter than Peyton. Marko is in full primal mode as Peyton approaches our booth.

I'm expecting clenched fists. Instead, Peyton is balancing four pie boxes in one hand and holding his keys in the other. He looks so comically domesticated I want to laugh.

"We're talking," I say.

"I'm Marko Gorski. You look familiar."

Neither man extends a hand.

"Peyton MacKenzie."

"From the Brooklyn wedding," I say for Marko's benefit.

"Is this who you're dating?" Marko asks.

"No," I say.

"Yes," Peyton says before I finish.

"We aren't—"

"Sometimes," Peyton says, making the conversation more incoherent for Marko to follow so that his head ping-pongs back and forth between us.

"What's with all the pies?" I ask brightly, in an attempt to ward off the menacing cloud of testosterone enveloping us.

"Lois is having an early dinner for her book club at Swill, and she demanded I serve Bonnie's pies. Why is he here?" Peyton studies Marko.

"This is between Talia and me," Marko says evenly and begins to sit down in the booth again to stake his claim.

"Like hell!" Peyton drops the pie boxes, grabs Marko by the shirt collar, and yanks him hard enough to send him stumbling out of the booth and against the occupied table next to us. The two senior women gasp and save their coffee mugs, holding them high above their table. Their empty plates are knocked off the table and smash to the floor. *At least they were done eating*, I think to myself.

Marko shoves Peyton back. Then they both step away from the women's table like they're about to square off for a real fight.

I have nothing to put between them to block any punches, so I act on instinct, grabbing a handful of individual creamers from our booth and begin pelting them. My aim is good, and they flinch when the little plastic containers hit them in the face, but they basically swat them away like flies.

"Peyton!" I grab his raised fist with both hands.

Marko looks at me and steps back to stop the altercation. Another attempt to show me he's changed.

"Peyton," I urge again, trying harder to pull his fist down.

"Goodness," one of the senior women says.

Pam and her husband, Mark, come running out of the kitchen to break up the fight. That's the moment when Peyton sees himself through my eyes, through the other customers' eyes. He releases his fist and steps farther away from Marko, raising his hands in surrender. Marko utters a string of Polish curses. I'm certain I'm the only one who understands him.

"Are you boys going to behave?" Pam begins to pick up the dish shards from the floor. Her husband has a big push broom in his hand. Most likely he was going to use it to break up the fight, but now he begins sweeping the shattered porcelain. Cherry filling from Peyton's pie boxes is smeared across the white linoleum floor.

"I apologize," Peyton says to Pam. He moves aside so she can straighten the table for the two women, who both surprisingly stay seated since they had ringside seats for the best show of the day.

"What were you thinking?" I ask Peyton.

His face flushes with embarrassment at losing control. I'm surprised Marko is so composed. If there were two likely people who would want to beat each other to a pulp with their fists, my vote would be for these two guys. Not because they'd be fighting over me, but because they both like to be noticed as the strongest alpha male in the room. I know Marko would revel in a fight, a trait I disliked in his family as a whole. Physical violence is common among the brothers and male cousins in Marko's family, and the parents brush it off as healthy, manly character traits. As much as I hated their sexist, violent behavior, it didn't deter me from willing to marry into their clan.

"I'm really very sorry, Pam," Peyton says. He pulls his wallet out of his back pocket and slides several hundred dollar bills out. He puts them on the table, and I think I see a slight tremor in his hand.

The urge to protect him, or at least reassure him that everything is fine, is powerful.

"You don't have to do that," Pam says, looking at the fan of large bills.

"Please take it," Peyton says gently. "Really, I apologize to all of you." He looks beseechingly at Pam and her husband and the two women sitting at the table.

The rest of the customers go back to chatting and eating, and the white noise of the diner resumes, cutlery against china and the hum of conversations. It all goes back to normal because people in Hera don't let a little barroom brawl interfere with their daily social hour.

Peyton tries to help Pam clean up some of the broken crockery, but I think he wants to say more. He keeps glancing at Marko. They're both holding back.

Pam wants to defuse this situation. "I'll bring new pies over to Swill, honey," she says cheerily. "Don't worry about a thing."

Peyton gets the hint to leave and starts to walk away, but then he turns around abruptly, and another hush falls upon the room.

"You don't deserve her," Peyton says to Marko and then walks out of the diner.

"Nice guy," Marko says with contempt. "He must be more than a friend. Did you fuck that guy?" he whispers sharply in my ear so no one else can hear.

I move away from him, affronted by his judgment after what he did to me. I adjust my bag on my hip so the strap rests evenly across my chest.

Marko watches me and shakes his head in disgust. "I've always hated that stupid telephone bag. I bought you that designer bag, a thousand bucks, and you choose this tacky phone thing over that."

This is all an act. He hasn't changed, and he still resents me for being imperfect and oh so flawed.

His remarkably kind behavior today was for show, manipulation. He was pretending so he could win me back. *Why?* I'm not sure. I still carry the defective gene, and somehow that would always be used against me if I were to be with him. That's how Marko's family operates. He would hold on to the Old Talia for the sake of ownership and power.

But Peyton likes the New Talia. The woman who is scarred inside and out. The woman who carries a weird purse shaped like a telephone because it is the most precious, sentimental possession she owns. Peyton likes these things about me.

Outside the diner, I abandon Marko at his car and rush across the street. I jog by the little Victorian storefront house being renovated into a library. Kim is outside talking to the contractor, and she waves as I take the shortcut behind the new library to Swill.

Peyton is in his office, sitting on the edge of his desk, putting a bandage on his forearm where some of the flying, broken china lacerated the skin. His grimace disappears when he sees me.

"He. Does. Not. Deserve. You."

"I agree. He doesn't."

When those words are out, Peyton visibly relaxes.

"I was crushed seeing you with him. Everything else disappeared, and I forgot about the damn pies. I had to go after him. I had to get him away from you."

I move closer and touch his arm. I trace my finger around the fresh abrasions that haven't been bandaged yet.

"Why were you with him?"

"He asked if we could meet. I thought we could be friends."

He flashes a wicked smile. "Did you now?" I'm relieved to see his humor return. "No real man would let his woman try to be friends with her former fiancé."

"That's the first time you referred to me as your woman. How traditionally barbaric of you."

He laughs.

"Am I your woman?"

"You were mine the minute you ran me over with your bike."

"I didn't touch you."

"You wanted to. That's why you sideswiped my ass. You were trying to get my attention. You were already crazy about me."

"I think I just had bad brakes. But you certainly have quite the imagination."

"I imagine a lot of things that involve you." He looks down at my fingers, which are involuntarily stroking his arm. I immediately remove my hand.

"Talia." He emphasizes my name with a pause. "Tell me why you're here. I've been waiting a long time for this."

"You don't even know what I'm going to say."

"I have a good idea. At least, I hope I'm right. I assaulted your former Polish asshole, who I'm guessing was trying to make amends with you. But you're here with me."

"Remember when you said I saved myself? That first morning at your home?"

"Of course, I remember. You told me about your scar. Your heart."

"Yes. You made me believe that I was my own hero."

"You are. You're one of the bravest people I know, and I admire you for what you've been through."

That makes me smile. I'm overcome, a joyful warmth bringing me close to tears. "That," I say shakily, pointing at him. "You say things like that, and it makes me—"

He stands up from the edge of the desk, and in one step, he swallows every inch of space between us.

"It makes you what?" he asks, looking down at me, patiently waiting.

"It makes me want to believe you. It makes me want to try ..."

"Try what? Come on; get the words out."

"To try with you. I'm considering what you said."

He smiles.

"But I want to take it slow, Peyton. Like actual dating. Not sleeping at your house."

"I can date."

"Dating without sex."

"I can do that."

"I'm not so sure, but I like that you keep trying to impress me with romantic gestures." I gaze at him and my heart swells. "Keep trying. Please keep trying."

"I will."

43

Talia

IT'S BEEN FOUR WEEKS of dating. Actual dating, along with furtive stolen kisses when we see each other at the restaurant, and lengthy texts when we are apart. It's like a bloom of first love.

I haven't spent the night at Peyton's home. We haven't had sex, and Peyton isn't suggesting it. He's following my lead and letting me see another side of him, the not-so-cocky version of the teenager he may have once been, less confident about girls but terribly romantic and sweet in his own way.

Unless Finn is staying at his house, Peyton has dinner at my place every night after work, and my mother gets to cook for everyone. Her kitchen, her rules, her dinners. Gavin is often there, too. Aleska seems to be enjoying the male presence in the household again. It's giving her more freedom to go out at night, knowing we're there to keep our mother company.

We're halfway through summer, and we both have businesses that depend on the influx of thousands of tourists. It's the time of year when a work day is more than fifteen hours, but we make time to be alone each and every day, even if it's just a ten-minute conversation in the parking lot of Swill.

Peyton has committed himself to Swill and Finn. He takes one day off each week to bike the trails with Finn. On the other days, he brings Finn to Swill, where Finn entertains himself by exploring the equipment in the brewery as Zander teaches him about the beer-making process. Peyton and Finn also spend much of their time overseeing the machinery being installed for the new bottling division. And Finn likes hanging out in the great hall before the dinner hours, getting served mock cocktails and drawing with Jess, who still escapes to the restaurant for quiet, personal time away from home. She gave Finn his own sketchbook and a set of charcoal pencils. Everyone, especially Peyton, was surprised that Finn looks forward to sitting down with Jess a couple of times a week for two-hour drawing sessions.

I signed on three new summer clients, big families with rambunctious young children running underfoot in large, expensive, new homes built by Carson's firm. It's a win for both me and Aleska. My menu has expanded to include dishes that accommodate even the pickiest of toddlers.

Word has spread, and now I have a waitlist. It's much more work, so Aleska hired two new employees, a young man to work with her cleaning crew and a woman with professional cooking experience to assist me.

It's an old-fashioned courtship. Peyton is the person I'm most excited to see every morning when I walk into work, and he's the man who kisses me passionately every night before we say our goodbyes.

When he wraps his hands around my waist, I wonder how long I can hold out. I want to be naked, in his strong embrace, in his bed. As if he senses everything I'm thinking, his arms tremble slightly when he holds me. Our bodies press together briefly. The lust and desire are intense.

Peyton is the one with willpower. He gently pries my body from his and gives me a quick kiss, leaving me to fantasize about him until I can fall asleep.

What we don't discuss is my ever-present doubt. The doubt Peyton knows I still harbor. He's trying diligently to show he's honorable and dependable, wanting to eradicate the distrust that was put in place by my father and Marko. If Peyton feels like he's being judged unfairly, he doesn't say so. He lets our relationship unfold slowly with romantic gestures, like handwritten notes left in the side pocket of my purse or slipped into my apron pocket before I arrive at work. It isn't poetry that he writes, but kind, loving words to: *Sunflower*. I realize now that it was a name he bestowed upon me, and only me. Sometimes I find small gifts, like a pot of basil in hand-thrown pottery positioned next to my workstation or a single sunflower stalk trapped under my windshield wiper. His gestures seem endless. He took me at my word that he would keep trying, and it keeps me in a heady cloud of swooning.

So, why am I still afraid?

By now I should be giving in to him and this romantic relationship completely without any reservations. Most women would, right? They would accept how much time Peyton has invested in being prime boyfriend material and his transformation from the egocentric man whose only true loves were work and sex into a man who puts all his effort into caring for his son ... and me. I am the only problem. I'm the one who can't believe this is real. Or, if it's real, then surely it won't last.

When will I stop being the doubter? When will I believe or trust fully, without an ounce of uncertainty?

"Where are we going?" I ask, plucking some french fries from the takeout bags between us. It's my day off, and Peyton is spending a rare lunch break with me. He picked me up at my house, stopped at BooHoo Burgers for my once-a-month junk food feast, and is driving me through familiar territory.

"We're going to your favorite place."

"My favorite place or your favorite place?"

"Mine would be my bed, and it misses you. However, it's confident you'll be back. Eventually. I hope."

"Really?" I tease. He's so ridiculously cute and sexy at the same time. I'm tempted to ask him to pull over so I can throw myself at him.

He grins. So wicked to have such self-control.

"What do you think?" He motions for me to look in front of us. It's Pickwick. We're entering the estate from the other side, a road I've never driven. Peyton must have known taking the back road was the only way to keep his destination a surprise.

"I love this place. Everything is so green." I look at the ancient trees and overgrown farmland left by years of neglect. "It looks so majestic."

"It looks decrepit."

He parks the truck and brings the fast food bags with us. We walk to the area where a small botanical garden used to flourish. Peyton places the food on a stone table surrounded by a half-crumbling stone bench.

"This is a beautiful spot," I say. "Imagine what it looked like a hundred years ago. See the three dancing cherub statues over there? That used to be a pond. Kimberly showed me some old black and white photos at the library."

"She told me. I have to confess she's the one who gave me the idea to bring you to this garden. Or, what's left of it. She had lunch with us the other day when Bash and I were going over business projections. Kim said the fountain garden has become your favorite place here." He pauses. "There's something I want to tell you—"

"I've decided to buy Pickwick," I say urgently, cutting him off.

"Sure, I get that it's your dream to reopen it as an inn, and when the time comes, I want to help you with the financing. That's what I wanted to tell you." He smiles, proud of his surprise, his grand gesture. And it is truly a surprise.

I keep seeing new sides to this man, and all of them are adorable ways to seduce my ovaries and my heart into a gleeful Rockettes chorus line of high kicks. It's only natural that visions of sex and marriage float around my head, maybe with some babies and puppies thrown in. Finn would be my stepson!

Peyton keeps upping his offerings, and it's making him pretty irresistible. However, this expression of his love to help me buy Pickwick is formidable as much as it is breathtakingly generous. This is his grandest gesture, and I'm going to squash it.

"Peyton, you've misunderstood me. I already decided to buy the home and the land, and the financing is being processed as we speak. I have the money."

His jaw twitches. He blinks a few times. "How? Did you get Archie to open his vault of cash?" he jokes nervously. "Please don't tell me you went to my brother and Carson for the money."

"No and no. Norma left me a little money. Not enough to buy this property, but it helps to show I have something in the bank. I have a secret investor."

"A secret investor? You mean a silent partner?" He sounds anxious. "Adam?"

"No, not Adam. He did help with the business plan, though."

"I bet," Peyton mutters.

I laugh and think back to two weeks ago, when my mother called me to the door to greet an unexpected visitor.

Harmony stands on the small front stoop, dressed in one of her designer suits, looking like a Vogue *model pretending to be a businesswoman. She wears a bold red lipstick, and I assume she must have reapplied it before ringing our doorbell because* no woman looks this put-together at the end of a long work day. I'm sure she's here to give me another lecture, warning, or threat because Peyton and I are dating.

When I cross my arms in defiance, instead of saying hello, my mother grumbles in Polish to me and leaves us alone.

Harmony extends her hand, and I look at it, wondering what Ms. Crazy Pants is trying to say.

"Take it," she urges gently with a smile.

I accept her hand, thinking the woman is going to go berserk on me at any moment. She's going to pull some kind of ninja move and throw me to the ground.

"Hello. I'm Harmony Davis. It's a pleasure to know you, Talia Madej," she says, shaking my hand.

"What are you doing?"

"Why should we dislike each other when it's easier to get along?"

"I thought you hated me."

"Hating is a lot of work, and it eats away at your insides. There was a time when I thought I hated my father. He would only support me and Finn in exchange for me cutting all contact with Peyton. I couldn't even tell Peyton about our baby without threats from my father. I hated him. For a while, I thought I hated everyone except my son.

"I heard you have problems with your dad, so maybe you understand how I felt. I was miserable for a long time until I accepted the fact that my hate could poison my son. So, no, I don't hate you. I could never hate someone who saved my son, and I could never hate someone who cares for my son in my absence. I don't hate you, Talia."

"I'm relieved. You must know I'm a little intimidated by you. Your strength as a mother. And your place in Peyton's life."

"You don't have to be jealous of my relationship with Peyton. I intentionally let you believe otherwise only because I was concerned about Finn's welfare. Peyton and I are co-parents, and we'll both be a part of Finn's life forever, but there is nothing other than friendship between us, as you know. I do trust you with Finn. You're really good with him."

"I was prepared for a tongue-whipping from you."

Harmony narrows her eyes. "A tongue-lashing from me? Why are people so afraid of me?"

"I have no idea." Because beautiful people who look like you tend to get what they want, lady! *I shake my head and shrug.* "I'm glad we can be friends. I really do like you, too."

"Well, let's not get carried away."

"Oh." Damn this woman. I can't win with her.

"I'm joking. You're growing on me, and I'm here because I also have a proposition for you."

"Really? I'm intrigued. I think."

"I hope you'll like my idea. I've been paying attention to how much Peyton talks about you, and he gave me some interesting information. That Pickwick estate, the place he says you romanticize. He said you go on and on about how you want to refurbish it and turn it into a working organic farm and a boutique inn. Peyton doesn't have your vision. He likes restaurants that are trendy and flashy for mass appeal. It's what he knows and what he's good at. But I was fascinated by your idea for this Pickwick place. I didn't get a good look at it the day I found you and Peyton there ... when we had the Finn incident."

I bite my lower lip, thinking about that awful day. I didn't like her then, and I certainly didn't like her threats. Nevertheless, it felt deceitful after her ultimatum, especially since Peyton and I did more than have lunch.

Finn's disappearance and the race to find him was my wakeup call. For better or worse, Peyton, Harmony, and Finn are a real family, and my little dalliances with him were starting to make me feel like a homewrecker. But that was then.

Harmony doesn't seem to notice my discomfort and continues, "So recently, one day after I dropped Finn off at Peyton's house, I made another trip out to the property. I walked around it."

"What did you think of it?" My heart starts racing to think she and I could have something in common! A love of historic farms and old houses? *Sounds strange, but I'll take any commonality I can find with her.*

"I think you're right, and Peyton doesn't get it. It's a beautiful piece of land and a magnificent old estate. It has so much potential. I also know you have a solid reputation as a chef, not only in Hera but in the surrounding towns. Not to mention, Pickwick's location is perfect as a destination spot. It would appeal to people in New York, New Jersey, and Connecticut who want to escape their urban lives."

"Yes, exactly. Hearing you talk about it makes me want it more, but I don't have the funds or collateral to acquire the kind of business loan I'd need. Unless I ask Archie or the Blackard brothers, which is what everyone else does."

"No. Forget the men. You can do this without them. They already have enough businesses going on. Those guys have their hands in everything."

"I agree, but I don't have the money."

"I do. My father left the bulk of his estate to me. I'm rich. Peyton may not understand the appeal of Pickwick. I do. I can totally picture what you want to do with it, and I want in. Fifty-fifty.

"A little bird, the loud brunette one—"

"Imogene?"

"Yes. Her. Finn's aunt." She chuckles. *"She said you have been meeting with someone about a business plan."*

"Adam. He runs a hedge fund, and he's helped me put together the numbers so I can present it to investors and a bank."

"There you go. You have a plan and an investor—me. I can put up all the money. I'll be the silent partner, and you can run the business."

I'm astounded. I want to scream yes!

"This is insane, Harmony. We barely know each other, and then there's Peyton. We started dating, you know. Is that going to be a problem?"

"Peyton has nothing to do with our business partnership. Maybe you two will end up together. Maybe not. Our business relationship is separate, and we can be professional about this."

"And we can be friends."

Harmony laughs lightly again. I'm determined to win this woman over.

"All right. And friends. I also want to rebuild the stables and have a few horses. They're expensive to keep, but I want Finn to have the experience I had—weekend riding lessons. I figure we can give him a minimum-wage job cleaning the stalls or something."

"I like how you think."

After listening to the story, Peyton contemplates this new information, stunning news to us both, and I'm worried he's somehow upset by the turn of events. Maybe he's hurt because I turned down his offer, or I come across as not needing him at all.

He could be one of those men who needs to have the upper hand in money and career. I think of Flora at her high-powered, legal firm and how she and Peyton had a very volatile relationship.

"It happened a couple of weeks ago. When she came to my house," I explain. "It happened so fast, and it was so surprising. Harmony and I agreed not to tell you or anyone until the paperwork was filed. I didn't want to bring it up with you until I knew it was real. That's why I'm telling you now. It's official. It's real!"

"So, Harmony is your business partner?" he asks as if he's trying to wrap his head around the idea of his current girlfriend being in business with the mother of his son.

"Yes, she is. This is already happening, Peyton. We signed the paperwork this morning."

"She never mentioned a word of this to me. She's good at keeping secrets."

If he thinks I'm going to feel guilty about pursuing this without him, it won't work. Marko cured me of macho guilt trips.

"You amaze me," he says. "I brought you here to wow you with something huge. A big gift is what I was aiming for. I thought my offer would convince you of my good intentions."

"I am wowed by your offer. I thought you'd be happy for me because I'm taking the initiative to pursue my dream."

"I am happy for you." He sounds unsure. "You're doing this with Harmony ... that's interesting."

"Remember, you're the one who told me I saved myself. Your words helped me do this. I *own* this."

"That's great. I mean it. It's absolutely remarkable what you're doing and that you took the initiative, but where does it leave me in all this? If I can't help you with major things like this, how are we supposed to be closer?"

"I didn't help you with Swill, and we became close anyway."

"Let me rephrase this. How do I earn your trust?"

"Oh."

We're still standing next to the stone table, the grease from the untouched food beginning to seep through the paper bags, and Peyton is looking at me with adoration now. I take all this in. It is the precise moment when I *know*.

"You have my trust. You support my wild ideas, and you do everything you can to hold me up. I lack experience and education in some things, but you never tear me down about my flaws. That's everything to me."

I hook my fingers into the belt loops of his jeans and rise on my tiptoes to kiss him. He lowers his head and kisses me thoroughly, a dazzling touch with erotic slowness. I caress the stubble on his chin with my lips when I come up for air, and then he claims them again, kissing me more urgently.

I am spent by that kiss. My lips feel bruised and worn out. It's only when I smile and look into Peyton's eyes that he finally smiles, and I see his confident swagger return.

Any doubts either of us has about a future together are forgotten for these few minutes. The only thing between us is the same chemistry that drew us together all those months ago when I followed him into Swill and he changed my life.

We sit and eat our burgers and cold fries, stopping every few minutes to kiss. Everything has changed. We've changed. All because of one small word. *Trust.*

"Let me guess; you and Harmony are going to call your new inn ... Tableside Dung?"

"Harmony would love that," I say dryly.

"Organically Overpriced?"

"You're hilarious. Make fun all you want."

"Oh no," he feigns worry. "We're not back to The Wounded Peach, are we? Please tell me you're not going to give it one of those sad, touchy-feely names."

"We haven't decided yet. I can assure you we will not be needing to consult you on the name."

His robust laugh is comforting.

He drives me home, and when he pulls into the driveway, I suddenly don't want to be separated from him. I don't want to walk into my home, where the walls close in on me, where I watch my mother try to navigate her life in square feet rather than miles.

"Thank you for today," I say. "You're pretty terrific. I'm rather fond of you, I hope you know."

He gives a low, throaty chuckle. "I have one more thing for you."

"Want to take me back to your place?" I say with a sly smile. We both know I'm only teasing.

"Yes, I do. However, I can wait until this dating stage is over and we enter the adult entertainment stage. Again. Until then ... I'd like you to go on a vacation with me ... and Finn."

"The big beach trip you planned with Jess and Carson? In two weeks?"

He nods. "And a few of the others. Greer and her kids, too. It would give us a chance to spend time together relaxing, instead of slicing out time for each other between our busy schedules. Cape May is a great beach town, and we'll be staying in a nice hotel. Historic and old, just what you like."

The word *hotel* conjures up a lot of images, mostly of me as a naughty mistress in front of a nine-year-old boy. Peyton notices my concern.

"I already discussed this with Harmony. She thinks it's fine. Finn says he's cool with it, too. He'd have his own room, and he'd be my priority, but we have enough relatives on the trip who can watch him when you and I want some alone time."

"I would love a vacation with you two," I say, thinking about me in a swimsuit for the first time in ages. With a big scar down my chest, and the questions and looks from others on the beach. Then there would be the room situation. "Finn doesn't mind being in his own room and not with you?"

"Hmm," Peyton says and lets out a deep sigh. "I was hoping we could enter the next stage. You and I will share a room, unless you think it's still too fast. I've got to tell you, though, I'm ready for more—"

"Me, too!" I say so fast that Peyton's mouth snaps shut.

"So, you'll go?" He perks up. "I was actually expecting you to say no, either because of work or because you would feel uncomfortable with everyone hanging out with us ... watching us."

"Aleska and my mom can fill in for me. My mother will love the work. As far as our friends, they know everything anyway. It's more important that we're appropriate in front of Finn. I don't even know what that is. Harmony told me whatever I have with you is separate from our business relationship, but we never discussed me going on vacation with her son."

"She's the one who encouraged me to ask you to go. I made a comment about wanting to take you somewhere because I need more time with you, and she suggested I take you on this trip. I was a little shocked, but Harmony has mellowed out a lot over the last month—she's more comfortable sharing parenting duties. I wasn't about to disagree with her, because I really do want you with me. After your little surprise today about Harmony, now her behavior makes perfect sense. She thinks you're good for me. She likes you."

"I think she and I are going to be good friends!" I squeal.

He rolls his eyes. "Could you focus on me first?" It's followed by a smirk.

I unbuckle my seat belt, throw arms around his neck, and smooch his cheek. "I can't wait for this trip. I'm going to go start planning! I need a bathing suit!"

"Want me to come in and say hi to your mom? We can make one of those lists you love so much."

"No. You can go back to work." *So I can take a cold shower and calm the hell down before I climb naked into your lap.* "I'll talk to my sister and mom and get everything arranged. I'm very excited."

He points to his crotch. "So am I."

I slap him playfully on his rock-hard bicep. Big mistake. That just arouses me more.

I have to get away. I'm delirious with lascivious thoughts and anticipation of this vacation. I jump out of the truck, slam the door, and wave goodbye.

"Your phone!" Peyton launches the telephone-shaped purse at me through the open passenger window, and I catch it against my chest.

I give him a thumbs-up, then run inside the house, breathless and giddy.

Everything is perfect.

Everything is *not* perfect. I enter the house to find my mother and Aleska in the front room. Aleska is brooding, and my mother is wiping her tears.

"You won't believe this," Aleska says, her arms crossed. She looks at our mother and shakes her head. "Tell her."

"Come sit down," my mother says.

"What's wrong?" I ask, stepping around the coffee table to sit next to her on the couch. "Did you and Gavin have a disagreement or something?"

"No, we're fine. I want you to listen to this. It's something I should have told you girls years ago."

Aleska's stony expression cracks, and a tear slides down her face.

"Is someone dying?" I ask.

"No." My mother puts her hand on my arm. "I was telling Aleska that you were not our first baby."

I look at Aleska. She's staring at the floor, holding herself together.

Another surprise baby? A child? Has my mother been inspired by Harmony's story?

"Are you going to tell me you gave a child up for adoption, and we have a big sister out there in the world? No, wait, let me guess. She was adopted by a farmer and that's really why you and Dad moved us to Hera, and our sister is the bitchin' blonde yoga instructor at Beyond the Pants."

"I wish," Aleska mutters.

"No," my mother says. "His name was Justek. He only lived for forty-four days. He died of heart failure."

"*Justek*," I say, sounding out his name and trying to picture him. Was he blond like me or dark like Aleska? "Why have you never spoken of him?"

"Your father and I were so young. We got married because I was pregnant."

Aleska sniffles.

I'm cautiously taking a deep breath to prepare for the tears I sense building. "Oh, Mom."

"We loved Justek so much. We were devastated. We didn't think to ask questions. Who were we to question the doctors? They were smarter than us. We only had Justek for forty-four days, but I think about him every single day. Your father was never the same. You wouldn't know that because you only know the man who buried his infant son. I saw him change. He was happy when you were born. Both of you girls made him happy, but bit by bit, I noticed him pulling away, becoming less involved, less responsible. He was becoming detached. From us. That's how he protected his heart from more grief. Then he stopped giving love."

My cheeks are wet. My sister hands me a fistful of tissues, and I bury my face in them. My mother rubs my back, and we all sit there for a few minutes to wring the grief from ourselves.

"Is that why you took care of me—after my surgery—like a baby? Sometimes I felt like an infant. You monitored everything I did, watched every move I made, and kept that chart on me. You wrote down all my medication doses, the steps and time I spent on the treadmill, my bodily functions, and everything I ate."

"I had to. I'm your mother. You and Aleska will always be my babies."

"Is it the guilt that made you so afraid?" I ask. "Did you feel guilty about Justek? Is that why you're so afraid to leave this house?"

"No. There were several things that triggered this—my problem. It started when things between your father and I got worse. We weren't talking to each other. He didn't want to be near me. I was thinking a lot about Justek then—even though he's been dead for more than twenty years, he is always on my mind. I became very depressed about our family situation. I tried not to let you girls see all this. We weren't doing well as a family, and I started to have panic attacks when we moved to Hera. Because my relationship with my husband was so strained over money and employment, my fears were heightened. Under those conditions, when my thoughts turned to Justek, it started to build to a certain level of paranoia. It went from regular concerns about money, marriage, and work to where I was constantly scared about how I could keep my daughters alive. Everything became terrifying. The day I finally gave up and didn't leave this house, I thought it was a minor little breakdown that would be resolved with a long, hard sleep. I really thought it would only last a couple of days, at most."

"Days turned into years," I say.

"Grief and fear are very powerful. I should have seen a psychiatrist, but I was too afraid to talk to a professional, to revisit all the things I was carrying around in my head."

"You're taking care of yourself now; that's what matters," I say. "Justek …"

"I'll never get over Justek's death. And the guilt of not paying more attention to how he died, how it could affect his sisters.

"When you were born, the doctors never detected a heart murmur, and we never thought to tell the new doctor who delivered you about your brother's death. It never occurred to us that there could be a family connection. When you came home from the cardiologist last December and announced you needed surgery, then I knew that you and Justek probably had the same heart defect. I felt responsible. I should have told you about your brother."

"It wouldn't have changed anything, Mom. I still would have needed the surgery."

"Maybe the surgery could have happened when you were younger, and then you wouldn't have been hurt by Marko, and you wouldn't be struggling with these fears today."

"Marko is an asshole," Aleska says.

"Aside from Marko's assholishness, we weren't in a position to have this type of surgery back in Poland. Our doctors didn't diagnose my murmur. I don't know if there was a doctor in Lublin twenty years ago who would have been able to perform the type of surgery I had. And if this had happened while we were living in Queens, Dad probably would have left sooner."

"Definitely," Aleska adds. "He runs away. He's weak, Mom. You're afraid to leave the house, but you're actually a strong person."

"You are strong." I grasp my mother's hand. "Justek's death wasn't your fault, and you could not have predicted it would have happened to another one of your children. I don't blame you for this."

My mother pulls out the little, double-sided heart locket she keeps tucked inside her blouses and T-shirts and opens it. I recognize the newborn baby, eyes wide open, wearing a green knit cap and swaddled in a hospital blanket. The other photo shows a sleeping infant, in an identical hospital blanket, with a yellow knit cap.

"You told us those were our baby photos. I remember asking you when I was little."

"I did tell you that. It was easier than the truth."

"That's Justek. You've been carrying him next to your heart all these years," I say.

"We only had the two photos of him while he was alive. I saw this locket at a little street fair, and it immediately made me think of these Justek photos I kept hidden in a drawer. I bought it. I finally had a proper place for my Justek's memories. When I showed the locket to your father, he cried and left the room. Two days later, I found out I was pregnant with you. Justek would have been twenty-seven today, and I still wonder what he'd look like as a boy, as a man, and what kind of person he would be today."

I wonder, too. I could have used a big brother to help me navigate through life.

"When the outside world became too much for me, when I was afraid of every unseen thing, I tried to put more effort into being your mother. I had to watch over both of you. I'm not very good at it. My daughters support me."

"You're still young, and you have your whole life ahead of you. With your therapy, it will get easier, and you'll eventually get a job, too. You'll be okay. We'll all be okay, right?"

"Right," Aleska says.

"And you have Gavin," I say. "He's better than Dad."

"I wish you had known your father as the man I fell in love with. Then you wouldn't hate him so much."

"I don't know if it matters who he was. What matters is who he became and how he treated you and us after a terrible tragedy. Is this why you've always been so forgiving toward Dad? You accept his phone calls as if we're lucky to have him grace our days with long-distance calls from wherever he's currently hiding."

"He's the only other person who knew and loved Justek. I suppose, in some way, I thought if I lost that connection, I'd also lose the memories of Justek altogether."

"You went through a traumatic event, losing your baby," I say. "I can't imagine."

"Then you lost your husband and you lost yourself," Aleska adds.

I lean into her. "I'm never leaving you."

"I hope you do," my mother says brightly, now recovered from her crying. "I want you to get married and have your own family."

"Let's not go there."

Aleska raises an eyebrow. "Trouble in Peyton Paradise again?"

"I'm going on vacation with him and Finn. Plus, with a dozen of our closest friends and his family."

"Oooo," they say together.

"That's what I thought." *Until I found out I really am not marriage material for any man looking to have biological children.*

I thought this was difficult with Marko. It's much worse with Peyton because I'm in love with him. I convinced myself that my heart defect wasn't going to be an issue. Aleska doesn't have it, so I decided I was a one-off in our family.

Maybe after he spends a few days with me on vacation, our appeal as a couple will lose its luster and he'll want to go back to the freedom of being single.

At least I'll have Pickwick and Harmony!

44

Talia

"JESUS, WHAT FRESH HELL is this?" Peyton looks at the black coach bus taking up half of Swill's parking lot. The purple lettering painted across the side of the bus says *PARTY!*

Jess hired a bus company to take all the families down to Cape May, New Jersey, for our beach vacation. She thought the idea of having all the babies and children enclosed in one space would make it easier for the adults. It's obvious she's a new mother and has had no experience with children.

I plunk down my suitcase next to his. "It will be fun. It's a party bus."

Everyone is pulling luggage and pool toys out of their vehicles. The large bus looms over them with a deceptively sinister aura, like it's waiting to swallow little kids whole. Something is off.

Peyton cocks an eyebrow with his smirk. "Seriously? Do you have any idea who rents these things?"

"I did!" Jess exclaims as she drags a suitcase by us. "Isn't it great! The kids are going to have a blast on the way down to the shore."

Carson follows close behind her with Scotty on his hip and another suitcase in hand. He shakes his head at Peyton. "Don't say anything. This stuff is all new to her. God, I just hope the inside has been bleached," he says grimly, catching up to his wife.

"What's the big deal?" I ask Peyton.

"Guys tend to rent these buses and … you know."

"I don't know. It's a kiddie bus. For birthday parties."

450

"No, I don't think this is that kind of bus."

Harmony's Mercedes pulls into the lot and parks next to us. When she steps out of the car, she studies the enormous bus with a frown.

Finn, with wide eyes and a big grin, jumps out of the car and runs to us.

"Hey, buddy." Peyton slaps him into a big hug.

"Do you think we'll get to swim in the ocean today?" Finn asks.

"We'll see. It depends on traffic and how long it takes to get there. We can still take a walk on the beach, even if it's night."

Harmony retrieves Finn's suitcase from the trunk and, still eyeing the bus warily, walks over to us with dismay. "That thing is huge."

"Hi, Harmony!" I say brightly. We're business partners now, so I feel I can say hello without cowering.

"Hello." Harmony gives me the slightest smile, a tidbit really, but I'm grateful to have anything from her. She's a tough woman, but I'm determined to have her like me as more than a business partner. "Will you make sure Finn puts on sunscreen and reapplies it several times a day?" She addresses this to me rather than Peyton, and it gives me a lift. She trusts me. She wouldn't go into business with me if she didn't. But trusting me with Finn is a whole other level.

"Yes, I will."

"I'll stay on top of the sunscreen." Peyton says.

"I think Talia will do a better job of it," Harmony says. Then she gives Finn a hug goodbye. "No offense, Peyton, but I don't see you as the type to keep track of the time and when to reapply."

"It's sunscreen. We have to track the time?" Peyton asks.

"I'll do it," I reassure her.

"That's certainly some bus. You have fun," Harmony says to Finn. "Listen to your father and Talia. No swimming alone, got it?"

"I know, I know. Can I go check out the bus now?"

"Yes," she says, and Finn takes off running. "Have fun!" Harmony shouts after him.

Dylan catches Finn and wrestles with him, pretending to stash him with the luggage below the bus, and then they disappear into the bus and we hear Dylan's outrageous laughter.

"Do I want to know what's inside there?" Harmony asks.

"Probably not," Peyton replies.

"We'll take good care of Finn," I say, eager to please her.

I'm thrilled I'm going on this trip with Peyton. Last night, I woke up *on* his bed when he came in late from the restaurant. I was fully clothed, waiting up for him while I dozed off. I turned on the bedside lamp, and when he came through the bedroom door, his smile upon seeing me waiting for him made me melt.

He sat on the side of the bed, took me in his arms, and kissed me like he hadn't seen me in years, when in fact we had only been separated for a few hours. The moment overwhelmed me. I am deeply in love with this man, and his look of gratitude and relief at seeing me made everything right. This may not end up the way I want, but at least I'm no longer afraid to try.

I woke up this morning wrapped in Peyton's arms. He was dead tired after only three hours of sleep, and we were still dressed in our clothes from the night before. The last thing I remember was being snuggled in his embrace as he murmured, "Let it be like this forever. It's perfect."

After Harmony drives away and we help stow the rest of the luggage for Greer and the twins and help Leo and Lauren squeeze in folded playpens and strollers, Peyton and I board the bus.

First, I'm assaulted by a freezing cold breeze, giving me goosebumps. The air conditioning must be set at Antarctic levels. And it's fairly dark inside. A glitter disco ball is mounted on the ceiling, spinning, creating swirls of white orbs flashing across everyone's face. But it's the two shiny, chrome poles in the center of the bus that startle me. The poles are the stage.

"Are those ...?"

"Yes," Peyton answers me without missing a beat.

Imogene is laughing and wrangling kids onto the leather seats that flank the sides of the bus.

"Isn't this great?" Jess says gleefully. "They have fireman poles so the kids can slide down them!"

Finn takes that moment to show off to his younger cousins. He climbs one of the poles with ease, then slides down, landing on his rear and laughing.

Peyton watches his son, speechless.

"Jess." I begin laughing. "Those are stripper poles."

"What?" Her brow furrows, and she looks at me as if I'm speaking another language. Then she turns and looks back at the poles. The disco ball is spinning wildly, emitting splashes of neon light. Her smile fades. "Oh my God! I hired a stripper bus. No wonder it was cheaper and available on such short notice!"

"It's okay, honey," Imogene says. "A bus is a bus. It will get us where we're going."

"I can't believe my son has gone up and down that stripper pole at least ten times now, and I'm just standing here, watching him do it," Peyton says.

"We don't want to ruin the kids' fun," Lauren adds.

"Who knows what's on those poles and the seats?" Peyton mumbles.

I can't contain my laughter.

"Oh, gross!" Jess squeals. "Carson! Carson, quick, throw me the box of wipes by my purse!"

Carson, with his baby strapped to his chest, locates the deluxe box of wipes and launches it at Jess. She catches it. Then, like a crazed, overprotective mother, she begins wiping down every surface, starting with the stripper poles. Then she scrubs down all the kids who touched said poles.

"Hello, everyone!" The bus driver steps out from the flimsy door that leads to his driver's seat cockpit. He has a big smile plastered on his face, most likely hoping Jess doesn't scream at him.

"Hi!" all the kids shout back.

"My name is Alejandro, and I will be your driver today! Welcome!" He begins passing out business cards. "Please, everyone, take one. Not only am I a driver, I'm also an ordained minister. I do a little of everything. I'm looking forward to this drive, too. After I drop you off in Cape May, I'm meeting my wife in Wildwood for some beach time, so let's get this party started!"

The kids cheer, and Jess gives up on trying to sanitize everything and everyone.

"Hey, Alejandro, why is it so cold in here?" Carson asks. "Can you turn the A/C down a bit?"

"Okay, that's a very good question," Alejandro says, then holds up two fingers. "Here are the two problems with the bus. One, the air conditioner is broken and permanently running at high. This means we'll be chilly and stopping for gas, maybe more than once. Two, the toilet is broken. With the kids, we may need to stop a few more times for bathrooms."

"What?" Jess's face begins to burn with the red flush of pissed-off-mother-on-a-stripper-bus. She's holding up the box of wipes as if it's a weapon she's ready to use.

"It's fine, babe," Carson says, grabbing the box of wipes from her. "We'll pull out some sweatshirts for the kids and crack some windows to let the heat in. And we'll stop as much as we have to. There's no rush. The kids love the bus. You did great. We'll get to the hotel on time and safely, so just let this go."

• • •

Two and a half hours later, we're traveling down the Garden State Parkway in New Jersey. The novelty of the stripper poles has worn off, and now they stand empty, covered in grimy kiddie prints. The sound system craps out, and then Alejandro announces over the loudspeaker that the stereo is no longer functioning.

It's good timing, though. The adults are sick of the dance club bass giving us all headaches, and the children are crashing, lounging lengthwise across the seats, coming down from their sugar highs from too many juice boxes and Twizzlers that Emma and Dylan kept passing out. The babies are asleep. Unfortunately, they both unloaded in their diapers after we left the second rest stop, so we are subjected to a potent, putrid stench for the rest of the trip.

Finn sits across from us, exhausted from his pole work and entertaining the smaller kids, dozing in his seat.

Peyton smiles at me. *This is perfect.* He picks up my hand, studies it, and then holds it firmly on his lap.

"I'm already having fun," I say. "I've never had a real vacation."

Peyton chuckles. "I'm sorry this is your first vacation. I really wanted to make it more special."

"You mean more romantic?"

"Yes. I didn't expect a giant freezer on wheels, stripper poles, and a disco ball."

• • •

Cape May is a small, pretty seaside town bustling with tourists playing on its vast, clean beach, walking its charming streets with beautifully restored Victorian homes in whimsical colors, and filling every restaurant to capacity. The only other beach I have been to is Coney Island. Our father would take us out there on the train for a day trip, and we would camp out on the crowded beach among all the other city dwellers, fighting for a few hours of surf and sand.

When we arrive at the hotel, Cooper takes our bags so Peyton and I can take Finn down to see the beach before it gets dark. We squish the sand between our toes and listen to the crashing waves. I can smell the breeze and taste the salt on my tongue.

Peyton puts his arm around me as we watch Finn run into the water up to his knees, making up for missing a day of swimming.

I'm delighted by our hotel. Congress Hall is a historic resort overlooking the ocean, a grand Victorian hotel painted in a welcoming yellow. When we enter the lobby, I immediately decompress. It's like stepping back in time. Wood floors that creak and a sort of vintage seaside decor that makes you want to order a cocktail and lounge about.

I release my breath, my shoulders relax. I have no supplies to buy, no orders to cook, no deliveries to make, and I don't have to exercise or think about what's best for my heart. I'm here with Peyton, the first man to take me on a vacation.

I was ready to marry Marko, yet I had never gone on vacation with the man, never experienced what it would be like to be with him when he wasn't working and scheduling his life around his own goals.

Finn's room, sandwiched between Greer's and Jess's, is a few doors down from us. Finn seems fine with the arrangement.

After we unpack and have a sunset dinner at The Rusty Nail, we all take a walk on the beach, followed by an evening stroll through town until the babies get fussy. On the walk back to the hotel, Peyton and I trail behind the others, holding hands, buoyant, riding a wave of exhilaration of what will come.

Peyton has been forthright with me, and I will have to be the same with him. My turn will come. I will have to tell him the family history my mother shared. Not tonight, though. I've been waiting for this night for too long, fantasizing about being with Peyton. I need this again, before I put all my cards on the table and lose—I've been dealt enough terrible hands in those poker games with Lois to know.

He closes the door to our room. "Finn is out," he says, placing his keys and wallet on the dresser. "I wanted to say goodnight, but he was already asleep on top of his covers. His feet are filthy."

"He's happy." I shrug. "He'll probably be filthy all week."

"I like the way you say *filthy*." He approaches me slowly, his eyes roaming my body. "I've been waiting for this night, thinking about it every day ... for weeks."

"The whole dating-without-sex thing was good." We both nod, unconvincingly. "It really makes us appreciate ... Who am I kidding? It was torture."

"I'm glad I'm not the only one who thought so."

He grasps the waistband of my jeans and tugs me toward him. I throw my arms around his neck and kiss him. We've spent weeks kissing, and we're damn good at it. We know each other's sensitive points, where one lick can turn us on. The kiss does all that, fires us up. We begin pulling our clothes off.

Peyton yanks the zipper down on his jeans and it stops halfway. "My zipper is stuck," he grunts in frustration.

He keeps tugging harder. The zipper won't budge. He tries shimmying out of his jeans, but he needs the zipper to slide another inch for that to work. I'm down to my bra and panties, and I watch him, fascinated with his naked torso and how his arms and shoulders bunch up with tight muscles and popping veins as he battles with the zipper.

"Look at you!" I say, amazed. "You're doing the Hulk pose. Your arms and elbows ... and you've got his angry scowl—"

"Arghhhh!" Peyton rips his zipper open with his fists, tearing through the jeans all the way down to the knee of one of his pant legs. He kicks off the shredded jeans.

"Hot," I say, completely aroused. "We'll buy you new jeans tomorrow."

He picks me up and carries me to the bed where he strips off his underwear, then reaches for mine while I toss my bra. Naked and pressed together, we resume our kissing and add in the much-anticipated groping. That's when the bed legs start pounding against the floor and the headboard begins tapping against the wall.

"We can't have sex in this bed," I say, pushing him off me. "Everyone will hear. We'll be that couple, the one who everyone says, 'They're at it again. Always humping.'"

"Is that what people say?" He's breathless and frustrated with my interruption. "Screw the bed, then."

He pulls me off the bed so I'm standing as he tosses the pillows, comforter, and sheets onto the floor. I immediately kneel down to straighten the bedding out on the carpet.

"What are you doing?" he barks. He has a full hard-on and is looking at me like I'm sabotaging his opportunity for sex.

"I'm arranging it. So it's like a bed."

"We're not here to decorate." It's somewhere between a growl and a laugh.

He pushes me into the soft pile of linens, and when he's naked on top of me again, all my decorating sense evaporates. I wrap my legs around him, and thus begins our foray back into friends who have sex. Except this time, it's different. We're two people in love.

"I haven't seen this crazed, beastly side of you in a while. It's sexy."

"Hmm," he says into my neck.

His tongue is doing its thing again, lighting little fires on my skin, making my nipples peak, and all those other parts I don't think about come alive.

"Where are the condoms?" I ask, expecting him to pull one of his magic lifetime-supply boxes out of thin air.

He tenses and stops kissing my throat. "No," utters in a low voice.

"What? Get them." I'm more demanding.

"No, no, no." He abandons my neck, looks up and around the room. "I can't believe this. I packed them in my kit bag. I left it in the bathroom."

"All right." It's not like he's never had to hobble to a bathroom with a raging hard-on before.

"At home."

My enthusiasm deflates.

"No, no, no." He shakes his fist, then throws his head back and looks up at the ceiling, enraged, with tendons popping out of his neck and shoulders. "Noooo!"

"Now you look like Superman. The old movie version when he finds Lois Lane ... dead." I place my hands on either side of his face. "We can still do *things* tonight, and then tomorrow we'll run to CVS for lots of condoms. Boxes and boxes of them."

"No." Peyton shakes his head. "No, we planned on this. I need this."

"We could ..." I have no idea what we can do besides pleasuring each other with hands and tongues—which is damn awesome—but he wants every item on the menu tonight.

"What can we do?" he asks. "It's not like I can make something out of a coffee filter." We both look around our room for signs of a coffeemaker.

"We can't even make coffee."

The humor of the moment goes over Peyton's head. He's having none of this.

"Shit!" He pushes himself up off the floor and looks down at me, all serious. "I'll be back."

"Now you sound like the Terminator. Where are you going? Stores are closed."

"My brother is trying to have a kid—no condoms there. I'll have to try Carson." He wraps a sheet around his waist, bunched up in front to hide his erection. *Good thinking, honey.*

Less than five minutes later, Peyton's back, running into the room, tossing the sheet aside, and ripping open a condom package. I don't bother to ask if he encountered anyone on his run down the hotel corridor and if he frightened them.

Within minutes, we're on the floor again and he's positioned between my legs, looking at me with reverence. My breath hitches when he begins stroking himself before he enters me. I completely fall apart when he's inside me. He was right. We needed to have everything on the menu tonight.

45

Peyton

M Y HEART LURCHES AT the sight of Talia and Finn being launched off the boat. Our party takes up two boats for our parasailing excursion, and although I've done this before and know it's nothing more than a ride—no skills required—I feel helpless watching the two people I love the most being catapulted into the sky.

Talia and Finn are laughing and waving at us as the parachute takes them higher and higher into the bright blue sky.

"This is horrible," I say. "This is so wrong." They have become indistinguishable specks. So far away. Too far away from me.

This is a picture-perfect, tranquil ocean scene, but our group is loud. The sound of the motor and the boat splashing against the water, along with the loud chatter of the others shouting to the other boat, I feel like the lone person who is concerned for my two people jetting into the sky.

"What's wrong?" Greer asks.

"Why do we send the people we love ... away... like that? She needs more sunblock," I say, looking back at Talia soaring above.

Greer's laugh jolts me from staring up into the sky. "Welcome to the real world. Where every day is about worrying. You worry about your kids and—" Greer looks at me hard, and her surprise turns into a warm smile. "Oh, sweetie, you've really fallen hard for Talia, haven't you? You're in love."

I look over at our two-man crew. One is steering the boat; the other has finished reeling Finn and Talia up and is now filming them so we'll have a souvenir video. I'm happy to give them this experience and feel sick to my stomach at the same time.

"Is there an antidote for this?" I ask Greer, wiping the sweat from my forehead.

She laughs and puts her hand on my shoulder. "No, absolutely not. Lucky you."

• • •

We survive two more days of parasailing and jet skiing. Or, rather, I should say that *I* survive. Talia is blissfully happy, tearing up the ocean on her jet ski, breaking every rule and getting whistled at and reprimanded by the guy in charge of monitoring all the skiers in the bay. Finn is underage, so he has to ride on the back of my jet ski. I feel that dad pressure of trying to impress your kid who is past the toddler phase of thinking their dad is a hero. We break a few rules of our own, taunting others into racing and taking fast, hard turns to blast Talia with some rocking waves. The monitor is blowing his whistle at everyone, but eventually gives up.

"If they knew you had a record for grand theft auto, you wouldn't be allowed on that jet ski!" I shout to Talia as we zoom past her.

Her look of shock turns into laughter as she races after us.

"For real?" Finn shouts from behind me. "Talia stole a car?"

"For real," I shout back. "But she was a kid. Don't go getting any ideas."

Just then, Talia drenches us with a heavy spray of water as she sidles up to us fast, almost crashing into us. That's the end of our jet skiing privileges. We're officially banned. But the owner of the company pulls me aside before we leave and says I can come back anytime with Talia as long as we're willing to be sequestered away from the other skiers and the general public.

• • •

We spend every day on the beach and every afternoon at the hotel pool. Talia, despite wearing big floppy hats and cover-ups over her bikini when she isn't swimming, manages to acquire a light suntan. Her hair is blonder, with sun streaks of white, and her cheeks have a rose tint against her light, caramel-colored tan. It's the spattering of the tiniest freckles across her nose that does me in. She's beautiful.

Every night, after everyone is exhausted and the children have been tucked into their own rooms, I look forward to pulling her naked body with her white bikini outline into our bed. My hands get caught in her tangled, windblown hair as I kiss her. She smells like ocean, sand, and the hotel soap. And her skin tastes extra salty, even after the showers she takes between the ocean swims and dinners out each night. I can't get enough of holding her, touching her, smelling her hair and skin, and kissing her.

"You're intoxicating," I say on our fifth evening when we're back in our hotel room, naked in bed.

"It's because you're away from work. All you can do now is play and have sex with me." She smiles while she strokes my arms.

I prop myself over her so I can look her over. Her scar stands out, white against her tan, but when she's flushed or aroused like now, the scar turns a light pink. I lean down and run my tongue from the base of it up to her neck. She shivers, and then I begin kissing her neck. It will be a long night of slow, gentle moves—maybe not so gentle if my libido has any say—and I will be in a drug-induced-like rapture. I have fallen so hard for her that my chest hurts thinking about her.

"It's because I'm in love with you," I whisper into her neck.

She takes my face in her hands. Her eyes are a vivid blue against her sun-soaked skin and the white-blonde wisps of hair framing her face. She doesn't say anything, but she kisses me with a demanding hunger.

Any doubts I had about her feelings toward me or any childish jealousy I may have felt about other men interested in her have evaporated completely. She doesn't have to say it, although I wish she would. Her heart is mine. We belong to each other.

• • •

"That's not very impressive," Finn says, looking at the velvet box holding a key to my house.

"Are you sure? I'm asking Talia to live with me. You don't think that's a big deal?"

"She and her sister already have a key to your house. They have a few. I mean, Aleska is always there with her cleaning people, and you gave Talia a key a long time ago. I've seen her use it."

"This one is shiny and polished. It's brand-new. It's symbolic."

"If you say so." Finn takes a big lick of his double-scoop ice cream cone.

We're sitting next to a three-tier fountain where tourists are posing for photos and tossing in coins for wishes. It's in front of the boutique where Talia and Jess are shopping—their seventh store—while I'm holding all the shopping bags.

I took Finn out this morning, just the two of us, for a little father-son time, walking on the beach and talking. At seven in the morning, we had the beach to ourselves. I wasn't concerned with work and hadn't made any calls to Bash or my father and uncle to check on any of the restaurants.

I needed to ask Finn first, to get his approval about bringing Talia into his life permanently. Apparently, though, asking Talia to live with me isn't the big deal I thought it would be for him. I consulted with parenting books and articles to prepare him for what I was asking, but it all became moot when he simply shrugged and said he was surprised how slow I was when it came to Talia. *Unoriginal*, he said. He didn't elaborate, and I didn't ask. Fortunately, we were distracted by the enormous dead horseshoe crab brought in by the morning tide.

I have Finn in my life, and I am going to ask Talia to live with me—I have everything. He's right, though. Another key to my house, a home I rent from Carson, isn't that impressive. I need another option, a better offer to give her. I also need a certain nine-year-old to weigh in with his ideas, and I know how to bribe this kid.

"Got room in that cast-iron stomach of yours?" I ask.

"What do you have in mind?" He tosses his napkin and the bottom half of his ice cream cone into a nearby trash bin.

"These women are going to be at least another hour. How about we walk over to Tommy's, and you can have as many hot dogs as you want? In exchange for some advice."

"That I can do." He stands up and grabs some of the shopping bags. "Just so you know, the quality of my advice is directly correlated to the number of hot dogs consumed."

"Where did you learn that kind of language?"

"Mom helps me with math and science. She always uses terms like *quantity* and *quantify*, *correlation* and *correlated*, *cause* and *effect*. She is a scientist, you know."

"She's very intelligent. How do you feel about your mother and Talia going into business together?"

"I think it's great! They're going to give me a job—with horses!"

"Ah, yes, breaking all those child labor laws, I bet." I chuckle.

"Dad, you owe me some hot dogs. We're on the clock."

"No expense is too great. I'm prepared to meet your demands, buddy."

46

Talia

"Yᴏᴜ ʜᴀᴅ ᴀ ʙʀᴏᴛʜᴇʀ," Peyton says, looking down at our clasped hands on the restaurant table where we're having dinner. He looks genuinely sad about the story.

I could sense that this vacation was a prelude to something more. Peyton was building up to ask me something, a bigger commitment for both of us, and I felt this could go no further without divulging the truth about what my family's hereditary condition brings to the table.

"I thought you should know about Justek."

"Of course, I should. Your brother died. You must have been devastated when your mother told you. I'm so sorry this happened to you, to your family. Mila, Jesus, your poor mother."

"Yes, it explains so much about us. And to be fair to you—"

"Fair to me? What do you mean?"

"This affects you, too. If you think you can have a future with me, this changes everything."

"What are you talking about? Changes what?" Something flares in his eyes.

He's so goddamn gorgeous. He has a dark tan, and his hair has grown out a bit again, making him look like one of the surfers who devote whole days to the ocean.

"I think you brought me on this trip because you do want more for us. You said you love me."

"And you haven't exactly said it back. Why do you think I arranged to have dinner here without the others? Why don't you tell me what I want to hear, Talia?"

464

Our table is on an open porch overlooking the ocean. We have a buffer of privacy created by the customer chatter of the busy restaurant and the sound of the crashing waves. Except for the people who take an extra-long look at Peyton—a tall, handsome man stands out anywhere—no one pays attention to our conversation.

The words rush out in a forced, nonchalant manner. "I feel the same way."

"What was that?" He laughs. "Could you be more *specific*?" He squeezes my hand and traps me with those startling gray eyes. The man knocks the wind out of me, and my heart flutters, a terrible combination if you're prone to imaginary heart attacks like I am. "*Talia.*" That deep voice and the way he says my name slowly, like it's something precious, give me goosebumps. His smile disarms my ability to stay tough.

"I love you," I say, barely above a whisper.

"I'm sorry. What was that?" he says, and we both laugh.

"I love you!" I say too loudly, and a couple at another table smiles at us.

"Good. Then we're set." He reaches into his pocket and pulls out a small, velvet box. It's fairly large for a ring, but it's alarming, nonetheless.

"Wait! We still haven't discussed this."

"Getting nervous already? It's just a box."

"Peyton, I told you about my brother because it means my heart condition is hereditary."

"*Was.* You're fixed. You're perfectly healthy."

"I'm healthy, but I carry the gene for mitral valve prolapse. If I have children, they would inherit this, and they could die before they're diagnosed, or they could have to go through the same invasive surgery I had. It's dangerous."

"*Could* inherit. Not *would*. Everyone carries all kinds of things in their DNA, but it doesn't always guarantee the outcome. Having children carries all kinds of risks. You never know what your child will be born with or how they'll turn out after eighteen years with their parents."

"Those are small risks people are willing to take because the odds are in their favor that they don't have something bad in their DNA," I say. "I do know what's in mine, and it isn't good."

"Want to know what's in my DNA? Twins. Beastly twins. Look at my brothers, Evan and Neil. Terrible, horrible twins."

I laugh. "They are both lovely. Nice brothers and good fathers."

"My mother passed it on to Greer. You've met little Owen and Nikki. Also, beastly children. They destroy houses, and you've seen their handiwork at restaurants. We have to leave an extra couple of twenties just for the table cleanup."

"Stop joking. Having twins is considered a good thing."

"My brothers' birth almost killed my mother," he says flatly. "She was in the hospital for the last two months of the pregnancy, and she lost a lot of blood during labor. The boys were breech. It was a long, difficult delivery, and my mom almost died. If she had, I wouldn't exist." He's somber, talking about his mother.

"It sounds harrowing."

"Greer also had breech twins, and a very difficult pregnancy and delivery. There's a reason she doesn't want more children. So, you see? We all bring something to the mix. Just because Aleska doesn't have a bad valve doesn't mean it's not in her DNA."

He's right. I was so relieved my sister was cleared during her checkup, but it doesn't change our genetics.

"Talia, I'm not asking you to have children. I'm asking you to be with me."

"I don't know if I'll ever have children. I want them, but I'm not sure I can go through with having them, because I'm so afraid of what I'll pass on to them."

"I know you are, but again, I'm not asking you to have children if you don't want to."

"Someday you may want more. You missed out on Finn's birth and childhood. You can say one thing now, but in a few years, you may want another son or daughter, and I might not be able to do that."

"I'm not Marko. I don't have any standard requirements in order for us to be together. Finn is crazy about you, and I know you're fond of him. I have everything I want."

"You make it sound so simple."

"It is."

He slides the box toward me. "It's not what you're thinking. Finn already told me it's kind of a dud offering. Open it anyway." He releases my hand, and I pick up the box and pop open the hinge.

Sitting on a satin bed is a familiar-looking key.

I look at Peyton's grin.

"You guessed it. It's a key to my house. And yes, you already have one. I was planning on asking you to live with me."

"And you changed your mind?"

"Nope. I still want you to live with me, but Finn said my plan was lame. He said it wasn't going to impress you since you already have a key and full access to my house. So we came up with a new plan."

"We?"

"Finn helped me come up with an offer you can't refuse."

"I haven't refused you. I'm simply putting all the cards on the table so you don't rush into something you'll regret later."

"I love you. Do you love me?"

"Yes."

"Good, because I'm not going anywhere. I know what I want. You have serious trust issues, but you can trust me. I won't break your heart."

"You have to be sure because, when I'm with you, I'm excited and terrified at the same time. I'm *terricited*. It's a real thing. My heart flip-flops all over the place, and medically speaking, it could kill me."

Peyton laughs.

"If we get more serious, and then break up later, my heart would shatter."

Peyton shakes his head, smiling. "You give your poor heart a workout. But I'm so sure about you and me that I got us a new house. Well, not new, but ... I got off the phone with Archie a while ago. You and I are going to take over Norma's house. We can renovate the kitchen or whatever you think needs work, or we can leave it as is. It's your call. Are you okay with that? Being in Norma's old house?"

"Really?" I haven't really thought about how Norma's home has been sitting vacant. "Sometimes, I walk through her house so I can feel her close to me. Not that I believe in ghosts, but her house has familiar scents, and it brings back nice memories."

"I know. Your mom told me. I also called her today while you were shopping. I told her I'd like for us to live next door to her. We'll be there to help her, at least until she becomes more independent again. And we can take Baby off her hands. She can't handle that huge dog when you're at work, so Baby will be back in his old house, too."

"I'm not sure Harmony will be thrilled that you're moving her son next door to your girlfriend's mother. She may feel like you have an unfair advantage."

"Nah, we're not like that. She was my third phone call today. We spoke for over an hour. Do you know how long it takes for you to shop for a dress?"

"It took three hours to find this dress," I say, looking down and admiring the silky blue material clinging to my waist.

"And it was worth every minute." He leans over the table and, in a conspiratorial tone, says, "I can't wait to take it off you."

"So you're saying you called all these people and just like that, we're moving into Norma's house?"

"And Harmony is moving into the house on the other side of Norma's, the one that's been vacant the longest. She said she's going to have to gut it completely and renovate before she can live there."

My eyes must have bulged wide, because Peyton barks a deep laugh, and more customers glance our way.

"You're not joking, right?" I ask.

"Not joking. We're going full-on cuddle-parenting with Finn. She's giving up the big, expensive house in Westchester, and with her next door, Finn won't have to do that long-distance shuttle between our houses. He's going to switch to the public school in Hera—his idea. We had to agree to invite his new Westchester friends to Hera for sleepovers and video game weekends. That's how everything else fell into place."

"You orchestrated this whole thing today while I was out shopping?"

"*Sunflower*," he says slowly. "I'm on a mission. What do you say?"

"I'm considering it," I say, but I hardly sound like I'm going to refuse him.

"Hmm, you do that." He smirks. "Come on; let's get out of here."

We leave the restaurant and walk along the boardwalk, swinging our clasped hands, feeling silly and happy.

We all have those moments where an idea or an answer comes to us with crystal clarity and assurance. This is my moment. Suddenly, all my doubts are gone.

Peyton is the one. *The only one.*

I don't have to be scared of defective hearts and future children. I don't have to make that decision today, because Peyton is with me. He's my person. We'll go through everything together.

I stop walking and pull his hand toward me. "Peyton." He turns to face me with a pleased but questioning expression. "I'd like to ask you something."

"Ah, more cross-examination. Whatever it takes to convince you. Go ahead, give me your toughest questions."

"Will you marry me?" It's so easy to ask.

He doesn't say anything. He stares at me as if I'm going to finish with a snappy joke. When he realizes I'm serious, his face breaks into one of those devilish grins. "Sunflower, the point of living together is that we'll eventually get married, right? Do you really think I'm the kind of guy who'd put you and my kid through years of playing house without—"

"No, will you marry me *today*?"

Peyton clams up. Either he's caught off guard that I'm actually proposing, stealing his thunder as they say, or perhaps this is all too soon for him.

"I know a certain bus driver who also happens to be an ordained minister. He's in Wildwood, and I bet he could be here in the next hour or so if I ask."

A little twinkle flickers in Peyton's eyes. "You're asking if I'll marry you now?"

"Yes, I am. The house key gift was sweet. I like everything you said. I also know what I want."

"Yes." He grasps my waist with his strong hands, and my feet leave the ground. *He's one of those men who can actually lift and twirl a girl.* "Yes, I'll marry you."

Peyton wants Finn to be our only witness. He explains that to Cooper and Greer over the phone. They are at the hotel with Finn, relaxing after playing in the ocean all day. Peyton says it's only fair he not have his family present since my sister and mother can't be here.

I call Alejandro, who's so overwhelmed that I would ask him to officiate that he says he can be here in twenty minutes, ten if he drives fast. He assures me that he's driving his wife's car, not the party bus. Peyton says he needs more time and asks Alejandro to meet us in an hour.

"Where are you taking me?" I ask as he pulls my hand.

"Stop trying to ruin all my surprises, woman."

Across the street from our hotel is a cute, pink Victorian house, Victorious, a store that carries fashionable clothing and accessories. It specializes in vintage estate jewelry—notably, engagement rings—and my eyes glaze over when I see all the pretty diamond rings encased in the glass counter. I peer down at them while the saleswoman explains different styles.

"I thought you'd like this shop. You love *old* stuff," he says when I gape at a stunning ring the saleswoman holds out for me to inspect.

"*Vintage*," I clarify, and he laughs. "Some woman wore the ring before me. The ring has its own story. I wonder if they had a long, happy marriage."

"Isn't that beautiful?" the saleswoman asks as I slide the solitaire on my finger and hold it up for Peyton to see. "It's a three-carat center diamond, white gold."

"Do you like it?" Peyton asks.

"It's very pretty, but I'm not sure it's me. It's big."

"What about this one?" The saleswoman takes a small, white box out of the case and rests it on the counter. Nestled in a worn bed of faded blue velvet, this ring has a smaller diamond than the previous one, but it sits in a square setting and has more detail. The style looks more old-fashioned than anything I've ever seen. I imagine this ring belonged to a woman who wore Edwardian-style dresses and coiffed hair like someone out of *Downton Abbey*.

"It fits perfectly," I say as I admire the ring on my finger.

"Then you're a size five," she says. "It's a center diamond, a little less than two carats. It's platinum, and the band has ten smaller diamonds."

"Is it Edwardian?" I ask, eagerly wanting this ring to suit me.

She looks at a notecard next to the box. "Circa 1920. About a decade later than Edwardian."

"Is that all right?" Peyton asks me. "Were you looking for a specific time period?"

"No, just curious." I rotate my hand back and forth, mesmerized by the pretty antique ring. "It's exquisite." I look at Peyton for confirmation.

"It's you." He smiles. "It's definitely you."

Behind Peyton, I notice a young woman standing in front of a floor-length mirror, turning side to side to get a better look at the very short, black lace dress she's modeling. She's taller than me, and that dress was made for her. Without thinking, I walk over to the mirror.

"Oh, I'm sorry," the woman says. "I'm hogging the mirror." She moves aside, and I step in front of the mirror.

"I actually just want to see what I look like wearing an engagement ring." I show off my hand.

Peyton laughs at me.

A brief, kind smile skirts across the young woman's face. She's dazzling, and that's when I recognize her. She's Zerina Baldwin, famous because her grandfather was one of the most popular US presidents before he died of cancer in the middle of his second term, and her father is an outspoken career senator who wants to run for president in the next election.

There are always photographs of Zerina on popular blogs and entertainment shows, and she always seems to be running from the cameras, trying to hide from the press that is obsessed with her and her famous family. She is someone I would seek out in tabloid news ever since the cameras started following her when she was a child. I grew up reading everything I could about her, admiring how she handled herself in television interviews and spoke so eloquently about her family's political legacy and humanitarian work. If I could be anyone, I always imagined having Zerina Baldwin's life, her family, and her expensive education. I would mark time from my elementary school days, through my teens, to now by events publicized in Zerina Baldwin's life. I would mimic her fashion sense with designer knock-offs and try to carry myself in certain situations as I imagined she would. To me, she was the epitome of perfection, and I thought all my attempts at copying her would improve me and my life.

But here she is, in front of me. No entourage, no cameras, she's alone. She's just as beautiful in person as I expected, but this woman, who has lived an exciting life, seems to have an aura of someone who's lonely, and it seems wrong that I notice this. I have inadvertently been given a glimpse into her private world, like an intruder. I don't think Peyton has recognized her. He's too busy watching me as if I'm the only woman in existence.

Out of guilt for my own happiness, I avert my eyes from Zerina Baldwin and look at the woman in the mirror, dressed in her lazy, summer day attire, flashing a diamond ring at herself because she's getting married.

"It's a beautiful ring," Zerina says. "You should get that one."

"Thank you." Our eyes meet in the mirror. "You look lovely in that dress. You should definitely get it."

Peyton swings a heavy arm around my shoulders. "Come on, beautiful. Let's pay for the ring. We have a wedding to get to."

We complete the transaction with the saleswoman, and as we walk away from the register, Zerina approaches the counter, ready to purchase the black dress. A brief smile passes between us, and I wonder if seeing her in this shop, in this little beachside town, is a coincidence or if the universe is giving me a sign.

I wouldn't think I'm significant enough to warrant such symbolism from the heavens. I've spent so many years picking out my flaws and comparing myself to this particular celebrity that being in her presence and seeing that she is a mere mortal is a revelation for me. The woman I thought who had it all doesn't seem to have half of what I have, which makes her human.

I'm a stranger to her, but this encounter makes me feel closer to her. Even if this is merely a coincidence, she has a profound effect on me, and I would tell her this if it didn't make me sound like every other stalker.

"Congratulations," she says as Peyton and I walk toward the store exit.

If I only had half of the happiness I'm feeling at this moment, it would last me a lifetime and exceed any expectations I ever had. Who would have thought I would ever be in this position with this much love? I wish I could throw some Zerina's way, but I know she'll be fine.

I thank her as we head back out into the sunshine.

· · ·

A half hour later, standing on the mostly deserted beach under a brilliant sunset, Peyton and I stand in front of Alejandro and repeat the simple vows. I hold a small bouquet of wildflowers Alejandro brought for me, and Finn stands next to his father, holding the little box with my ring.

This is not the wedding I imagined. Ever. This is more beautiful. It's better than a church full of women in layers of makeup and hair product, concerned about their dresses; men complaining about stiff tuxes; and the general anxiety that accompanies a tightly scripted wedding service meant to entertain a hundred spectators.

My wedding is intimate and lovely. Finn in board shorts and flip-flops, the minister in khakis and a brightly flowered pink shirt, and me and Peyton in jeans and T-shirts. No guests, no reception, just a warm breeze and fading sunlight with the ocean as our backdrop ... and love. So much love that my heart feels like it could burst.

This wedding is for the three of us, my new little family. Later, we'll do it again in Hera at a party so our friends and family won't nag us for a lifetime about not being witnesses to our vows.

Finn covers his eyes when we kiss, and then I hug Finn and kiss the top of his head with the promise that I won't do it again, certainly not in public.

Later that night, we sit on Adirondack chairs on the hotel's great lawn, sipping cocktails and discussing our future with the rest of our friends and family who are already planning the party they will hold at Swill to celebrate our nuptials. Finn is running around with the other cousins, chasing Dylan in the dark.

I close my eyes and listen as Greer and Imogene talk about the invite list and the band that they want to perform at the party that has now become *their* party, hardly letting Jess and the other women join in. Cooper and Carson are holding a lively conversation about football and beer and anything not related to weddings and parties.

Peyton hasn't stopped holding my hand since we stepped off the beach as husband and wife. We keep smiling when we look at each other.

"You know that thing you said earlier today?" he asks quietly so only I can hear him.

"What *thing*? We talked about so many things today, and then we got married." I laugh. "I still can't believe it."

"You said you weren't sure if you want to have children."

"Yes?" Where is he going with this?

"Surprise." He chuckles. "You're a mother. It's a boy. There, you got the same initiation as me."

"We're proud parents of a nine-year-old boy," I say.

"*Almost ten!*" we say in unison, mimicking Finn's usual retort.

"I have to get you a wedding ring," I say. "Would you wear one?"

"If you want me to, I will. Whatever you want."

"You've given me everything I could ever want. You. A family. A really big family."

He lifts up our clasped hands and kisses the back of my hand.

"I love you." I lean across the wooden armrest to kiss him.

He meets me halfway, and then we have our twenty-fourth kiss as a married couple. Yes, I'm counting.

"I should have told you weeks ago. Months ago." I look into his eyes. Night has descended, and his features aren't as clear, but I can see all I need in his eyes. Those eyes.

"Let's make a deal not to have any regrets." His deep voice sends shivers through me. "I love you, and we have years and years to say it every day."

Epilogue

One year later...
Talia

FIND HARMONY ON the porch, settled back in one of the wooden rockers, sipping a cocktail. Over the past six months, we've become close. *Friends.* I remind her of that constantly. Renovating and restoring a large Victorian home and starting a business together could have made us mortal enemies, but it has had the opposite effect. We both found the place where we truly belong.

"Look at those two jokers." She points at the tractor that Peyton and Finn are riding across the field below.

I laugh and walk over to the porch railing, leaning against a post to take in the majestic view that never gets old.

We settled on retaining Pickwick as the name of the estate. Naturally, many people were surprised that we weren't more inventive in the name department. Only Kimberly appreciated our attention to historical preservation for an estate that was in ruins and about to lose to bulldozers if a developer had his way.

We started farming the land months ago, but officially opened the inn and dining room three weeks ago. The whole operation is fully staffed with a farm manager, a few farmhands to manage the horses, the goats, and the crops, and an inn manager and housekeeping and restaurant staff. I'm the CEO and run the kitchen, too, and I oversee my catering business and own staff, which was relocated out of Swill to Pickwick. Aleska is the CFO and still runs the housekeeping business, formerly under the now defunct T & A Services. Like any business venture, we hit a lot of bumps along the way, but with Aleska's business skills and Harmony's common sense and venture capital, we worked out all our issues in a timely manner and surprised the skeptics.

Our living arrangements, while odd by conventional standards, have worked out brilliantly. Four homes side by side: my mother and sister, though Aleska plans on moving into the remaining vacant home within the year; Peyton and me; and Harmony and Finn. Baby runs freely among all the houses, which means we all keep shovels and garbage bags on hand for those special Baby piles that dot our yards. It's as if Norma's spirit is still with us, having the last laugh. And her strength and humor are present, tying us all together as one large family.

"Do you want to give Peyton the third degree on this, or should I?" Harmony's voice breaks my reverie.

"They're sure having fun. I'll tell Peyton to lay off the tractor, and you can remind him that Finn is an impressionable boy."

Harmony stands up to join me. Even in casual clothes—jeans and a wrinkled linen shirt—she looks elegant. "Peyton loves being the fun dad. He thinks you and I conspire behind his back."

"We do." We both laugh in that way friends develop with their own inside jokes. "How's the drink?"

"Excellent. Mila really excels in mixology. I like every version she's given me with the different berries she picked. These could become our signature drink at the inn once word gets out."

"My mother will love hearing that from you. She's becoming quite more comfortable with the guests. She's starting to work the front desk so she can find reasons to leave the kitchen and socialize."

"That's wonderful. She has such a gracious presence and makes everyone feel welcome."

"True, but she's also bad for profits. You need to watch her. She likes to walk around with trays of champagne flutes or glasses of wine, handing them out like cheap breath mints."

"She may be on to something. People come here to relax, and they enjoy sitting in the lounge downstairs. That old fireplace makes it cozy. Why don't we fill the beautiful hutch Cooper made us with bottles of wine and glasses? People can serve themselves. It won't be the same expensive wines we sell in the restaurant. Good wines, but less expensive, and Mila can bring down a tray every afternoon with some of her homemade cookies or lemon bars. The lounge is only for guests of the inn, and they're already paying a premium for the rooms."

"Adding a perk like a wine lounge and afternoon treats would be a good addition to our publicity pieces."

"Now you're thinking like a businesswoman instead of a chef." Harmony toasts me with her glass, then takes another sip. "Hmm, we're definitely not giving these yummy things away for free, though."

The sound of an approaching car makes us turn toward the front of the inn. It's Adam's red Bugatti.

"Adam!" I wave and step toward the front staircase of the wide porch.

He gets out of the car with a big bouquet of flowers in his arms and bounds up the stairs, looking energized and tan from his vacation in Thailand.

"Just a little housewarming for the new innkeeper." He kisses my cheek. Then his smile grows bigger when he looks over my shoulder at Harmony.

"*Innkeepers*. There are two of us," I say. "Thank you. This is huge. I'll have my mom put them on display at the front desk."

He's still staring at Harmony, and she's staring back.

"Wait. Have you two never met?"

"No, I'd remember. Hello. Adam Knight." He reaches out his hand, and Harmony takes it.

"Harmony Davis." She suddenly sounds coy and sweet—nothing like the Harmony I know.

"Harmony is Finn's mother," I add, assuming he can do the math and figure out that she was Peyton's high school fling.

"It's a pleasure," he says. "I'm sorry I missed the opening party. I was out of the country for over a month."

They're gazing at each other as if I'm not standing between them, so I slip away to give them a chance to talk and see if their meet-cute goes any further.

I walk to the stairs and stand on the top step, watching Finn and Peyton leave the barn where the tractor is kept. They make their way up the hill toward the inn, talking and laughing. My heart swells—in a good way. They are my family. My husband and my stepson.

"Wifey!" Peyton shouts when he sees me.

Finn charges up the stairs with a quick hi.

"Give these flowers to Mila, please!" I say as he tries to rush by me. I thrust the bouquet in front of his face, and he grabs them as he makes a beeline for the kitchen, knowing my mother, his only grandmother, and her gentleman suitor, Gavin, will have fresh cookies ready for him.

"You have flour on your face." Peyton puts his hands on my waist. The sun glints off his wedding ring as he reaches to brush the flour from my cheek.

"Figures Harmony wouldn't tell me."

"And you smell like butter. And this floor-length apron is oh so sexy."

"Don't get too excited there, horny boy. Check out Harmony's new friend."

Peyton looks past me and frowns. "Knight."

"Be nice and don't screw this up for her. Those two were starstruck when I introduced them."

"Really?"

"Yep. Can you imagine if they start dating? What if he starts spending some nights at her place? All of us in our own little cul-de-sac of *Dynasty* meets *Desperate Housewives*."

"Please, don't give me those images. I can't think about that now. I've been waiting all day to take you up to the Hera Suite so I can have my way with you." He fiddles with my wedding ring dangling on a delicate platinum chain at my throat. It's the safest place to keep it while I cook.

"I'm helping with the family dinner tonight. Everyone is coming. I'm setting up the tables outside by the new hedges we put in. Stop pretending that you don't remember. Besides, all rooms are booked, including the Hera Suite. It's the most popular room. A Mr. Edward Van Hulane booked it for tonight."

A deep belly laugh rumbles through Peyton. "It's Edward Van Halen. Of course, you didn't get that one. You know Chopin and The Beatles, but you've never heard of Eddie Van Halen."

"You know this man?"

"I am this man. I booked and paid for the room tonight. For us. Finn is going home with Harmony after the dinner, and I want my wife to take a night off."

"You did this? But I have to help my mom in the kitchen, and I have to help set and serve. We have a lot of people coming. Imogene and Cooper and their three kids, Greer and her kids, Jess and—"

"I know who's coming. Aleska and I went over the list. She'll be here soon to help your mom cook. She enlisted Imogene and Lauren to help serve. And I got Cooper and the other guys committed to helping with the cleanup. Dishes and all."

"If you say so, Eddie. I'm impressed with your plotting and scheming."

"Thank you. Now how about a quickie before the dinner?"

"Oops, can't. Look who's here."

More cars arrive. Aleska's in our new catering van, Kim and Bash have a carload of book boxes for our library room, and behind them are Cooper and Imogene and their three foster children—all siblings, all girls under the age of ten. Harmony told her to arrive early so she could teach Imogene how to care for the girls' hair, all of whom have afros. Harmony plans to instruct Imogene on the proper hair products to use.

Bash and Kim approach, both carrying a heavy box.

"Peyton, you wanna grab one of these boxes?" Bash asks.

"Oh, you can call him Mr. Van Halen," I say.

Bash laughs. Of course, he's in on Peyton's ruse.

"You should be carrying all those boxes for Kim," Peyton tells Bash.

"He's been so helpful," Kim adds, giving Bash an adoring look.

"Great. Who's running the kitchen at Swill?" Peyton puts his arm around me.

"Our excellent kitchen staff, Mr. Van Halen. Thanks for asking." Bash shakes his head as he and Kim pass us and head into the inn.

"Why do they get to go into the library? My mother told me yesterday no one was allowed in there until the new stain on the end tables dries."

Peyton chuckles. "You fall for everything."

"What are you talking about?"

"I'm here! I'm here!" Aleska grouses as she jogs up the stairs. "Thanks for calling and texting me every thirty minutes, Peyton! So happy I can help you two celebrate your monthly anniversary *again*! Every fudging month!" She doesn't wait for a response, and Peyton just smiles smugly as Aleska storms into the inn.

"This time it's officially our one-year anniversary!" Peyton yells after my sister.

"Looks like you've been planning this for a while," I say. "You're going to owe your sister-in-law big time."

"Don't worry. I know how to get back in her good graces. A superior gift is in the works."

"Well, I'm a mess. Not about to sneak upstairs with you. And look at our mangy dog. Someone has to clean him before dinner." I point at Baby, who is galloping in from who knows where after chasing who knows what. He's panting with his tongue hanging out, and the fur on his chest is matted with sweat and drool.

"Oh, for Christ's sake. Please tell me someone is doing a tick check on that beast before he comes back to the house."

Baby paws Peyton's foot, and when he doesn't get the human hugs he relishes, he takes off down the veranda toward Harmony and Adam.

"I hope Gavin will hose him down. He loves Baby," I say. "Finish what you were saying before Aleska interrupted us."

He smirks. "What's that?"

"Stop it. Yesterday my mother told me to stay out of the library, and you just said I fall for everything. What did you mean?"

Peyton sighs, a sly smile blooming. "I have something for you. For our anniversary. I wanted to give it to you a year ago, when I thought you'd never speak to me again."

"After *The Kitchen Incident*?"

He chuckles because I always use The Kitchen Incident as a marker of our time together, the before TKI and the after TKI. It's become legendary, thanks to Imogene's colorful storytelling.

"Yes, after the *incident*, there was something I wanted to do for you. I didn't have the knowledge I needed, and I didn't have a location."

"This sounds very mysterious. Did you put something in the library for me? A gift? Is that why my mother locked it and hid the key?"

He nods. "She's helping me."

"Then how are Kim and Bash getting in there?" I ask, already leaving the veranda and heading inside.

He grasps my hand and takes the lead down the long hallway that crosses the inn and ends at the library door. "I have a key," he says, pulling it out of his pocket.

When we reach the library door, Kimberly's book boxes are stacked by the door. Peyton unties my apron, slips it over my head, and tosses it onto the boxes.

"I hope you like it," he says, unlocking the door.

I walk in ahead of him. It's a beautiful room, painstakingly restored woodwork, a floor of wide pine planks, floor-to-ceiling bookcases, and large, French doors that provide plenty of natural light. Kimberly helped us acquire used and new books for the shelves, but little furniture has been put in the room because Aleska and my mother said it was on order and delayed.

There's still no new furniture; however, across the room is the most dazzling grand piano I have ever seen. I walk slowly toward this thing of beauty.

With the exception of Adam's piano, I haven't had music in my life for years. The old upright we used to have was downright shabby, but I still played it until my fingers and hands ached and the instrument needed to be tuned. The absence of a piano and being unable to play every day has left a void in my life.

I touch the glossy, ebony surface with a fingertip and turn to Peyton, who's watching me intently. "How did you do this?"

"They parked the truck out on the side lawn and brought it in through the French doors."

"I figured out why my mother kept me in the kitchen for five hours today. I get that. I mean, how did you buy this? Did you buy it? Are we renting it? Can people rent Bösendorfers? This must be worth at least fifty thousand."

Peyton blinks.

"A hundred thousand?" I ask, alarmed.

"The cost isn't important. I can afford it. *We* can afford it. Sit down."

I slide onto the bench, and Peyton sits next to me. My fingers are dying to play the gleaming keys, but I hesitate. "How did you do this, Peyton?"

"When I saw you play Adam's piano, you looked so natural at that keyboard. I'm not an expert, but I know talent when I see it. I wanted to get you a piano to pay you back for the kitchen—"

"*The Kitchen Incident.*" I nod, and he chuckles.

"Yes, that. So, I called a guy who's an expert. I thought he'd tell me to invest in a Steinway. It's the only name I recognize other than Yamaha. He and I talked for a while." Peyton speaks in a soft, gentle manner, telling his story slowly. "I told him that you're a professional chef, and you're going to start another business soon, but playing the piano is part of who you are. You need the music, the piano, the same way other people need their TVs or cars. He gave me good advice because he has a natural talent like you. He helped with the research, and when I settled on this one, I said maybe some time he could come hear my incredible wife play."

"That would be nice. Does he live in Hera or nearby?"

"He's kind of a sad man. We've only spoken on the phone. For the past three months, I've gotten to know him pretty well. He asked me if my wife was happy. And he asked about her health." Peyton pauses. "Because he's been worried about her for a long time."

A soft gasp escapes from me. I search his face. He's nervous about telling me this. With good reason.

"What did you tell him?"

"I told him you're very healthy and very happy. He told me about losing his first child. He told me how he thought he was teaching his oldest daughter how to play the piano, but he realized she had no interest in reading music because, as he discovered, she could play by ear. He said he loved his daughters and was delighted when his ... when *you* came home from school and played the piano for him every day. You made him happy." He waits, gauging my response.

"Oh my God." My lower lip trembles.

"He said he hurt his family, and he regrets that."

"How much does he regret it?"

"Deeply." Peyton takes my hand and cups it in both of his. "I really did reach out to him because I simply wanted to get you a nice piano. It evolved from there. We've been talking every week. He is deeply flawed, sunflower, but I like him. He wasn't trying to be someone other than the man who he is. I assumed he would help me find the right piano to buy, and then we'd be done. Instead, we kept up the phone calls. We spoke this morning, when I told him the piano was being delivered today, and I offered to fly him up here and put him in a hotel sometime—it doesn't have to be yours—and only if you agree to it."

"I don't know. I don't know if I'm ready to see him."

"That's all right. You don't have to know." He lays a gentle kiss at my temple. "You think about it. You have enough going on with this place. It's the busy season. No one expects you to do anything you don't want to do."

I nod. "Maybe late autumn would be better."

Peyton gazes at me with loving tenderness. "That would be nice."

"Maybe you could get him a room at Mohonk. Maybe he can stay here—I don't know."

"All you need to know is that I love you." He kisses my cheek, then puts the key to the library in my hand. "This is yours. The key, the room, and the piano. It's yours. You can play here anytime. I bet the guests would love your performances."

"I like that idea. Did you actually reserve the suite tonight?"

"We have the suite. Happy anniversary, beautiful."

"Happy anniversary. I didn't get you anything."

"You're giving me what I want tonight." He grins. "There's another gift. You get that one tomorrow."

"Why tomorrow?"

"It's at the house. It's an upright. Not as flashy as this one, but you need one at home, too."

"My thoughtful, amazing husband. I wish I had gotten you something."

"How about I say being with you every day *is* my gift?"

"That's so corny. So sappy." I laugh. "You're easy to please. I'm going to wait to play this tonight after dinner. We'll bring everyone in here to see this work of art you've given me, and my first song will be for you." I kiss him, but the peck turns into a full-on, heart-thumping kiss as we wrap our hands around each other, groping for more.

Peyton pulls away, breathless. "You need to stop molesting my mouth or we're going to have to go use that suite now." He shoves a hand down the front of his jeans and adjusts himself.

"You know what? We can be fashionably late to the dinner," I exclaim, standing quickly and banging my thigh hard against the piano. "We're going to the suite now."

Wincing, Peyton is still adjusting himself, and then I accidentally step on his foot. His soft canvas Converse is no match for my steel-toed boot, and he groans in pain.

This is no time for injuries!

"Let's go! Now!" The pain in my thigh takes my breath away, and I begin to collapse. Peyton lunges forward and catches me. My extra weight on his foot causes him to curse.

"We excel at bad timing, but we'll get to that suite." He winces when he takes another step. "Eventually ... But I dread the staircase. And let me be very clear. I'm not carrying you up two thousand steps. It's every man for himself."

"I'll make it up to you in bed. I just need to get off this leg." I howl when my tender thigh bumps his leg.

We both laugh at our predicament, at the intended seduction suite that promises an evening of cold packs, aspirin, and maybe some attempts at sex, likely very gentle and ungraceful.

Together, we limp and shuffle our way toward the library door, laughing and holding on to one another.

Author's Note

The first book in my Fearsome Series has an undiagnosed autistic heroine, the second book has a bipolar hero, and the third book has an over-the-top, inappropriate, snarky heroine who was written to humor me during a difficult period in my life. With this book, I decided to flip all the characters from the way I originally outlined them and make their lives even more difficult. The heroine shares my personal experience of mitral valve prolapse, and I gave the hero constant obstacles, so he doesn't get to be a knight in shining armor who saves the damsel in distress. And the antagonist is really more of a modern-day Glinda the Good Witch with a twist.

Regarding mitral valve prolapse, mine was diagnosed a few years ago, and like Talia, I had to have my heart valve repaired as soon as possible. I was in the middle of raising two young children, one of whom is autistic with severe issues, and, in addition, I was dealing with my own challenging behaviors which put me on the autism spectrum alongside my son.

I was terrified to have open heart surgery, and despite all of my OCD-DEFCON-1-level research, planning, and preparation—to help my family through my hospitalization, or the worst-case scenario of my death—I carried around a significant amount of post-surgical trauma which I still have today. But unlike Talia, I had an amazing husband who sat by my hospital bed, day and night, and put up with an un-medicated wife who yelled at him for breathing too loudly. I was, indeed, horrible to him. Fortunately, I still have that amazing husband, and it's his humor that shines through in Talia's witty vocabulary gaffes because English is also his second language.

So to spare the reader, I removed a whole chapter from this book which was devoted to Talia's hospital ordeal. It was laced with amusing incidents, but I decided that nobody needed to read about blood bags and all the other grim details. No matter how cathartic these scenes were for me to write, they would be a miserable read for anyone else. Hence, the chapter was cut. You're welcome.

I have to point out that my mitral valve surgery at Mount Sinai in New York City only represents my experience, so I don't claim to be an expert on the topic. That said, a big shout out to the talented surgical team who saved my heart and the amazing nursing staff who kept me alive.

I also want to mention Harmony because I didn't just want to wing it with this character. I chose to base her on my friend, Dez, who gave me permission to craft Harmony in her likeness in every way. I definitely didn't want Harmony to be *the other woman* or a villain. That would have been too easy, and too lazy. After consulting with Dez on her background, I was able to shape Harmony in an authentic way and avoid stereotypes. At least, I hope I did her character justice. In the story, she is the person with the strongest education and the greatest wealth, but more importantly, Harmony is vital to Talia's and Peyton's personal growth by way of her compassion and generosity.

As far as our hero is concerned, I wrote the first draft in 2015, and at the time, I was worried that I was making the hero stumble and fail too much. However, in light of real world headline news over the last two years, I knew I wanted Peyton to be a man who screws up and exposes his own vulnerabilities before he could, or would, evolve into a real hero. Peyton is not a hero because he saves the heroine—because he doesn't—his hero status is defined by how he supports the people he loves.

In the end, I hope my intentions for the characters come across in ways that are relatable.

Sincerely,

Sara

Acknowledgements

I owe endless buckets of love and gratitude to my readers. Thank you for spending your precious time on my stories, and thank you for all of your kind messages.

To Emma - You're always there for me. Even when you're supposed to be taking care of yourself, you manage to lift me up. You are awesome, woman.

To Anima, Michelle, and Becky - Your beta reads help me tremendously. Thank you for stepping into the murky depths of my messy, first drafts.

To Alisha and Damon - Thank you for the beautiful cover and for all the stunning new covers you designed for the whole series.

To Kris - Thank you for coming back to work as an editor. I love working with you.

To Elaine, Eliza, and Jovana - Thank you for all of your hard work and making my book better.

To bloggers and reviewers - Thank you for your support and sharing your passion for reading with the world.

To my husband and kids - Thank you for putting up with me.

To Dez - Everything.

Much love,

Sara

About the Author

S.A. Wolfe spent many years working in corporate finance and television advertising, but she always wanted to be a novelist. After 12 years of participating in autism-related programs for her son and working with professionals in the ASD field, she was inspired to write her first contemporary romance in 2013 (*Fearsome*) with a heroine who has Autism Spectrum Disorder.

You can find her on Facebook at:
https://www.facebook.com/sawolfe24/

Visit her website at: https://sa-wolfe.com/

Other Books by S.A. Wolfe

(All Standalone Novels)

Fearsome (Book 1)

Freedom (Book 2)

Faithful (Book 3)

Flawless Book 4

www.ingramcontent.com/pod-product-compliance
Lightning Source LLC
Chambersburg PA
CBHW020606040726
47498CB00003B/659